RESTLESS DREAMS, ❧ ETERNAL LOVE ❧

"Oh my God, Keith! You can't believe that Daniel Haverston is still in love with me, after all these years and all that's happened?"

"And why not? Any man would admire and covet you, however discreetly he might handle himself. Haverston lost your affections before—maybe he thinks he can win them back again."

"How, for heaven's sake?"

"Who knows, with a desperate man! He'll think of something, Devon. And if he knew the true extent of his loss, how much he really missed, he would surely want to kill me—and even be justified in doing so..."

Devon and Keith... their surging love... their glorious marriage... threatened beyond hope?

꧁ ꧁ ꧁ ꧁ ꧁ ꧁ ꧁ ꧁

ON WINGS OF DREAMS

PATRICIA GALLAGHER

BERKLEY BOOKS, NEW YORK

ON WINGS OF DREAMS

A Berkley Book / published by arrangement with
the author

PRINTING HISTORY
Berkley edition / January 1985

ISBN: 0-425-07446-3

A BERKLEY BOOK ® TM 757,375
The name "BERKLEY" and the stylized "B" with design
are trademarks belonging to Berkley Publishing Corporation.
PRINTED IN THE UNITED STATES OF AMERICA

Dedication:

To my editor, Nancy Coffey, who encouraged me to continue the story of Devon Marshall and Keith Curtis, which began in CASTLES IN THE AIR

AND

To my many loyal fans who beseeched me to do so in numerous letters.

PART ONE

Oh, woman! lovely woman! Nature made thee
To temper man; we had been brutes without you;
Angels are painted fair, to look like you;
There's in you all that we believe of heaven,
Amazing brightness, purity, and truth,
Eternal joy, and everlasting love.

Thomas Otway (1652—1685)
VENICE PRESERVED

Woman is the shelterer, the nourisher, the life-giver, the medicine-woman, the potter of cosmic vessels, the spinner of the threads of life.

Elizabeth Mann Borgese
ASSENT OF WOMEN

That which is eternal in Woman lifts us above.

Goethe (1749—1832)

Variability is one of the virtues of a woman. It obviates the crude requirements of polygamy. If you have one good wife you are sure to have a spiritual harem.

G. K. Chesterton
VIKING BOOK OF APHROSIMS

We love being in love, and that's the truth of it.

Thackeray (1811—1863)
ESMOND

Nature, for the preservation of the human species, has conferred on woman a sacred character, to which man naturally and irresistibly pays homage, to which he renders a true worship.

Alexander Walker

WOMAN PHYSIOLOGICALLY CONSIDERED
AS TO MIND, MORALS, MARRIAGE,
MATRIMONIAL SLAVERY, INFIDELITY
AND DIVORCE (Published in 1840, New York)

Terrible and sublime thought, that every moment is supreme for some man and woman, every hour the apotheosis of some passion!

William McFee (1881–1966)

CASUALS OF THE SEA

❧ 1 ❧

IF THE weather was a good omen, all would be calm and fair for the eagerly anticipated event at the Curtis estate on Manhattan Island. June arrived in a splendor of brilliant skies, lofty white clouds, and gentle zephyrs scented with roses, lilies, and Persian lilacs. The hanging gardens of the great stone escarpment were lushly green, the terraces massed with vivid blooms, the vigorous vines trailing to the deep blue rolling river.

Now in the ninth month of her pregnancy, Devon Marshall Curtis could no longer negotiate the stairs of the beautiful old Dutch manor of fieldstone and silver-aged timbers called Halcyon-on-Hudson. She spent her leisure in the parlor of the master suite, reading, embroidering, or merely gazing wistfully at the scenery—a magnificent panorama changing with the seasons. An almost constant parade of river vessels passed below the windows: commercial ships and barges, fishing boats and scows, small pleasure craft, large private yachts, and great passenger steamers with churning paddlewheels, puffing smokestacks, and ornamental wood trim as artistically carved as scrimshaw. Watching them provided a pleasant pastime, and she could recognize familiar names by the sounds of their whistles and horns.

The captive lives in her body had recently become less active, a medical sign, according to the obstetrician, that they were moving into position for birth. Dr. Ramsey Blake and his nurse were already in residence, along with a well-referenced nanny to take immediate charge of the new heirs, and the prospective mother was attended like a cherished queen-in-waiting. Trays of delicious food were brought to her, including rare, imported delicacies and rich pastries, much of which Devon declined in deference to her figure. And she kept many of her physical discomforts to herself, lest her attendants suffocate her with solicitude.

Her husband and his friend were out riding this morning, as they had done every pleasant day since Ramsey Blake had left his Manhattan practice temporarily to his partner and moved into guest quarters at Halcyon, when he deemed his special patient's time imminent. Never again would Keith risk the frightening prospect of delivery without a competent physician in attendance, as had inadvertently occurred with his son. Scotty, who had recently graduated from his Shetland pony to a gentle Arabian mare, accompanied the men now, with the big shaggy collie bounding alongside in the bright green meadows splashed with wildflowers.

Karl and Lars Hummel, the handymen, could easily contact them with the hunting horn if necessary. It carried for miles, and Devon still shuddered at the memory of this medieval trumpet echoing eerily across the countryside during the dreadful search for their abducted child. God forbid that they should ever hear it blown on such a tragic mission again! High fences and a lookout gatehouse, armed guards and watchdogs had become permanent fixtures on the estate, and potential trespassers were duly forewarned. All these expensive and confining precautions because a fanciful press insisted on labeling Keith Heathstone Curtis "the richest man in America" after the demise of Commodore Cornelius Vanderbilt. Manhattan Midas, Golden Emperor, King of Wall Street—little did they seem to know or care about the enormous problems and burdens inflicted upon him and his family, nor how much he abhorred the imaginary crown, mantle, and scepter depicted in the caricatures of him.

Devon opened *Daisy Miller,* the latest novel by the popular writer Henry James, which was selling like hot chestnuts on a cold day in Central Park. The heroine, a naive young American girl baffled by sophisticated Continental society, reminded Devon of herself when she had first come to cosmopolitan New York, and she reflected on her own literary dreams so long in abeyance. The public had developed an avid interest in romantic literature, especially about the antebellum South, and some enterprising Southern ladies had already published successful memoirs, diaries, romances. Would she ever be able to resume her ambitious career?

After a discreet knock, the housekeeper's daughter entered carrying a thick slice of fudge cake and a glass of milk on a silver tray. Fair, plump, and still single, with her butter-colored hair-braids hanging on her sturdy shoulders, Enid Sommes looked even more like a farm girl than the first time Devon had seen her. "Oh, no!" she cried, frowning at the midmorning nourishment. "I'm not the least bit hungry, Enid. It's only been a couple of hours since breakfast, and I'm still stuffed. Sit with me and enjoy the cake yourself. I know chocolate is your favorite."

"There's more in the kitchen, ma'am. And Mama is churning vanilla ice cream for luncheon. Master Scott loves frozen desserts, you know."

"He doesn't have a weight problem, Enid. But I can't exercise now and don't want to gain another ounce. I feel as if I'm wearing a tent," she complained of the pretty shell-pink silk smock collared and cuffed in Honiton lace.

"Mr. Curtis thinks you're more beautiful than ever, Miss Devon. We all do. You're simply radiant, with your skin and eyes glowing, and your lovely hair curlier than ever. I hope you have twin girls and they look just like you."

"Bless you, dear." Devon suspected a household conspiracy to elevate her spirits whenever she appeared the least bit depressed or impatient. "I just wish they'd hurry and get here! Nine months is an awfully long time to wait."

"Well, it can't be much longer. And you'll be slender again soon enough with two mouths to feed. You'll have to eat like the farmhands, or hire a wet nurse to help out."

"We'll worry about that when the times comes," Devon told her. She had not considered that possibility, any more than she had that of bearing twins. But the idea of a strange woman suckling her babes was as repugnant to her as would have been that of providing a sexual substitute for her spouse when she became physically unable to accommodate him. "Besides, there's always a fresh cow or two on the place, Enid. I trust you and your mother understand why we've employed a nurse for the new infants?"

"Oh, yes, ma'am! Mama says one is an armful, but two! And we all like Nanny, including Miss Vale, even though she's a mite concerned about her own position, after Master Scott goes off to school."

"Nonsense! She'll simply become governess to the twins, that's all." Devon sighed, feeling an odd malaise. "I'd like to rest now, Enid. Don't disturb me if I'm asleep at noon. I'm wearier than usual today."

"Mr. Curtis will hover over you if he learns that, ma'am. He's been restless the last week or so. Mama hears him walking the floor at night."

"He's worried, Enid. One would think we were the only couple since Adam and Eve to have children! He plans to be with me during the delivery. Remember the first time, when he and your mother had to do it alone?"

The maid nodded. "I was fifteen then, and scared silly. But they managed very well, didn't they? Mr. Curtis never left you for a moment. How he loves you, ma'am! I think you must be the luckiest lady in the whole world."

Devon smiled. "I think so too, Enid."

She picked up the tray. "If you need anything, just ring the bell. We test it every day in the quarters."

"You can bring me the latest papers," Devon suggested. "I like to keep abreast of the news, here and abroad. It's been so long since I've been away from Halcyon."

"Yes, ma'am."

When the latest New York journals were brought to her, Devon reached for the *Record,* which she regarded as her alma mater. Although not as large or flamboyant as some of its daily competitors, it was an established and well-respected oracle, with a strong feminine appeal. Carrie Hempstead and Tish Lambeth were still on the staff, in better and higher-paying positions. Tish had replaced Devon midway in the world tour of former President and Mrs. Grant, and Devon followed her current reports on the Orient faithfully: from the magnificent Taj Mahal with its glorious singing birds of Aigre, to the fabulous amber palace and belly dancers of the Maharaja of Jaipur, to a thrillingly dangerous Bengal tiger hunt riding in an elephant howdah; sailing across the turbulent, pirate-infested China Seas to the teak-jade-pearl splendors of Singapore and Hong Kong, thence to the fantastic gold palace of the King and Queen of Siam, and finally to exotic, mysterious Japan, where the much-celebrated American general planted some memorial trees at Nagasaki. And Devon thought wistfully of all the wonders, excitement, history she had missed—all the marvelous, incredible opportunities that might never come her way again. . . .

In the political columns she learned that the governor of Texas had persuaded the junior senator, Reed Carter, to withdraw his resignation and remain in his appointed seat in the Senate. Nellie Hutchinson, whom Devon knew quite well from her own capital correspondency, wrote: "The ruggedly handsome young Texan, who still prefers his Western duds to those of his Eastern colleagues on Capitol Hill, has vigorously renewed his fight against the menacing monopolies. The brave David of the Lone Star State is drafting yet another antitrust bill, with which he hopes to slingshot and fell the Wall Street Goliaths, and specifically the biggest giant of them all, whose initials are K.H.C. With his usual candor, Senator Carter has vowed to 'go after the ornery varmints hell-bent for leather!' Whatever that means in Texas."

Devon knew very well what it meant for her former husband. Like Don Quixote, Reed Carter liked to tilt at windmills. He also fancied himself a cowboy Robin Hood, champion of the poor and oppressed citizens of his state. He longed to crush the robber barons of the North, retrieve the fortunes he felt had been stolen from the South, and return them to their rightful owners.

Whimsy touched Devon's features. She had expected Reed to marry his paramour, Melissa Hampton, immediately after his divorce, but apparently he was still single. Playing the field? The ladies of the Washington Press Corps, privileged to watch the political knights joust in the congressional arena, no longer referred to New York's aging Senator Roscoe Conkling as the Apollo of the Senate. Evidently, the valiant Texan in his unique leather armor had become their new idol, and they were enamored of him.

Turning to the Business Section, where her present spouse commanded so much attention, Devon was surprised to notice yet another familiar, unforgotten name. A new tobacco factory had recently gone into production in Richmond, Virginia, and the proprietor was none other than Daniel Haverston! Tobacco was an energetic commodity and industry since the advent of the increasingly popular cigarettes, and its stocks were trading high on the current market. Surely Keith had seen this particular item, for he habitually turned first to the financial pages. But Devon knew he would never intentionally mention it to her, nor that of Reed Carter, either. The men in her past were taboo in their conversations.

Good luck, Dan, and more power to you! Have you a wife and heir for Harmony Hill?

Nostalgia suddenly washed over her like a tidal wave, nearly drowning her in reminiscence of Virginia. The good days before the apocalypse of the Bluecoats, and the Confederate Armageddon at Appomattox. Her father happily publishing his newspaper, the *Richmond Sentinel*. Her carefree days and special friends. Plantation barbecues and balls and fox hunts and excursions on the James River in gaily decorated boats. A splendidly uniformed cavalier galloping off to war on a white steed, so confident of swift, triumphant return that the opposite never even occurred to him. . . .

But what did any of that matter to her now? Her dreams had come true, her wishes were fulfilled. She had the man she loved and the life she wanted. Everything she desired, and more. Didn't she? Of course, she did!

♂ 2 ♀

IT WAS shortly before midnight when the first true indications of labor alerted Devon: mild preludes, easily borne. Exhausted after a week of restless nights, Keith lay soundly asleep beside her, allowing himself only about one-third of the mattress, and she hated to disturb him. Nothing drastic could happen with the physician and nurse in residence, and the entire household prepared for the confinement.

She lay awake, counting the melodious Westminster chimes echoing through the still house from the grandfather clock in the foyer, and waiting for additional physical signs. Moonlight slanted through the windows, silvering the room and creating friendly shadows. Devon was familiar with the way the curtains waved and danced when blown by the river breezes, and the silhouettes of every beloved piece of furniture. The masculine garments on the mahogany valet provided comfort and security simply by their presence. The sight of them always made her want to touch him in the dark, assure herself that he was really there and she wasn't just dreaming. Feeling another slight pang, she glanced at the onyx clock on the nightstand, able to tell the time without lighting a candle. Placing her hands gently on the sides of her belly, as if cupping a huge melon from beneath, she realized what the doctor meant about the fetuses descending toward the birth canal. She had little doubt that this would be their birthday.

For several months now, since learning that she was carrying twins, they had wondered about their sex and what to name them. Would they be a pair of boys, girls, or one of each? To Scotty, his mother seemed to be waiting forever for the babies. During the interim, the animal population of the farm had increased by a new foal, a new calf, several litters of puppies and kittens, and batches of new chicks hatched in the henhouse almost every day.

Yesterday he had asked Devon, "Did I take so long to get here, Mommy?"

"I'm afraid so, darling."

"Was I much bother getting born?"

"Not much," Devon lied, reflecting on the long, terrible ordeal and suspense of that parturition. "No more so than is supposed to be natural, Scotty."

A frown puckered his small brow. "Will the babies be blind? The new kittens can't see yet. Daddy says it takes nine days before they open their eyes, and it's the same with all cats, even lion and tiger cubs."

"Well, I'm sure Daddy knows all about felines. But human infants see right away, dear, and cry almost immediately upon entering the world. You'll hear them."

"I can hardly wait," he declared and dashed outside to check on his most recently acquired pets.

Devon knew Miss Vale would have to keep her curious charge busier than usual today, lest he make a nuisance of himself during the travail. And though she hoped for at least one girl, she knew she would be pleased as punch with two more boys exactly like him.

At one o'clock she experienced another sensation, sharper and more significant, originating in her lower back and radiating to her abdomen. No false alarm, this signal, but she still could not bring herself to wake Keith. Let the poor darling sleep. She lay as quietly as possible, mentally marking the time, gritting her teeth and clenching her hands as labor inexorably advanced. Familiar with the various stages, she recognized the preliminaries and knew far worse developments were yet to come.

The ethereal light at the windows dimmed as the moon slipped away, surrendering the sky to dawn. Would it be over by noon, or at least by sunset? She prayed for a shorter, less difficult time than her first. Why must women linger and suffer in childbirth, anyway? Was it really by divine decree—God's angry, perpetual curse on the daughters of Eve? It seemed so cruel and unfair and merciless, even vindictive! If man and woman were not to procreate, why were they created in the first place? Merely as toys and pawns to play with in Paradise? Oh, the vagaries of pregnant ladies! She certainly had her share.

A faint pink luminescence brightened the rectangular frames of gray daybreak, and the cocks were crowing in the barnyard when a severe, piercing pain shot through Devon's being, evoking a spontaneous gasp and movement.

Instantly, as if his senses were attuned to hers, Keith was awake and inquiring anxiously, "What is it, darling? Pains?"

"Yes," she murmured, relaxing as it passed.

"Since when?"

"About midnight."

"Jesus, honey! Why didn't you tell me?"

"You know it takes a while, Keith, and you needed your rest. Go back to sleep."

He ignored that as ridiculous, rose, and began to dress. "I'll get Ramsey."

"Oh, I don't think that's necessary yet, dear."

"That's what he's here for, Devon! And the nurse, too. Hell, I'm going to wake the entire household!"

"Not Miss Vale and Scotty, please? Anna and Enid are

already up and in the kitchen—they always rise early. And I assume Karl and Lars are tending to their chores. This *is* a farm, isn't it?"

"Partly," he agreed, fully clothed now and walking out the door. "I'll be back promptly."

Dr. Blake returned with him, conducted a preliminary examination, and confirmed the onset of labor. But he did not expect rapid progress. "Six or seven hours yet," he estimated. "Go have some breakfast, Keith. Devon's going to be a very busy lady most of this day."

"I want to be with her, Ramsey."

"I know, and I have no objection. You can even assist if you like, although that's my nurse's duty. I remember the excellent job you did before, without medical assistance. And your housekeeper is a competent midwife, so we won't lack for assistants. Relax, man! Nothing will happen for quite a while, believe me. Let's both go downstairs and have some coffee."

Keith agreed, albeit reluctantly, kissing Devon lovingly before leaving. And soon Nurse Ellen Mayfield, in a crisp white uniform, apron, and cap, was preparing the lying-in chamber. She was in her early forties, with gray-streaked dark hair, pale brown eyes, and a pleasant professional manner. Devon knew Mrs. Mayfield had assisted Dr. Ramsey Blake in numerous deliveries and had accomplished many on her own in midwifery.

"Good morning," she greeted cheerily. "So this is the big day?"

"Evidently, and I certainly hope so, Ellen. I don't want any breakfast, however."

"You can't have any food, Mrs. Curtis. Only sips of water. It's a medical precaution, in case you should need some ether at the last, which can only be administered on a fasting stomach."

"You mean twilight sleep?"

"No, that's a different and prolonged procedure, which Dr. Blake practices only under certain conditions. Trust him to know what's best for you. Having experienced labor before, I'm sure you realize you're still and only in the initial stage of three?"

"Yes, but the discomfort is getting harder to grin and bear.

Too bad it can't be banished with magic words."

The nurse was preparing the instrument tray: surgical scissors, speculum, forceps, scalpel—the tools of childbirth, formidable and often frightening even to the initiated.

"Well, a French magician claims to have alleviated his wife's suffering through hypnosis. The experiment was reported in the medical journals last year, and now he's besieged by *enceinte* Continental ladies seeking his services."

Devon winced as another fierce contraction gripped and ultimately released her uterus. Mrs. Mayfield checked the watch hanging on a silver chain around her neck and asked sympathetically, "That was a hard one, wasn't it?"

Devon nodded and tried to divert her mind. The sun was rising, a heavenly glow in the east, promising a glorious day. Mrs. Sommes and Enid brought up extra supplies for the patient and the nursery, which Scotty had long since vacated. Two cradles and other accouterments were in readiness there now. Soon Devon heard the governess rousing her charge, informing him that classes would be held in the library this day. He protested sleepily that it was too early to get up, but Miss Vale persisted.

"Does the child know what's happening, Ellen?"

"No doubt his father will tell him. Your husband is a remarkable man, Mrs. Curtis. Most don't want to be present during labor and find excuses or escape in a bottle. Giving birth is woman's lot, you see, and they prefer to forget their role in her agony. My husband was not with me when any of our three children were born. Count your blessings, ma'am, and cherish your spouse."

"I do," Devon said, flinching at another brutal pain. It came sooner than expected, like a cruel vise clamping her pelvis for several excruciating moments that made her writhe and groan.

"Shall I summon the doctor?"

"Only when you consider it necessary, Ellen."

"Talk if you like. Sometimes it helps to pass the time and renders it less tedious."

"I suppose. How do you manage a career, marriage, and motherhood? Do you have domestic help?"

"A charwoman once a week. My youngest, a boy, is ten. My seventeen-year-old daughter is in control of the household while her father and I are away, and aided by her younger sister. We were never able to afford a nanny or governess. You are so very fortunate, in so many ways. Surely you don't miss *your* career?"

"At times," Devon admitted. "Journalism can be very interesting, and I had some fascinating assignments. Maybe I'm *too* fortunate in having so little to do now. But I'm sure that's not a familiar complaint from the majority of your other patients."

"Hardly. Most are overburdened with their marital and maternal duties. They all seek reliable methods of contraception and beg the doctor to abort unwanted pregnancies, which, of course, must be denied by law. Then they resort to quacks, or try to operate on themselves, with hatpins and crochet needles and even shoe-button hooks, often with dire consequences. The horrors and mutilations I've seen when they come, sometimes too late, to the doctor!" Nurse Mayfield shuddered in grim reflection.

Her information was not news to Devon. While active in the Women's Movement, she had heard and read numerous accounts of such tragedies, of the pathetic victims of desperation, both wedded and unwedded. Certainly she could never forget her own fears and anxieties when first caught in womankind's oldest and most painful trap!

"I can imagine," she said, grimacing at more cyclical progress and punishment.

"Scream if you like, dear. I always tell my patients that. Why try to be brave and noble about it? Some strong men roar like bulls at the removal of a splinter from a finger and faint at the sight of a little blood. But I've also seen severely wounded soldiers suffer and die valiantly. Battlefield nurses could never understand the male enigma, any more than the men could understand women ministering to them under fire. Quite a paradox, we humans, all in all."

For an indefinite space Devon's mind drifted back to the war: Richmond under siege, her father dead of his own volition in the office of the *Sentinel,* the victorious Union Army marching into the defeated Confederate capital; herself fleeing in terror and panic to Capitol Hill, clutching the few personal possessions she could salvage, and watching with other horrified, bewildered citizens as the once proud and beautiful city on the James River trembled and exploded and burned through the longest, most awesome night of her life. So many years ago... and yet so vividly realistic!

Swept back to the present on waves of rhythmic pain, she found herself still lying in the great Flemish oak bed in her home on the Hudson—the wife of a handsome, enormously wealthy Yankee, not the ruined, limping Rebel fiancé she had left in Virginia....

"Water, please," she whispered, licking her parched lips. "My throat is awfully dry."

Nurse Mayfield held the cup to her mouth. "A few sips only, Mrs. Curtis. No more."

Devon obeyed and asked, "Have I been raving?"

"Mumbling a bit, incoherently. It's common in the throes of labor."

Intense physical torture induced intermittent delirium, and a kaleidoscope of memories spun desultorily in her head. She was on a dark train chuffing northward, surrendering her virginity in a princely private coach; then, a fine hotel in Washington and more forfeited virtue. Next, she was alone in New York, modeling exquisite lingerie in a French boutique. Working in a Broadway bookshop and fending off the prurient old proprietor in a blizzard. A supper club on Chatham Square, posing in fabulous bird costumes in gilded cages, until recaptured by the determined Yankee and whisked off to a lovely apartment in Greenwich Village to become his mistress. They were sailing up the Hudson in a luxurious steam yacht, to Saratoga Springs and the elaborate Mountain House in the Catskills, where they made wild, reckless love in a storm. She was marching with Susan B. Anthony and the suffragists through Wall Street and the Bowery, arrested and jailed—and rescued by the furious but forgiving Yankee lover, whom she could never quite forget nor long escape, no matter where perverse fate led her, including unwed pregnancy....

Then she was traveling through the war-ravaged South with Reed Carter, leaving her precious baby and his father behind... a desolate little ranch near Forth Worth... a friend named Carla Winston... coyotes attacking the crude wilderness cabin at night... a raging prairie fire and miscarrying in a jouncing buggy . . . living in Austin, where Reed Carter was Speaker of the Texas House of Representatives . . . reporting Nellie Grant's wedding at the White House . . . meeting Keith and Scotty again . . . returning to Texas . . . a boat race on the Colorado River and plunging through foaming rapids and over a steep waterfall into a treacherous whirlpool. . . .

Screaming, thrashing, struggling to survive the vicious maelstrom—Oh, God, she was going to die! She was being wrenched and torn apart with hideous pain, and she couldn't fight any longer. . . .

Vaguely, as if from another world, she heard voices and felt hands shaking her back to consciousness. She wasn't perishing in a wild river, after all; she was giving violent birth in bed, and people were surrounding her.

"Help her, Ramsey!" Keith demanded as the doctor and nurse worked with her. "Give her something! We've discussed twilight sleep—"

"Yes, and I've used scallopine successfully in single births, Keith. But I don't consider it wise in this case. Devon has been carrying two healthy fetuses for nine months—we can't take any unnecessary risks these last minutes just to alleviate some natural pain. She's well dilated, it won't be much longer. Less than an hour, and I think she's strong enough to bear it. Why don't you go downstairs, open a bottle of cognac—"

"You know damned well I'm not going to take that advice, Ramsey!" Keith flinched as Devon moaned again and clutched at the birthing straps attached to the bedposts during her delirium. "Yell, darling," he urged, aiding her. "Bring the goddamn roof down, if it'll help!"

He felt helpless, powerless, and it frustrated and infuriated him. She was suffering because of his pleasure, and he silently swore that he would never bring such agony upon her again. Yet how could he keep such a vow, loving and desiring her as he did? The past few months of sexual abstinence had been sheer hell for him, and only the alternative of infidelity was more abhorrent. The mere thought of ever betraying her with another woman sent Keith back to her side and bending to kiss her moist, flushed cheek in mute, humble apology.

Perspiration drenched her body as she pulled frantically on the strong leather straps, straining with all her dissipating strength and grit, grimacing and groaning. Her saturated gown had been thrown up and back, her legs parted widely and bent at the knees. The water sac ruptured, and hot, bloody fluid gushed out onto the protected mattress. Keith spoke tender words of encouragement, his own muscles aching in sympathy, and angry with Ramsey for withholding the comforting drug until expulsion of the first fetus. The second followed rapidly, and Keith could not contain his relief and elation.

"Thank God!" he exclaimed, mopping his own sweat as Devon gazed up at him groggily. "Girls, darling! We have two beautiful little daughters!"

There seemed to be a large crowd in the room, but Devon recognized only her husband's face and voice. Smiling weakly, she closed her eyes and sank into a sea of exhaustion. As if in a dream, she heard the lusty cries from the nursery, where the competent nanny tended them, while the physician and nurse cared for their exhausted mother. Soon Mrs. Sommes and Enid came in with fresh linens and lingerie, but Devon was unaware of their presence and ministrations.

"It's over, my darling," Keith whispered close to her ear, his lips brushing hers gently, "and everything is just wonderful. You were so strong and brave, and I'm so proud of you." Then a vial of ether was wafted under her nostrils, and Devon sailed into swift, merciful oblivion.

ঝ 3 ৎ

SCOTTY WAS on noon recess, watching the newborn cats, which were meowing and stumbling over one another to get to their mother's milk. So far only one of the litter of seven—an aggressive tom, striped and fuzzy—had opened its eyes enough to see. Scotty feared the others were in danger of starving, but somehow they found nourishment.

His father joined him, bending a knee to the ground. "Do you realize what you're observing, son?"

"Hungry kittens," he answered.

"The miracle of life, Scott. And your mother has just accomplished that miracle again herself. Two new lives, twin girls, and they're beautiful."

"Two girls?" He frowned in disappointment. "One would have been plenty. I wanted a brother. We'll be surrounded by petticoats and hair ribbons, Daddy!"

Keith smiled. "Believe me, son, the time will come when that won't be a matter of complaint. Eight or nine more years, and you'll enjoy the rustle of perfumed skirts."

"If you say so, sir," he said dubiously. "When can I see my sisters?"

"As soon as they're presentable, Scott. That's another thing you must learn about girls: they like to be seen at their best, always."

"Is Mommy all right?"

"Fine, but tired, of course. She's sleeping now, and we mustn't disturb her."

Scotty peered at his father. "Do you like the girls better than me, Daddy?"

Keith gave him a reassuring hug. "Certainly not! But I don't love them any less, either. I'm just happy they're here, safe and sound, and we are a nice little family now. Maybe you'd better get back to your lessons, son. Miss Vale is waiting for you in the library. Nanny will look after your little sisters." Her name was Penelope Tewkesbury, she was as British as tea and crumpets, but the Curtises would always refer to her simply as Nanny, at her request.

"I'm learning algebra now," the boy confided. "But it's all Greek to me."

"That's what I thought, at your age. But you'll catch on quickly, son. I wish you were old enough to drink a toast with me, but I'll have to do it with Dr. Blake. And tomorrow— well, I'm going to Manhattan and give every man on Wall Street *two* Havana cigars!"

"What will we name the twins?"

"Mommy and I haven't decided yet, Scotty. But we will soon and christen them at Grace Episcopal Church, where I was baptized."

"Me too, when I was born?"

Keith hesitated, a trifle too long, perhaps. "No, you haven't been through the formal rites of Christendom yet, son, but you will with your sisters. And we'll have a fine family celebration afterward—won't that be nice?"

"I guess so. Am I a heathen now, Daddy?"

"Heavens, no! Where did you get such an idea?"

"I must be a Jew, then. Because Miss Vale says all Christians are baptized."

"You're a Gentile, Scott. And you'll be christened, not circumcised."

"What does that mean?"

"So Miss Vale didn't explain circumcision? Well, it's an operation performed by rabbis on Jewish males, as an important ritual of the Hebrew faith. It won't happen to you, boy. Nor will you be immersed in water, like Jesus when the Apostle John baptized him in the River Jordan, merely sprinkled with it at the church font. I don't have time to go into detail now, but that's the gist of it."

Scotty pondered the blind kittens, scuffing the toe of one high-stopped shoe in the earth, stirring up dust. He still did not understand why he wasn't baptized in infancy, but his father seemed disinclined to discuss it further. His hand was on Scotty's arm now, gently propelling him toward the house and his education.

Not until much later that afternoon was he allowed to visit the new arrivals. Never having seen a newborn human, he didn't know what to expect. They were asleep in their frilled cradles, their tiny faces rosy-pink, soft fuzz of different shades covering their heads. Since all the adults said they were pretty, they must be. But their brother thought the baby animals were cuter, and certainly more fun, for he could not imagine much pleasure in playing with these little creatures. They appeared much too small and delicate, fragile enough to break on touch. But his father was beaming on them, and inquiring, "How do you like your sisters?"

He shrugged, unimpressed and uninterested. "They're all

right, I suppose. Awfully little, though, aren't they?"

"Oh, they'll grow, just as you did and are still doing! It's different with people, you know, and takes much longer to reach maturity. Shall we go see Mommy now?"

Devon had just awakened and wore a fresh blue silk nightgown and jacket ruffled in lace and fluttering with satin ribbons. Her honey-gold curls were neatly brushed, her amber-flecked green eyes smiling at her son. She opened her arms to embrace him, drawing him lovingly to her bosom. Scotty responded with a shy kiss on her cheek. After months of paternal cautioning to be gentle and careful with Mother, he wasn't quite sure just how to act now that she was no longer "in a delicate condition." But at least her first words were about him, not the bundles in the nursery.

"Scotty darling, I missed you this morning! Did you have a good day?"

"Yes, ma'am. I got ninety on my arithmetic test."

"Congratulations! Miss Vale says you're a wizard in all of your subjects. I hope your sisters will do as well."

"Why should they? Girls are not supposed to be as smart as boys, are they?"

Devon smiled, patting the mattress for him to sit down beside her. "Well, that's something of a myth, dear, which girls have to live with. It's not necessarily true, and often unfair. Many teachers are women. Miss Vale is quite smart, isn't she?"

"But Daddy says I'll have male professors in college."

An upward glance caught Keith's grinning countenance, which he promptly altered to a more serious one. "That's because you'll go to Harvard, an all-male university. There are some female professors in women's colleges. There are even a few lady doctors and lawyers, and no reason why they couldn't learn architecture and engineering, too. But you haven't mentioned your sisters yet, Scotty. Aren't they adorable little dolls?"

"I really wanted a brother," he said honestly.

"Maybe next time," Devon soothed.

"We mustn't tire Mommy," Keith told him firmly. "Besides, I think supper is ready. Go along, Scott."

"Aren't you coming down, sir?"

"No, I'll keep Mommy company up here."

"May I stay, too?"

"Not this evening, son. Mother and I need to talk about things that wouldn't interest you."

"Yes, sir. Nighty-night, Mommy."

"How about a kiss?"

He obliged, mumbled goodnight to his father, and walked out reluctantly, head bowed.

Keith frowned. "I'm afraid he's not very happy about the twins, Devon."

"Just a bit jealous, Keith—worried that they may supplant him in our affections. Nanny says it's perfectly natural, when there's so much space between children. His attitude will change once he's assured they're all of equal importance to us. We just can't fuss over them too much in his presence. I never had any siblings, hence no rivalry. How did you feel about *your* sister?"

"I don't honestly remember, but trust not resentful. Elaine and I were closer together in age, and she died of cholera at sixteen. Remember my telling you that?"

"Yes, you lost your mother in the same epidemic. Yellow fever took mine when I was twelve. I worry about childhood diseases, Keith. I was frantic when Scotty had measles in Washington. And I worried constantly all the time I was away from him."

Keith pulled up a chair. "Scott hasn't forgotten those separations, Devon. He's developing some curiosity about it, in fact. One day we may have to tell him the truth."

Her face blanched, her jaw fell. "Oh, no, Keith! How can we do that, *ever?*"

"He's already curious as to why he wasn't christened at birth, Devon. Unwittingly, I brought the subject up myself earlier today, concerning the twins, and his keen mind immediately focused on the baptismal aspect. I answered his questions as best I could, but I don't think he was completely satisfied. His intelligence is far above that of the average child his age, you know. He's something of a prodigy, according to Miss Vale. She has already started him on algebra."

"Dear God." Devon sighed. "My past is going to haunt me, isn't it?"

"Oh, now, darling, that's nonsense! Don't recant and upset yourself—it'll affect your milk. Ramsey thinks you'll be able to nurse both babes, for a while, anyway."

The sun had set and it was that tranquil time of evening, between twilight and dusk. The sky was faintly purple, the trees shadowless, doves already nestling under the eaves. Keith rose to light the kerosene lamps, noticing the strip of light beneath the closed nursery door, where Nanny was tending the infants. Devon gazed pensively at the flickering wicks in the polished crystal globes, mulling her past.

"Say something, Devon."

"Like what, Keith? That I sold myself to a married man to get to New York, became his mistress, and bore his child out of wedlock? And the rest of it? Will we explain your marital situation to him, and mine with Reed Carter? What does that say about me? My ethics, morals, decency?"

"There were extenuating circumstances, Devon."

Tears surfaced in her eyes, trickling down her cheeks. "But will he understand them? What does he know of my poverty and desperation after the war, my desperate ambition to support myself in journalism? The kind of witch Esther really was, and the vindictive bitch she became when she learned about our affair and child? Oh, he'll forgive you your trespasses! He's male, after all, and will experience his own masculine passions and transgressions in time. But how will he regard my mortal sins, my unconventional behavior?" She wept, brushing helplessly at the gushing tears. "I'm his mother, for God's sake! That one supposedly sacred image of woman to man!"

Keith moved immediately to comfort her, kneeling by the bed, drawing her tenderly into his arms and holding her head against his chest while she sobbed wretchedly. "Darling, that's in the distant future, if indeed it happens at all. And you're omitting the one fact that could rationalize our relationship to any intelligent, sensitive person: love. Intimate, complicated details shouldn't be necessary, and wouldn't be divulged, in any case. Scotty will never be told anything at all, Devon, unless I think he can handle it properly. Now, please, stop crying and fretting. Our trays will arrive soon, and you must eat heartily."

"I'm not hungry, Keith."

"You have to recoup your strength, Devon."

"To make milk?" she asked wryly.

"Well, there are two little mouths depending on you to feed them, Mommy."

"And a fresh cow in the barn if I fail them."

Remorse flogged Keith. He had been incredibly thoughtless to bring up the issue at this tedious time, even though his only intention was to prepare her, should Scott broach it himself and catch her off guard. But her emotions were still highly vulnerable in that respect, even after all these years. He kissed her tearful face, then her tremulous lips, suppressing his swiftly rising ardor. "I love you, Devon. You're my whole life. Nothing can change that. Look at me and say it's the same for you."

"You know it is." She sniffed. "What else could possibly have brought us to our present situation?"

"Well, I'm not sorry about it, Devon. I never have been and never want you to be. I'm fatalistic enough to believe we were destined for each other, and that mere mortals have no real control over their destiny. We're actually blessed, you know, and doubly so today. Let's have enough faith to assume the Almighty planned our lives this way." While he blotted her tears with his handkerchief, a knock sounded at the door. "Suppertime, darling. Smile?"

Devon obliged, touching his face briefly, never doubting the sincere love in his eyes, and confident that he realized *her* love was eternal. "Come in!" she called after the second tapping, and Mrs. Sommes and Enid pushed in a teacart heaped with a prodigal celebrational feast.

After her long fast, Devon's appetite was better than she expected, and she ate enough to please Keith. But he seemed to slight the delicious food, and she chided, "What's *your* trouble, Daddy? Isn't the roast beef cooked to your liking? It's certainly rare enough, and the Yorkshire pudding is excellent."

"Everything's fine," he said, pouring vintage champagne into crystal goblets. "I'm disciplining another kind of hunger, suddenly."

"Suddenly? You've been wrestling with *that* appetite for months, haven't you?"

"Don't worry, I have orders from the doctor."

"I'm not worried, so have I."

"Just the same, I think I'll sleep in a guest room for the next month or two."

Her silver spoon of dessert stopped midway to her mouth.

"No, Keith. I want you beside me. We slept together even when I hogged most of the bed. You insisted on being near, should I need you. Well, that could happen tonight."

"All right, I'll use the trundle." He drained and replenished his glass.

"Keith, I'm acquainted with your laudable self-control! There's something else bothering you now. What is it? My fertility?"

"You're still young, Devon, with many childbearing years left. I'm pleased and content with our little family. But I was frightened when Scotty was born, and more so today. I don't want to inflict that kind of ordeal on you again."

"That pregnancy wasn't accidental, Keith. Ramsey removed the pessary at our request—don't you remember? We were so afraid we had lost Scotty in the abduction. I—I thought you might want to try for another son in a year or two."

"I'd like that, of course. But while you conceive readily, you don't give birth easily. There's too much risk and danger involved, Devon."

"What are you proposing—abstinence? We can't live together without sex, unless you become an ascetic!"

"Well, I've been pretty much of a monk lately."

"Poor darling," she sympathized. "But I've been deprived too, you know. And we'll make up for it, just as soon as possible. I'm feeling much stronger already. Forget the trundle tonight. Just lie with me, hold me close, and I'll fall asleep quickly. I'm really quite exhausted and just want your presence. How can that hurt?"

Was she actually that naive? And did she imagine that he, too, would find quick slumber with her in his arms? Was she totally unaware of the kind of dreams he'd experienced recently, the carnal desires that frequently sent him into a cold tub, or galloping off on a horse!

"I think I'll fetch another bottle of champagne," he decided, rising. "Would you like some warm milk, or a wine caudle?"

"Perhaps later, darling. The babies are certainly quiet, aren't they?"

"Waiting for two A.M. to cry," Keith surmised, smiling. "If memory serves, that's when our firstborn usually chose to have colic."

"Oh, but we have an experienced nanny now, Daddy! I

know the doctor and nurse have gone on another case, but
would you tell Anna that I'd like a sponge bath, cologne rub,
and fresh nightie before retiring?"

"Anything else?"

"Just my husband."

"I want to visit Scott before his bedtime," he temporized.
"Cheer him up a little."

"Give him my love."

"That's what he needs most now, Devon. Our love."

She nodded, blowing him a kiss.

$\approx$ 4 $\approx$

MANY MOTIVATIONS spurred Devon's postpartum recovery,
none more effective than Keith's reluctance to resume conjugal
relations. A few weeks after the twins' birth, her figure was
back to normal and further enhanced by the larger, lactating
breasts. The doctor recommended another month of recuper-
ation, however, before mounting a saddle—a definite privation
for the excellent and avid equestrienne. Like any other potent
man, Ramsey Blake appreciated feminine beauty and accom-
plishment, and remarked that he was seriously considering a
wife-hunting expedition in Virginia. A personable bachelor in
his vigorous prime, and coveted by some of his female patients,
Ramsey still had not found his ideal mate. He visited Halcyon
frequently on weekends, riding or driving over from his own
estate in Washington Heights, and examining Mrs. Curtis and
the children on his calls.

"How many more of other men's heirs will you deliver, my
friend, before begetting one of your own?" Keith chided as
they stood in the nursery waiting for Devon.

The big, blond physician laughed jovially, replacing the
stethoscope in his alligator satchel. "Oh, until I find an irre-

sistible lady like yours to wed! Does Devon by any chance have a sister in her image back home? Or even a facsimile cousin?"

"Not to my knowledge, although that state, like most in the South, is noted for its charming belles. Certainly mine is proof of that. And though our daughters are not identical, I think they resemble their mother more than me. Don't you?"

"Who can tell, at this age? At least you won't need labels to tell them apart. Can't be positive about the permanent color of their eyes and hair yet, but I predict they'll have different shades of both. One may be fairer, however. Not less pretty, just more blond." He paused. "By the way, when is the christening?"

"Soon, probably."

"Summer is coming on hard in the city, Keith, and infantile diseases are always more prevalent and virulent in hot weather. Don't wait much longer."

"For what?" asked Devon, joining them after her examination, lovely in a buttercup yellow robe-de-chambre cleverly camouflaged for nursing.

"To take the twins on their first trip to Manhattan," Ramsey answered, his Nordic blue eyes frankly admiring her. "What did you think I meant?"

"Oh, that you were warning my husband further, even though you just pronounced me in excellent health. He's becoming a celibate, Ramsey. We both are!"

"Well, it's a little early to insert a pessary," the physician explained, glancing at Keith. "But you needn't martyr yourselves until then. There are other precautions, you know."

"See, darling?" Devon addressed Keith, as if they had not previously discussed the matter, most recently last night. "You needn't spend so much time at Gramercy Park." And turning again to Ramsey, "His Halcyon weekends are very short, starting on Saturday instead of Thursday. Talk to him, Ramsey. You will stay to dinner?" she invited, for it was Sunday.

"With pleasure," he accepted, "and Keith and I will be riding together this afternoon. If I'm to be godfather to your brood, I want to feel like a member of the family."

"We already regard you that way," Devon assured him.

"Then I should also know all the names of my future godchildren, my dear. For the vital statistics, anyway."

"Didn't Keith tell you? We're calling the girls Sharon and Shannon."

"Charming! Which is which?"

Devon indicated the nearest cradle, its ruffled net hood lined and bowed in a lighter shade of pink than the other. "This is Shannon."

"Cherubs, both of them," Ramsey declared. "Keith, you lucky devil! I envy you, in more ways than one."

Keith slapped his shoulder in comradely fashion. "You surely know how God sends such little angels to earth, Doctor? And it's high time you took a helpmeet!"

Nanny appeared on the threshold then, with nippled bottles of water for the infants, nodding to the gentlemen as they departed her domain.

Devon remained for her maternal duties. Nanny insisted on regular feeding schedules and advised Mrs. Curtis to alternate breasts during nursing. But suckling two babes was a demanding drain on her body, and everything she ate seemed absorbed in the production of milk. How much longer could she provide proper nourishment for two mouths? "I may have to wean one of them," she told Nanny, picking up Shannon and sitting in the wicker rocker.

"I suggest simultaneous weaning, madam."

"Why, if I can continue to satisfy one?"

"They're twins, Mrs. Curtis. Which would you choose to breastfeed?"

"You're right, Nanny. I couldn't slight either one." Unfastening her bodice, Devon guided a gorged nipple into the tiny, puckered mouth. Angel, indeed! she thought, gazing lovingly at the pink, cherubic face haloed with pale, silky curls. "You've seen many newborns, Nanny. Will she grow up blond?"

"I would say so, yes. More so than her sister, anyway. Sharon will have darker hair and perhaps gray eyes, like her father. But they'll both be beauties! How could they not be, with such handsome parents?"

"Thank you, Nanny. Shannon came ahead of Sharon, didn't she? By only a few minutes, but still the first to enter this world."

"And with a veiled head."

"Oh?" This was surprising news. "No one told me that."

"Nurse Mayfield promptly removed it. But it's no cause for concern, madam. Quite the contrary! Cauls are rare and supposed to portend good fortune."

"That's superstition, Nanny. Old wives' tales."

"Perhaps," said the Englishwoman, who was not as skeptical about such mysteries and phenomena as Americans. "It's a nice coincidence that they were born in June, too. Twins under the sign of Gemini. How fitting!"

"I'm not an astrological buff, Nanny." Devon rocked slowly, lest Shannon lose the nipple. Her small jaw did not clamp the breast as firmly as her sister's. Nor did she suckle as long, or seem to gain weight as rapidly. Soon satiated, she slacked and released her hold, and fell asleep before Devon could belch her. This would likely mean colic later, but Nanny knew how to cope with it. Floor-walking was a last resort, after peppermint oil or paragoric.

Sharon woke, wet and wailing. Nanny changed her diaper before delivering her to Devon, who went through the same ritual with her other breast. But Sharon clung tenaciously to her nourishment, trying to cup it with both hands, working her strong jaws busily. Her opened eyes were indeed a grayish hue, a rather smoky cobalt, and no golden flecks such as Shannon's glinted in the irises. Sharon's thatch of hair would probably darken considerably in time. Her father's child more than her mother's, just like Scott, and Sharon would likely resemble her brother more than her sister.

As it was obvious from birth that they were identical twins only in their sex, it was also readily apparent that they possessed other distinctive characteristics. If Sharon was more aggressive, Shannon was more cunning. She could cry just as long and lustily as Sharon, and did so oftener for mere attention than the necessities of life. Sharon yelled more demandingly for food and dry clothing, ceasing her complaints once these creature comforts were satisfied, and tending to amuse herself. Shannon wanted to be carried, rocked, cuddled, played with, and she smiled winsomely much earlier than did her sister.

"Her mother all over again," Keith declared, observing Shannon's antics with doting delight. "Adorable when she coos, and cute even when she drools."

"You didn't know me as a baby."

"I didn't have to, my pet. Shannon is undoubtedly an exact replica in miniature. Haven't you noticed? Her eyes are changing from blue to green, and the sparkles are more pronounced, like gold dust on aquamarines. Can you doubt that her champagne-colored curls are the same? The little minx already knows how to charm and coax her daddy, too."

"Oh, really, Keith! At five months?"

"Feminine instinct." He grinned. "Sharon has it too, though not as much. I assume she gets most of her looks and reserve from me. I was never much of a flirt."

"Just a rogue," Devon teased, crinkling her pert, retroussé nose at him.

"See what I mean? When I chuck Shannon under the chin, her button nose does the same thing."

They were sitting on the bedroom carpet, the infants on a pallet between them. Both girls had already discovered their fingers and toes and found them fascinating, although Sharon was the first to get her foot in her mouth. Bored with her rattle, Shannon impulsively tossed it away, accidentally striking her twin. Without crying, Sharon simply retrieved the toy and flung it back.

"Separation time," Keith decided expediently. "Nanny can take them strolling in the buggy. Did I tell you I'm having a double carriage built? And when they're old enough, I'll buy a fancy pony trap, white leather with gold trim, like the one that ballerina, Maria Bonfanti, drives in Central Park."

"You're determined to spoil them, aren't you, in spite of their sensible nurse? I pity poor Miss Vale when they become her responsibility."

"She manages Scott well enough, doesn't she? And boys are supposedly more difficult than girls."

"Not always," Devon said, rising to summon Nanny. "I wasn't exactly docile."

"That's a fact!" Keith sighed, symbolically clapping his forehead. "What a merry chase you gave me! I despaired of ever catching, much less taming, you."

"I wasn't wild, Keith. Just stubborn and fiercely independent."

A nod and arched brow acknowledged that. "And still not completely gentled-down or resigned, eh?"

"Is that what you want?" she countered with a coy smile.

"I thought you admired my spirit."

Outwitted, Keith grinned and slapped her buttocks. "You haven't changed much, Devon. That spunky, feisty little rebel I met in Richmond still resides in the woman, and emerges often enough to challenge my mental agility. Indeed, that free spirit is an integral part of your charm, my love, and you've always had more than your share."

"How else could I have captured such a clever Yankee?" she quipped, playing the game. "Perhaps I should have served the Confederacy as a spy, like our detective friend, Carla Winston?"

Mistaking her reference to the war and Carla Winston, whom he had hired to protect her in Texas, his manner sobered, and he waited until the babies were on their way outside before speaking again. "Would you like to spend the weekend on the yacht, Devon?"

"I'd love it, Keith! The children, too?"

"Just Scott. The twins couldn't appreciate it. And now they're weaned, we can go a few places together again. You must have felt terribly confined since our marriage."

"Well, I have missed the city," Devon admitted. "The restaurants and theaters and shopping. Visiting my friends at the *Record* and the Women's Bureau, too."

The last two admissions disturbed Keith, and he sought other distractions for her. "We shall have to do some entertaining at Gramercy Park," he proposed tentatively. "My old friends are beginning to wonder about us. We've declined so many invitations in the past."

"With good reason, Keith."

"It's different now," he reminded.

"Even so, your old friends were also *her* old friends, and the house in Gramercy Park—"

"Was my mother's home first," he interrupted. "You can redecorate it any way you please, Devon. Or we can build a new town residence. Some fine mansions are rising on Fifth Avenue. I think we should have a cottage at Newport, too."

"My word! You didn't talk that way ten years ago."

"I didn't have a family ten years ago," he reasoned. "Lord knows I'm no social lion, Devon, and I never want us to become whirling dervishes constantly spinning in party circles. But you don't have to seclude yourself in the country anymore, Mrs.

Curtis. Our children will need the companionship of others in their position. Scott has already been too long deprived of suitable friends. He'll meet some at the right schools, of course."

"Oh, of course, dear! I forgot that your heirs have noble blood in their veins. But what about their maternal ancestry?"

"Are you being sarcastic? There's nothing wrong with your lineage, Devon. Your father was a highly respected publisher. An intellectual."

"Who killed himself," she lamented, "rather than face reality. My mother's family were gentlefolks, but not landed gentry. Not Southern aristocracy! We were not wealthy, we owned no plantation or slaves. I was not to the manor born!"

His arms circled her waist in an effort to calm her sudden agitation. "My sweet innocent, you're confused about the antebellum caste system; it doesn't prevail in the North. Every journalist is aware of the backgrounds of the Astors and the Vanderbilts; they came out of butcher shops and off ferryboats! I'd stake your genealogy against theirs anytime, along with that of many other prominent citizens of this country. Most of Manhattan's 'elite' really are robber barons—even your husband, to some extent."

"You didn't admit that when Senator Reed Carter was gunning for the Wall Street monopolists, as he still is!"

"Hell, I didn't care when he attacked my wealth and business tactics, Devon. I was far more concerned that he might hurt you and our child. That's why I fought him so hard, with lobbyists and friends in Congress. And I'll do it again, if he revives our old vendetta and starts shooting at me from the hip!"

She faced him, endeavoring to fathom the smoky-gray depths of his eyes. "You still hate Reed, don't you? And you'd enjoy clashing with him over any issue. Too bad you can't settle your grievances with fisticuffs, as you did with Daniel Haverston."

"*That* was never settled," he said grimly. "Your Virginian cavalier never retracted his challenge to duel, you know. And no doubt the Texan would have issued one, too, if we had met in his lawless territory. But you seem to forget, my dear wife, that both of your Southern gallants initiated the feuds."

"And you seem to forget, my dear husband, that neither one

is *my* Southern gallant anymore."

"No matter. If they expected to confront a Yankee coward, they were disappointed. And should our paths be so unfortunate as to cross again—"

"Kiss me," she interrupted, slipping her arms around his neck and rising on tiptoe to offer her lips.

His mouth remained poised above hers, not quite touching, only their breaths mingling. "The eternal temptress, up to her old tricks? I say something you don't like, you shut me up with temptation. Always works, doesn't it?"

"Does it?"

"Not often enough lately, but you know why."

"I'm wearing my gold stud again, dear. We can indulge more freely. Unless you have some personal problem?" she teased, undulating her pelvis seductively against his and thrilling to his potent response.

"Oh, yes, it works!" he muttered, seizing her.

Their mouths fused, tongues probing and sharing. Instantly ignited, their volatile passions spread like molten fire in their veins, intense and consuming. As he parted her negligee, his head dropped to her breasts, nuzzling the deliciously warm and fragrant flesh, tasting the taut coral-tipped nipples. Stimulated to erotic frenzy, Devon wished she were still nursing the babies, for Keith would never be weaned from this particular pleasure. Expecting to be swept off her feet and into bed, she felt herself instead sinking to the floor with him, on the patchwork quilt.

"Take that thing off," he ordered, swiftly disrobing himself, ripping off buttons in the process.

Devon mutely obeyed, casting aside the lacy garment and preparing herself eagerly for him. As always, she encouraged his prompt entry and vigorous action. Love and desire merged in perfect harmony and sequence, generating waves of exquisite nuance and crescendo, cresting in her first orgasmic rhapsody. Thoroughly familiar with her sexual nature, Keith induced a series of such vital ecstasies, rotating deeply and rhythmically inside her, before surrendering to his own desperate and demanding urgency.

"Oh, darling," she whispered, clutching him to her quivering bosom. "Just like in the Catskills!"

"Yes," he groaned, relishing the last throbbing sensations

of his finale, then turning on his side with her, tête-à-tête. "And you know what happened during that violent storm in those mountains?"

Sweat glistened on his marvelously virile body, as it had on that unforgettable occasion in the Mountain House, when nothing had mattered but the wonder and joy of copulation. She still remembered the lustful glitter of his eyes in the flashes of lightning, the ravishingly brilliant smile, and the convulsive, climactic explosion that had undoubtedly impregnated her with his son.

Now she worked her fingers in the dark, moist hair at the back of his head and stroked his shoulders, soothing the same anxieties she knew had assailed him after that other unbridled indulgence. "We had no protection then. But I wouldn't care if it happened again, Keith. Truly, I wouldn't."

"I *would*, Devon. It's too soon. I should have taken extra precaution."

"That Don Juan thing?"

"It's called *coitus interruptus.*"

"And you've always hated it. Married men don't have to practice withdrawal, Keith."

"Damn it, Devon!" he swore impatiently, pulling away from her. "Can't you understand? I don't want to make you pregnant again. These wild, reckless episodes are dangerous to your health. I damned near raped you."

"Or vice versa—and I loved it."

"We'd better get dressed," he suggested. "I wanted to wait until we were on the yacht for this kind of action, and even then I intended to be careful."

"Darling, stop worrying! I feel marvelous. Wonderfully relaxed, as if I'd just bathed in warm oil."

"That wasn't warm oil I gushed into you, lady." He gathered his garments and stood to replace them.

Devon stretched languidly. "Didn't we sleep on the floor that night in the Catskills?"

"Will you get your mind off that subject?"

"Yes, dear. And I promise not to seduce you again, until we board the *Sprite.*"

"That's this afternoon!"

"Well, I might spare you until tonight." She smiled up at

him provocatively. "Give you time to recuperate."

"Spare me?" He laughed, shaking his head. "Cover up your pretty little ass, my brazen enchantress, before we test how exhausted I am! Haven't you learned yet that I don't like challenges? Well, you will on the cruise. I'll have you begging for mercy."

"Promise?" she asked, chuckling.

❧ 5 ❧

IT WAS their first vacation together in over a year, and their first ever as man and wife. So much had happened since the May evening in 1875, when Keith had come to the Brooklyn Hotel, where Devon was staying while reporting on the trial of America's most famous clergyman, the Reverend Henry Ward Beecher, accused of adultery with the pretty young wife of his best friend. A *cause célèbre* even before it went to court, the long, bitter, sordid case provided front-page news and national sensationalism for over six months. And after several days of pondering Keith's invitation to sail around Long Island with him, Devon had acquiesced during a weekend court recess. Her legal spouse was in Washington then, busy with his antimonopoly bill, which he hoped to introduce in the Senate.

That particular cruise was especially memorable to Devon, because it marked the resumption of her love affair with Keith Curtis. Until then, she had successfully resisted him, despite their emotional meeting at the White House on the occasion of the social event of the year—the marriage of President Grant's daughter, Nellie, to a British diplomat; and even afterward during their long, worried vigil at their ill child's bedside in the Clairmont Hotel. It was while celebrating Scotty's recovery that Devon had come perilously close to surrender, fleeing from Keith's comforting embrace to weep miserably and alone in her separate suite. If only she had known *then* of Reed's in-fidelity with Melissa Hampton in Austin while Devon was away, and of their later flagrant episodes in the Carters' own home in Georgetown!

Lying in Keith's arms in their stateroom now, as the yacht cruised the moonlight waters off Long Island, Devon wondered how she could ever have imagined that she might eventually forget Keith by marrying Reed and going to Texas with him. What desperation, despair, what utter madness had possessed her! Her bewildered sigh woke Keith, who was just dozing off. They had retired early after a delicious meal, made marvelous love in the commodious double berth, and then shared a night-cap from the same snifter, tasting the brandy on each other's lips in the good-night kiss. Her life seemed so blissfully happy and perfect, she feared some sudden calamity might mar or even destroy it.

"Bad dream?" Keith asked, alert now.

"No, I haven't fallen asleep yet. But you were about to, darling, and I'm sorry for disturbing you."

"Can't you relax, Mrs. Curtis? Before our marriage you worried about the crew knowing we were in my quarters at night. What's the trouble now—too much lovemaking?" His teasing recalled her earlier sexual challenge.

She shook her head on the pillow, smiling. "No, you proved your point adequately, Mr. Curtis. Appropriately, too, for a man should be masterful in his master cabin. I hope you always are with me, in that respect."

Sitting up, Keith reached for the decanter in the handy rack above the berth. "You know very well it's a mutual conquer-ing," he said, pouring another single potion and offering her the first sip. "But that doesn't explain your insomnia now. I sense some tenseness and anxiety, Devon. Shall we talk?"

"Oh, it's silly of me, Keith. But I was thinking how won-derful things are for us now, when suddenly a dark cloud passed over the moon."

He glanced at the portholes. "It's a brilliant night, darling, almost luminescent."

"I meant my personal moon, Keith. Maybe I'm a masochist and can enjoy happiness only so long before tormenting myself with ominous doubts of its continuance. We've never had smooth sailing for long in the past, you know."

"And you're afraid it's too good to last?"

She nodded, moving into the curve of his arm. "Promise me it'll never change?"

"My dear, you made that same request in Saratoga once, remember? I couldn't guarantee it then, and I can't now, because life is not immutable and change is inevitable. I can only promise to love, honor, and cherish you until death."

"Oh, don't say that! I couldn't live without you."

"Dearest, yours fears are somewhat premature. I'm not planning to expire anytime soon."

"Neither was your Wall Street friend when he dropped dead last week in the Gold Room of the Stock Exchange."

"He was sixty, Devon, and engaging in wild trading in mining stocks. His heart simply couldn't endure the stress. Such strain has felled more than one bull and bear. You should have seen them collapsing on Black Friday. Several leaped out of windows. I try to keep a level head and avoid the hazards of imprudent speculation."

"Is that why President Grant so frequently besieged you to become Secretary of the Treasury during both of his administrations?"

"Well, the Curtis Bank has maintained a stable monetary pulse for three generations, and Grant's fiscal policies were always in chaos. The military genius was a financial dud and dupe. The country is booming now, but another bust is predictable. The market functions on cyclical crises, and the greediest speculators usually get hurt the most." He paused, trying to lighten her mood. "Hell, honey, you think I want to leave a beautiful young widow for some other man?"

"Don't joke about this, Keith. I know you're under pressure sometimes, whether you admit it or not, and involved in many other industries besides banking. Railroads, shipping, oil, metals, utilities. You invested heavily in the Bell Telephone Company and will probably do the same in the Edison Electric Light Company now forming."

"Definitely. They're not risks or gambles, they're sure things. Their stocks will skyrocket, and the early investors will reap fortunes. The Wizard of Wall Street," he said, reminding her of one of his journalistic tags, "would be a dunce not to cast some lots with the Wizard of Menlo Park! Bell's and Edison's inventions will rank with the steam engine in historic and economic importance. But I won't be flirting with apoplexy when the laggards are vying for their stocks in the Exchange, because my certificates are already secure in my vault. And having a competent agent to act for me, I don't even occupy my seat in the Gold Room much anymore. So banish your worries, my beloved. I should survive at least as long as Commodore Vanderbilt, who made it to eighty-three."

"Despite his vices," Devon murmured.

"Or maybe because of them," he suggested, his left hand cupping her bare breast. "He liked his wine and women, and was seventy-seven when twenty-four-year-old Tennie Claflin became his mistress. Weren't they together on his yacht when her sister, Victoria Woodhull, the biggest whore since her Babylonian predecessor, conducted a seance to contact Margaret Fuller's spirit in Davy Jones's locker? Wall Street roared with laughter for weeks after that escapade, in which my adorable little rebel participated without my knowledge. Maybe we'll sail over the exact location when we pass Fire Island."

"Don't you ever forget anything?"

"Not where you're concerned. More cognac?"

"I'll get drunk."

"No, I wouldn't let that happen to either of us. As you know, I agree with Shakespeare that 'alcohol provokes the desire but takes away the performance.' I try to avoid such handicaps."

Devon cuddled closer to him. "What time is it?"

"Just past midnight, if the ship's bells are correct. We can sleep late tomorrow and breakfast in here."

"Lovely idea," she agreed.

"Just one of the many marital benefits, Mrs. Curtis."

Flinging back the sheet, he feasted his eyes on her nudity: the firm, conical breasts and erect coral nipples; the perfectly molded hips and thighs and triangle of golden hair that never failed to arouse him. Moonlight streaming through the portholes gave her smooth, creamy skin a pearly opalescence, inspiring erotic fantasy. "You look like a naked sea nymph," he said, caressing her from head to toe. "I'd love to chase you in the surf that way. Maybe tomorrow evening, if we can find an isolated beach. . . ."

Devon was silent, enchanted by his passionate voice and skillful fondling. The prelude was almost as intoxicating as the ultimate intimacy, and he knew precisely how to prolong and intensify it. Pausing for a sip of brandy, he did not swallow all of it, and soon Devon savored it on his tongue in a voluptuous kiss. Repeated with her breasts, the exotic stimulation sent them both into rapturous tremors. His mouth moved slowly down her body, kissing every sensitive nerve and fiber, and finally accomplishing an incredibly joyful experience for her. Desire mounted swiftly, running rampant, urgent, demanding. As he knelt between her parted thighs, she arched her pelvis and positioned her legs around his torso, taking all he could give her and eager for more. He luxuriated in her pleasure, she gloried in his, and once again Devon thought nothing on earth or in heaven could equal this magnificent act of love. She wished it could be so for every woman with her man, although she knew it was not and pitied those so deprived. How fortunate she was!

They lay melded together for a quiet interlude, making appreciative gestures. Devon's happiness bubbled up irrepressibly, and she chuckled contentedly, as his face nestled between her warm, sweet breasts.

"That's a satisfied gurgle," he remarked, "if ever I heard one."

"Oh, Keith, this must be God's greatest gift to humanity! I can't believe life offers anything better, and I hope it lasts forever for us."

He smiled. "No doubt the Creator receives many such petitions, darling."

"Well, we shouldn't take our blessings for granted, and I shall thank Him every night in my prayers."

His eyes glinted in amusement. "Before or after the glorious climax?"

"During," she quipped, hitting him with a pillow, and their playful laughter echoed in the quiet ship.

Wearing an exquisite apricot satin peignoir, Devon allowed herself to be pampered with breakfast in bed. Nautical in white flannel trousers and dark blue blazer, Keith sat on a leather captain's chair beside the berth, smiling at her ravenous appetite for the luscious Persian melon garnished with fresh peaches and strawberries.

"Rufus always remembers what I like," she said. "He's a

marvel, Keith, and I hope he never leaves us."

"Why should he? He's well paid and has no duties beyond the yacht and rail coach. But I agree, he is a culinary genius and could make a reputation for himself as a chef, if the fine hotels and restaurants weren't convinced that only the French know how to cook."

Devon poured thick sweet cream into her tea, then spread orange marmalade on a hot split buttered English muffin and offered him a bite.

He declined, savoring his strong black coffee. "I'm sure there's more in the galley, honey."

"And I'm famished!" she declared, removing the silver cover from a mushroom omelet.

"My love, are you eating for two again? If not, you're going to get rolypoly fat, and I'll divorce you."

"Would you, really, for obesity?"

"You know better, just as I know you'll never be obese. You have too much pride."

"You mean vanity?"

"That, too, in small measure. But a completely humble woman is usually also a dull one," he added before she could protest. "And I probably *would* divorce you for dullness."

"I'll never bore you, sir—especially not in bed," she promised, winking.

"Careful, my alluring little mermaid, or I'll dive back into the bunk. Finish your meal, get dressed, and come on deck. Scott must be wondering if we slipped overboard last night— which, in a sense, we did." He bent to kiss her cheek, retrieved his yachting cap, and left.

The boy, a miniature of his handsome father in identical regalia, was at the ship's helm with the captain when she arrived. Sighting Devon, he ran to greet her. "Good morning, Mother!"

"Good morning, son! Are you enjoying the cruise?"

"Aye-aye, ma'am! I always do, don't I, Daddy? Heck, I never even got seasick when we went to England!"

"You're a fine sailor," Keith complimented. "You proved it on the Atlantic."

Reference to that voyage, which had excluded her, always saddened Devon. Now she glanced entreatingly at Keith. "When are we going abroad?"

"When the twins are older."

"They're old enough now, dear. Babies are born at sea, you know. The *Mayflower* arrived with children on it, and every immigrant ship since brings more. We'll take Nanny and Miss Vale along, of course."

"We'll see," he hedged, indicating the comfortable lounge chairs under the new green-and-white striped awning, scalloped with breeze-fluttering fringe. Large, thick canvas cushions scattered on deck invited convenient sunning by day and stargazing at night, and the overall effect was that of a sultan's luxurious barge. Silver carafes of steaming coffee and tea and a pitcher of iced milk for the child stood on the anchored serving cart, along with a tray of tempting pastries.

Eyeing her favorite napoleons, Devon declared, "I swear you *want* me to get plump!"

"Oh, no, Mommy!" Scott intervened, associating fatness with pregnancy. "The sweets are for me, mostly."

"Then don't eat too many, dear, and brush your teeth afterward. Where is Miss Vale?"

"In her cabin, preparing some tests for me."

"At college level, I presume?"

"Preparatory school. Daddy says I'm going to Groton when I'm twelve, and I have to be ready."

"That's still a few years off, Scotty." Devon did not like to think about his leaving them at all, being at home only on holidays and vacation. Taking a seat, she told Rufus, "Just tea, please. No cream or sugar."

"Yes, ma'am. And you, sir?"

"Nothing, thank you. I want to smoke."

It was perfect sailing weather, and other pleasure craft were on the water, some familiar to Keith. A gracefully rigged schooner drifted on the wind, her master signaling as she passed, and Bowers returned the salute.

"Do you know them?" Devon asked.

"Courtesy of the sea, darling. But yes, I know the owner, and so do you. James Gordon Bennett, Jr."

"I hardly thought you and the publisher of the *New York Herald* were friends."

"We're not, just members of the same yacht club. The bastard was accepted after he won that race to England some years ago. To give the devil his due, Bennett's a damned good yachtsman. Unfortunately, he's also a yellow journalist, with the carnival instincts and tactics of P. T. Barnum. I know he offered you a job when you were with the *Record*. Did you ever consider working for him?"

"Not seriously. He has a terrible reputation as a drunkard and womanizer, and is incredibly crude and unethical. I couldn't ever work for anyone like that."

"Good, because I wouldn't let you, Devon."

Fishermen trawled in dirty, battered old boats, dragging huge nets or drying them on the masts and rails. A Coast Guard cutter patrolled offshore, reminiscent of the United States vessels that had menaced Southern ports during the war blockade. Great steamships resembled toys receding on the distant horizon. Other silhouettes enlarged as they approached New York Harbor, and through her binoculars Devon viewed one flying the French flag.

"Oh, I hope new Paris fashions comprise her entire cargo!" she cried excitedly. "After all those smocks and hubbards and buttoned bodices, I'm ready for the latest fall creations from Monsieur Worth's salon!"

"By now, Madame Demorest has already copied the best of his collection for her Emporium," Keith surmised, nonchalantly puffing his cigar.

"Perhaps. She and Jenny June were abroad again this year. But I still want some originals."

"As many as you like, darling, including his most elegant evening wear. I was serious about attending some social functions—and even hosting a few of our own."

"As you wish, master."

"None of that now!"

"But I would like to sail south sometime, Keith. To Baltimore, Charleston, Savannah."

"And Richmond?"

"How did you guess?"

"I seldom have to guess with you, Devon. You want to go to Richmond most of all, don't you?"

"Well, I haven't been back since . . . since you took me away so long ago."

"At whose request, my pet? You were so desperate to leave then, I think you would have tried to stow away or hobo on that train to New York, if Rufus had not admitted you to my car under false pretenses. What a chain of events we started that night!"

"Any regrets?"

"None, although I know you've had some."

"I won't deny that, Keith. As I said before, you never forget anything. But that's all in the past now."

"Then why do you want to return to Richmond, even for a visit?" he inquired, quirking a dark brow at her.

"It's my birthplace, after all, and I guess I'm a mite homesick. Isn't that natural?"

"Yes, of course."

"I wonder if any of my old friends are still there, and why Mrs. Chester stopped writing to me."

Keith pondered the glowing ember of his Havana cheroot before tossing it overboard. "Renewing old acquaintances might be somewhat embarrassing with your Yankee husband along, Devon. You might prefer to go alone."

"Don't be absurd! I'm proud of my Yankee husband. And my beautiful half-Yankee children, too. I'd love to show off my whole wonderful family."

"Captain Bowers could alter our course."

"Mercy, no! I only packed for the weekend, and my jewel case is virtually empty. I left Richmond in rags, without even the gold locket and cameo brooch from my father, which I sold to a Union officer for his sweetheart. And my mother's jewelry was donated to the Confederacy—" She broke off, unable to pursue that memory.

Keith nodded, understanding: she wanted to present a different image on her return. "We'll dock at our Hudson berth after the cruise and stay in town, Devon. You can buy a complete new wardrobe, all the latest styles, and I'll pick up a few new trinkets for you at Tiffany's."

"Darling, I have loads of jewelry in the safes. Your mother's, and the fabulous pieces you bought for me."

"A lady can't have too many jewels or furs, my dear. Don't deprive me of the pleasure of giving you more. Besides, it helps to solve my gift problems."

"You're so good to me, Keith."

He reached for her hand, pressing it lovingly. "And you reward me amply, Devon. Do you have any particular date in mind?"

"For what?"

"The journey to Richmond."

"Oh, that. Next spring, perhaps. Virginia is beautiful in April and May, and that's also when most outdoor entertainments are held."

"You expect us to be entertained?"

"Why not? Not everyone in Dixieland perished in poverty. As publishers, the Marshalls knew a good many people, and I've read that some of them are quite prosperous now, even renovating old family homesteads and estates."

"Indeed?" Keith frowned, curious about one particular plantation. "Could you be more specific?"

"I wasn't thinking of Harmony Hill," she denied.

"Weren't you?" he asked skeptically. "And would you decline an invitation from the proprietor?"

"Would you?" she parried.

"And affront Southern hospitality? No, if the Virginian can swallow enough of his pride and arrogance to make the effort, I shall be the soul of tact and courtesy."

"Truly, Keith?"

"Word of honor."

"That sounds tongue-in-cheek and crossed-fingers," she accused.

"Such skepticism wounds me here." He grinned, touching his heart.

Detecting cynicism in his casual geniality, Devon prudently changed the subject. For all his suave sophistication, he could not totally conceal or disguise his jealousy of her old beau. Was he remembering their bitter confrontation at Halcyon-on-Hudson? Did he expect another one, perhaps, should they meet again? And did he know more about the prosperous Haverston Tobacco Factory than they had both read in the *Wall Street Journal* and other business news?

"I think Rufus is preparing to serve luncheon, dear. More special surprises, I trust."

"Your famous Virginia ham with cherry sauce," Keith apprised. "We just received a shipment from Smithfield, and I asked him to prepare some for you."

"Thank you, darling. What shall we do afterward?"

"Oh, I might do a little target practice."

"What?"

He smiled, though without much humor, and rose to escort her to the dining salon. "Skeet shooting, darling. The crew will operate the trap."

<h1 style="text-align:center">⚜ 6 ⚜</h1>

DUSK HAD settled over Manhattan Island by the time they arrived at Gramercy Park on Sunday evening. The tall, pedestaled bronze gaslamps illuminated the Curtis address, and Devon would never forget her first sight of this imposing brownstone mansion on the south side of the exclusive park. She had nearly died of shame on that foggy, freezing November afternoon when her employer, Madame Janette Joie, had unwittingly taken her there, in a hackney piled with boxes of extravagant French lingerie, which Devon had to model for the "invalid" mistress of the house—and the master had returned early from his bank on Wall Street, surprising her before the showing was completed. . . .

The domestic staff, still headed by the aging British majordomo, welcomed them warmly—and especially Devon, whom they had not seen in almost a year. On Dr. Blake's advice, the family had remained aboard the yacht when the children were brought to the city for christening and sailed back up the Hudson promptly afterward.

"Madam," said Hadley, bowing his gray head respectfully, "how very good to see you again! It's been a long time."

"Yes, it has, Hadley. But, as you know, there were valid reasons. I expect to be here more frequently from now on, however."

This announcement obviously pleased the housekeeper and maids, who still remembered the tyranny of the first Mrs. Curtis and her equally despotic mother, Hortense Stanfield, who had assumed management of the ménage upon her daughter's terminal illness, for they had heard nothing but praise of their new mistress. And the elderly butler, whom Esther had despised for his staunch loyalty to his master and whom Mrs. Stanfield had attempted to discharge, was especially grateful and appreciative. Keith had promised Hadley a home for life, with continued salary and medical benefits after retirement, which both men hoped was still in the distant future.

As always in the residence, Devon felt uneasy, remembering the years of horror and unhappiness it had encompassed for Keith, and the few occasions of extreme unpleasantness for herself. Was there a premature autumn chill in the air now, or only her imagination? No one else seemed to notice, and Scotty was actually removing his jacket. Hadley surely knew when to order the basement furnace into service. And she certainly had not felt cold on the *Sprite,* even with the ocean breezes blowing in the portholes at night; a light coverlet had provided sufficient comfort in the berth.

Yet she shivered now, mounting the stairway with Keith, and huddled in her wrap. In the master suite, he immediately shucked his twill blazer and started toward a window.

"Don't open it," Devon said quickly. "It's rather chilly in here, don't you think?"

"Why, no, it's just the opposite to me. Unseasonably warm." He went to her, felt her brow; her skin was cool and unflushed. "You don't seem to have any fever, Devon. Do you feel ill?"

"Not physically."

He gazed at her, puzzled. "What does that mean?"

"Nothing, Keith. I'm a silly goose." How could she tell him the strange effect this house had on her? That she invariably felt like an unwelcome visitor—indeed, an intruder! She was not superstitious enough to believe in ghosts, yet here she was shuddering at the mere possibility....

"You are, darling, if you still have qualms about this place, or harbor any guilt and misgivings about your position in it. You're my wife, Devon, and you belong in any domicile of mine. I'm happy about it, the servants are happy, my friends are happy for me."

And with his strong arms around her, Devon was happy, too. His embrace was a powerful shield, a magic barrier protecting her from all that was unpleasant even to contemplate.

She felt this wondrous protection in his bed, through the night, and while they breakfasted in the dining room the next morning. Their life-style was much more formal in the city than the country, not because either of them preferred formality, but these servants had long ago been accustomed to it and meticulously trained in their duties. Every meal was served as if guests were present: fine china, crystal, silver, fresh flowers and glowing candles and immaculate linen. The magnificent tapestry over the mahogany sideboard, an English fox-hunting scene commissioned for Heathstone Manor in Sussex, reminded Devon of that favorite Virginian sport. She had ridden in hunts at Harmony Hill and other plantations, and must purchase some traditional habits before their trip to her native land.

"I have to dash," Keith said, finishing his meal. "The usual Monday-morning board meeting!" He stood and came to her end of the long, damask-clothed table, bending to bestow a parting kiss. "Take a respite from your shopping and meet me for luncheon at Delmonico's, at one?" He waited for her answer. "Devon?"

"Sorry, dear. I was woolgathering. I'll be there," she promised. "Bye-bye, love."

Hadley handed Keith his hat and monogrammed portfolio, which he jokingly called his *vade mecum,* because he was rarely without it. The coachman and footman were waiting to drive him to the Curtis Bank. In his dark, custom-tailored suit, conservative cravat, gold studs and cuff links, he was the epitome of gentility, wealth, and success. To Devon, he looked much as he had on that long-ago, fateful day they had met in the ruins and rubble of Richmond, and she still felt the same deep, strong, magnetic attraction of that first memorable encounter. Nor did she ever expect that feeling to change, no matter how long she lived.

She remained seated for another cup of coffee, pondering the tapestry so reminiscent of her beloved Virginia, and soon nostalgia receded into melancholy. Was it because Keith had taken the reassuring warmth of his love with him that the atmosphere of the house seemed suddenly cold and forbidding again? And why did it only affect her? The domestics, going about their chores, had their sleeves rolled back to the elbows; all except the sedate housekeeper, Mrs. Sturges, whose neat dark poplin gowns never exposed more than her hands. The scullery maid, polishing silver in the pantry, had even removed her cap and pinned her hair atop her head. Miss Vale and Scotty, already busy with his lessons upstairs, were in summer-weight garments, the boy in short pants, which he scorned except in warm weather.

It's just me! Devon scolded herself. Stop this idiocy and dress appropriately for shopping, or you'll suffocate in the crowds on Broadway! The Ladies Mile, from Eighth Street to Twenty-third, was usually jammed on weekdays with female shoppers attired in whatever the prevailing fashion: bustles of varying size and design now that hoopskirts and crinolines were passé. Devon knew from past experience that one could get crushed in the stampede to the Monday sales in the better shops and department stores. But she needn't search and compete for bargains anymore. How nice it was to purchase anything she wished without consulting price tags!

As she lifted her skirts to ascend the stairway, the heavy bronze knocker sounded urgently at the front door. Hadley, who insisted on wearing his handsome livery, went to answer it. Devon heard a feminine voice speaking but couldn't understand her words. Pausing on the third step, she turned, one hand on the polished banister. Hadley crossed the tessellated marble foyer and presented an unfamiliar calling card on a silver slaver.

"A visitor, madam."

"At this hour?" Devon read the name. "I don't know any Sabrina Carlton, Hadley."

"She claims to know Mr. Curtis, madam."

"And what is the nature of her call? If it's business, direct her to the bank."

"She says it's personal, madam. Will you see her?"

Devon hesitated, perplexed. "I suppose I must, Hadley. Give me a few minutes, then send her to the drawing room."

When the visitor appeared on the threshold, Devon all but gasped, not in recognition, but at her astonishing resemblance to the late Mrs. Curtis. Sabrina Carlton was tall and walked with a regal bearing. The thin veiling of her peacock-feathered hat did not conceal her delicate facial features, nor the brilliant deep-purple eyes, nor the raven tresses. She smiled slightly, apparently secretly amused by Devon's amazement.

"You look startled, Mrs. Curtis? Did you imagine you were seeing an apparition?"

Devon composed herself. "Not knowing you, Miss Carlton, naturally I'm surprised by your call. And your purpose?"

"Aren't you also curious about my identity?"

"I assume you know my husband."

"Not personally, unfortunately. We never met formally, although we were related by marriage. I am Esther's first cousin. Our mothers are sisters. I've lived abroad since I was eighteen."

"I see. And are you just visiting in America now?"

"That depends, Mrs. Curtis. May I sit down?"

"Please do," Devon invited. "Tea?"

"No, thank you. I had breakfast at my hotel."

Devon sat opposite her, on the twin to the brocade-and-rosewood sofa. A low satinwood table adorned with a Wedgwood bowl of white roses from the conservatory stood between them. "How did you know I was here, Miss Carlton?"

"I didn't," she replied, arranging the bustle of her turquoise moiré gown in a more comfortable position, so that she sat sideways with her silk-hosed legs crossed at the ankles. "Actually, I was hoping to catch Mr. Curtis before he left for his office."

"Do you have business with him?"

Even her smile was reminiscent of Esther's, embodying the same complacent secretiveness. "Possibly. I just arrived from Boston last night."

"You should have gone to the bank, Miss Carlton. Mr. Curtis does not conduct business at home."

That sly, superior smile again, as if she held some unknown advantage. "I think he'll make an exception in this case, Mrs. Curtis."

"Do you enjoy being mysterious, Miss Carlton—or are you engaged in some sort of intrigue? I don't intend to play games with you to find out."

Sabrina lifted her veil, and Devon saw that she was not as young as she had first appeared. In her late thirties, perhaps, but still highly attractive and shapely. Her tight basque revealed an hourglass waist, obviously severely corseted to thrust up her more than ample bosom. She glanced about the elegant room enviously, mentally calculating the value of the furnishings and art, precisely as Esther might have done of another's possessions.

"My cousin was a very lucky woman, marrying Keith Heathstone Curtis! And a stupid fool, playing him false. With a mediocre artist yet!" Her violet eyes peered at Devon, slanting under dark, wing-swept brows. "I'm not surprised, however, that he turned to you. You're quite beautiful, and so fair—a definite contrast to Esther's brunette beauty. Is that a portrait of your son above the mantel?"

"Yes, at age four."

"Spit and image of his handsome father."

"I thought you'd never met him?"

"I've seen photographs," she explained. "Aunt Hortense has their wedding portrait hanging on the wall, and smaller framed pictures scattered about her home. She still resides in that red brick Bulfinch relic on Beacon Hill. A total recluse now, and not always in command of her faculties, she rocks and stares through the amethyst-paned windows at Louisburg Square."

"You haven't enlightened me yet about your visit," Devon reminded.

Sabrina hesitated a few moments, collecting her wits. "I can't do that, Mrs. Curtis, without relating some of my personal background." She grinned wickedly. "But the story of my life shouldn't shock you too much, since in some respects it's comparable to your own."

"How dare you!" cried Devon indignantly. "We are total strangers, Miss Carlton!"

"Ah, but Aunt Hortense told me a great deal about you, Mrs. Curtis! Everything, in fact, that she had learned from her daughter. I've been living with her for several months now. I could no longer sustain myself abroad. I'm broke, you see, disinherited by my father, when I disgraced the family at the tender age of seventeen. My lover was married, but I wouldn't have wed the fool even if he weren't. Mother took me to Europe, but my pregnancy was too far advanced to abort, so I bore the child—a puny little creature that died before her first birthday. I refused to return to Boston with Mother. She sent me money without Father's knowledge, and I managed to live rather well with the assistance of my gentlemen admirers.

I married one of them, but it didn't last. I found wealthy keepers in Paris, Rome, London, Vienna. Europeans are more broad-minded than Americans about *affaires d'amour,* you know. And about abortion, too."

Devon might have been listening to Janette Joie, so closely did their stories parallel. She bitterly resented any comparison to her own life, however, and considered asking her to leave. But the woman was still skirting the principal issue—her reason for being there—and Devon prompted, "I have plans for the day, Miss Carlton, and would appreciate your coming to the point."

"Very well. I need financial assistance to return to Europe. Frankly, I enjoyed my exile. It was an interesting and exciting adventure. I never realized how truly dull Boston could be, until I came back to it. I'm afraid I would perish of ennui to remain!"

"Exactly what does all this have to do with my husband, Miss Carlton? You are not in any way his responsibility! What do you want of him?"

"Didn't I make that plain enough? Money, of course."

"He owes you nothing," Devon declared, furious at the brazen hussy's blatant request. In appearance, character, voice, mannerisms, she was Esther incarnate! "He has contributed to Mrs. Stanfield's support since her daughter's death, but why on earth should he add you to his numerous other charities?"

"Because I have some highly damaging evidence against him," came the smug reply.

The impact of that announcement stunned Devon for a few moments. She stared at her, nonplussed. Keith had once mentioned a letter Esther had supposedly written to her mother, accusing him of threats on her life, when he was pressing too hard for a divorce. Devon assumed this was the "damaging evidence" to which the cunning witch referred. But she shrugged, pretending disbelief and lack of interest, even when Sabrina removed a packet of envelopes from her reticule and waved it significantly in the air. "I think you'd better leave, Miss Carlton. The butler will show you out."

"As you wish, but I'll return."

"You won't be received."

A complacent smile. "Cousin Keith might feel differently,

when he learns of my visit. If he should, I'm staying at the Hoffman House."

Devon's response to that was a steady glare and bell-cord summons to Hadley. But immediately after Sabrina's departure, she fled upstairs to the third floor. Overwhelmed by her vulnerable emotions, she feared a contretemps before the servants. Entering the luxurious suite, which Esther had referred to as a prison after her accident, Devon closed the door and stood surveying the rooms in the dim light penetrating the tilted slats of the Venetian blinds. Redecoration emerged as her first priority, taking precedence over a new wardrobe. Everything must go, including the heirloom furniture and *objets d'art*. Keith would understand, for he had given her carte blanche on this project. And yet, even as she made the irrevocable decision, she visualized the imperious lady in the queenly canopied bed, her intense amethyst eyes mocking her as had her cousin Sabrina's only minutes ago. Devon wanted to pound her fists on the lavender-blue satin bolster, crush the delicate bric-a-brac, smash even the gorgeous lapis lazuli lamp—and she would have instantly, if violence could eliminate the memory of her forever.

"You bitch!" she murmured, twisting her hands. "You incredibly cruel, malicious, vindictive bitch! Have you become the devil's consort punishing us from hell? Will we never be free of your evil spirit? Do you still live in your wicked cousin? How many letters did you write, how many lies did you tell? Will you never be satisfied until you destroy us all!"

She paused, appalled by her fantastic monologue. As if her spectral nemesis could hear and materialize to taunt her! Feeling foolish, she left and went to the master suite. But she did not dress to go shopping; the incentive, the enthusiasm were gone. She reclined instead on the velvet chaise longue, knowing she would have to tell Keith about Sabrina Carlton, and dreading it. Although useless in her terrible dilemma, tears offered some solace, and she indulged herself.

Keith found her there, weeping, when he arrived home posthaste shortly before two o'clock. "Did you forget our luncheon date? I waited for you an hour at Delmonico's, and worried. Don't you feel well?"

"I'm fine, Keith. And sorry about the luncheon. I should have sent you a message."

"Devon, you're lying here crying. You forgot our appointment. That's hardly fine! Indeed, you're quite pale. Still having chills? I'll summon Ramsey."

"No, please. I'm not ill, Keith. But something very bizarre happened. We had a visitor...."

He sat down on the chaise, placing her legs across his lap. "Who, for God's sake, to affect you this way?"

"Sabrina Carlton. Is the name familiar?"

"Vaguely." He nodded. "Esther's first cousin, on the distaff side. What did she want?"

Devon told him, halteringly, and then burst into tears again. "I—I ordered her out of the house."

"That was a mistake, Devon."

"Why? She was very nasty, Keith! And she's Esther's blood kin, all right! Their resemblance is startling."

"Their characters, too, apparently. Greediness is a family trait. How many letters did she have?"

"I couldn't count them, Keith. She brandished them so swiftly before me. Perhaps five or six."

"She didn't offer to let you read them?"

"I didn't want to," Devon said, drying her eyes.

"Another mistake, darling. They may have been empty envelopes, or old correspondence in Esther's hand."

"She inferred that you had written at least one incriminating letter to Mrs. Stanfield when you were trying to force Esther to release you."

"So I was warned, but I never saw it or any other. That doesn't mean none exist, however, or that Sabrina Carlton doesn't actually have the originals. She may be in conspiracy with her aunt Hortense, although the old lady is suffering from senile dementia. More likely, her unscrupulous niece stole the letters, if any, from her. What's a little theft and blackmail to a woman who has confessed the sordid life she did to a perfect stranger? God knows what crimes she committed in Europe!"

Devon marveled at his calm rationality. But she also knew that his temper had a long fuse, when it suited him, and his anger could smolder undetected for a good while before surfacing.

"Did she appear hysterical? Unreasonable?"

"Just sly and confident, as if she held the secret to the Rosetta stone. What will you do?"

"Talk with her. Examine any potential evidence. She could be bluffing in desperation—that's another inherent family characteristic. Esther tried it on me often enough."

Still the same prudent voice, the contemplative eyes, the capable manner. He would handle it, Devon assured herself. Somehow, with his usual finesse and competency, he would foil the cunning cat, extricate himself from her conniving claws. *But how?*

"She said she'd be back, Keith, but I'd rather not see her again."

"You won't have to, Devon."

"Oh, but you can't go to the Hoffman House alone, Keith! She may have an accomplice, a thug with her. . . ."

"What good would that do her, unless he has the combination to my vault? If so, she would have come to the bank in the first place."

"You have guards there, since the rash of bank robberies in the city."

"And I'll have one with me, in plain clothes, down the corridor from her room. I don't intend to be taken hostage, Devon, or the victim of any other extortion plot."

"When are you going to her?"

"This evening, after dinner. No sense letting her think I'm anxious or concerned. Why don't you get dressed now? I'll take you shopping."

"It'll keep until tomorrow, darling. I'd rather stroll in the park, while Scotty plays with the other children." She would feel safe there, behind the locked gates, which opened only with the golden keys of the privileged residents of Gramercy Park.

❧ 7 ❧

THE DIN and dazzle of Manhattan's night life was already in progress when Keith drove himself to the Hoffman House, an imposing marble structure north of Fifth Avenue, chosen for its Continental atmosphere by the Grand Duke Alexis of Russia on his celebrated visit to America. No other city in the New World offered finer lodgings or more exciting entertainment than New York. Theaters, casinos, brothels—the facilities for pleasure and perversion were almost limitless, and the Grand Duke had availed himself of them all, especially the gorgeous prostitutes, whose skills were unsurpassed even in the notorious French and Roman bordellos. European royalty and nobility invariably sampled the Gotham fleshpots via their state visits to Washington, and Sabrina Carlton hoped to encounter one or two during her stay there.

Tossing the reins of his sports rig to a hotel lackey, Keith entered the impressive lobby with its crimson brocade walls, Empire furniture, and great crystal chandeliers. He proceeded to the discreetly lit bar, which was famous for its large painting of voluptuous women *au naturel,* one of the few nudes on public display in the city. The conservatively dressed bank guard was already there, having a drink. Keith took a seat next to him and ordered Scotch whisky, neat. They conversed in low tones for a while, then the other man left and climbed the marble staircase to the third floor. Keith rode the Otis steam elevator. They did not acknowledge each other in the corridor leading to Sabrina's room.

She opened the door immediately upon his knock, obviously recognizing him, but her deshabille surprised Keith. It was an expensive boudoir costume of soft, shining fabric that clung seductively to her body, the décolleté revealing the deep cleav-

55

age of her breasts. No doubt her confessions to Devon were true. She was, among other things, a harlot. And she resembled his late wife enough to be her twin sister!

"Miss Carlton?"

"Yes, Cousin Keith. I've seen your photographs. Come in, please. And call me Sabrina. I'm sorry I couldn't engage parlor accommodations, but we can talk as well in a bedroom, can't we?"

Keith imagined most of her business was conducted in boudoirs, and seduction was one of her ploys. He glanced warily about the room, and his caution amused her.

"We're alone," she assured him. "Search for yourself, if you wish. Under the bed, in the wardrobe, wherever."

To her surprise, he conducted an impromptu inspection, including the water closet.

"Satisfied?" she chided. "Would you like a drink?"

"I had one in the bar downstairs."

"While admiring the nude? It was painted in Paris, you know. Have some absinthe with me?"

Keith despised this vile, bitter concoction of wormwood and anise known to cause mental aberrations in its devotees. "No, thanks. Were you expecting someone?"

"Only you, Cousin Keith."

"Well, I'm not here socially, Sabrina—and certainly not for an assignation, despite your apparent preparation. That is your profession, isn't it?"

"More or less," she replied candidly. "My nature, too, which is the essential difference between me and Cousin Esther, rest her soul. But how she could support that gigolo paint dauber, Giles Mallard, when she had a spouse like you is beyond me! Incidentally, her replacement does you credit, Cousin Keith."

"I'm not your cousin, Sabrina."

"Cousin-in-law?"

"We're no relation whatever anymore. I came to warn you never to come to my home again! You upset my wife tremendously. What in hell do you expect to accomplish with such tactics?" he demanded, taking one of the two chairs in the room without her permission—a deliberate insult which no gentleman would have committed in the presence of a respectable lady.

Sabrina sat on the bed, then partially reclined on her side, bracing herself on an elbow. The sleek satin molded itself to her form as if it had been applied damp, and it was obvious that she wore nothing beneath it. Her exotic purple eyes, so like Esther's, surveyed him languidly, and her sultry voice might have been an echo from beyond. "Surely Mrs. Curtis told you?"

Keith nodded, crossing his long legs. "But you appear reasonably intelligent, Sabrina. If you need money, why didn't you apply for a loan? I'm a banker, after all."

"Oh, yes! Manhattan Midas and Wall Street Croesus, according to some of your colorful sobriquets. But I couldn't borrow the amount I need without security, and I could never repay even a small loan. I want a hundred thousand dollars, Cousin."

"Just like that?" He laughed, snapping his fingers. "Extortion is against the law, Sabrina."

"So is attempted murder," she quipped.

"Have you tried it?"

"I've considered it on occasion," she admitted, "just as you have, sir. I have proof of that in poor Cousin Esther's letters to her mother."

"If so, they're mere delusions of a deranged mind, Miss Carlton. Esther was insane—several physicians could attest to that fact."

"Not always, Keith. Indeed, she had a keen mentality when you married her—clever enough to fool her spouse for quite a while! She may have suffered some brain damage in her accident, for which you were responsible. And according to her mama—"

Keith interrupted, "Hortense Stanfield is senile."

"Partially, due to age, although she remembers a great deal more than you might imagine, Cousin Keith. Her daughter confided in her freely, after learning about your mistress and illegitimate son. You adopted the child at age three or four, I believe, and married the mother just last year. Devon Marshall is—or was—a noted journalist and formerly a Texas senator's wife. Even the Boston papers reported her marriage to the reputedly richest man in America, who would never miss the moderate sum I'm requesting."

"Moderate? That's a king's ransom! And regardless of their content, those letters are worthless, Sabrina. Esther died of natural causes."

"A lingering, hideous death, Keith, with hallucinations such as might result from an insidious drug or poison administered over a long period of time. Aunt Hortense told me about the books on the subject in your library, and that Esther's personal maid acted as a food taster. She also had the gas jets in her rooms sealed, and slept with her pistol handy."

"Hysteria and suspicion"—Keith shrugged—"common in mental illness. Her maid, Lurline, is still quite healthy and in my employ. But if you really believe I murdered her somehow, why don't you go to the police?"

"What would that benefit me?"

"Precisely my point."

"Then you're a fool, Keith Curtis! Hardly the monetary genius and wizard I've read about in the business journals, if you can't grasp the significance and intrinsic value of my proposition! But surely your wife has enough intelligence and journalistic sense to realize it? My word, didn't she cover the lurid adultery trial of that pious hypocrite, the Reverend Henry Ward Beecher? And didn't one of his paramours, the clever Victoria Woodhull, sell his steamy love letters to her to the *Chicago Tribune* for a tidy profit? Would you like me to peddle Esther's accusatory missives on Publishers Row? No doubt James Gordon Bennett would be interested in them for his lusty scandal sheet. Aha!" she cried jubilantly as his sanguine expression changed to wariness. "That got your attention, didn't it? Struck a sensitive nerve! Guilty of a crime or not, the public would try you in print. Is that what you want for your precious family?"

He had underestimated her. She was a crafty, treacherous bitch who would not be easily outwitted. Nor was she offering any options or alternatives.

"Where are the letters?" Keith demanded, eyeing her shrewdly.

She did not waver under the challenging scrutiny. "In a secure place, naturally. I'm not foolish enough to carry them on my person."

"Nor I to buy a pig in a poke! Which was what you undoubtedly brought to my home this morning."

"A few samples," she conceded, "primarily to whet her feminine curiosity."

"Certified copies?"

"Samples," she reiterated.

"You mean forgeries of your own composition?"

"Don't gloat, Cousin Keith! I have the originals."

"I want to see them, Sabrina."

"You'll have to come to Boston, to the Stanfield home. With the proper amount of cash! That shouldn't inconvenience you too much, considering the methods of transportation at your disposal. We could travel together, in your rail coach or yacht." She gazed at him enticingly, lips slightly parted, and assumed a sensual pose. "I would be happy to entertain you to the best of my ability—which, I assure you, is considerable."

"Once a whore, always a whore, eh? Is that how you've lived all these years abroad? Selling yourself and employing blackmail whenever feasible?"

She shifted her position, jiggling her breasts so that they almost bounced out of the loose garment. "I was kept, mostly, by some very fine gentlemen—one as powerful in the Paris Bourse as you are on Wall Street. And a member of the British Parliament with as much noble blood in his veins as in yours. There was even an Italian count for a while, in Rome. If a woman has a pretty face and shapely body—"

"And the morals of an alley cat in heat?"

"You should know, with all the tomcatting you've done! Are you faithful to *this* wife, monsieur?"

"Stick to the issue, Sabrina."

"This is the issue now. Don't you find me attractive, Cousin Keith?"

"I told you not to call me that!" he growled, his anger rising. "And you're wasting your talents and my time. I feel nothing but pity for you, and we're not going to Boston or anywhere else together."

"Then I'll just have to go to the publisher of the *New York Herald* tomorrow," she threatened.

"With what? Fantasies you pieced together from gossip with your strange old aunt? Hortense Stanfield realized her daughter was insane, during all the months she helped to care for her in our home. But she never wanted the truth known, and I doubt she would have preserved any evidence of it in Esther's own handwriting. Nobody would buy or publish hearsay and forgeries, Sabrina. There are libel and slander laws, you know." He grinned at her dismay. "Your extortion plot has failed, madam. Try your luck—and your charms—with someone else."

As he stood to leave, Sabrina bounded off the bed and planted herself firmly before the door. "Esther wrote a will, on her monogrammed stationery, in which she expressed fear of your intentions to harm her. Aunt Hortense did not destroy *that!* She merely misplaced it. I found it while straightening her closets and drawers."

"Seeking money and valuables to steal?"

"Putting her things in order."

"Of course," Keith muttered cynically. "Unfortunately, it's her head that's in disorder." But Sabrina's last news was something of which Esther herself had made him aware, and somewhat disquieting. Had Mrs. Stanfield forgotten and unwittingly kept the will after her daughter's death, or merely described it to her niece in conversation? "I don't believe you," he challenged.

"But you're not as positive as you pretend, either! You want tangible proof? Come to Boston. I'll give it to you before a witness."

"I'm not interested in your games, Sabrina."

"But you're still curious and playing! That tells me something." She put her hands on his broad shoulders, then let them slide slowly, sensuously down his arms. "My God, but you're a handsome animal! Just looking at you excites me. I don't know how any woman could resist you. Don't be angry with me, dear. Stay a while. Let's get better acquainted. I remind you of Esther, don't I, and I know how much you loved her in the beginning. We could have some wonderful fun together. I know how to please a man in bed. . . ."

"Most whores do," he muttered, brushing her hands away just as she felt the derringer in his coat pocket. Never had he encountered a more flagrant attempt at seduction, nor been less susceptible. "Forgive me, madam, but you don't appeal to me. I'm not interested in anything you have to offer, for sale or otherwise."

Sabrina sighed, deflated, unaccustomed to that kind of male rejection. "Well, just give me some money, then? I'm desperate, Keith, can't even pay my hotel bill. You're so generous with Esther's mother—won't you help me, too? I beg of you, please?"

"You could have had a loan," he reminded her.

"Can I still, if I come to the bank?"

"I'm sorry." He shook his head, opened the door. "Good-bye, Sabrina, and good luck."

"You'll regret this!" she warned him, more disappointed than humiliated by his scorn. "I promise you that, Cousin Keith!"

He ignored her, giving the sentry down the corridor a signal to abandon his post.

Devon was in the library, trying to concentrate on a new novel, when Keith returned. "How did it go?" she asked anxiously, closing the book.

"Not exactly as I hoped," Keith admitted. "But well enough, I suppose. The wily jade had blackmail in mind, all right. She wanted a hundred thousand dollars, for the initial installment. She got nothing."

"What about the letters?"

"Since she produced neither originals nor copies, I assume none exist, although she claimed to have them in safekeeping. I was ready to leave, when she made a rather startling revelation."

Her eyes widened. "Tell me!"

"Sabrina may actually have that crazy will Esther wrote and sent to her mother," he informed. "She quoted essentially what Esther told me she put in it, but she could have gleaned that information from her aunt. Evidently, though the old woman babbles in senility, she's also lucid and coherent at times. Her niece undoubtedly takes notes on these rational occasions, for she's fairly well versed on my life with Esther."

"Then nothing is resolved?"

"Not unless I go to Boston, toting a satchel full of green-backs. I'll just procrastinate on the premise that she's bluffing, Devon."

"And if she's not?"

"I may have to deal with her."

"How?"

"With money, of course. That's what she wants, isn't it?

She threatened to go to the newspapers. You know what that could mean."

Her chin trembled. She knew the power of the press, the reputations and lives ruined by unscrupulous journalists and publishers. "It's like sitting on a powder keg, Keith, wondering if and when it'll blow up."

"Never, if her powder is damp."

"How long can we endure that kind of uncertainty and suspense, Keith? Give her the damned money, if she can provide the evidence."

"You think that would end it? The woman is a conniving courtesan, Devon! She was half-naked when I arrived, and tried to seduce me throughout the meeting. The fact that she aroused only revulsion didn't stop her. I suspect she's really seeking a wealthy keeper and hoped I would prove vulnerable. She suggested that we travel to Boston together—shall I continue?"

"Not unless you did with her."

"Good God!" he swore, opening the cellaret. "Would I be telling you this if I had?"

"I'm sorry," she apologized, watching him pour a stiff potion of Scotch. "But having met the creature, I can't bring myself to trust her."

"Trust *me*, Devon, and trust my instincts about Sabrina Carlton. She's as skilled as Esther was at intrigue and conspiracy, and as avaricious. But, ironically, the same greed that motivates people also often incapacitates and defeats them."

"Is that a riddle?"

"Just one of nature's peculiar puzzles," he replied, smiling at her perplexity. "I solved it long ago by studying would-be embezzlers at the bank. Sabrina is a potential extortionist, and there's not much difference in these two criminals. They betray themselves, ultimately. Sabrina did so when she tried to compromise me. Presumably this was her alternate strategy should the other fail."

"You may be right, dear. And I guess I can't honestly blame her for trying to seduce you, whatever her reasons. You do look devilishly debonair tonight."

He laughed, tossing off his drink. "That's essentially what the purple-eyed snake in her slinky green satin skin said, as she offered her big ripe apples."

"And you weren't even a little tempted?"

"Oh, a little, maybe."

"Keith!"

He laughed again. "Jealous?"

"Enough to cut your heart out."

"Darling, I'm teasing you. Don't you know yet that I'm impervious to any other woman's charms and enchantment?" Setting aside his glass, he pulled her to her feet. "Is it too early to go to bed?"

"It's never too early—or too late—with you, my love," Devon invited, before his ardent kiss. She only wished she were as confident as he that they were permanently rid of the insidious serpent that had suddenly slithered into their paradise.

❧ 8 ❧

DEVON ENGAGED the same New York firm, Brown & Spaulding, commissioned by Mrs. Grant to renovate the White House, which had fallen into disgraceful disrepair during the lean, hard years of the Civil War, when all available funds had necessarily gone to the military. During her exciting Washington correspondency, Devon had reported the successful transformation of the deteriorating Executive Mansion into an elegant and stately residence fit for the President of the United States, and the numerous brilliant, innovative entertainments there for foreign luminaries, including British and European royalty. She did not miss reporting on the dull, unimaginative Hayes administration, which was such a disappointing contrast to its predecessor, although she was definitely beginning to miss her journalistic career.

After giving the decorators carte blanche in the redecoration of her own predecessor's apartments, she absented herself from Gramercy Park as much as possible. She did not observe the removal of the third-floor furnishings to be sold at an auction gallery, nor inspect those that would replace them. Aware of her adamancy in this respect, Keith inquired, "What if you don't like the finished results?"

"Oh, I'm sure I will, dear. These people are experts, you know, and I trust their judgment implicitly. Look what they did for the mansion on Pennsylvania Avenue! Our renovated floor will be for guests, however, and perhaps we'll have some distinguished ones in the future. It must have been very exciting when President and Mrs. Grant were here."

"It was a madhouse," Keith recalled grimly. "Secret Service agents everywhere, curious mobs outside barely restrained by the police, the servants in awe and anxiety over their duties. I wouldn't care to experience it again, ever."

"Nor I, what I experienced the next day," said Devon, reflecting on the hideous confrontation with Esther Curtis, when she had come at the latter's invitation, naively expecting an exclusive interview with the First Lady for the New York *Record*.

"I know, Devon. But you must try to forget all that, pretend it never happened."

"Have you forgotten it, Keith? Can you pretend none of it ever happened?"

His mood turned somber, brooding. "I've tried, Devon, and was beginning to believe I'd succeeded in banishing the bitter memories. Then that witch, Sabrina Carlton, who also had ancestors in Salem, suddenly appeared like some abominable incarnation of her Cousin Esther. . . . Thank God, she hasn't returned!"

"Yet," Devon cautioned. "Maybe she's planning some new mischief with her aunt."

"Hortense Stanfield is a fool confiding in that cunning slut. If she has willed her estate to Sabrina, she could be robbed of it before death—and lucky if she isn't suffocated prematurely in her sleep. But that's not our problem, Devon. Try not to worry about it. Do you miss the twins?"

"Dreadfully."

"Me, too. I told Captain Bowers to prepare to sail up the Hudson for the weekend." He scanned the sheaf of mail Devon had placed on his desk, discarding the trivia. Of the several engraved invitations, only one seemed of any importance to him. "The Belmonts are opening the autumn season with their usual grand ball," he noted. "I think we should accept, Devon."

"She's a haughty lady, Keith—one of Gotham society's grandes dames. I met her in Albany some years ago, while covering the inauguration of Governor Seymour. The Belmonts attended most of the state affairs, including Boss Tweed's reception at the Delevan House, where he lived like a potentate during the legislative sessions."

One dark brow arched sardonically. "Just what in hell were you doing in the Albany den of Ali Baba and his Tammany thieves?"

His tone took her aback. "I just told you! The Tweed soiree was one of my journalistic assignments for the *Record*. And since his puppet, Horatio Seymour, couldn't have won the governorship without the support of Tammany Hall—"

"And ballot-box stuffing," Keith interrupted. "I'm aware of the Tweed Gang's machinations, as well as August Belmont's political affiliation and reasons for kowtowing to the Wigwam chiefs! But you neglected to inform me of your presence at their campfire celebrations, Mrs. Curtis."

"You just forgot," Devon dissembled. "It was so long ago, Keith, and I wasn't your wife then. Anyway, that's where I met Mrs. Belmont and learned that her husband and some of those other mighty Democrats were pro-Southern during the war and had actually despised President Lincoln. Not one of them paid their respects to the Lincolns during their brief sojourn in New York after his election."

"That discovery could hardly have disconcerted a native Virginian," Keith muttered, peeved because he had never known exactly how she acquired her position with the New York *Record* and rose so rapidly in her field. He knew the publisher, Samuel Fitch, was at that time an unwilling tool of Tammany Hall, beholden to the City Chamberlain, Peter Barr Sweeny, for the advertising that helped to keep his journal from sinking in red ink. Now he wondered if one of the notorious Tweed tigers, who actually wore this ruby-eyed gold emblem on their lapels, had sponsored Devon Marshall. The mere idea of such a possibility rankled in his flesh and aroused cynical criticism of her career.

Stung by the barb, Devon reciprocated with one of her own. "No, indeed! It pleased me immensely."

"Then it should also please you immensely to attend the

reception of the Democratic, pro-Confederate Belmonts."

Devon shrugged, still hurt by his nasty remarks and disturbed by their tendency to quarrel in this house, as if both were somehow possessed. "I don't care about their politics, Keith! And I wish you wouldn't act as if our daughters were ready to debut. They're still in diapers."

"But our son is not, and I don't want him alienated from society because of his parents' seclusion."

"Is this a command performance?"

"An expedience, my dear. Must I remind you that August Belmont is the American representative of the House of Rothschild?"

"So what? You're allied with the Bank of England."

"The French banking connection is equally important, believe me. Buy a fine gown, darling; I want to show you off."

"Display your new possession?"

"Goddamn it, Devon! You know I hate such sarcasm and insinuations—why do you persist in provoking me on this particular issue?"

She shook her head, herself confounded. Then, in the interim of tense silence, she heard the workmen upstairs and instantly perceived the reason for her caprice and tartness. Esther's domain was being remodeled, and her tenacious spirit resented it! The decorators had complained of difficulty in removing the ornate, thronelike bed from its dais, where the "mad queen" had ruled so many despotic years, and Devon feared now that she would never permanently abdicate the premises under any circumstances.

"Forgive me, Keith. I don't mean to be a shrew."

"Nor I a tyrant, Devon." His voice softened in humble apology, and he seemed as puzzled and distressed as she by their quick clash of temperaments over insignificant matters. "Send our regrets to the Belmonts, if it's an imposition."

"It's not," she relented with a conciliatory smile. "We haven't danced together in ages, Keith; attending a ball would be very nice." And tapping her chin pensively, "I wonder if the brougham would be roomy enough for all my purchases."

"Take the clarence," he suggested, kissing her cheek perfunctorily.

"Oh, you can do better than that!" she chided, hoping to mend this argument more intimately, in bed.

"Sorry, honey. I have an important appointment. I'll try not to be late for dinner. Have a nice day!"

As it developed, the brougham was more than adequate, for Devon did not go shopping after all. Instead, she ordered the coachman to drive to Publishers Row, feeling a surge of excitement upon her arrival. A sense of urgency always prevailed in Printing House Square, and her journalistic blood pulsed like the clicking telegraph keys. Every serious reporter learned how to decipher Morse code, and some even figured out how to tap the trunk lines. In New York, the newspaper industry's proximity to City Hall and Wall Street was not accidental. And curious citizens invariably congregated there, awaiting the latest editions.

Devon spent a few minutes viewing her alma mater, to which a new garnet brick story had been added, along with a dignified bronze plaque marking the ornamental white limestone entrance. Entering the refurbished lobby, she proceeded directly to the Women's Department, on the second floor, which was now honorably listed in the directory. This recognition pleased Devon, who remembered when the "petticoat pages" had been virtually ignored in most daily journals.

Carrie Hempstead, once relegated to an open corner of the large, bare-floored rooms previously cleaned by the female staff members, had finally acquired a private office with her name and title on the frosted-glass door. Her young assistant, delighted at meeting a lady who had become something of a legend in the profession, happily announced her to the editor.

It was a joyful reunion for both women, and they hugged and kissed cheeks. "I hope you've come seeking employment," said Carrie, admiring Devon's chic fall costume of topaz wool, modestly bustled in the new walking length that no longer swept dust off the sidewalks. "We could certainly use your glamor and fashion in our beauty column."

Devon smiled. "Don't think I haven't considered it, Carrie. The essence of ink and newsprint will always intoxicate me; my father used to say it was in my blood."

"Mine, too." Although older, grayer, plumper, Mrs. Hempstead had lost none of her enthusiasm or energy, and her wise eyes still sparkled behind her bifocals. "You're still the loveliest lady in journalism, Devon. More so even than Kate Field at the height of her youth, and she'd be the first to admit it. Will you join us at the Sorosis Club meeting today? You've neglected us the last year or so."

"Not intentionally, Carrie. As you know, other matters have taken precedence."

"Yes, dear. We've kept abreast of the newsworthy developments in your life, although you certainly surprised your colleagues by marrying Keith Heathstone Curtis. We assumed you were at his country estate merely to cover the abduction of his little son and, true to the press code, you never revealed any of your informational sources."

"Oh, Carrie, there's so much I'd like to confide!" Devon cried, for the older woman had always seemed as much a mother as mentor to her. "And probably shall, someday."

"Whenever you're ready, child." Carrie was perusing Tish Lambeth's latest dispatch on the Grants, wired from San Francisco, which had just accorded the travelers a tumultuous welcome on their return to America after two years abroad. "Our girl with the globetrotters has become quite adept at her job, hasn't she?"

"Excellent," Devon agreed. "I've read all of her reports, sometimes envying her experiences and imagining myself in her place. But I couldn't have done better, Carrie."

"Except in image, my dear. I'm afraid poor Tish has never acquired a flair for fashion. Words interest her far more than appearance."

"Perhaps that's as it should be, in this profession."

"Not necessarily. You and Kate Field managed to combine them successfully, outstanding examples even on the most glamorous occasions. Your coverage of the Washington social scene increased our circulation enormously, and we still receive inquiries about you. Unfortunately, the White House is a dull beat now, with its incredibly lackluster couple, and the media expects their exit next election." Carrie paused, editing some copy. "The gossipmongers would have been hard pressed to fill their columns without that scandalous triangle in Newport this summer. Imagine Governor Sprague running amuck with a shotgun after his confessed cuckold! Could his wife and Senator Roscoe Conkling really have been clandestine lovers for over a decade?"

"So rumor claimed when I was in Washington, and Mrs.

Sprague was his most ardent admirer in the Senate gallery, when she wasn't competing and conspiring to replace Julia Grant as the capital's foremost hostess."

"Sad, the lurid turn of events in Kate Chase Sprague's once brilliant life," Carrie lamented. "The poor soul is more to be pitied than envied now, and I tone down our reports on her."

Never keen on any woman's public disgrace and humiliation, Devon staunchly approved of such journalistic compassion. "What is the major project of Sorosis now, Carrie?"

"Oh, we have a number on the agenda! Our committees are coordinated with those of the Women's Bureau on child labor abolishment, shorter hours and improved working conditions for women, and as always, suffrage. We'll never give up on that issue! We're also still striving for acceptance in the New York Press Club, which continues to bar our sex. But the Movement needs financial assistance badly, Devon. Our treasury is constantly on the verge of bankruptcy, and Miss Anthony and Mrs. Stanton have a hard time meeting their travel expenses with lecture fees and donations."

"I'll make a substantial contribution, Carrie." Keith was so generous with her allowance, and so heedless of how she spent it, Devon felt she could afford to support all of the feminists' worthy causes now.

"The Bureau will be most appreciative," Carrie told her. "And I have some other news which may interest you. Remember your series on Five Points, *Missions in Hell*?"

"Yes, of course! Mr. Fitch wouldn't publish it."

"Not then, because he feared political reprisal. But now the *Record* is no longer dependent on financial aid from Tammany Hall, and Samuel Fitch has become something of a crusader. The industry hasn't had a real one since Horace Greeley, you know. Anyway, Sam deplores the wretched conditions of the local slums, and thinks your in-depth articles were not only accurate but excellently written—and still timely. Those milieux don't change much, despite the efforts of a few churches and charities. After all, how long can rain wash the gutters of sewage? The filth soon returns, and government should help to clean the urban cesspools. Mr. Fitch feels that your inflammatory series could have some effect on our own City Fathers, at least."

A year ago Devon would have leaped at the opportunity to

prove herself a serious, capable journalist. Now she hesitated, worried about Keith's reaction. Her account of New York's most infamous district had encompassed all of its worst aspects: crime, prostitution, poverty, disease, suffering, sorrow, and the politicians' blatant disregard for the hapless victims trapped in its hellish horror. Keith had been furious upon first learning about *Missions in Hell*, amazed that she had actually ventured into that dangerous area alone, interviewed whores and hoodlums on the streets, as well as waifs and refugees in the few religious shelters, and relieved that it was not published. But she was his mistress then, not his wife—how much more displeased would he be now!

"We'll need your permission," Carrie was saying, "and you'll be paid, of course. Sam is at City Hall now, wrangling about the long-promised improvements. He'll be pleased to hear of your visit, Devon. We can send the release, or you could sign it today."

"I'll do it now," Devon decided, afraid she might weaken in procrastination. She would deal with the consequences, if any, of her impulsive agreement later.

Carrie beamed. "Sam will be delighted, Devon! Is there any possibility that you might return to work for us on a regular basis?"

"Don't tempt me, Carrie. Mr. Curtis thinks my career is behind me." She paused, listening to the noise of the press rolling off the evening edition, and the sound was like music in her ears. "Oh, Carrie, I have everything I've ever wanted, or any sensible woman could want! A loving husband, a beautiful family, financial security, social position. And yet, some pesky, restless imp of ambition plagues me! I'm happy, content—why does my hand itch to write again? Why do I miss the pursuit of an exciting story, the often frustrating interviews with obnoxious people, the hard discipline of deadlines, and even the ridicule of some of our male colleagues? I should cherish my good fortune. But I occasionally feel idle, useless, even parasitic. Something is missing, Carrie. I realized it immediately upon coming here this morning. It's like the giant picture puzzle I worked on during my pregnancy with the twins. Thousands of pieces, but one is missing—and nobody else notices. Others see a complete scene, I see a vacant space."

"Do you attach any significance to this vacancy?"

"I try not to dwell on it."

Carrie studied her with knowing eyes. "There are some women who need more than the things you mentioned for total fulfillment, Devon. Apparently you are one of them. You have a God-given talent for something more than love, marriage, and motherhood. The emptiness, the void you see in that otherwise complete picture puzzle is the denial of self, of individuality, of innate personal freedom and independence. The fragment missing from that lovely, seemingly perfect family portrait is probably yourself, my dear: your own identity. And if that's the case, perhaps you should share this perception, this knowledge with your spouse."

Devon plucked a pencil from Carrie's holder and toyed with it in restless hands. "That's easier said than done, Carrie. He's so involved with business—"

"You don't think he'd understand your sense of too much leisure and dependence?"

"Do men, especially husbands, ever understand these feminine feelings? Don't they usually regard them as dissatisfaction and rebellion, or some sort of peculiar female ailment?"

"Usually," the women's editor nodded, "and even the most intelligent of their sex seem incapable of comprehending some aspects of ours."

"Promise me one thing, Carrie? My series won't be sandwiched between advertisements for feminine health and hygiene products?"

Raising her right hand in solemn oath, Carrie vowed, "No remedies for menstrual cramps and vaginal itch on the same pages! I'll put it in the release, if you like, and make certain the male pranksters in layout are aware of it."

"Thank you, Carrie. That's a great relief, remembering some of the embarrassing tricks played on us in the past."

"I didn't have as much editorial clout then, Devon." Consulting her lapel watch, Carrie rose to don her hat and gloves. "Come along, dear. Lucy Stone is our honored speaker today, and afterward we'll drop in at the Women's Bureau. Won't the girls be delighted to welcome back a comrade in arms? You'll receive many Croix de Guerre embraces and kisses!"

But not from Keith, thought Devon, following the stalwart leader into renewed action on the battlefield.

✤ 9 ✤

IT WAS an emotional day for Devon, meeting old friends and making new ones at the Sorosis meeting and later at the Women's Bureau, renewing her dedication, pledging financial support, and volunteering her services on the Child Labor Committee. Ironically, a league for the defense of animals was already in existence, but none for the protection of children. They could be legally exploited, brutalized, victimized, while the most influential preachers of the era railed primarily against sin and vice in the pulpits. And why didn't Harriet Beecher Stowe write a book about the Simon Legrees of industry, who abused their employees—and especially the helpless minors— as cruelly as any Southern slavemaster had ever done?

Devon had addressed the issue in *Missions in Hell*, and Carrie Hempstead's announcement of its imminent publication brought applause and congratulations from everyone present. Elizabeth Cady Stanton encouraged them to combine and concentrate their efforts and abilities on this particular social evil and injustice.

"It won't be as glamorous as covering the White House was," she told Devon, "but eminently more important to humanity and history. How are you at public speaking, dear? Perhaps you could grace our lecture platforms?"

"Oh, I don't think so, Mrs. Stanton. Writing is my forte, and we do need help in the press."

"Desperately, Devon! And with the New York *Record* as your oracle, you'll reach a large and mostly sympathetic female audience. You can accompany our next delegation to Washington."

Devon was shaken by that suggestion, convinced that Keith would object, as he would to any activity that would take her away from him even temporarily. Once again she had impulsively involved herself, without due consideration of the possible consequences, and as so frequently before, she was trapped by her own impetuosity. She explained that definite travel commitments were presently unfeasible, for she had brand-new twins, but she would gladly assist in every other respect.

A mother herself, Mrs. Stanton understood and did not press for promises. "Your editor is a true Joan of Arc," she commented as Carrie Hempstead returned to her desk and duties. "Ready to go to the stake for her beliefs! Unfortunately, we don't have many like her in the Fourth Estate. Men dominate the presses and the pulpits! Indeed, as Victoria Woodhull so accurately observed years ago, nowhere is the phallic symbol more powerfully evident than in publishing and preaching. Even our few supportive women's publications must be careful of what they advocate, lest dominating males in their subscribers' families cancel their subscriptions." Her sigh was a lament. "Thank heaven, Mr. Stanton supports my viewpoint, for even with six children, I would not live in marital bondage. How tragic when the wedding band becomes a shackle! And what a greater tragedy is the average woman's willingness to docilely accept the yoke, victim of her own subservience, and consequently her own worst enemy."

The lady was a human dynamo, her spirit undiminished after twenty arduous years on the lecture circuit with Miss Susan B. Anthony, suffering ridicule and indignities even from some of their own benighted sex, rallying their beleaguered forces after repeated repulses and humiliating defeats on all levels of government, determined to prevail against the seemingly impossible odds and overwhelming tides of prejudice and persecution.

Her zeal was so infectious, Devon wanted to go out recruiting with the drum and fife corps, organize troops in marches on Albany and Washington, jump on the bandwagon regardless of the obstacles and hazards along its routes, be arrested and incarcerated again, if necessary. She had not done her part in the campaign recently, and was ashamed of her laxness and complacency, paying lip services while writing social trivia with no more substance and durability than soap bubbles.

"You're so right," she said, feeling inadequate in the presence of such eloquence. "And it's grossly unfair that so many of our sisters are reluctant to fight for their own liberation, yet have no hesitancy or compunction about accepting whatever benefits derive from the labors and struggles of others."

The standard bearer smiled and lifted a symbolic torch. "Bravo, Devon Marshall Curtis! And welcome back to the embattled ranks! If you still have some influence with Senator Reed Carter...?"

"I'm afraid not, Elizabeth. It wasn't a very amicable divorce, you know."

"But surely you have much persuasion with your present spouse, and he in turn with some members of Congress?"

Mrs. Stanton could not perceive her dilemma. Devon Marshall's long premarital relationship with Keith Curtis was still a guarded secret, which could never be publicly revealed. The few prominent or influential people who suspected the truth were unable to confirm their suspicions and would remain forever in doubt. Thus, not even her closest colleagues were aware of her beloved's relentless opposition to her career, and Devon expected fireworks to explode in their domicile when he learned that she was resuming it.

Nervous about her commitments to Carrie Hempstead and the Women's Bureau, Devon was a paragon of wifely perfection when Keith arrived home that evening. She met him at the door, taking his hat and portfolio before the butler could do so, and kissing him ardently. Pleased but surprised, since she was usually shy before the servants, Keith searched her face for a few moments, smiling. "What have you been up to today, Mrs. Curtis?"

She blushed. "Didn't you like my greeting?"

"Very much, but we've only been apart a few hours. That was more than a welcome-home kiss. Compensation for spending too much money?" he teased.

"No, I just felt like it."

"I'm glad—and hope it becomes a habit." And to Hadley, who had just put his things in the foyer closet, "Fix me a double Scotch, please."

"Yes, sir."

"Hectic day?" Devon asked solicitously.

"The Stock Exchange was a bedlam," he replied as they

strolled to the library. "The gold brick swindle finally hit the city, and the bulls and bears went crazy."

"I don't understand."

"Did I forget to mention it before? Gilded lead ingots and counterfeit currency are selling briskly on the New York market and driving the Treasury and mints up the walls. The imitations are clever enough to fool all but the experts, and the operation has been successful in Chicago and New Orleans for some time without detection. We're not accepting any gold bricks at the bank and having those in the vaults scrupulously examined. We haven't discovered any fakes so far, although some have already turned up even in the Federal Reserve Branch across the street."

"And some folks think banking is dull!" Devon exclaimed.

"Not those who sit in the Gold Room of the Exchange! There was near panic there today—much yelling and some fisticuffs." Taking his drink from the butler's tray, which also contained a glass of Madeira for the mistress, he toasted, "To a calm, peaceful evening!"

"And many more," Devon added with her wine. Breaking the news to him then was out of the question, and she was relieved. She could not actually relax, however, having discovered in the past that temporary reprieves were often harder to bear than immediate confession.

"When do they expect to finish upstairs?" Keith asked as the workmen departed via the back entrance.

"A few more weeks, I think."

"God, I hope so! I'm tired of strangers in the house, and especially that odd little fellow who obviously curls his hair and can't talk without fluttering gestures. We met on the landing this morning, and he had some kind of sexual spasm. After admiring my 'sartorial elegance,' as he phrased it, he proceeded to readjust my cravat, smooth my jacket lapels, and pat my shoulders, presumably testing for padding. I swear I thought he was going to embrace me before I could escape!"

Devon chuckled. *"Embrace?"*

"Well, he's too small to succeed at rape."

Maids were lighting the gaslamps and chandeliers in the various chambers, for the autumn days were growing shorter. The trees in Gramercy Park were turning color, the asters and chrysanthemums bursting into brilliant bloom. Was the night air chilly enough for a fire on the hearth? No, she was just being superstitious again!

Soon Hadley announced dinner, and Keith escorted her to the dining room. Seated at the head of the table, he inquired, "So how was your day, madam?"

"Comme ci, comme ça."

"Any luck finding a gown for the Belmonts' ball?"

"Not really." Unfolding her snowy napkin, she laid it across her knees. "Some of the Paris fall collections are still on the high seas. I may have to engage a modiste."

Two servants, unobtrusive as shadows, served the leg of lamb and mint sauce, the potato soufflé, and other vegetables, all from silver utensils.

"If so, get the best and offer a bonus."

"Of course, dear. Madame Demorest has a marvelous designer at her Emporium."

"Why aren't Scotty and Miss Vale dining with us?"

"He got hungry early, and we didn't know how late you'd be. But you're right about his needing companions his own age, Keith. He seems to enjoy playing in the park, with the neighborhood children."

Dessert and coffee were brought in, and Keith waited until the domestics disappeared into the kitchen again. "I'm glad you agree on that."

Devon tasted the Bavarian torte, an elaborate pastry garnished with cherries, whipped cream, and slivered almonds, and then gazed pensively at the tall white tapers flickering in repoussé silver candelabra. The crystal pendants and prisms of the ornate Marie Thérèse chandelier overhead shimmered iridescently in the gaslight. There was a propitious moment, an opportunity for significant conversation, but she let it pass. She had fibbed to him about shopping, dissembled, and the realization disconcerted her.

"Aren't you having brandy in your coffee?"

He glanced up. "Didn't you notice Hadley prepare it on the sideboard?"

"No, my mind was elsewhere."

"The country? That's where mine is, too. I hope the twins will recognize us."

"Darling, it's only been a few days! I'm sure they're still

crawling, drooling, wailing, and wetting."

"I can't wait for them to walk and talk and ride ponies. I'll buy a beautiful pair of matched Shetlands and hand-tooled leather saddles. You'll choose their habits, naturally. I assume we'll dress them alike in every respect?"

"Well, shopping for them is certainly simpler in duplicate," Devon agreed. "And the seamstress who stitched their layettes is conveniently located in Inwood Village."

"Would you like to attend a drama or concert this evening?" Keith invited, finishing his demitasse.

"Do you have tickets to either?"

"Darling, we have boxes!"

"At the opera, too?"

He nodded. "There are no more available at the Academy of Music, and people are offering as high as thirty thousand dollars for one. We should either take advantage of ours or lend it to others less fortunate."

"We will, dear, but not tonight."

The fingerbowls were presented, used.

"Chess?" Keith suggested, rising and ushering her back to the library.

"Oh, darling, I'm terrible at chess! No challenge at all for you. Hadley is your best partner."

"Checkers, then?"

"All right, though you always beat the chemise off me in that, too."

He laughed, winking. "Good! You're adorable sans chemise. Two games out of three?"

"Just don't let me win—I'll know if you do."

"Why should I try to fool you?" he inquired, his tone suddenly serious. "You wouldn't fool me, would you?"

Did she dare pursue that? "Well, you're acquainted with feminine wiles."

"Yes, indeed! Few men since Adam have probably had more experience with them. And I'll know if you make a rash move, or one without prudent deliberation." He grinned at her, setting up the board. "Red or black?"

"Red," she decided, swallowing tensely. "Keith, are you pulling my leg?"

"No, that'll come later." Another covert smile, as if baiting her. "I intend to win, my pet—and I always collect on my bets and play for keeps."

She played wretchedly, unable to concentrate, puzzled by his ambiguity. "I'm a dunce!" she exclaimed at a bad strategy that gave him a triple jump and another crowned king. "But I'm not doing it purposely."

Raising his smoky-gray eyes from the board, he peered at her intently. "You're in a corner, darling, with no way out. Might as well concede. One down, two to go."

"I'll do better next time."

"Not if your mind keeps wandering. You're about to lose your chemise, my pretty little charmer."

"I'll lose it anyway in the end. I always do—and the sooner now, the better. It's much more fun playing with you in bed. I *know* the proper moves there. At least I don't make many false ones, do I?"

"None," he complimented. "I taught you quite well. Never try to beguile me in the boudoir, *chérie.*"

Her tension mounted, her nerves drawing tight as bowstrings. She flubbed another move, frowning as he practically cleared the board of her men. "I surrender, maestro."

"Unconditionally?"

"How else?"

"Oh, there are degrees of surrender, Devon. It can be primarily physical, with mental reservations."

"Why the analogies and cryptograms, Keith? Are you subtly baiting me?"

He sighed heavily—the kind of reaction she had come to associate with personal disappointment or frustration. Abandoning the game table, he rose and circled the room, flexing his hands in suppressed anger. "I was on Publishers Row this morning and recognized a familiar equipage."

Finally! The crux, and she was at the center of the marital crucible. "I—I was going to tell you about that, Keith."

"When, Devon?"

"Tonight."

"Before, after, or during lovemaking?"

"Does it matter?"

"Hell, yes! Because you still think I can be led by the penis, and that I'll forgive you anything in bed! And because I suspect you were doing more than just visiting your old friends at the *Record,* to which you know I have no objection whatever, else you would have told me."

"It began as a visit, Keith. Then Carrie Hempstead invited me to lunch with the Sorosis Club—"

"And?"

She hesitated. "You won't like the rest."

"Nevertheless, I want to hear it."

Devon told him everything, wishing she could have first removed the whalebone constriction that impaired her breath, for it was like swimming underwater in a swift current.

"Pray continue," he prompted at her breathless pause.

"That's all," she murmured, one hand rising to her palpitating bosom. She felt faint.

"And more than enough, wouldn't you say?" He scratched a long sideburn, bemused. "Were you going to keep your little secret until the first installment of *Missions in Hell* was published?"

"No. Maybe. Oh, I don't know, Keith! I—I was afraid you'd forbid it."

"I would, and I will. My lawyers will slap an injunction on Samuel Fitch tomorrow."

She stared at him in disbelief, her spine stiffening in sudden defiance. "That series was written before our marriage, Keith! I signed a release and accepted payment, which I have already donated to the Women's Bureau. If you try to prevent its publication, I shall have to return the money and be humiliated before my colleagues and friends with more liberal spouses. I won't willingly abide that kind of domination, Keith! Nor be docilely punished for my principles! Despite my love for you, my spirit would rebel against such despotism, and I—I would have to defend my conscience." Head held high, eyes flashing emerald fire, she was the image of the same brave little Rebel who had declared her firm independence to him in the defeated, surrendered capital of the Confederacy.

Shocked out of his pacing, Keith stood immobilized as a stone statue. "Are you saying you would leave me?"

Devon nodded, uncertain of her voice.

"And our son and baby daughters?"

The enormity of her predicament struck painfully, as maternity fought feminism—and conquered. She swayed irresolutely, her vision blurring in distraught tears, her heart fluttering in her tight throat. Spinning in sudden vertigo, courage and conviction collapsed in dark oblivion.

She awoke on the bed in the master suite, with the acrid odor of ammonia in her nostrils, and the housekeeper and a maid ministering to her. Her slippers were off, a pillow elevating her feet. Lurline held a vinaigrette of smelling salts. Mrs. Sturges, applying a cool wet compress to her forehead, inquired, "Are you all right, madam?"

"I—I think so. What happened?"

"You swooned," Keith answered, pouring some cognac.

"How stupid of me!"

He dismissed the hovering servants, who departed quietly and closed the door. His arms then supporting her back, he urged her to sit up and drink some stimulant. Devon obeyed, meek as a kitten now. Noticing her deshabille, she asked, "Who undressed me?"

"The women. And it's no wonder you fainted, laced so damned tightly! You should know better."

"Even Miss Anthony wears a corset," Devon murmured. "But it's not my tight stays you're angry about, is it?"

Stacking several pillows against the headboard, he eased her against them. Then he sat beside her, but did not touch even her hands. "Do you feel like talking?"

"If you do."

"You gave me a hell of a scare, Devon. Have we reached an impasse?"

"I trust not, Keith."

"Do you remember your threats?"

"I hoped you would ignore them," she quavered, picking at the embroidered flowers on the sheet. "Oh, Keith, you know I couldn't ever leave you and the children! I did once, with Scotty, because I had no alternative. I couldn't even acknowledge him! You had a sick wife, and you had taken my baby by adoption."

"But that's not the case now, Devon. *You* are my wife, and I thought you were perfectly happy and content in that status. Was I living in a fool's paradise? What's lacking in our relationship? What are you seeking outside of it?"

"Nothing cosmic, Keith. Just a little personal liberty and integrity: freedom to pursue matters of importance to me. An opportunity to do something for humanity. What the French call *raison d'être*: reason for being."

"I know what it means, Devon. And you feel you must justify your existence via causes and crusades?"

"Is that so terrible? Would it be better to devote all of my leisure to social functions, become one of those absurd matrons vying with one another to host the most extravagant entertainments? Society is fine, and we'll be a part of it, for the sake of the children. I want the best for them, just as you do, and they'll have it. But what about the thousands of less fortunate youngsters in this world?"

"I've endowed an orphanage, Devon. Also homes for the blind and mentally disabled."

"I'm speaking of child labor, Keith. Mrs. Stanton convinced me that I could be of service in the Movement's efforts to abolish it."

"How? By writing a few inflammatory articles and soliciting funds and signatures for petitions to Congress?"

"It's a start."

"It's a political issue, Devon. Why didn't you get involved in it when you were married to a politician?"

Her jaw fell. "That's a low blow."

"I'm sorry, but I don't want my wife traipsing back and forth to Washington with those wild-eyed firebrand feminists, whatever your particular mission. Unfortunately, they're all branded with the same iron. All classed as revolutionaries!"

"So were the colonists," she reminded.

"Touché, my little spitfire! But I've had enough rebellion for one day. Don't try my patience."

"May I write some pamphlets on the subject?"

"Write some fiction instead," he suggested. "Try to deliver that long-gestating antebellum novel. It'll keep you out of mischief."

"And at home?"

"A woman's place, traditionally." He smiled at her petulance. "I think I'll go downstairs and read."

"I may be asleep when you return."

"I'll try not to disturb you."

"You're still angry with me, aren't you?"

"More disappointed," he said. "And somewhat disillusioned, perhaps. This thing hit me like a bolt of lightning. I am wounded and will need some time to recover. Do you understand?"

She shook her head, weeping at his rejection.

"Crying won't help, Devon. Not this time, anyway."

"Do you still love me?"

"I'll always love you, Devon."

"Then don't leave me now. I need you, Keith."

"My darling, beneath your veneer of sophistication, you're still a pathetically naive child. Do you imagine male sexuality operates on command—or a spring lever, like a jack-in-the-box? I couldn't make love to you now if I tried. I feel castrated, about as potent as a eunuch."

"Too impotent to even kiss me good night?"

"Get some rest," he said brusquely, opening the door.

Devon clamped her hands over her mouth, lest she cry out to him. Dear God, what had she done to his manhood and their marriage? And how could she accomplish a reconciliation without his cooperation?

Her emotions were in turmoil, precluding sleep. The porcelain clock on the bureau sounded mockingly loud, ticking away precious minutes and hours of lost time with him. Nothing was worth this agony and loneliness. Fool! she admonished herself, sobbing in remorse.

Finally, she dozed off, tormented by nightmares in which she missed the comfort of his arms. But not until morning, seeing the empty space beside her, did she learn that he had slept on the long leather sofa in the library. Hadley found him there, with an open book on his chest.

✧ 10 ✧

"MY DARLINGS!" Devon cried, hugging and kissing the twins effusively. "My precious little girls! Mommy missed you dreadfully. And Daddy, too," she added as Keith swooped them up to bestow his affections. "How have they been, Nanny?"

"A wee bit cross, Mrs. Curtis. They're teething, you know. Enid and I had to walk them last night, before I rubbed their gums with paragoric. As usual, Shannon needed more pacification. How old was Master Scott when he cut his first tooth?"

"Five months," Devon said, remembering that she had had to wean him for biting her. Then he had chewed the rubber nipples on his bottles, the pacifier and bone teething ring, the crib rails, rattles, toys, and anything else he could get in his mouth. "Well, I hope they haven't been too fretful, Nanny."

"Oh, no, madam! Caring for babies is my profession, after all, and Mrs. Sommes and her daughter are willing aides. We managed nicely. But they may be a trifle more spoiled than before." And their fawning father won't help matters much, she thought.

Keith's shirt-bosom was damp with tears and drool, but he didn't seem to mind. One cherub in each arm, he carried them outdoors, which always seemed to placate them. Devon accompanied him, enjoying the autumn landscape. Nature's magic brush had gilded the elms, bronzed the oaks, splashed the meadows with goldenrod. A big tom turkey strutted about the yard, unaware that he had been marked for the Thanksgiving dinner. His raucous gobble amused the twins, who tried to imitate him with gurgles. They pointed at everything that caught their attention, cooing, chuckling, endeavoring to form coherent syllables. And as parents had always done, Devon and

Keith praised and encouraged their efforts to speak, identifying the animals and objects and enunciating names and sounds, teaching by rote.

Scotty was already in the stables, assisting in the saddling of his horse. Nothing at Halcyon gave him more pleasure than riding, and his skill steadily increased.

"Shall we join him later?" Devon asked, waving as their son cantered off toward the yellow fields.

"If you like."

His perfunctory politeness was wreaking havoc on her taut nerves. He had remained on deck during the trip upriver, conversing with Captain Bowers at the helm, with the crew, Rufus, Scotty. After coffee and croissants with him in the dining salon, Devon had strolled alone on the promenade, pausing at the port railing to admire the familiar but invariably gorgeous New Jersey palisades, brilliantly hued in the late October sunlight, and then slipping off to the master stateroom. But her husband did not follow her there, as she had hoped.

"Don't do me any favors, dear."

"I know you think I'm sulking, Devon, which is primarily your province, and that I'm chastising you for not previously informing me of your plans."

"Well, aren't you?"

"No, just meditating. Maybe I've been too selfish and possessive with you. So I've decided to be more lenient, give you more leeway in your career and feminist activities. I don't want you feeling deprived, stifled, unfulfilled."

"Oh, darling, I don't feel any of those things! At least I didn't until last night, when you preferred the library sofa to our bed. . . ."

He scowled in embarrassment. "Never mind that! We were discussing your individuality—your freedom to express yourself intellectually, or however you prefer, but you don't seem too pleased. Not exactly overjoyed."

"I'm surprised, I guess. Your capitulation is rather sudden, isn't it?"

"Why prolong it, Devon? I would concede eventually, anyhow, in the interest of domestic harmony. Don't I usually? Celebrate your easy victory, Mrs. Curtis."

Devon contemplated a grove of trees in shades of scarlet and crimson, sienna and burnt orange. Ironically, she felt no triumph, no exuberance or jubilation. Perhaps it was *too* easy. And suspicious of his acquiescence, she questioned it. "Are you humoring me, Keith?"

"What else does a man do with a temperamental woman, if he loves her and values his peace of mind?"

"I see," she murmured, recoiling. "And do you think I was just being capricious last night? Having feminine temper tantrums?"

"You riled yourself up enough to swoon!"

"I had a rare attack of the vapors."

"Precisely, my dear. Your rare fainting spells are invariably induced by emotional upsets. I learned that years ago, during one of our tiffs on the train from Washington to New York, when I proposed an unconventional arrangement. First you fuss, then pout, then cry, then faint."

"Thank you for that brilliant psychological analysis! My victory seems somewhat hollow now. As usual, you've managed to disarm me without my knowledge."

"Oh, come now! We've been fencing mentally, and some of your dire threats last night were mere bravado. I just called your bluff, that's all. But you've succeeded in blunting my sword, so why not sheathe yours?"

"Are you comparing my tongue to a saber?"

"Not at all, darling. I just prefer a different kind of action from that particular part of your anatomy. How about a conciliatory kiss and embrace?"

"Your arms are already full." As Devon reached over to wipe Sharon's drooling face, Shannon's fingers became entangled in her mother's loose curls. "Naughty girl," she scolded, extricating the tenacious little hand.

"She's just a baby, Mommy."

"But pulling hair is a bad habit, Daddy, and I think it's jealousy of my attention to her sister. Sharon's no better when she's not the center of attraction. They'll snatch each other bald-headed before their first birthday! And look how they cling to your neck. They know *your* weakness."

"For humoring females?" He grinned sheepishly. "Guilty. So when will you relaunch your writing craft on the waves of printer's ink?"

"When the right assignment presents itself," she replied, pretending nonchalance.

"No doubt *Missions in Hell* will provide some. Couldn't you use a less explosive title?"

"Probably, though hardly a more suitable one. I shan't change it, but I can't say the same for your wet little leeches. We'd better return them to the nursery, Keith. They're ruining your shirt."

"It's washable." He waited, gazing at her. "Have the bugles blown truce in our marital conflict?"

Tempted to resist a while longer, for the sheer erotic stimulation of it, she finally relented and smiled at him. "Oh, you rogue! You know I wouldn't forfeit our love again tonight! But I think I shall make you pay double for neglecting me last night."

"Ah, you've scored again! But that's hardly a penalty," he said, grinning, as they strolled toward the house. "And you still haven't dropped your guard completely, nor surrendered your double-edged blade."

"Nor you yours! We're well matched, darling. Highly compatible."

"I hope the years won't change that too drastically, Devon. I have a few up on you."

She patted his magnificent shoulders in mock sympathy. "Poor old fellow! I suppose you'll be needing a cane and aphrodisiacs before long? I understand raw oysters and ginseng mixed with powdered ram's horn are effective."

That observation evoked hearty, virile laughter. "Who told you that? The lecherous little bookseller, Ephraim Joseph, who tried to seduce you when the great blizzard trapped you in his shop?"

"Uh-huh. And he was twice your age! Fortunately, he gave up chasing me without much of a struggle."

"Like Madame Janette Joie, after you repelled her peculiar advances on Christmas eve? You had some fantastic experiences your first years in Sodom and Gomorrah! Served you right, too, for defying me after I ensconced you in the Astor House with unlimited credit; running away and leaving no forwarding address, only that infuriating promissory note for the money you imagined you owed me. You have much interesting material for an autobiographical novel, my dear."

"Would you let me publish it?"

The answer was an unequivocal "No."

"Then what's the point? Self-amusement? That's a waste of talent. It's siesta time for the bambinos, dear. And their nappies, as Nanny calls diapers, are saturated. Take them inside, doting Daddy."

The weekend passed swiftly and enjoyably. Dr. Blake made his usual Sunday visit, and he and Keith went sculling after dinner. Devon rode with Scotty for an hour. Then, with a mounted and armed guard trailing the buggy whenever it left the property carrying a member of the family, she and the boy drove along the country lanes, through Inwood Valley toward Sputen Duyvil Creek, crossing many shallow, meandering streams, the wheels splashing through the water or rumbling over picturesque wood or stone bridges. Ferns, rushes, and cattails flourished in the marshes, rustling when the wind swept through them. Brightly colored leaves, tokens of the waning season, drifted across the path, forecasting an early winter. Scotty was already anticipating sleighing in the snow. When her gloved hands tired, Devon let him handle the reins, cautioning him to slow down. "You're not racing a sulky in Harlem Lane, son!"

"I wish I were," he said. "And I will when I'm old enough, like Daddy told me he used to do. I want to be just like him in every way, Mommy."

"Nothing could please him more, Scotty. But you're still my little boy, too, remember."

Her adjective piqued him. "The twins are *little*, Mother. Miss Vale says I'm growing like a reed!"

"So you are." Devon sighed. "And soon I must let you go off to that boarding school in Connecticut...."

"It'll be good for me," he declared, obviously quoting his father. "And college will make a man of me!"

"Just don't lose the years between boyhood and manhood, Scott, for you can never retrieve them. Shall we pause by the next stream, take off our shoes, and wade?"

"Isn't that rather childish?"

"No more so than romping in the surf, which we all did on that Long Island beach during our last cruise. Besides, I know you want to wade as much as I do. Then we'll pick some cattails and autumn foliage to decorate the house. The holidays are coming, you know. Time to make out our Christmas lists! I suppose you're too old to write to Santa Claus?"

"Really, Mother!" He frowned, embarrassed. "That's a myth, like elves and fairies, and storks bringing babies. Daddy explained that to me, though I don't quite understand everything about it yet."

"You know enough for now," his mother assured him.

"But I'm sure he left out some important things."

"I'm sure he did." Devon nodded. "There's a nice clear brook, Scotty. Draw rein and take off your boots."

To Devon's dismay, she could not return to Gramercy Park with Keith on Monday. Despite Nanny's assurances that the teething infants' slight temperatures and digestive upsets were natural, she could not bring herself to leave them. Keith left the *Sprite* moored at Halcyon Landing and boarded a train at the village station.

Rapid transit for commuters was becoming a reality on Manhattan Island. The Hudson River Railroad became elevated on its approach to the bustling city, traversing some of its worst slums, the puffing engines showering soot and cinders and fiery sparks that occasionally set fire to the dry wood shingles of the tenement roofs along the route.

Passing over Hell's Kitchen, the most notorious of all the metropolitan milieux, abounding in crime and vice, Keith pondered Devon's past foolish bravery in venturing into the equally dangerous Five Points for her series soon to be belatedly published. What if she decided, again alone and without his knowledge or consent, to venture in Hell's Kitchen for a follow-up feature? And how could he cope if the resurgence of her journalistic ambition became obsessive? Why couldn't she be satisfied to write about motherhood, homemaking, and fashion! Most newspapers had at least one section catering to such bland, harmless fare. Why must his wife aspire to lofty ideals and noble crusades—and why did he indulge her whims and fantasies?

Arriving at his office, he found a cluster of excited employees around his elderly secretary, who had just suffered some sort of seizure. Martin Stacy, a small bald man, had served Keith's father, Cameron Curtis, in the same position for many years. Lacking the heart to retire him even at seventy-two and in failing health, Keith realized his benevolent mistake as the hastily summoned physician pronounced Mr. Stacy dead of apoplexy. Soon a hearse arrived to transport the black-shrouded corpse to a morgue, and Keith told the attendants to bill him for the funeral expenses.

A Wall Street employment agency was notified of the opportunity at the Curtis Bank, which was temporarily occupied by an anxious clerk from the accounting department. A host of eager applicants appeared: twelve young men all claiming education and experience in finance, and one young woman who had worked in various government offices in Washington until her present resignation.

Marnie Ryan had thick titian hair, alert vividly blue eyes, and a lilting Irish voice. She also possessed incredible audacity, seeking a job traditionally reserved in the profession for qualified males. During the interview, Keith learned that she was twenty-five, single, educated in a convent school, and ambitious for a career in banking. Informed that he knew of no financial institution with a confidential female secretary to the president, she simply inquired, "Why not, sir? It seems to me that women are far better suited to the position than men! Business schools are training them in secretarial work, shorthand, and the use of the new Remington machine, and I am skilled in both. If you are still using handscript for your correspondence, I could print it neatly on the typewriting machine."

Keith surveyed her across his large polished mahogany desk. She sat decorously in a leather armchair, conservatively dressed in a dark wool skirt, gored and only slightly bustled, an immaculate white linen blouse, and short dark jacket. Her hat was anything but frivolous, her white-gloved hands folded demurely in her lap. Apparently she had not been screened in the proper department, and he was curious as to how she had accomplished that. "Tell me, Miss Ryan, how did you get past the Supervisor of Personnel?"

"Why, I came directly to you, sir! My father always told me, 'If you want something badly enough, colleen, go to the top!' 'Twas good advice?"

"'Twas." Keith nodded, caught between amusement and amazement, since her sex would automatically have been disqualified on a lower level. "And while I admire your ingenuity, Miss Ryan, I would be setting two precedents in employing you in this capacity."

"Sure now you don't discriminate against the fair sex in your hiring practices, Mr. Curtis?"

"Have you seen many working in this building?"

"Only with brooms and mops," she replied, her tone and manner resembling Devon's in accusatory moments.

If there was one thing he didn't need, it was another strong-willed, defiant, ambitious female! Nor to be the first among his colleagues to install one in his ante-office, as his business and personal confidante. A masculine stronghold, Wall Street precluded even the wealthiest women from the Stock Exchange and Gold Room. No females had breached the barriers of the monetary citadel since the maverick Cornelius Vanderbilt had set up the brazen sisters, Victoria Woodhull and Tennessee Claflin, in a fancy brokerage-bordello on Broad Street, where they had dealt more in assignations than in stocks and bonds. The lascivious old Commodore's connection with the Bewitching Brokers, as the press labeled them, was no secret, therefore no really great surprise to the bulls and bears of the District, many of whom patronized them for similar reasons. Wives and sweethearts breathed sighs of relief when Old Corneel abandoned the beauteous pair of trollops to marry a young girl whose mother vigorously disapproved of such shenanigans; and without his support and expertise, the Bewitching Brokers soon went bankrupt.

"I'm sorry," Keith said, rubbing his chin ruefully. "Nothing personal, you understand, but it just wouldn't be an expedient arrangement."

"You dislike women, Mr. Curtis?"

"On the contrary, Miss Ryan."

"You like them in their place?"

"Well—"

"What is a woman's place, sir? Where does she belong? In the home and nowhere else? If so, why are they hired in factories and sweatshops? Is it because men think they have a menial mentality capable only of performing drudgery, or because they'll work longer hours for cheaper pay, without complaining?"

"That's impertinent, young lady!"

"Insubordinate," she corrected. "You see, I *do* know my place, Mr. Curtis, and I would certainly keep it in any gentleman's employ. But you're not going to give me a chance to prove either my ability or propriety, are you? If it didn't work out to your satisfaction, sir, you could always dismiss me, you know."

Damnation! She was challenging his integrity and business ethics, and he could end this incredible interview merely by showing her the door. What stopped him? The fact that her questions, however blunt and officious, were also honest and relevant? The rule against women in banking was an ancient custom, not covenant, carried over from the days of the goldsmith and the countinghouse, as if there was some great mystery about finance which the feeble feminine mind could not possibly comprehend.

While Keith hesitated, she made the one challenge most certain to test his masculinity. "Perhaps you would prefer to discuss this matter with your wife first, Mr. Curtis?"

Against his better judgment, and hoping he would not rue his rashness, Keith scribbled an executive order on his letterhead and handed it to her. "Take this to Personnel, Miss Ryan. Your hours will be eight to six weekdays, eight to one Saturdays. I'm here at nine, usually, and leave by five, usually, no Saturdays. You will be expected to manage my office efficiently in my absence, but you will make no important decisions without clearance. If you need assistance when I'm unavailable, you will consult the first vice president, Mr. Josiah Hammermill. Deviations from the bank's procedures, policies and code of conduct are not tolerated. Understood?"

"Yes, sir. And thank you very much."

"You haven't mentioned salary."

"I assume it'll be adequate," she said, her trusting smile appealing to his generosity. "I'm supporting my father."

"The smart Irishman, who advised you to go first to the top?"

"He's ill and crippled, Mr. Curtis, ever since a crate of goods fell on him in a dock accident. That's why I had to leave my job in Washington, to come home and care for him. But also because I couldn't accomplish anything, or foresee any future in the mazes of Federal bureaucracy and nepotism. It's not what, but *who* you know there that counts, and a relative in political power is one's finest recommendation. Pa and I live in a tenement in the Bowery."

"Advantageous information," Keith muttered, starting her

with five dollars per week more than he had intended. "Good day, Miss Ryan."

She extended her hand for a businesslike shake. "See you in the morning, boss!"

Keith frowned. "Don't ever call me that, Miss Ryan. The word 'boss' has an evil connotation in New York, as any Irishman living in a Tammany Hall ward should know."

"Mike Ryan—that's me old man's name," she said with an exaggerated brogue revealing a fine sense of humor, "never engaged in politics, Mr. Curtis. Sure now he never had the time or money."

"Sorry," Keith apologized, escorting her into the anteroom. "This will be your office, Miss Ryan. Unless my door is open, or the building is on fire, you will never enter my domain without knocking."

"Of course not, sir." Marnie Ryan was prepared to be the soul of discretion with this obviously well-bred gentleman. "May I put a few personal things in my space?"

"Such as?"

"A back cushion for the chair, a photograph on the desk, and a green plant or two?"

"Yes, but no visible feminine articles—hand mirrors, hair-receivers, cosmetics, et cetera. And when not in use, accessories of apparel are to be kept out of sight, too, in the closet. This is a bank, Miss Ryan, and dignity is an essential part of its decor."

"I understand, Mr. Curtis. Good day!"

She walked away briskly but sedately, holding her posture erect and controlling the natural feminine sway of her hips. She would not interfere with any male employee's morale, Keith thought, and he would fire anyone who trifled with hers.

✦ 11 ✦

MARNIE RYAN gave her best to her position in the Curtis Bank, determined that its proprietor should never have any regrets about hiring her. He could dictate rapidly to her, for she was as proficient in the Isaac Pitman method of shorthand as in the operation of the Remington typing apparatus. And though an excellent speller, she kept a dictionary handy to ensure both the neatness and accuracy of his correspondence. Possessing a natural aptitude for the profession, she also studied available texts on banking in whatever leisure she could spare, after caring for her semi-invalid father and the small flat they shared in the Bowery District. Always punctual in the morning, she never abused her luncheon period, nor left before the completion of her workday schedule.

Her presence at the executive meetings, which she recorded for reference, was dignified and unobtrusive. And though some male jealousy and resentment of Miss Ryan still existed in the lower ranks, and especially in the clerk who had coveted a promotion to the president's office, it was not liberally or generally discussed beyond their washroom.

Increasingly pleased with her performance, Keith removed Marnie Ryan from probation to permanent status and raised her salary long before the customary six-month requirement. She opened a personal checking account and felt very fortunate and sexually advanced. She hoped to save enough to move to a better neighborhood—and toward this goal she brought her lunch from home, bought her clothes at bargain sales, remade outdated garments and hats, and repaired her own shoes whenever possible.

Marnie read the recently published series of *Missions in Hell* and considered it excellent, true of everything she knew about slums. She learned the identity of the journalist through in-house gossip, but determined never to mention Mr. Curtis's wife in any way unless he did. Apparently he kept track of the important dates in their private lives, such as birthdays and anniversaries, for there were no circled reminders on Marnie's calendar. But having heard and read that Mrs. Curtis, née Devon Marshall, was a talented and gracious beauty, Marnie wished for an opportunity to meet her. Wasn't she curious about her spouse's new secretary? In her place, with a man like Mr. Curtis, Marnie knew *she* would have made a prompt call at his office.

And so would Devon, had she been aware of his new confidential assistant. They rarely discussed business, and she certainly never browsed in his portfolio. But she had recently noticed, when he worked at home, that formerly handwritten documents were now printed on the typing machine first demonstrated at the Centennial Exposition, in Philadelphia, and which Devon herself could operate.

"Mr. Stacy's replacement must be able to type," she remarked casually, the evening of the Belmonts' reception.

Already formally attired, Keith was perusing a contract while Devon finished her toilette. She had managed to find a magnificent Worth creation, a perfect fit, in the Paris salon of Lord & Taylor. It was French satin in a luscious shade of ivory, overlaid with a mist of creamy Chantilly lace sprinkled with seed pearls, and she epitomized Keith's image of a fair and beautiful woman. His smoky-gray eyes glowed with admiration. "My God, but you're gorgeous tonight! The gentlemen are going to monopolize you."

"And the ladies my handsome husband! Just remember you'll be the favorite on my program, and don't forget to claim your dances."

"Not likely, my dear. What was your earlier question?"

"About your new secretary. Does he type?"

"Yes, she does," he answered nonchalantly, replacing the document in his monogrammed leather case. "Her name is Marnie Ryan, and she's also proficient in Pitman speedwriting. Quite an improvement over poor old Martin Stacy, God rest his loyal soul."

Devon, just opening her jewel case, paused and gazed at

him. "You hired a female replacement?" she inquired, as if she had misunderstood him.

He nodded. "A highly competent one."

"Were you saving it as a surprise for me?"

"Not exactly. Miss Ryan was employed on a trial basis. I wasn't sure she could handle the position, and I was also setting a precedent on the Street. Bankers' private secretaries are traditionally male and middle-aged, you know. Mine should please the feminists!"

"Including your wife?"

"Why not? Don't you subscribe to their theories and goals? Equal rights, in employment and everything else? Actually, women are probably superior to men in secretarial work, even in financial institutions."

Devon held up a three-strand necklace of Oriental pearls. "Will you fasten this for me, please?"

"With pleasure," he obliged, gauging her reaction in the mirror. "Do I detect some objection, darling?"

"Only in your neglect to inform me," she replied, further adorning herself with pearl earrings and bracelet. Pearl-headed hairpins nestled like translucent dewdrops in her shimmering pale-blond hair fashioned in the latest and eminently becoming *al greco* style.

"I told you the reason, Devon. Had I not hired her, or subsequently had to fire her for inefficiency, it would have smacked of sexual discrimination. And then you would have accused me of prejudice."

"Probably."

"Probably?" He shook his head, confounded. "Damned if I'll ever understand women!"

"Is she pretty?"

"I knew *that* was coming, however, and she's certainly not ugly. Auburn hair, blue eyes, a few freckles across her nose. Very Irish, including her accent. Miss Ryan is in her twenties, single, and somewhat buxom," he added, anticipating her next questions.

"So much younger than Mr. Stacy, and yet so well qualified at that age?"

"I'll admit, I was skeptical, too."

"But no longer?"

"You're conducting an inquisition, dear."

"Sorry, *dear*," she murmured, realizing that she was indeed nagging and badgering him. But suddenly the shoe was on the other foot, and it pinched. And she couldn't resist asking, "Do you find her physically attractive?"

"I find her work eminently satisfactory," he replied, frowning at her persistence.

Standing, Devon surveyed herself in the cheval glass, checking every minute detail of her reflection, as she donned the elbow-length ivory Kasan gloves.

Bending to kiss her delectably bare shoulders, Keith proceeded to drape the sable-trimmed matching satin cloak over them. "Look at yourself, Devon! How could any other woman compare or compete with you? I'd like to take you to bed now...."

"Then do!" she cried passionately, turning to him.

"And spoil that stunning coiffure? Besides, we're late already. But perhaps your first appearance in Manhattan society as my wife should be an entrance, Mrs. Curtis."

"I don't care about that, Keith, or my hairdo. Make love to me before we go."

"Stop tempting me, my adorable little minx! Anticipation will only intensify the longing and pleasure, later. Come along now, and make me the envy of every man there."

Like that of so many wealthy New Yorkers, August Belmont's residence was a grandiose pile of brownstone on Fifth Avenue, overdecorated in the splendor and opulence of the era. There was simply too much of everything, an overabundance of marble, gilt, crystal, paintings, sculptures, furniture. Too many liveried servants, too much gourmet food and liquor, including a golden fountain with a continuous flow of premium French champagne from the Rothschild cellars.

Except for Devon, most of the ladies were conspicuously gowned and jeweled, seeming to flaunt every precious gem in their collections. When they were not dancing together, Keith's eyes followed her uxoriously on the waxed parquet floor and in the mirrored walls reflecting myriad flickering candles, for Mrs. Belmont refused to employ harsh gaslight in her sybaritic ballroom. Even their aging host, never known for his marital fidelity, was visibly smitten and verbally envious of his Wall Street colleague's good fortune with respect to his mate.

"Lovely creature," he remarked to Keith at the bar. "Even the young bachelors squiring this season's debutantes are admiring her."

"Why not? She puts them all in the shade."

Belmont, a short, homely man with a slight limp, agreed. "An eclipsing beauty, all right! You must be very proud and protective of her."

"Absolutely."

"And jealous?"

"Murderously, my friend."

Her self-confidence reassured, Devon forgave Keith's negligence with regard to Marnie Ryan. Intentional or not, it seemed insignificant now. Indeed, she should be happy to report this feminine progress in banking to the Women's Bureau and the Sorosis Club, and proud that her husband had initiated a pleasant prospect. Less so, however, was the realization that the Curtises would, ultimately, have to reciprocate the numerous invitations they were receiving.

When she mentioned this to Keith on the way home, he soothed her anxiety with a simple solution. "Darling, that's the caterer's problem! You don't imagine Mrs. Belmont fretted over their gala, do you? Or that the First Lady worried about the social events you covered in the White House? If Ward McAllister has his way, even the guest lists will be simplified by the special register he's compiling."

"A Blue Book? Oh, surely not! He's a snobbish, insufferable man? A toad in tails, with two left feet, and he asked the most personal, impertinent questions."

"Like what?"

"How long we had known each other before our marriage. And how well, if at all, I knew the first Mrs. Curtis. He emphasized 'first' as if it were a Roman numeral attached to a queen's name, obviously still much impressed with her Boston Brahmin peerage."

"The arrogant, officious bastard! What did you do?"

"Changed the subject to *his* background."

Keith laughed heartily. "I bet *that* shut him up. Mr. McAllister was nobody and nothing before he ingratiated himself with the

Old Gotham Guard. Now he thinks he can dictate to them. Well, maybe the Astors and Vanderbilts and Belmonts will kowtow to him, but not the Curtises. He'll court our favor, not vice versa."

The coachman drew rein before their carriage block, and the footman leaped down from the perch to assist them. They entered the house, chuckling and holding hands.

The Belmont affair was duly reported in the society pages, where Mr. and Mrs. Keith H. Curtis were listed "among the prominent and illustrious guests." Devon hardly recognized herself in the various detailed descriptions, so glorious and effulgent, including the *Record*'s, where Carrie Hempstead's new social reporter seemed to overdo her piece. She thought Tish Lambeth would have done much better, but Tish was traveling in the South with the Grants, where Ulysses was testing his ambition for another nomination for the presidency in next year's election. Northern Republicans favored James A. Garfield, however, and Devon marveled at General Grant's courage in soliciting political support among Southern Democrats whom he had conquered militarily. His reception to Dixieland had to be described in euphemisms, for the most part, and Evon was glad it was not her assignment.

She was currently involved in researching the history of child labor, and discovering that it was an incredibly long and cruel one. Worse, it seemed likely to continue for many years to come, its abolishment depending primarily on the efforts of the Women's Movement. She wrote some meritorious pamphlets for the steering committee on which she served, and several comprehensive articles, which were published verbatim in the New York *Record* and reprinted with editing in other publications. But the surface was barely scratched, the goal a distant dream.

They celebrated the holidays at Halcyon. Ramsey Blake, still a bachelor, shared their Thanksgiving feast. At Christmas, he arrived like Santa Claus, bearing expensive gifts for everyone, and especially enjoying his three godchildren. He fawned over the twins, a pair of adorable live dolls in frilly pink silk frocks, with bows in their curls, as much as their parents did.

An abundant snowfall transformed the landscape into a pristine whiteness, and the adults went sleighriding on the country lanes, laughing and singing carols. Devon wore a charming red velvet gown and hooded cloak trimmed in white fox, her hands tucked into a huge matching muff, and Ramsey could hardly keep his eyes off her. They built a debonair snowman with a tophat and cane stuck under one arm, and engaged in a jolly battle of snowballs. Later, while Scotty played outside with his new red sled, they sat before the blazing Yule log, imbibing delicious eggnog and watching more feathery flakes drift past the diamond-paned windows.

"It's not fair," Ramsey complained good-naturedly, refilling his cup from the silver wassail bowl circled with red-berried holly. "I hung a pair of silk stockings on my mantel last night, hoping they would be filled by the legs of a lovely lady when I awoke this morning—but no such luck! And you have too much good fortune, Keith; so much happiness, such a fine family. May I console myself by kissing your beautiful wife under the mistletoe?"

"You mean you haven't yet?" Keith chided, "with it so convenient everywhere? You've been cheating yourself, *mon ami!*"

It was treated as a joke, until their guest was ready to leave. As they walked him to the foyer, Devon inadvertently paused in the arched portal, directly beneath a large sprig of mistletoe. The doctor kissed her, not on the cheek or forehead, but the lips, and his hungry intensity surprised her. But she pretended not to notice his familiarity and hoped that Keith would ignore it, too. They thanked him for the gifts and waved him off to his own estate.

"Did you enjoy that?" Keith casually inquired as they returned to the cozy hearth.

"What?"

"Ramsey's kiss; it was more than platonic, you know, and you're blushing."

"He was tipsy, I think. Perhaps the eggnog was too strong."

"He wasn't drunk, Devon. Far from it. The poor devil is in love with you."

"Oh, I doubt that, Keith! He has never made the slightest advance or gesture."

"Until today."

"That was traditional," Devon temporized. "It's the season of good will, after all, and he's our friend."

"Also your physician," he said, embracing her. "The best in his field, and if you should get pregnant again—"

Their son burst into the house, bravely suppressing tears. He had crashed into a tree and scraped his face on the bark. Seeing the blood on his cheek, Devon rushed to him, crying, "Darling, you're hurt!"

"Just a scratch, Mommy. But I broke my new sled. Will you come outside and fix it, Daddy?"

"Speaking of ill-timed accidents," Keith murmured to his wife, before obliging the child.

They returned to the city for the New Year's festivities, and Dr. Blake had another fortuitous opportunity to take advantage of tradition. They met at a fabulous ball at the Metropolitan Hotel on New Year's Eve, where Devon glittered in silver lamé and diamonds, and there was much merriment: dancing, drinking of toasts, singing "Auld Lang Syne," and kissing of mutual friends and strangers.

As spring came on, Devon prepared for the sentimental journey to Virginia. Scotty and Miss Vale would accompany them on the *Sprite*, but Nanny insisted that the twins would be better off at home. Their parents agreed and planned to be back at Halcyon in time to celebrate their daughters' first birthdays in June.

One mild March day, while shopping for the trip, Devon decided to drop in at the Curtis Bank before noon and invite her husband to luncheon. Keith was in conference when she arrived, and she had to wait in the reception room for him to finish. She finally met his secretary, liked her pleasant personality, but wished Miss Ryan were not quite so young, attractive, and amiable. A glass bud vase on her tidy desk held a single pink carnation, and Devon inhaled its spicy fragrance. Had Keith, in his gallantry, bought the flower? Did he give her small tokens of appreciation?

As if reading her mind, Marnie said, "I bought the carnation from the old woman vendor on Wall Street. I really wanted violets, but the first of the season are too high."

Twenty-five cents a bunch? thought Devon. Surely she could afford that much. Then she remembered times when she, as a working girl, could not afford to waste a penny, much less a quarter, on nonessentials.

She indicated the plainly framed group photograph. "Your family, Miss Ryan?"

"Yes, when we were all together. My mother is dead now, and my older sister is a nun in a St. Louis convent. I take care of my father, who can't work anymore. I'm so grateful to Mr. Curtis for giving me this good job."

"But surely you have a serious suitor, Miss Ryan, and want to marry someday?"

"Someday, perhaps, when Pa is no longer dependent on me. But I just may be a spinster. Some folks might already consider me so, at my age."

"Nonsense!" Devon scoffed. "It's foolish to marry too young, or just for the sake of custom."

Marnie nodded in agreement, adding succinctly, "Or for any reason except love." Her round blue eyes gazed at the exquisitely groomed Mrs. Curtis, somewhat awed by her incredible beauty and slenderness. Suddenly conscious of her own figure, Marnie felt that her breasts were too large and her hips too broad. She imagined the other woman had trim, shapely legs under the graceful skirt, while her own were perhaps too fleshy in the thighs and calves. But no matter, since no one but herself could view her naked form.

The door to the president's chambers opened, and he emerged with a rotund, monocled customer, speaking in low tones and shaking hands in parting. Evidently, a deal had been consummated. Then, approaching his wife, Keith bestowed a husbandly kiss on her cheek.

"Sorry to keep you waiting, darling."

"Not at all, dear. Miss Ryan and I had a chance to get acquainted."

"Good! Any preference in restaurants today?"

Devon proposed the St. Nickolas Hotel, popular for the gourmet cuisine served in its multiwindowed fourth-floor dining salon overlooking Broadway, and Keith consulted his secretary about his next appointment.

"Two-thirty, sir. Mr. John D. Rockefeller."

"Thank you." And taking Devon's arm, "At least we won't have to rush too much. This is a nice surprise, Devon, but less convenient than advance notice."

A uniformed guard attended the massive intaglioed bronze portal for them, and as they descended the marble stairs to Wall Street, Devon pettishly inquired, "Should I have made an appointment to see you, Mr. Curtis?"

"Well, I'm not always available during business hours, Mrs. Curtis. Nor can I always rearrange my schedule accommodatingly. Nevertheless, your spontaneous visit is most welcome and refreshing," he hastily assured, glimpsing her rueful expression. "But your arms are empty. No purchases?"

"They'll be delivered. And you'd better check with your tailors, about the suits and other garments you ordered. Hadley thinks you need more cravats and shoes, too, and another pair of riding boots."

"I'll take care of it," he promised, signaling a hansom cab. "Are you excited about the trip?"

"Fairly. Are you?"

He shrugged noncommitally, giving the driver the address. Managing a desirable table from the maître d'hôtel, he pondered the French menu and suggested a few entrees: "Chateaubriand? Poulet aux champignons? Truite amandine?"

"Nothing rich or heavy for me, darling. Just mushroom soup and a green salad."

"Suddenly lost your appetite?"

"Watching my weight," she replied, slanting her emerald eyes at him. "I shall even forgo one of the chef's famous pastries. Indulge yourself with the steak, if you wish, but we're having prime rib for dinner this evening."

"Then I'll have the broiled flounder," he decided, relaying their order in French to the white-coated Gallic waiter, along with a request for a bottle of vintage white wine.

Devon was observing the continuous parade of traffic and pedestrians from their vantage when he nonchalantly inquired, "What do you think of Miss Ryan?"

"Why, she appears to be everything you said, including buxom. Her hair is more titian than auburn, however, and the few freckles are becoming to her Irish complexion."

"Robust stock, and quite healthy. No absenteeism for illness yet, not even the common winter cold that downed just about every other employee."

"Lucky lass! Never suffers from the female complaint or

vapors of her more delicate sisters?"

"She doesn't discuss such things with me, Devon. And if she doesn't swoon, maybe it's because she laces her stays sensibly."

"Or doesn't wear any?"

"How would I know *that?* I was referring to your penchant for binding yourself in whalebone."

"I thought you liked my figure."

"Darling, I *love* your figure! It's perfect, and you certainly don't need to diet or deprive yourself of any dessert. And if we don't change the subject, we'll have to rent a room here for a few hours. . . ."

That pleased her, and a sensual smile encouraged him. "Sounds like fun, sir. Deliciously wicked!"

"Too bad I have that important appointment," Keith lamented. "Now do you grasp the advantages of prior notice, madam?"

Her head bobbed in disappointment. "Have any of your peers employed female private secretaries?"

"Not yet, although some would no doubt like to appropriate mine for their offices," he said.

"They'd never succeed."

"Why not?"

Devon sipped her Montrachet. "I'm sure Miss Ryan is completely loyal to the Curtis Bank."

"I should hope so, for God's sake! She's privy to much confidential information."

Was he honestly unaware of the lady's personal attraction to him? It was immediately apparent to Devon, as it would have been to any sensitive wife, and she only wondered about the essence of Marnie Ryan's feeling for her boss. Was it just respect and admiration? Gratitude and appreciation? Or was it more, much more, and far deeper?

"Naturally," she murmured as the delicious food was Continentally served. Keith ate zestfully, while Devon forced herself. And she spent the rest of the afternoon in the boudoir boutiques, buying fabulously expensive, exquisitely seductive lingerie.

PART TWO

Women, in truth, are not only intelligent; they have a monopoly of certain of the subtler and more utile forms of intelligence.

H. L. Mencken
IN DEFENSE OF WOMEN

What is truly indispensable for the conduct of life has been taught us by women—the small rules of courtesy, the actions that win the warmth and deference of others; the words that assure us a welcome, the attitude that must be varied to mesh with character and situation: all social strategy. It is listening to women that teaches us to speak with men.

Beatrice Forbes-Robertson Hale
WHAT WOMEN WANT

No woman is an absolute fool. . . . No woman is ever completely deceived.

Joseph Conrad (1857–1924)
UNDER WESTERN EYES

From the greater part of men's acts the deep soul of women stands aloof with a puzzled tolerance, as a mother watches the ingenuous make-believe of her little son. . . . To women it seems that men play with life.

Remy de Gourmont
VIKING BOOK OF APHORISMS

Love does not consist in gazing at each other but in looking together in the same direction.

Antoine de Saint-Exupery
VIKING BOOK OF APHORISMS

The woman's cause is man's; they rise or sink together.
Lord Tennyson (1809–1892)

A woman is a marvelous creation.

Elizabeth Cady Stanton
(1815–1902)

✣ 12 ✣

VIRGINIA WAS a paradox, in some ways vastly changed, in others scarcely at all.

The *Sprite* steamed leisurely from the Atlantic Ocean toward Hampton Roads, past Newport News, then up the broad yellow James River. Emotions almost overwhelmed memories as the years dropped away and Devon was back in her beloved native land again. She was pensively silent as the handsome green-and-white vessel traveled slowly up the wide deep-water channel to its ultimate destination. At some distance from the banks, camouflaged partially by groves of trees and rank shrubs, plantations were visible, a few in skeletonic ruins with charred frames and gaunt chimneys silhouetted against the brilliant April sky, others rebuilt as grandly as ever, and some even enlarged and refurbished.

Great ships, foreign and domestic, lay at anchor in the harbor or moored at the wharves. Giant black stevedores, former slaves or their sons, loaded and unloaded cargoes of tobacco, cotton, lumber, turpentine, tar, wheat and grain from the prolific Shenandoah Valley, Smithfield hams, barrels of salt pork, kegs of apple cider. And as if it were yesterday, Devon remembered the Yankee destruction of the port: the foul odors of the blazing warehouses and clouds of acrid black smoke blotting out the sun, and exploding ammunition dumps rocking the very foundations of the surrendered capital of the Confederacy. The horror of defeat, the terror of Union occupation, the pain and poverty and despair and desperation of Military Rule—all so vivid and incredibly real again, and yet so different, too.

New wood and sheet metal constructions lined the river, and eighty percent of the razed area of Richmond had been rebuilt, or was in the process of rebuilding. Fresh paint covered

the smoke-darkened stucco and frame structures. Chalky whitewashed fences surrounded new clapboard homes and gardens
shaded by survior trees: hardy linden and elm and chestnut and
oak. Business was brisk on Main Street and its environs. Commercial wagons and vans, horsecars and buses, buggies and
surreys, and even a few stately private carriages rumbled over
the cobblestones. Blue military uniforms no longer predomi-
nated on the streets, and few people were abroad in the wretched
rags of humiliation so prevalent when Devon had left Richmond. Black vendors hawked various wares from pushcarts,
or baskets toted on heads and hips, and she heard the familiar
poetic haunting chants of fresh catfish, vegetables, fruits, flowers, shoestrings, notions. Knife-grinding, window-washing,
chimney-sweeping, gardening were offered "cheap" by former
slaves turned tradesmen.

Capitol Hill, its high elevation visible from all sections of
the city, presented a magnificent and inspiring sight when approached from the south. The lofty Ionic portico and fluted
columns towered above the spring-green trees and tall bronze
statues of notable Virginians: Washington, Jefferson, Patrick
Henry. Heroic monuments to Robert E. Lee and Jefferson Davis
were under construction.

From the hackney, Devon solemnly observed her birthplace,
wondering what would have been her destiny had she remained.
Seeing Richmond for the first time, her son was not much
impressed, however, for it was dwarfed and eclipsed by New
York. Scotty couldn't understand why his mother's eyes misted
at certain sights and locations; why she wanted to linger in
some places and not in others; why his parents exchanged
wistful glances at a certain address on Main Street. It was only
a hardware store, after all, with a tin awning and tools and
utensils hanging on the walls, and buckets and tubs and kegs
stacked on the sidewalk.

"This is where your father and I first met each other, Scotty,"
Devon told him quietly.

He looked puzzled. "In a general store?"

"It wasn't any kind of store then, son," Keith informed,
seeing Devon's chin quiver. "It was the burned remains of the
Richmond *Sentinel*, your maternal grandfather's newspaper
building, which had been in the family for generations. Hodge

Marshall wrote about the American Civil War, which you'll study in your history books."

"I already learned about slavery and President Lincoln, sir. About the great generals and battles on both sides, like Gettysburg and Atlanta, and how Lee surrendered to Grant at Appomattox. But I suppose I still have a lot to learn about the War Between the States."

"A great deal, son. And you're in the cradle of the Confederacy now—its most sacred shrine, in fact."

"Is that why we're visiting Virginia?"

"One reason," Keith answered. "It's also Mommy's native state. She was born and reared in this very city."

"Do I have grandparents and relatives here? Will I meet them?"

"No, they're all dead, unfortunately, and we can only visit their graves. Right now, I think we should check into our hotel," Keith decided, anxious about Devon's sudden pallor, and bade the driver take them to the Richmond House, the grandest hostelry in town.

The child was somewhat amazed at the vast numbers of Negroes everywhere, for he saw comparatively few in the city of New York and none in the country around Halcyon-on-Hudson. Rufus Brady was, in fact, the only colored person he actually knew and was accustomed to seeing. All the other Curtis domestics, including the coachmen and footmen, were white.

Here, Negroes drove the hired and private vehicles, tended the portals of the public establishments, toted the baggage, cleaned the streets and stables. But there were many idle males, too, standing on street corners, speaking their colorful idiom, laughing, hustling, occasionally brawling. They lived in dire poverty in squalid shanties that had mushroomed around the Freedmen's Bureau, still waiting, nearly two decades after the Emancipation Proclamation, for the glorious promises and visions of freedom and prosperity to materialize, as if by divine miracle.

The Curtis accommodations, the finest in the hotel, had been engaged in advance. Several porters carried and trundled their numerous leather valises and trunks, most of which belonged to Mrs. Curtis, to their respective suites, which were on the same floor but not adjoining, for the assiduous governess continued her pupil's education even on vacations. Virginia would be no exception.

Several chambermaids were assigned exclusively to their rooms, and Devon took a liking to the one called Pansy—a most pleasant girl with a shiny ebony face, huge sparkling jet eyes, and startlingly white teeth. "Does you need a valet, suh?" she asked Keith as she unpacked and stored articles in the armoire and bureau. (As usual in port, Rufus remained on the *Sprite,* as he did with the private railroad coach at the depots.)

"No, thank you," he replied. "But we would like dinner served here this evening. Is there a menu?"

"Dinnah was served at noon, suh. I s'pects you means supper, and I'll bring up a bill o' fare." Finishing her tasks, Pansy bobbed her turbaned head politely, straightened the long white apron over her dark uniform, and went to perform the same duties in the other suite.

The decor was flamboyantly Victorian, with marble-topped furniture, gilded mirrors, and crystal chandeliers, such as had appealed to the Union officers and their ladies previously in residence. Sitting beside Devon on the red plush sofa with carved black walnut trim, Keith remarked sardonically that it resembled the parlor of an expensive bordello.

"Oh? Have you been in many, dear?"

"Some," he admitted. "Years ago, however. Long before I met you, my love, so remove that pout from your pretty lips. Now that we're in this Southern 'metropolis,' how shall we entertain ourselves?"

In the past, as Devon knew, Southerners did not entertain themselves, they were entertained—and there was a distinct difference. Friends and relatives hosted various social affairs, formal and informal, according to season and occasion, but outsiders other than visiting kin and guests were rarely, if ever, included. Did Richmond society still function on that same antebellum principle? Was it still an inner circle made even smaller, tighter, more circumspect and exclusive by the consequences of the war?

Surely the arrival of so luxurious a private yacht, out of the port of New York, could not have gone unnoticed by the local news media? Every Manhattan journal recorded the visits of personages to the city, if only for posterity, and they had far more numerous and illustrious names to chronicle than did Richmond. She had not expected an elaborate welcome, such as accorded to foreign dignitaries and heads of state, but certainly the businessmen were too intelligent and expedient to long ignore the presence of the wealthiest man in America in their community.

"Oh, let's just rest this evening," she said, kicking off her high-heeled slippers. "We'll do some more sightseeing tomorrow. Things have changed, Keith, far more than I expected. I guess I've been away too long. Except for Capitol Hill and Linden Row, I hardly remember how it was before the fire. It's not much like home anymore."

"That's because it's not your home anymore, Devon, and never will be again. At least, I hope not."

"No," she assured him, but her sigh was pure nostalgia, and she had to swallow a sentimental lump in her throat. "Do you regret not buying any property here, now that it's so obviously prosperous? So many new commercial establishments on Main Street, so much activity on the waterfront! Manufacturing and shipping must be major industries. You should have invested when there was just rubble and twisted iron and sunken vessels in the harbor."

"I did," he advised matter-of-factly.

"You *did?*" Devon was astonished. "When?"

"On my first trip here, after the war. I own a nice stretch of those new wharves, warehouses, and factors' buildings on the James River."

"I might have known! A shrewd Yankee speculator would not have missed such an opportunity. But why didn't you ever tell me before?"

"I didn't want to infuriate my little Rebel further at the time, and there seemed no point later. But property was dirt-cheap then, and only a blind fool wouldn't have realized its potential. Richmond, of all Southern cities, had to rise like the phoenix out of its own ashes, or remain forever a symbol of the South's defeat. I also invested in the future of other Confederate citadels—Charleston, Atlanta, New Orleans—which had to be resurrected, if only to defy the conquerors."

"Invested how, Keith?"

"Real estate, mostly. City blocks around the depots and other transportation facilities, available for a pittance then but which will sell by the square foot before the century is out. I also purchased wilderness land for two cents an acre that will be settled when the railroads traverse it, and ultimately valuable. The surveyors' maps and routes aided me in those investments."

"Dear heaven," Devon breathed, amazed by his acumen and ingenuity. "You really *are* the richest man in America, aren't you?"

"So they say, Mrs. Curtis. I trust you don't find that idea too distasteful?"

"Frightening," she murmured, gazing at him in awe. "So much power concentrated in one individual—why, it's almost obscene, sacrilegious! You could play God with other people's lives and fortunes! Naturally, you have interests in the major banks of the cities you mentioned?"

"Naturally. Northern bankers helped to finance the Union's war. Devon. When the Confederacy went bankrupt, who do you think financed Reconstruction? But the proud and noble Southern gentlemen wouldn't borrow from the damn Yankees up North, so banks were established in their own communities, with their most respectable citizens in charge, and they never knew the difference."

Her gold-flecked green eyes widened, then narrowed suspiciously. "Do you own the Bank of Richmond?"

"Only fifty-one percent of the stock."

"The controlling interest!" Devon gulped, thinking of the Haverston Tobacco Company, a large buff brick building on Cary Street, which she had glimpsed in passing. Was its proprietor indebted to the Bank of Richmond and, unwittingly, to Keith Curtis? Overwhelmed by curiosity, which she knew he would not gratuitously satisfy, she asked the question outright.

Keith dissembled. "Every entrepreneur in the country, the world, owes money to a banker somewhere, Devon."

"That's ambiguous and evasive."

He crossed his long legs. "You want directness? Very well. Mr. Daniel Haverston has a large loan from the local bank. He established his factory with it, and leased storage and shipping facilities with an additional loan."

"Some of your buildings?"

Keith nodded, striking a sulfur match to light one of his favorite Havana cheroots, and wishing someone would invent an easier method to make smoking more enjoyable. He seemed amused by the irony of the Haverston situation, and even intrigued. "I doubt that his cigars will ever provide much competition for Cuba's, but he'll do quite well with his other tobacco products. The British have always preferred Virginia bright leaf and burley in their pipes. Naturally, your friend is not aware of any of this information, Devon."

"How can he *not* be aware?"

"Most of the Curtis Enterprises' Southern investments are managed by holding companies," he explained. "That's how Northern banks infiltrated the entire financial system of the South, in fact, and are repeating the process in the West. Banking is a devious business."

"Indeed, it is! And I tell you frankly, Keith, Daniel would rather be dead than indebted to you, of all Yankees, for so much as a dime."

"Who's going to tell him? Not I. He's doing just fine, Devon. Meeting all his obligations, not just the interest payments but reducing the principal, too. The planter is also a damned good businessman."

"Is Harmony Hill mortgaged?"

"Not anymore. He paid it off on schedule, which makes him a good risk for future loans."

Devon was speechless. Never in her wildest dreams or imagination did she perceive anything like this, and Daniel must never learn the truth. It would destroy him, in spirit and reality.

﴾ 13 ﴿

THE NEXT morning a small but select delegation representing the local business community called at the hotel, requesting an audience with Mr. Curtis. The well-dressed, courteous group of gentlemen included officers of the Chamber of Commerce, directors of the Bank of Richmond . . . and Daniel Haverston. Keith met them in the lobby, whence they retired to a conference room. He agreed to address a special meeting of the Chamber, to dine with several committee members, and to tour the city's newest tobacco enterprise. Only the latter invitation surprised him, as he knew it would his wife, and Keith suspected that its proprietor was acting at the behest of his colleagues. Neither man acknowledged prior introduction, and their perfunctory handshake was brief and something less than cordial.

Keith said, "I've read about your factory in the *Wall Street Journal*, Mr. Haverston. It promises to be one of the largest and best equipped in the South. Congratulations!"

"Thank you, Mr. Curtis. We had an auspicious beginning, with some of the finest tobacco grown in this state. Our special pipe mixture, Harmony Hill, is selling exceptionally well, both in America and abroad. In fact, British tobacconists report good sales on all Haverston products." He paused sheepishly, as if regretting his boastfulness. "Will you be touring the plant?"

"If our schedule permits," Keith replied tentatively. "Mrs. Curtis and our son are with me."

If this information disconcerted the Southerner, only the Yankee realized it. "The invitation includes your family, of course."

"We appreciate your kindness, sir. I'm sure the boy would be interested in the operations, and perhaps Mrs. Curtis, too. When would it be convenient for you?"

116

"I'm at *your* convenience, sir," Daniel drawled, barely perceptible mockery in his tone. "And may I take this opportunity to extend an invitation to be my guests at Harmony Hill Plantation?"

It sounded vaguely like a renewed challenge, which Keith could not gallantly decline. "We'd be delighted, sir."

The president of the Bank of Richmond requested the honor of the Curtises' presence at a reception in his home, others followed suit, and another round of handshakes concluded the meeting with the commercial ambassadors of good will.

Returning to their suite, Keith found the maid lacing Devon into her stayed corselet, and advised, "Not so tightly, Pansy."

Unaccustomed to such admonitions from a husband, the tignoned Negress continued pulling the strong strings, while Devon clutched a bedpost for support. "Missus wants 'em tight, suh."

"Loosen those knots," Keith ordered in an authoritative voice, and the astonished girl promptly obeyed.

"You may go now," Devon told her, slipping into a mauve satin negligee fluttering with marabou, her tiny feet already tucked into matching mules. "I'll call if I need you later, Pansy."

"Yessum." She bobbed a curtsy and disappeared like an obliging shadow.

Keith, who had been leaning against the door frame, arms crossed nonchalantly while observing the whalebone encasement, now walked with Devon into the parlor.

"No doubt that was a novelty for Pansy," she remarked crossly. "I don't imagine many gentlemen supervise their wife's dressing in the boudoir."

"Why not? They watch them *undress* there, don't they? I've warned you repeatedly, as has the doctor, about those damn corsets, Devon! I don't want you fainting on the street here—and especially not in a public factory."

"What are you talking about?"

"That welcoming committee. Your Southern cavalier was one of them."

"You can't be serious."

"Cross my heart"—he grinned, making the symbolic gesture—"although I think his hospitality had a little nudging. But we're invited to several social events, Mrs. Curtis, at different places. And Haverston not only asked us to tour his tobacco factory, but to visit his plantation."

"That's incredible! Did you accept any of the invitations?"

"All of them, tentatively. If you're agreeable."

"Oh, Keith, I don't know about Harmony Hill!" She seemed suddenly flustered. "Was Daniel friendly?"

"Courteous enough, before his associates, but not exactly congenial. He hasn't forgotten you, Devon, nor that incident at Halcyon."

"Is he . . . married?" Mrs. Chester never mentioned Devon's former fiancé in her letters, which had ceased coming some time ago, and she hoped to discover for herself what had happened to the dear old lady.

"He didn't say, and I certainly didn't ask. I suppose we'll learn in due time."

"Must we, Keith?"

"Must we what?"

"Attend these affairs?"

He quirked a dark brow. "When we first discussed this trip, Devon, you wondered how we would be received. And you seemed disappointed yesterday, when there was no brass band and tophatted mayor to greet us."

"Not at all!" she vehemently denied. "Indeed, I was apprehensive of any such political attention, and would have been appalled by it. Besides, no local politicians had advance notice of our visit, did they?"

"Not to my knowledge, nor did the Chamber of Commerce. But word got around somehow, and rapidly."

"That's hardly a mystery, Keith. The announcement was undoubtedly trumpeted like a proclamation by the officers of the Bank of Richmond. Their largest stockholder is in town, after all, and they could hardly ignore him."

He smiled wryly. "Sometimes I think you actually resent my wealth, Devon."

"Don't be absurd! I'm your wife, Keith. But Curtis money does seem to be everywhere, not only in this hemisphere, but the entire world. It's pervasive and invasive, and can make or break almost any person anywhere."

"Beautiful dreamer! You still believe in fairy tales, don't you? Am I the villain in Daniel Haverston's success story? Would it be more appealing to your literary sense if he had not had to borrow from a bank which I control? He could have, you know—I don't own every financial institution in the country. He went to the Bank of Richmond simply because it's the soundest one in this state. Give him credit for enough intelligence to have investigated its solvency, before mortgaging his property and depositing his profits. Don't you realize the number of bank failures that occur every year?" He paused, shaking his head. "Evidently, your major concern is his pride, should he ever discover the truth. Well, it might smart a little, but he'd have to be uncommonly stupid to sacrifice all his gains because of it. To cut off his nose, as it were, to spite his face!"

"You don't know Daniel Haverston," Devon said, picking nervously at the marabou on her flowing bishop sleeves.

"Come now, darling. Even the most rabid Rebels of the past must have mellowed by now."

"I don't mean the war, Keith. That's long over, and Dan was reconciled and resigned to the South's fate soon afterward. He realized he'd have to start over again."

"But he didn't expect to do it alone, eh? He wanted you by his side, helping him pull up his bootstraps—but more importantly, in his bed. And if I'm any judge of character, he'd still like it that way. That's what he can't forgive me—what he couldn't forgive any man, even one of his own breed. This should be an interesting odyssey!"

"We can leave tomorrow, if you like."

"Oh, no! Coming here was your idea, Devon. Meeting Haverston again was almost inevitable, and declining his invitations would not only be impolite, but might convey some erroneous impressions about where all of us stand. Frankly, I'm curious to see what develops."

"Nothing is going to develop, Keith, and where we all stand won't change one iota, either," Devon declared emphatically. "You'll see, when we go to the plantation. Take Scotty with you to the factory, however. I want to visit Mrs. Chester."

"Alone?"

"I'm not a young maiden in need of a chaperone, dear. And since barbaric Bluecoats no longer prowl these streets, preying upon our tender females, I think I may safely go abroad in my hometown." Her last statement was made in jest, but Keith did not appreciate its humor. She had to kiss the frown from his face.

* * *

Devon had no difficulty locating or recognizing the Chester residence, which had only further deteriorated in her long absence. There were zigzag cracks in the red brick walls, slates missing from the roof, and slats from the rotting shutters. The shrubbery grew rankly, and weeds choked the flower and vegetable gardens, which Devon had helped to cultivate when she lived there. The place appeared vacant and abandoned. She hammered on the front door, noticing the peeling paint and rusting hinges. Peering into the dirty windows, she saw the same tattered lace curtains and torn shades hanging helter-skelter. She called Mrs. Chester's name several times, loudly enough for a neighbor to hear, and soon an elderly man in patched clothing came out on his porch and beckoned to her.

Devon strolled over to his fence. "Good morning, sir! I'm looking for Mrs. Agnes Chester. Does she still live here?"

"Nobody lives there, ma'am."

"Did she move?"

"Died."

"Oh, I'm so sorry!" Devon clutched the gatepost, feeling a bit giddy. "When?"

"Last year. Don't rightly remember the date."

"Was she sick long?"

"Invalid," he said. "Fell, broke her hip. Never walked again. Neighbors looked after her."

Devon felt wretched. Mrs. Chester had never mentioned her health in her correspondence, and she had consistently refused financial aid from Devon, who assumed she was managing somehow. When she stopped writing, Devon assumed the old lady simply felt they had nothing more in common.

"Did Mrs. Chester receive a Confederate widow's pension?" she asked hopefully.

The old soldier snorted, scratching between his rangy legs. "Us veterans don't get no pension, much less widders and orphans. You must be from up North? Southerners know better."

Devon swallowed hard. Had she lost all of her Virginian accent and mannerisms? Or did her fine clothes fool him?

"How did Mrs. Chester live? Support herself?"

"Took in boarders while she was on her feet."

"Do you happen to know where she's buried?"

"Potter's field," he grunted. "Where else, for poor folks?" And, as if resenting the rich lady's curiosity, he turned and shuffled back into his home, which was only slightly less dilapidated than his late neighbor's.

Climbing back into the waiting hackney, Devon returned to the hotel. She was having tea in the parlor when Keith and their son joined her. Brimming with information about his jaunt to the tobacco factory, Scotty innocently announced, "You should have gone along, Mommy! We saw how cigars are wrapped and cigarettes rolled, and lots of interesting things! Mr. Haverston asked about you—he's a really nice gentleman. I can't wait to see his plantation! Won't it be fun? He's glad we like to ride, because he has many fine horses. His daughter is just a year younger than I. Her name is Fawn, and he says she's as graceful as a little deer."

"Really?" That was all Devon could manage. "Take a pastry, Scotty, and go along to your own suite. Miss Vale is waiting for you."

"Yes, ma'am." Grabbing a fistful of cookies, he went obediently, obviously disappointed at his mother's reaction to his enthusiasm.

"Tea?" Devon offered Keith.

"I'd prefer something stronger."

"Didn't the tobacco tycoon offer you a drink?"

"Bourbon is not my favorite whisky. I hope he keeps some Scotch at his estate. We'll sail downriver tomorrow, with a map he provided for Captain Bowers to locate his landing. Did you find Mrs. Chester?"

Her mouth trembled. "She passed away."

"I'm terribly sorry, darling. I know you were fond of her. But you mustn't feel too badly. Wasn't she quite old?"

She nodded. "Past eighty. I just regret not visiting at least once after leaving Richmond."

"Remorse is pointless now, Devon."

"But I can't help it, Keith." She stirred her tea pensively. "Someone should mourn Agnes Chester, and I was the closest person to her, after she lost her family. She didn't die of old age; it was an accident from which she never recovered. And she's buried in potter's field, like poor little Malley O'Neill. Dear Lord! What an indignity to a dignified lady!"

"It's not your fault," Keith sought to console her. "And you can't feel guilty, Devon, as you did about the suicide of your young friend, Miss O'Neill, because you weren't around when *she* needed you. None of us can assume the responsibilities, or alleviate the misfortunes, of everyone we've ever known, however briefly."

"I'll be all right, later." She gazed into her cup, as if reading the tea leaves. "Scotty seemed to enjoy his experience today."

"Yes," Keith said, eager to change the subject. "It was his first visit to any kind of factory. He found busy industry decidedly more interesting than staid banking. Green-visored gnomes with black sleeve protectors, pondering heavy ledgers, are not very exciting to a youngster. And vaults of silent money can't compete with noisy machinery."

"I suppose not," Devon concurred, "and he can't witness the bedlam of the Stock Exchange until he's older. Maybe he'll come of age before the next panic hits Wall Street."

"That's hardly a pleasant prospect, my dear, and certainly not one to anticipate."

"Of course not! But inevitable, isn't it, in the crazy world of finance? Will the weaker Southern banks be the first casualties?"

"Are you concerned about any particular one?"

"Well, it's rather awesome knowing that my husband is the nation's exchequer!"

"You're confusing me with the United States Treasury," he said somewhat testily.

"Of which you could be secretary! How many times have you actually declined that cabinetcy?"

"What does it matter? Rest easily, Mrs. Curtis. Your Croesus won't ever let the Bank of Richmond fail," he promised, smiling at her affected shrug of indifference. "Nor am I much beguiled by this persiflage, which is simply a disguise for your real curiosity."

"Oh? What am I curious about, my clairvoyant mate?"

He grinned, amused by her continued pretense. "I saw your expression when Scotty spoke of Haverston's daughter. You're anxious to know if he's married."

"Well, is he?"

"Presumably so, though he didn't mention a wife."

"He's married, or was," Devon insisted. "Daniel Haverston would never father a child out of wedlock."

His face blanched under his tan, and his mouth twisted grimly. "Unlike Keith Curtis, who sires bastards without any qualms?"

She bit her tongue, appalled by her thoughtless remark and his cynical dismay. "Oh, Keith—forgive me, please. I'm not myself."

"That's obvious, Devon, and has been since you set foot again on your native soil. The question puzzling me now is, *Who are you?* We were strangers in bed last night, speaking inanities, trivia, not touching each other intimately. I wanted to make love, but—"

"You made no advances."

"I hoped for some from you," he muttered, frowning. "As you know, I don't often indulge in legal rape. I believe in marital privileges, not *rights*. But you were distant, even cold, for the first time in our long relationship. How could I proceed against that mood?"

"Darling, you're imagining things! We should never have made this trip."

"On the contrary, my dear. It may have been imperative, and too long delayed. It'll probably teach us a lot about each other . . . and ourselves."

"Do you want to go to bed now, Keith?"

"That's not very subtle, Devon, and I don't think either of us would enjoy it much. Besides, we have to dress for Mr. and Mrs. Clinton's reception this evening. In case you have forgotten, Harold Clinton is chairman of the board of our local branch," he explained at her blank look. "Wear the Heathstone emeralds."

"Would you like to choose my gown?"

"Don't be snide! You know I have the utmost confidence in your taste. I just happen to like the way the emeralds complement your eyes, and they're noble jewels."

"Fit for the wife of a man of noble ancestry?"

"Fit for the daughter of Hodge Marshall, who seems to have misplaced her own identity in the noble Commonwealth of Virginia."

The cup trembled on its saucer as the gist of the argument struck her, and Devon set them down on the low, marble-

topped table before the sofa. How could she apologize enough
for her lack of perception? "What a dense dolt I am, Keith!
And you're so marvelously patient and understanding of my
insensitivity! You should turn me over your knee and spank
me like a spoiled brat."

He surveyed his open hand, smiling. "That thought has
occurred to me, my pet, and more than once recently."

At dusk a chill wind swept up the James River from the
sea, perfect for the white ermine cape Devon wore over her
magnificent Paris gown of silver brocade intricately draped with
diamond-dusted tiffany. And Keith was right about the Heathstone jewels: the fabulous emerald parure and tiara transformed
elegance into splendor.

Feminine whispers behind fans and discreet elbow-nudging
were rampant in the fine old antebellum mansion on Linden
Row as the liveried Negro butler announced, "Mistah and Miz
Keith Heathstone Curtis, of Noo Yawk City!" to the expectant
assembly of Richmond's Old Guard.

The epitome of Southern beauty and grace, like a vision
from the glorious past, Devon was admired by the appreciative
gentlemen and envied by the less fortunate ladies. Cognizant
of this conclave of Old Dominion ancestor-worshipers, and
nobody's fool anywhere in the South, Keith proudly escorted
his native Virginian wife. And even those guests who did not
remember that her father had published the *Richmond Sentinel,*
or that the Marshall clan had been in the genteel profession of
publishing for a century before that, one of them witnessing
the British surrender at Yorktown, and another the Redcoats'
burning of Washington in 1814, pretended to be familiar with
her family history.

To his own credit, Keith had never been more princely in
appearance, more courtly in manner. A coterie of belles, not
all young and single, gravitated toward the tall, dark, suave
Yankee who had no peers in wealth or gallantry. Certainly
none was better bred or educated, more sophisticated, nor more
accomplished in the art of ballroom dancing and flattery of the
fair sex. Several ladies flirted outrageously with him, arousing
Devon's jealousy, for she was as proud and possessive of him
as he was of her.

"So," she chided petulantly as they waltzed to a medley of

Strauss, "the picaresque Yankee has captured a few feminine hearts this evening."

He grinned, whirling her gracefully about the candle-lit room. "And I suppose Milady is not aware of her numerous male conquests? As many, or more, as she conquered at the Belmonts' soiree! Not that I blame them, even the old codgers leering and lusting like young gallants. You're incredibly lovely and irresistibly charming tonight, Devon. A glorious goddess, no less!"

She smiled at the extravagant chivalry, wondering what sort of compliments he paid the simpering, fawning coquettes. "How much champagne have you had, dear?"

"Sufficient, love. And you?"

"My quota, I think. I want to be alert when we return to the Richmond House. . . ."

Her wink both teased and promised, and Keith held her closer, whispering in her ear, "Put a fresh strawberry in your next glass—I like the taste on your lips. It does wonders for a kiss."

"So you taught me, our first night in Washington," Devon reminisced. "Oh, Keith, I'm so glad we found each other! And so happy tonight!"

"Remember that tomorrow," he advised, his tone suddenly sobering, "when we visit a certain plantation."

Although he was conspicuous by his absence, neither of them referred to Daniel Haverston by name, assuming he had his reasons, for surely he had been invited to this lavish affair honoring the New Yorkers. Before the reception was over, and the Clinton carriage was again at their disposal, the Curtises received more invitations than they could possibly accept without extending their journey indefinitely. And Devon's earlier apprehension vanished in triumph.

Stimulated by the success and excitement of the evening, they rushed into each other's arms the moment they were alone, even before Devon discarded her regal fur and Keith the dashing opera cloak he had affected. Now he was pushing the gown off her shoulders, to caress her breasts, and the exquisite jewelry was only an impediment to the impatient fingers searching for the clasp.

"Darling, be careful, you'll break it," Devon cautioned,

slipping off the earrings and fumbling with the bracelet, having already removed Lady Heathstone's splendid coronet from her head.

"Then we'll get it fixed," he muttered, finally succeeding and tossing the necklace aside like a mere bauble. "God, how I want you! Every man there envied me, Devon, and longed to be in my bed tonight. Don't let me ravish you. . . ."

She giggled at such an absurdity, for she was as eagerly amorous as he. Strewing their elegant garments from parlor to boudoir, both were naked when they reached the bed. They luxuriated and indulged over an hour in rapturous love and shameless lust, Devon straddling him at times, stroking his chest and belly and groin to inflame him anew. When finally he declared himself spent, she swished some brandy in her mouth and went down on him, providing pleasure so intense and unique he moaned and shuddered and clasped her with effusive appreciation.

"I love you," he whispered huskily, pulling her body upward and full-length onto his, tasting his seed on her lips. "But I don't think I fully realized how much you love me until now. I could never ask you to do that, although I know you like it when I oblige you, and I always hoped . . ."

"I know, darling. Did the liquor burn?"

"Like fire—good, hot, marvelous fire! You're the most wonderful wife and lover a man could ever have, Devon. You have everything, and more. And there's nothing I wouldn't do to keep you . . . including murder. . . ."

❧ 14 ❦

THE TRANSFORMATION Keith had observed in Devon upon their arrival in Virginia became even more apparent as the yacht cruised down the broad yellowish-gray stream that flowed be-

tween the junglelike banks of native flora. Widely spaced docks
marked the water entrances to private property, although few
of the old plantation manors were actually visible from the river
on which they had thrived for generations, from Colonial set-
tlement to the Civil War.

Captain Bowers had little difficulty locating the Harmony
Hill landing even without the Port of Richmond navigation
charts. He had piloted a Union gunboat on Chesapeake Bay
and Hampton Roads, participating in attacks on Confederate
fortifications and camps in the Tidewater region, and assisting
in the blockade of the Virginia coast.

Apprehensive about meeting her first suitor again, Devon
changed costumes twice en route, and Keith pretended not to
notice her nervous indecision about her appearance. At last,
coming on deck as the *Sprite*'s distinctive whistle signaled the
final approach, she was charmingly Southern in a jonquil-yellow
muslin gown, with a heart-shaped neckline, short puffed sleeves,
and a triple-flounced skirt piped in black velvet ribbon. A black
velvet bow adorned her hair, yellow silk gloves graced her
hands, and she swirled open a matching ruffled parasol. Her
marital rings and a gold locket nestling in the vale of her ivory-
textured breasts were her only jewelry. She looked ten years
younger than her age, and Keith was visibly proud and impressed. He and Scotty sported their traditional sailing garb:
white trousers topped with dark-blue, brass-buttoned jackets
and black-billed white seacaps cocked at jaunty angles.

Evidently, sentries had been posted at Harmony Hill, which
crowned a promontory partially secluded by giant and ancient
trees, to observe the vessel's arrival, for a welcoming party
headed by the master of the house waited on the scrubbed
landing to greet them. A new warehouse and wharf had been
built in the last five years, and several Haverston boats and
barges were moored nearby.

Daniel, in a frock-coated suit of tobacco-brown broadcloth,
swept off his high-crowned hat and bowed from the waist as
Devon debarked. And though he shook hands with Keith and
Captain Bowers, and acknowledged Heather Vale and the boy,
his blue eyes lingered intently on his lost love, and his full-
lipped mouth smiled sentimentally. Although some gray showed
in his sandy hair, the minié-ball limp in his left leg had dis-

appeared through surgery, and he had long since regained his outdoor ruddiness. Except for the few sun-squint lines in his face, Daniel Haverston very much resembled the same dashing young captain of the elite Tidewater Guard who had galloped away to join the Virginia cavalry that long-ago April day when the momentous news had come from Fort Sumter, South Carolina.

"Welcome to Harmony Hill," he said softly, taking Devon's hand and caressing it as much as possible through the silken glove.

"Thank you," she murmured, conscious of her husband's gaze and cynical smile. "We were sorry to have missed you at the Clintons' delightful reception last evening."

"I was preparing for your visit here," he explained, and then addressed her son. "Well, young man—I trust you are ready for an enjoyable holiday?"

"Yes, sir!" Scotty replied, glancing at the Negroes standing at a distance, and wondering why Mr. Haverston's daughter wasn't present.

A small caravan of vehicles conveyed them along a lane flanked by cedars, locusts, and tulip trees in gorgeous bloom. Devon and Keith rode with their host, vis-à-vis, in a fine maroon-gilt landau recently purchased from Richmond's new carriage factory. A freshly painted gray buggy accommodated the governess and her charge, followed by a bright red-and-yellow wagon carting the trunks, valises, hatboxes. Devon was greatly surprised, for nothing much seemed to have changed at Harmony Hill, after all. How had Dan managed to recoup his fortunes so effectively? Surely not entirely on mortgaged land and borrowed capital? Of course, it had been fifteen years since the war, and other industrious Southerners had survived and even prospered, many regaining their family estates and social status. The survival of the fittest, presumably—the cream of the Southern caste system rising again to the top! And the Haverstons had never been satisfied with any other position. . . .

The manor, almost totally restored to its original grandeur, was an arresting sight even to eyes accustomed to splendid residences. Occupied by a succession of Union generals during the many campaigns to take Richmond, Harmony Hill was spared the torch and serious depredations inflicted on some of its neighbors. Grant's order at Appomattox forbidding further destruction of Confederate property saved other plantations from vengeful destruction, and the troops, animals, and equipment soon departed the premises. Landscaping eventually restored the lovely gardens, which in the Tidewater were rivaled only by those of the Carolina Low Country near Charleston, and their beauty was enchanting in spring.

"Oh, Daniel!" Devon cried, trying to view everything at once. "Harmony Hill is beautiful, just like before! However did you manage?"

"It's a long story," he replied, "which I hope you'll stay long enough to hear."

"I hope so, too!" said Scotty. "Gee, this is a swell place, Mommy? Isn't it, Daddy?"

"Very nice," Keith agreed, "what we've seen of it so far."

"Well, I want to see it all!"

Vast, verdant fields of tobacco waved in the warm spring sun. But there were also acres and acres of thriving wheat and other grains, revealing that Harmony Hill was not a single-crop plantation. The rows of neatly whitewashed slave cabins, preferred to leaky tents by the bivouacking Federals and thus not maliciously destroyed, now housed sharecroppers and free Negro laborers, including some former Haverston slaves and their descendants. Women and children worked alongside the men in the fields and cultivated their personal vegetable patches in addition to other chores. Numbers of colored youngsters scampered in play over the rambling emerald-green lawns tended by their elders.

The mansion was built in wings, the garnet brick walls latticed with English ivy and symmetrically balanced by six tall graceful chimneys. There were numerous leaded and stained-glass windows and elaborately carved oak doors with bronze fixtures. Ornate friezes, frescoes, and fine wood paneling decorated the interior of the thirty castlelike rooms. Miss Vale was sedately impressed, and the boy was awed by the suits of dully gleaming armor, ancient fencing masks and swords, lances, halberds, maces, and other knightly paraphernalia in the enormous central hall. Greedy thieves and scavengers, seeking gold and silver and jewels and other easily concealable loot, had overlooked these cumbersome antiquities. Nor had they recognized the value of the heirloom furniture, master paintings, marble and jade and ivory sculptures, the rare books and manuscripts. Illiterate farmboys, villagers, city slum dwellers had no use for such things, no conception of their worth—and the proprietor of Harmony Hill was eternally grateful for their ignorance.

"Will your captain be joining us for supper this evening?" Daniel asked Keith, who was trying to keep watch on his wandering son. Scotty seemed utterly fascinated by his surroundings.

"Was he invited?" Keith inquired, a little vexed by the belated courtesy.

"It's understood, Curtis. Your darky valet, too. We have quarters for our guests' servants, and they are served in the kitchen. Custom, you know."

Keith nodded. That same custom prevailed in the North, regardless of a domestic's color. And though Rufus was free to dine with the Curtises and Captain Bower on the yacht if he wished, he seemed to prefer the formal master-servant relationship.

"Daddy, Daddy!"

A delightful child bounded down the main stairway, wearing a frilly blue pinafore and bows in her coppery hair. Fresh from her nap, her skin glowed pinkly and her chestnut eyes were wide and shining in her delicately featured face. She had a pretty mouth and a saucily tilted nose, and she appeared to bounce and bubble with radiant health.

"This is my daughter, Fawn," Dan proudly introduced her. "These are our guests, darling: Mr. and Mrs. Keith Curtis, of New York. And their son, Master Scott."

"She's adorable," Devon complimented, and Keith agreed.

Her manners, imposed *de rigueur*, were impeccable. She smiled, bobbed a curtsy, spoke the proper amenities. But her eyes, like sherry sparkling through crystal, concentrated on the stalwart young lad in his yachting attire. Fawn thought he resembled his handsome father far more than his beautiful mother, who was the prettiest lady she had ever seen. Her own mother, whom she barely remembered, was not nearly as lovely. . . .

Devon was still intensely curious about Daniel's wife, but apparently she would have to wait on his discretion for any information. If he had a portrait of her, it was not prominent among the familiar and recognizable Haverston ancestors in the foyer gallery.

Negro servants escorted them to the guest chambers in the north wing. Mr. and Mrs. Curtis were assigned an especially fine suite of rooms, with an inspiring view of the manicured gardens sloping down to the riverbank. Masses of brilliant flowers, with tulips and Virginia's beloved jonquil predominating, bordered the meticulously restored walks, fountains, reflecting pools, statuary. There were mimosas in gorgeous bloom, and the intoxicating fragrance of jasmine and magnolias. English boxwoods, without which no formal Southern garden would be complete, were shirred into perfect geometrical designs, and included an intricate maze for romantics to explore. Devon was sweet sixteen when Daniel had first kissed and proposed to her in that clever, secluded labyrinth.

Standing at the windows, gazing out wistfully, she felt Keith's arm circle her slender waist. "I must say, this isn't quite what I expected, Devon."

"Nor I," she admitted.

"A great deal of time and money have been invested in restoring this place," he said, mentally calculating the expenditures. "And damned if Haverston doesn't act the part of the antebellum plantation master! Looks it, too. He may not own the Negroes, but they don't seem completely aware of it. His people must have been kings in this country."

"More or less," Devon said, recalling the family's long reign in Tidewater society, which was different from that of any other section of the state.

"Well, too bad he didn't get the queen he wanted for his kingdom!" Keith said, privately rejoicing.

"That sounds smug," she admonished him.

"It is," he conceded. "I wonder what sort of woman he actually did marry, in order to get an heir, and what happened to her."

"A fever, probably. She bore a lovely child, though."

"But not the son he undoubtedly wanted! That must have been a blow to his masculinity. Men like Haverston just naturally expect male offsprings and only token females. How can he not envy our handsome specimen?"

"Oh, stop gloating! He's obviously well pleased with his

darling daughter, and very proud of her, too."

"Ah, but I beat him there, too! Wait till he learns we have *twin* girls!" Keith chuckled, like a naughty youth having bested a rival. "I'll allow you the privilege of informing him, Mrs. Curtis."

Despite his jovial banter, Devon detected an anxious edge in his voice. "Do you feel uncomfortable in his home, Keith?"

"Yes," he admitted, after some hesitation. "Because I know my presence here is only because of you. His desire was to invite you alone, but that was impossible, so he had to settle for my company too, however displeasing to him. Furthermore, I have a nagging suspicion that he is going to attempt to revive any dormant feelings you may still have for him."

Devon stared at him, her coral mouth forming a surprised O. "Then he won't succeed, for none exist, latent or otherwise."

"Your positive attitude pleases me, my dear. But I still recall his remarks upon leaving Halcyon the day of our brawl, mounted on his rented steed like a knight even in his torn and bloodied clothes. I told him to find another lady to fight over, because you were mine, and he sneered, 'Don't be so sure, Curtis! She's still a Virginian, remember!' That stuck in my craw, Devon, and has given me more than one case of indigestion."

She abandoned the leaded glass oriel window and its serene and enchanting view. "Now I know we shouldn't have come! Promise me, Keith, there won't be any trouble between you and Daniel?"

"Not unless he starts it, Devon. Which I don't think he will, being a 'Southern gentleman,' and we his invited guests."

"Oh, my God, Keith! You can't believe that Daniel Haverston is still in love with me, after all these years and all that's happened?"

"I'm afraid so," he nodded. "And why not? Didn't I continue to love you in spite of hell and high water? Even after you married that Texas cowboy politician and son of a senator, who tried to crucify me on a monopolistic cross! Why should the Virginian give up, or surrender any more graciously than any other of his breed? He's no less tenacious than this Yankee, and just as goddamned determined to have you for his own, one way or another, and better late than never!"

"Darling, you talk as if I were still a young belle, with two jealous swains vying for my affections!"

"No doubt that's precisely how he still sees you, Devon. And you're certainly just as beautiful and desirable, if not more so, than you were then. Any potent man would admire and covet you, however discreetly he might handle himself. Haverston lost your affections before—maybe he thinks he can win them back again."

"And you imagine that's possible, after last night?"

"No, I'm just convinced he'll try."

"How, for heaven's sake?"

"Who knows, with a desperate cavalier! He'll think of something, Devon. And if he knew the true extent of his loss, how much he has really missed, he would surely want to kill me—and even be justified in doing so."

❧ 15 ❧

DEVON APPEARED for breakfast dressed to accept their host's invitation to ride afterward. Keith had politely declined, on the pretext of something important to do on the yacht, which Devon suspected was merely an excuse to escape the plantation for a while. He had hoped to take his son with him, but Scotty wanted to ride with Daniel's daughter.

Despite her tender age, Fawn could handle her small mount, a snow-white Peruvian mare with a gorgeous mane and tail and prancing strut, quite well, and she looked like a little princess in her pretty blue habit and plumed hat.

"Fawn has the makings of an excellent equestrienne," Devon observed as she and Daniel cantered across a riotously blooming meadow, their progeny some yards away.

"Virginia planters' daughters are traditionally accomplished horsewomen," he reminded, quoting almost verbatim from a manual Devon had studied at Rosewood Female Academy, where he evidently intended to enroll his daughter. "We started her lessons at age two, sidesaddle, and she never had any fear of her Shetland pony, nor larger mounts to which she graduated before six. She'll begin training on jumpers and hunters soon. I want her to ride to hounds in the next season's hunt. Your son is a fine rider, too. Takes after his mother in that respect, no doubt."

"Oh, his father is quite a horseman, too!" Devon defended her absent spouse.

"Then why didn't he come with us this morning?"

"Some business on the *Sprite*."

"That's a grand steamer," he complimented grudgingly. "Seaworthy, I trust?"

"Absolutely. We plan to sail her abroad, when our daughters are older."

"Daughters?"

"We have twin girls, Daniel. Sharon and Shannon, not quite a year old. They're adorable."

His eyes glanced away, focusing on the horizon. Negroes were laboring in the tobacco fields, which required almost constant attention to produce the high grade of bright leaf and burley to justify the increasingly famous Harmony Hill trademark on his tobacco products. Other hands toiled on the many acres devoted the ancillary crops, especially the vital grains, necessary to sustain any large plantation community. Women and adolescent children worked in the vegetable gardens and fruit orchards, the latter a veritable paradise when the apple, plum, peach, and cherry trees were in bloom. Fat cattle grazed in the green pastures, and sleek, blooded horses exercised in the log-fenced paddocks. Devon had seen the renovated stables, the kennels of hounds descended from the best English breeds, and thought that Keith's earlier observations were accurate. Daniel Haverston was again the country squire living in ease and luxury. He plainly preferred to ignore the devastating interlude in his orderly existence; to forget the inconvenient interruption and pretend as best he could that it had never happened.

"Congratulations," he offered, after a few moments of brooding meditation. "So you have three children now? Do you plan to have more?"

"If we receive the additional blessings."

"Gifts from heaven?" Cynicism played across his features.

twisting his jaw muscles. "Ah, Devon! We don't find babes in the bulrushes, despite the biblical story about Moses."

It was an opportunity to pose the question that puzzled her, and she took it. "When did you marry, Dan? I used to correspond with Mrs. Chester—and learned only yesterday of her passing—but she never mentioned anything about you in her letters."

"That was at my request," he apprised, "after my impromptu trip to New York."

The gossamer veil of her postilion, which protected her delicate complexion, also disguised her embarrassed blush. "Did you tell her the truth about me?"

"Of course not! I could hardly believe it myself, Devon. It was so unlike you, so contrary to your rearing. I wanted to kill Curtis, though I'd hang for it in that state. My life seemed over anyway, and I cared little about myself. But I never blamed you, only him. The scoundrel dazzled you with his gold and promises, no doubt, and whisked you away in that splendid transportation like a ruthless Arabian sheik to join his harem. It was white slavery!"

Devon protested his version vehemently. "No, Daniel! You're grossly mistaken in that assumption. *I* boarded his 'magic carpet' on false pretenses and actually *begged* him to take me to Bagdad-on-the-Hudson. All I wanted then was a career in journalism, to make my own way, and be free and independent. But I fell desperately in love with him—and things developed quite differently."

"It was still illegal," he insisted bitterly. "Did his wealth and political power and influence elevate him above the law in New York?"

"I resent your implication," Devon reproached him indignantly. "Keith Curtis never enslaved me sexually or any other way, Daniel. We couldn't marry because he had an ill wife and other obligations." She paused, refusing further details. "Incidentally, what about *your* marriage? You didn't answer my question."

"Caroline is dead," he replied somberly. "A miscarriage in her fifth month, four years ago. Profuse hemorrhage. The physician couldn't save her."

"I'm so sorry, Daniel. Was she a Virginian?"

"No, a Marylander, born on her family's plantation on the

Potomac. They weren't ruined in the war because, as you know, that state remained neutral. In addition to tobacco, the Caldwell Plantation raises some of the finest hunters in the country. I met Caroline when I went there to purchase a pair for breeding. We were married three months later, in her home."

"I'm sure she was a fine lady. And beautiful."

"A great lady," he affirmed, "but not beautiful. Not like you! Maturity has only enhanced your beauty, Devon. You're even lovelier than in girlhood, if that's possible."

Devon's thank-you was barely audible, for she did not wish to encourage such personal conversation. And her mind still dwelled on his marriage, wondering what exactly had inspired it, since it did not appear to be true love. Was it expedience, necessity—a *mariage de convenánce* in the Continental custom? And if so, did he consider such a marital alliance more honorable than her premarital relationship with Keith Curtis?

"You must miss your wife dreadfully, and the child her mother."

"Fawn was too young to remember much about her," he said, again thwarting Devon's curiosity. "Her maternal grandparents have been most generous to her, however, and she will inherit Caroline's share of their estate. There's another Caldwell heir, Merilee, a spinster." After some tense reflection, he volunteered, "In case you're wondering, I wasn't Caroline's first choice as a spouse. She was betrothed to another man, a neighboring planter, who perished in a shipwreck on Chesapeake Bay. She mourned him for many years, probably until her death."

Her suspicions were correct, then, and Devon pitied him. Twice cheated out of genuine love! And except for his child, his only compensation was in the restoration of Harmony Hill, presumably aided by Caroline's generous dowry. How empty and even futile his life must often seem under these circumstances! She felt truly sorry for him.

They trotted their horses slowly toward the forest, without which no tobacco plantation could profitably exist, for the lumber was necessary to build the hogsheads to roll the cured weed downhill to the rivers for shipment. Loggers had to cut various lanes through the timber, removing the stumps to create bridal paths, and the hoofs crunched on generations of fallen leaves and mulch.

Daniel glanced furtively at his companion, so gracefully seated on the imported British sidesaddle. No lady in his acquaintance possessed such beauty, grace, charm, intelligence. Her body was still lithe and slender, only her bosom enticingly fuller beneath the tight basque of her pearl-gray faille habit, and she had the most compelling eyes and adorable profile in all womankind. His arms ached to hold her again, his mouth to devour hers, and his hands tightened on his reins. How could she not be aware of the tension in his loins, the desire surging through his veins, the emotional thunder in his heart?

Devon *was* aware and growing uneasy. They should not be riding alone together this far out, and especially not into the secluded woods. Prodigal wildflowers—blue lobelia, bluets, lupine, violets—edged the sun-dappled trails. Dogwood frothed prolifically among the dark green pines, and purple wisteria climbed into the hardwood trees. Wild berry bushes and vines were scattered throughout, and Devon wondered if the planters still threw parties to hunt and pick the fruit for jams and preserves.

Unwittingly, Daniel intruded on her reverie. "All those lost years, Devon! Where did they go for us? How did we lose them?"

"I think we both know, Dan."

He nodded, sighing. "I followed your career with the New York *Record,* Devon, including your coverage of the White House when the Grants occupied it. You were at the top of the ladies in the profession, when suddenly you married that Texan, Reed Carter. How could you do that, if you were so hopelessly in love with Keith Curtis?"

"Because I thought I *was* hopeless, then. There's no point in discussing it now, Dan."

"I guess not," he agreed. "Have you returned to journalism?"

"Not on a regular basis. Actually, I'm contemplating an antebellum novel, set in Virginia."

"Marvelous! You must come to Harmony Hill for your research. . . . I can help you. My library is still largely intact, thanks to the illiterate Yankees' uninterest in books, and my personal experiences and memories are indelible. I trust it'll be a serious literary effort, Devon, not a frivolous romance like some of our Southern ladies are scribbling?"

"The story is still in gestation," she said. "I'm not sure what my muses will deliver, if anything."

"How does Curtis feel about it?"

"He approves, because I can work at home."

"That place in the country?"

"We have a town house, too. And we're building a summer cottage in Newport, which is what they call even the most elaborate residences there. I'm afraid ours will be something of a palace."

"Which America's richest man can easily afford," he said grimly. "Richmond ladies will be buzzing for weeks, I'll bet, about the gown and jewels you wore to the Clintons' reception, which were detailed in this morning's papers. Daniel Haverston isn't even the richest man in Virginia anymore. No competition for the King of Wall Street!"

"It's not his money I love," she admonished him. "Can't you understand that?"

"And would it be the same for him if you were fat and ugly and barren? Do you honestly believe he would have taken you from Richmond, had you been some homely little waif in rags?"

"I *was* in rags," she reminded, "or almost."

"But not homely! Prettier in cast-off garments than most girls in their finest raiment. Don't delude yourself, Devon. Male lust got you on his train and into his bed! You sacrificed your virtue for that trip to New York, didn't you?" That seemed to enrage him more than any other propriety Keith Curtis had breached, for Southerners dueled as readily over a lady's honor as their own.

Manifest truth negated a reply. "Shouldn't we see about the children?"

"They're all right, and having fun. Getting along famously, too. That's a fine boy you have, Devon," he complimented, adding ruefully, "I wish he were my son, and he might have been, except—"

"No, Daniel," she interrupted with finality. "Shall we return to the manor?"

"Later, my dear. We haven't ridden together in years— don't deprive me of the pleasure now. I want to show you what I've done to our favorite brook."

He used "our" as if there were still some intimate unity between them, and Devon lacked the heart either to correct him or summarily abandon him. As the path narrowed, the flanks of their animals almost touched, and his roan stallion nuzzled his nose in the golden mane of her mare, until Devon decided to drop behind.

At the brook, Daniel dismounted and assisted her, his hands lingering on her waist until she disengaged them. Then they strolled to the rustic cedar bridge he had erected near the great oak in which he had long ago carved their initials in the symbolic heart pierced by cupid's arrow. Finally, he spoke, softly and tenderly: "I built the bridge myself, from scratch, and dedicated it to you."

Devon was touched but wary. Perhaps if she made light of the situation . . . ? "How sentimental, Dan! But you always were a sentimentalist, weren't you? About Harmony Hill, Virginia, horses . . . and me."

"Not in that order, Devon. And don't belittle my sentiment, or treat me like a schoolboy smitten with first love. My feeling for you was never a shallow, passing fancy. It helped to keep me alive and caring to live during the war, on the battlefield and in that damnable Union prison camp." He stepped toward her. "Do you feel anything at all, being here with me now?"

"Nostalgia, Dan, for the days that were, and can never be again! Surely you realize that? You must!" Her voice rose slightly, impatient with his continuing self-delusion and obstinate refusal to accept reality. Could she find her way out of these woods without his assistance? The sun had moved overhead, it was high noon, but the dense growth allowed only random shafts and beams of light to penetrate the obscure paths.

"Don't look so frightened, my dear. And don't confuse me with your Yankee rapist. I have no intention of forcing myself on you. I wouldn't touch a hair of your lovely head against your will."

"I know that, Daniel," she said, regaining her poise. "You always were the perfect gentleman."

A rueful smile touched his mouth. "Still am, darling. Does that also make you the perfect fool? How many Yankees would not press their advantage in a situation like this!"

So his geniality toward her husband was feigned, only pretense, and would never be more. He still harbored his grudge and resentment, his consuming hatred for the man he believed had stolen her heart from him. And she must never wander off this way with him again.

"I'm rather tired, Daniel," she dissembled, "and would like to return to the house."

His eyes focused on her lips. "May I kiss you once, for old times' sake?"

"That wouldn't be wise, Daniel."

"Perhaps not," he conceded, assisting her back onto her saddle and remounting his own. Then he grinned sheepishly, "But I can't promise not to try again, Miss Marshall."

"Mrs. Curtis," she corrected, with no visible effect on him. Lifting her reins, she clucked to Goldie, whose color blended with her own and was called palomino in Texas.

"Do you like that horse?" he asked.

"She's beautiful."

"Take her, with my compliments."

"Thank you, Dan, but we have our own stables. All fine thoroughbreds, though fewer than you have."

"Perhaps the boy would like to make a selection?"

Bribery through her son? "Not without his father's consent."

"Which means no," he said, digressing. "I haven't told you about the entertainments I'm planning in your honor. A barbecue, of course. A ball, naturally. And though the season is over, a fox hunt can always be arranged. . . ."

"Sounds delightful! But I'm not sure how long we can stay at Harmony Hill," she hedged.

"Don't tell me the Curtises must keep schedules," he chided. "You can stay as long as you please, milady. Or should I say, as long as His Manhattan Majesty decrees?"

Devon did not answer, but her eloquent eyes conveyed her knowledge of his game. He was testing her deference, her *subservience,* to her spouse. Well, let him wonder, hang on tenterhooks! She had to cogitate on her strategy henceforth with both men.

As they emerged from the forest, Keith galloped across an oat field toward them. He was casually dressed in tan twill breeches, brown cordovan boots, and a raw linen shirt opened at the throat on a V of thick dark chest hair. And though this was his usual attire at Halcyon, and admired by Devon, Daniel decided the Yankee was simply flaunting his flagrant masculinity. Undeniably a handsome devil, though, and a demon rider. Small wonder the innocent young maiden had yielded to him on his terms!

"Yahoo!" he hailed them. "Am I too late for a jaunt over the estate?"

As their mounts met, Daniel said, "We were heading home, Curtis."

"I'm a bit weary," Devon explained. "But I'm sure Dan would be delighted to show you around, dear. Have you seen the youngsters?"

"They're playing in the garden, I think. Scotty is amused by the boxwood maze. Fawn hides from him, but not for long. He already has all the angles figured out." He grinned complacently at their host. "My son is very clever, a budding genius. Just ask his governess."

"My daughter is no dunce," Daniel muttered.

"Definitely not," Keith agreed. "Cute, too. I can't wait for my little girls to reach her age, and sit a horse as well."

"Pardon me, gentlemen," Devon said, directing Goldie toward the stables, where a Negro groom awaited her. "Enjoy yourselves!"

⚜ 16 ⚜

"WHAT'S YOUR acreage here?" Keith asked conversationally as they rode along a dirt road away from the direction in which Daniel had taken Devon.

"Ten thousand, more or less."

"The original King James's grant?"

"No, that was over fifty thousand. My forefathers parceled it among their sons, some of whom didn't know much about raising tobacco, how it depletes the soil and eventually exhausts it to utter barrenness, and either lost their land or let it revert to wilderness. Those who learned conservation through crop rotation, fertilization, and the wisdom of allowing fields to lie intermittently fallow, prospered beyond any other class of planters. Fortunately, Great-Grandfather Haverston was among the wise ones."

"How many slaves did your family own?"

"The number varied due to losses by death, sales, exchanges, and runaways, but never less than a hundred and generally around two hundred. Not that we needed that many, because about a third of them didn't work, but Father hated to separate families."

"How compassionate of him," Keith remarked in a mocking tone. Extracting a flat monogrammed gold case from a concealed clutch in his customized boots, he flipped the latch and offered, "Smoke?"

Daniel declined, reminding bluntly, "I manufacture my own cigars, Curtis."

"Can they compare to Cuba's?"

"Not yet, simply because our land and climate are too different to grow the same variety and quality of tobacco. But we're experimenting"—he pointed to a small patch of plants staked under gauze to protect them from the hot sun and insects—"and hope to produce some comparable leaves, eventually. My chewing plugs, snuff, and cigarettes have good sales, however, and my pipe blend compares favorably with that Turkish Latkia you prefer in your briar. Try some before you leave."

"I'll do that," Keith promised, with no intention of smoking it in any of his seasoned pipes. "And may I inquire if you keep any Scotch whisky in your private stock? The Tennessee and Kentucky bourbons you sip and mix in mint juleps are excellent brands, to be sure, but I've never acquired a taste for sour mash. I order directly from a Scotland distillery, by the case."

"Everything imported, eh? Liquor, tobacco, clothes, boots. I'm surprised you didn't import your wife."

"I did, in a way," Keith said, unable to suppress a grin. "From Virginia."

Daniel scowled, despising him more by the minute. "More like confiscation, wasn't it?"

Keith's glare elicited a reluctant apology. "Forgive me, sir. I guess I'm a bad loser, but not in all respects. How about some poker this evening?" He could never be friends with a damned Yankee, not in a century or millennium. But he would have to try, for Devon's sake, lest they depart prematurely, for he had no doubt that Curtis could be as implacable and vindictive as himself.

"Fine," Keith agreed. "Set your own limits on the stakes. Do you happen to play chess?"

"Not as well as you, I'm sure," he replied, his tone sarcastic. "How are you at tilting?"

"At windmills?" Keith gibed, insinuating that this was precisely what Haverston was doing.

"In a tournament! Our local cavaliers enjoy jousting, and attend the Carolina and Maryland meets. I could arrange an exhibition for your edification, and perhaps you would like to compete in it. Naturally, our lances are blunted, and we are in costume, not armor."

"Well"—Keith shrugged—"if such antiquated sport still amuses the natives, gather your contestants. I'll participate, though it's alien to me. Tilting is not our game in New York, nor anywhere in the North to my knowledge."

"No, I reckon baseball is the national sport of Yankees now, isn't it? Batting a cowhide ball and running around a dirt diamond! It's a game more suited to little boys on vacant lots." A contemptuous smile curled one side of his mouth. "Tilting is for men and can get rough, but you might enjoy the feat, sir."

Keith was not beguiled. This was merely another scheme to test his mettle, another attempt to somehow best his rival for Devon's benefit. A preposterous challenge, but he could not decline it without appearing inept or cowardly before his wife and son.

"At your service, sir," he accepted mockingly, as if the traditional gauntlet had been slapped across his face.

"It should be a fair match between us," his challenger drawled. "We are about equal in age, agility, and horsemanship. There's no actual combat involved—it's primarily a contest of skills. You run the lists and try to insert your lance through the ring suspended on the crossbar before the judges' pavilion. I'd advise you to study the manual and do some practicing, however, because you'll be pitted against some experts fresh from the spring pageants."

Nothing more was said about it, and after an hour more in the saddle, they returned to the manor. Scotty met them in the central hall, with its intriguing museum, told his father how much he was enjoying their sojourn at Harmony Hill, and plied their host with questions about the ancient armor and weaponry.

Keith reminded him that he had seen many of these same types of articles at Heathstone Manor, in England, without adding that the heraldry on most of the helmets and shields there was authentic. "Your male ancestors on the maternal side fought with such equipment, son—some of them in the Wars of the Roses. And there were many knights among them. Don't you remember Miss Vale and I telling you about it?"

"Not very well, Daddy. I was rather small then, and more interested in the towers and drawbridge over the old moat, and hearing about the ghosts in the castle..."

Daniel pounced on the boy's last interest. "You like ghost stories, Scotty? Well, Harmony Hill has three resident spooks— pirates, no less! They used to infest these coastal waters and attack the plantations. Lynnhaven Bay was one of Blackbeard's favorite hiding places, and he was the worst of the lot. Finally captured and killed, his skull was made into a cup and still remains somewhere in the Tidewater region. Three of his villains were hanged at Harmony Hill, buried in the cellar, and on Halloween their spirits roam down there, making weird noises and, we think, hunting for rum."

"Really?" His eyes were curiously wide, his excitement high. "Golly gee! The ghosts at Heathstone Manor are all ladies, who just float around in white draperies. The servants hear them wailing, but I never saw or heard anything. I wish I could be here on Halloween night! Could we?" he beseeched his parents. "Fawn had invited me to come back for another visit."

"We'll see," Keith told him, trusting that he would forget it by then or be otherwise diverted. "It's just nonsense anyway, Scott. Ghosts don't actually exist, despite the tales that persist, including President Lincoln's supposed apparitions in the White House." His eyes importuned Devon to help debunk the fantasy, but she remained silent, sipping from a tall, iced glass of lemonade sprigged with fresh peppermint.

Having grown up in the South, where almost every old house

and plantation harbored at least one "haint," as the Negroes called them, Devon would not dispute or deny the folklore. Besides, didn't she have her own occult experience with a certain obstinate, though invisible presence in Gramercy Park? Complete renovation of Esther's apartments had not exorcised her spirit enough to suit Devon, although its prevalence seemed to depend primarily on her own moods, and no one else in the brownstone mansion admitted to sensing anything unusual. Miss Vale's only complaint, after spending a week in the suite, was that she could not feel comfortable in so much luxury, which logically bespoke her Spartan nature. And when Carla Winston was an overnight guest during a mission for the Pinkerton Detective Agency, she claimed to have slept like a log in the luxurious chambers.

Fawn had heard so much about haunts, dints, and witches from white and black people alike that she accepted them as natural, fascinated but not fearful of their supposed reality. Indeed, she found it convenient to blame some of her own mischief on them, as when she broke something she had no business handling, or was otherwise naughty. When it was to her advantage, Fawn also pretended to still believe in Santa Claus, the Easter Bunny, and the Tooth Fairy. But it was also apparent to their elders that the youngsters had a childish attraction to each other, had fun together, and enjoyed investigating the nooks and crannies, the myths and mysteries of the great plantation.

"Daddy, did you know there's a secret tunnel from the basement to the river?" Scotty informed excitedly. "It was used since Colonial days to escape from all kinds of dangers! May I explore it with Fawn?"

"You may not!" Devon interjected. "There may be snakes in there, and cave-ins and water seepage." Her eyes implored Daniel. "They're too adventurous for their own good. Forbid them to venture into that passage."

"Don't worry, my dear," he soothed the anxious mother, as if he were both children's father, and infuriating Keith. "It's been boarded up at both ends for years, and Fawn has never been allowed to enter it."

Keith spoke sternly to his son. "Those are orders, Scott. Don't disobey them!" He wished Daniel would discipline his precocious daughter more firmly, but instead he was ordering the butler, Moses, to serve some twenty-year-old Scotch to Mr. Curtis, bourbon and branch for himself, and anything whatever that Mrs. Curtis might desire. Sated on tea and fruit ades, Devon decided on a cup of planter's punch.

Her choice pleased Daniel immensely, and he reminded her spouse, "You can take the lady out of Virginia, but you can't take Virginia out of the lady."

Keith only frowned at the familiarity, still troubled that his bold and curious boy might defy his orders concerning the tunnel. "Did you hear me, son?"

"Yes, sir." Disappointed and thwarted by the paternal edict, Scotty was clearly unhappy with his father. He had been trying to impress Fawn with his bravery and prowess, how well he could ride and daringly climb the tallest tree. Now she might think him timid and afraid—and worse even, sissified. Seeming to understand his boyish embarrassment, and to sympathize with him, Fawn took his hand and led him outside to play in the yard.

That evening, as they prepared to retire, Keith suggested that perhaps they had been at Harmony Hill long enough. Devon protested mildly. "But Dan has so many entertainments planned for us, dear. We can't just pack and leave so soon! He has a social reputation to uphold in the county."

"And you enjoy the fuss he's making over you and the boy, don't you? Hell, Scott seems to regard him as some kind of hero! All this muck about ghosts and pirates and underground escapes. . . ."

"Notorious buccaneers did menace the entire Southern coast, Keith. Blackbeard *was* killed in the Tidewater, and Stede Bonnet *was* hanged in Charleston. But you know all this, for it was lengthily recorded in the Barbary Pirate Wars!"

"Yes, and Captain Kidd buried treasure on Manhattan Island, which some fools are still seeking. So what? That was centuries ago! Haverston has created a glorious legend for his family. And I don't like him telling Scotty about his Civil War adventures, his wounding at Gettysburg, and suffering in the Yankee prison on Rock Island."

"But that's all true too, Keith! It's history, and Scotty is studying it now."

"Well, I doubt he'll learn much about General Grant, or Richmond's Libby Prison and Georgia's Andersonville from your heroic Virginian! Nor that the Curtis Bank helped to finance the Union's victory, and I consulted with President Lincoln and the Secretary of the Treasury on the emergency bond issues. Scott is too young to understand or appreciate my position in that conflict, and I don't want him confused by Haverston's goddamn self-veneration. As far as I'm concerned, he's just another son of a slaveholder and traitorous rebel!"

He regretted his last remark, seeing its cutting pain reflected in her misty eyes, even as she tried to appease him. "Darling, Scotty's just a child—a normal, healthy boy exercising his curiosity and venturesome spirit. He'll outgrow it, and realize what a terrible period of American history that actually was, and how the nation was saved. Surely you don't imagine any man alive could win his affections from his father?"

"I think Haverston is trying his damndest to do exactly that, Devon. To make me appear something less than valiant and manly in my son's eyes. The bastard expects me to compete with him in a jousting contest. Pure and noble Sir Galahad, still seeking his Holy Grail in the person of Devon Marshall!"

"Devon Curtis," she corrected. "And you're making too much of this, Keith. But just send Captain Bowers word, and we'll sail tomorrow."

He pondered it, scowling. "Sure—and how would *that* affect Scotty? His father refusing to participate in a flamboyant, medieval display of courage and chivalry! Oh, he's a clever son of a bitch, your Southern cavalier in his archaic realm! I wonder how many Haverston slaves tried to escape to freedom through that hidden tunnel, only to be fetched back with bloodhounds."

"Shall I send for a maid to help pack?"

"You don't seem to understand, Devon. The tilting tourney is merely a public extenuation of the cartel he sent me in New York. All in fun and fellowship, he says, lying in his teeth. He's determined to embarrass me before you and our son, publicly if possible. Presumably he's well skilled in this knightly sport, still practiced in Virginia, Maryland, and the Carolinas."

Devon was familiar with these pageants, performed in costume, and harmless enough, if the contestant was an accomplished rider able to remain simultaneously aloft and accurate with his lance. Serious injury was rare, usually the result of recklessness and impatience. And though tilting was primarily a game for cocky young gallants, older men could compete if they chose, and Devon dared not mention the age factor to Keith, since there was no essential difference between him and Daniel in that respect.

"I hope you didn't agree. It's foolish for grown men! Besides, what do you know about jousting, except what you've read in books?"

"Thanks for the vote of confidence," he muttered. "You figure he'll beat me?"

"He's not a novice, for heaven's sake! Probably attends most of the meets every year. But the opponents don't clash physically in battle, merely try to unhorse one another and hoot them into missing the ring. That's the object of the modern version."

"Fine! Go off riding with him tomorrow morning, to the woods or wherever you spent so damned much time together today, and I'll tutor myself. I know the principle, all I need is practice."

Devon sighed. "You're worse than Scotty," she admonished him. "While he's forbidden to engage in daring deeds, his father performs even riskier stunts!"

He grinned at her dismay, but grimness tightened his facial muscles. "I won't get hurt or killed, Mrs. Curtis, unless my steed throws and tramples me."

"That has happened, Keith. Fatal accidents can occur in any sport."

"Then you'll be a wealthy widow, my dear."

Such cynicism appalled and angered her. "Don't talk that way," she scolded, getting into bed. "This is a regional folly, Keith, and I certainly won't love you any less if you stay out of it."

"But I wouldn't like myself much," he apprised, taking his place beside her.

Keith lay with his arms folded beneath his head, solemnly contemplating the shadowy canopy of the romantic bedstead. As he seemed uninterested in making love, Devon initiated it. And though at first his response was mild, it developed with more and greater intensity when he realized that Daniel Haverston was alone in his bed and perhaps jealously concerned about their intimacies. He laughed aloud, and Devon shushed him, "We'll wake the house!" But he only laughed again, louder, enormously pleased by the thought of disturbing their host in this fashion.

Later, lying in gratified embrace, Keith whispered mischievously, "Maybe we won't use blunted spears, after all."

"Oh, yes, you will! They have a code, Keith, and you'll adhere to it. The winner presents the white plume of victory to his favorite lady, after which the losers can vent their frustrations by tilting with sabers at cotton or straw-filled leather heads mounted on limber poles."

"Good God! That's barbaric."

"It's just more of their horseback games, and better than slaying one another with dueling pistols and swords."

"Haverston may reissue that old challenge if I fail to eliminate myself in a fall or other accident."

"No, darling. You're his guest, and that would be most inhospitable."

"Hah! I wouldn't put it past him, Devon."

She trailed a sensitive finger over his chest, down and around his navel and groin. "Sleepy?"

This time his arousal was spontaneous and urgent, and he had his satisfaction in her arms. He was a lucky man, a winner regardless of the results of the tournament. And that poor, covetous fool eating his heart out was just that: a poor, covetous fool.

⭑ 17 ⭑

ALONG WITH other invitations to social events at Harmony Hill, messengers delivered notices of a combined barbecue and tilting tournament. Thus, Keith had less than a week to practice his prowess against men skilled in the sport for years. Notified by telegram, some Maryland and Carolina champions were already en route by rail and water.

Furious with Daniel for what she considered a very unfair advantage, Devon still could not dissuade Keith from participation. Sardonically amused by his determination, Daniel happily prepared for the flamboyant entertainment, which would culminate in an all-night ball interspersed with romantic hayrides, for the moon would be gloriously full on that date.

Horse racing being common fare at the larger plantations, most had good clay tracks bordered with a post-and-rail fence and pavilions for judges and spectators. The crossbar with suspended gilded rings only an inch and three-quarters in diameter, which the "knights" riding down the lists at full gallop must transfix with their lances, was especially erected for the jousts. Observing the construction of this gallowslike contraption called the Rigg, Devon feared that Keith could not possibly perfect his performance with so little time and experience, and under such severe pressure.

"Darling, please don't engage in this strenuous feat," she pleaded to no avail, and wished desperately that they had not come to Harmony Hill. She had no worries about his horsemanship, for he was an expert rider, but she could not bear to watch him practice hour after hour with lance and ring. Daniel had offered him his choice of mounts, and after several tryouts, Keith selected one of the finest in the stables, comparable to Haverston's in speed and endurance.

The lawns were cut and rolled, the boxwood hedges and labyrinth shirred to perfection, weeds and faded blossoms cleared from the gardens. Women and girls came from the sharecroppers' cabins to assist the staff servants in the manor. Dressed in calico hubbards and aprons, with tignons on their heads, they appeared as much in slavery as in prewar days. Devon remarked on this to Daniel, who shrugged and replied that some of their elders had difficulty adjusting to their present economic status.

"One must realize their handicaps and limitations," he said, "the worst of which is illiteracy. Whites are back in control of the Southern state legislatures, of the money and power politics and influence, and the darkies are simply surviving now. Since agriculture is what they know and do best, you'll find them in the fields throughout the South. I pay the prevailing wages, and you wouldn't believe the savings on food, shelter, clothing, and medical bills. Planters are prospering more now than ever before. That's both a paradox and irony, isn't it? Negroes have become racial victims, enslaved by ignorance and prejudice, and will have even less freedom by the turn of the century than they have today."

"Because of organizations like the Knights of the White Camellia and the Ku Klux Klan?"

"Partially."

Her eyes measured him. "Do you belong to any such vigilante groups, Dan?"

"You should know better than ask a white Southern male that question, Devon."

"Why?"

"Because it's dangerous knowledge for a woman to possess, and he couldn't answer it honestly either way."

"I see."

"No, I don't think you do, my dear. Their membership is secret, under oath and pain of death. Suffice it to say that I have no fancy for white sheets and hoods and cross-burning, but that's not true of every visitor to this plantation. So beware of your curious, journalistic mind while here. Just remember, genteel Southern ladies never discuss such masculine subjects."

"I'll be careful," she promised. "I just wish you'd call off the tilting tourney, Dan."

They were sitting in the shade of the rose-latticed gazebo, sipping refreshing drinks. Devon glanced intermittently toward the track, where Keith had been diligently practicing since dawn, pausing only briefly for meals and to change his sweat-soaked shirts.

"It's too late, Devon." Plucking a perfect bloom from the crimson climber, he presented it to her. "I must admit Curtis has guts! But he's destined to lose, honey. Visceral courage is no substitute for experience. Doesn't he realize he'll be up against some champions?"

"Certainly, and he knows the odds. But they won't be his *real* opponents, Daniel."

He nodded, understanding her implication. "Well, I'm not

exactly a tyro at this game, either, you know."

"Yes, and I suppose it would be wrong to appeal to your chivalry for my sake?"

"Throw the contest?" he asked, gazing at her intently.

Embarrassed, Devon's skin flushed deeply. How could she even have hinted at such a conspiracy, impugning his honor and compromising her own? "No, of course not! That would be dishonest, and Keith would be furious with me for meddling."

"I should think so, Devon. At any rate, I couldn't prudently oblige you, or him. No willing forfeitures for Lancelot. . . . You look rueful."

"He calls you Galahad."

"Really?" He scowled slightly. "Well, let him do his damndest! It'll take a miracle for Sir Lancelot to win, but if so, it'll be fair and square."

"Believe me, Daniel, Keith would not want the victory any other way," Devon assured him, still mortified by her imprudence. "Please forgive and forget my *faux pas*."

"It's done, darling."

His endearments were growing more personal, and Devon wondered how to correct him. If he did not realize that love and concern for her husband had prompted her contemplated connivery, mere admonitions would not suffice to deter him, nor alter his attitude toward her. Wherever her eyes wandered, to Keith driving himself desperately, or to the children playing harmoniously, Daniel's eyes followed with the same attentiveness he had exhibited from the moment of their arrival. Devon could never long or effectively distract him, for it was a kind of humble, incessant idolization.

"Look, Daniel! Scotty is swinging Fawn—isn't that cute? We should take a picture of them together."

"We will," he said. "I've engaged a photographer from Richmond to capture some of Saturday's highlights and events. I'll send you a set, if you like. At least we'll have some memories for our family albums."

"That would be nice, thank you."

"Do you have any pictures of your daughters with you?"

"No, not even a daguerrotype. We'll have them photographed on their first birthday, and every year thereafter for our records. Their portraits will be painted when they're old enough to pose. We have a fine one of Scotty, at age four. What about Fawn?"

"When I can commission the right artist," he replied. "She should have been painted with her mother, but that's impossible now."

Devon hesitated, reluctant to intrude on his privacy. "Forgive my prying, Dan, but haven't you thought of marrying again? Surely you've had opportunities."

"Many," he admitted. "You'll meet some of them at the barbecue and ball."

"Any likely prospects?"

He shook his head with ponderous significance. "Not at present, my dear. Does that need explanation?"

"No," she murmured, glancing at Keith again. He was still running the lists with poised javelin, succeeding in transfixing the rings more often than she had expected, or Daniel appreciated. Her heart went out to him, and viewed through emotional mist, he resembled a mythical centaur, his body blending into the beast's.

"Your tilting challenge was cruel," she accused Daniel. "Keith is exhausting himself."

Chagrined by her wifely concern, Daniel rejoined brusquely, "It's self-torture, and he can cease anytime."

"But he won't, until after the contest."

"That's his prerogative."

"I don't want him hurt, Daniel."

"He's an adult, Devon, capable of making his own decisions. And he's surely aware of his own stamina and fortitude. Don't blame me if the defiant Yankee kills himself in this competition!"

"Oh, Dan, you still hate him, don't you? Still think of him in that awful, inimical way? Not only as a Northerner, but as your avowed enemy."

"And you wish me to regard him as a true friend, with brotherly love?" He smirked at the notion. "I'm sorry, Devon, but that's impossible. Geography has little to do with this situation. We are two men in love with the same woman and will be rivals as long as we live on this earth."

Devon was silent, slowly pulling apart the scarlet rose he

had given her, its velvety petals falling into her lap like great
red teardrops.

Scotty watched the preparations for the feast and tournament
with fascination and even awe. Nothing so spectacular had ever
taken place at Halcyon-on-Hudson, where the mostly family
entertainments were nice but hardly exciting. They never had
overnight guests, except for Dr. Ramsey Blake and a friendly
lady named Carla Winston. But hundreds of people, including
many children, were shortly expected at Harmony Hill.

Fatted calves and pigs, slaughtered the previous evening,
were roasting on hand-turned skewers over long pits of smoldering hickory coals, and delicious aromas filled the air. The
smoke whetted his appetite, and Scotty was eager to taste the
genuine Southern barbecued beef and pork. Chicken and fish
were frying in the outdoor and manor kitchens, between which
servants bustled with crocks of potato salad and cole slaw,
tureens of buttered and creamed vegetables, crisp dill pickles,
piccalilli, chutney, and other relishes. Long pine tables and
benches were set up beneath huge shade trees and spread with
clean cloths and cutlery. One special table heaped with cakes,
pies, cobblers, cookies, and puddings was attended by several
young girls with long-handled palmetto fans, whose only duty
was shooing away flies and other insects. Negro women were
churning freezers of ice cream—vanilla, fresh peach, strawberry—in the cool, screened springhouse, where the fruit ades,
planter's punch, and mint juleps would also be concocted and
iced.

Since dawn the routes to Harmony Hill had been crowded
with various vehicles: open carriages, buggies, fringed-top surreys, jaunty pony carts. Some guests arrived in gaily decorated
riverboats, prepared to spend the night. Everywhere were ladies
in bright spring dresses and floppy straw hats, swinging or
twirling dainty parasols, and escorted by nattily attired gentlemen. Youngsters mingled with others in their Sunday clothes.
Mr. Haverston was genially greeting his guests, but Scotty's
parents were nowhere in sight. He imagined his mother was
still undecided about what to wear, but it didn't matter, for his
attention was soon focused on the jousting contestants, most
of whom arrived in the colorful costumes and plumed headgear

generally reserved for official meets and pageants.

The local knights furnished their own steeds and equipment and brought stuffed leather heads, some painted with ghoulish faces, to mount on the willow poles. They were members of the elite Knighthood of the Southern Realm, with self-bestowed titles. Those from the surrounding counties masqueraded as the Knight of Richmond, the Knight of the James, the Knight of the Shenandoah, the Knight of Monticello, the Knight of Mount Vernon, the Knight of the Blue Ridge, the Knight of the Rapidan, and other such picturesque Virginian titles. Daniel Haverston would ride as the Knight of Harmony Hill. Keith Curtis, unceremoniously dubbed the Knight of Manhattan for program designation, was merely amused by his wife's romantic suggestion that he adopt the Knight of Halcyon, declaring that he would probably be regarded simply as the Damn Yankee Knight anyway. He declined the offer of a costume, his only ornamentation a Cochin rooster's tailfeather stuck in the band of his gray felt slouch hat.

"Christ," he remarked to Devon, observing the activity below their windows. "What a pompous bunch of peacocks strutting their stuff down there!"

"Not all of them, Keith, mostly the young cocks. Anyway, you look better than any of them to me! I like that defiant feather in your crown, even though it does give you a touch of the renegade."

"Yankee Doodle Dandy, eh? Would they mob me if I went into battle whistling that tune?"

"Probably." She smiled. "The band will play 'Dixie' as they parade before the stands. You can still withdraw, Keith, with honor intact."

His emphatic no was superfluous. "Never, Devon. I'm in this contest, though my Southern adversaries make Yankee mincemeat of me."

"How many rings do you expect to capture?"

"Several, at least. I have a fine mount, which I've mastered, so being unhorsed is not likely. I won't lose by default, anyway. Will you and the boy be there?"

"I'm not sure I want to watch, Keith, but Scotty is thrilled about the spectacle—and certain his father will acquit himself well."

"I hope I don't disappoint him, Devon. But you must be present too, *if* you can get dressed in time," he added chidingly. "I'll need some support, since I don't expect many natives to cheer me."

"Captain Bowers and the crew are coming to the barbecue, and they'll be on your side," Devon reminded. "And so will your most ardent admirer, darling, in the front row. And no matter the final score, I'll give you a special trophy in private. Our loving cup will runneth over!"

"Thank you, my sweet. But what if the Knight of Harmony Hill is the victor and presents you with his white plume?" he asked, gauging her reaction.

"Well, I couldn't refuse it, without flouting tradition. Nor could he make the gesture without doing so. That honor is strictly reserved for the privileged knight's own fair lady, be she sweetheart or wife, neither of which I am to Daniel Haverston."

"Too bad he can't seem to realize that," Keith muttered, unable to resist an affectionate pat of her French-chemised derrière. "Finish dressing, Mrs. Curtis, so I can go down and meet my competition. Maybe I can get in a few practice runs against the champions, pick up some valuable pointers before official time is called."

"Go ahead, Sir Knight of Manhattan! I'll be another hour or so yet." She still had not definitely decided on her costume, though the bed, settee, and chairs were strewn with gowns and bonnets, and a maid was patiently waiting to assist her. "But first a good-luck kiss, beloved..."

Devon's belated appearance, in crisp coral taffeta and flattering picture hat with coral ribbon streamers, created a mild sensation, stealing some attention even from the courtly knights. She recognized people she had met at the Clinton reception, along with some former classmates at Rosewood Female Academy, and girlhood friends who happily renewed their acquaintance. But most of the guests were like strangers with familiar faces, their appearance and character so altered by time and circumstances that they had little in common anymore. Did they feel the same way about her?

With Keith beaming proudly at his wife's side, Daniel could

barely conceal his chagrin in introducing them properly, invariably adding, "Mrs. Curtis was the former Miss Devon Marshall, of Richmond, and the publishing Marshalls of Virginia. She resides in New York at present, and Mr. Curtis plans to ride in the meet as the Knight of Manhattan." The latter information could hardly gain the Yankee much favor with the spectators, he reasoned, and might even distract and disconcert him in action. But Daniel regretted being lax in his own practice, for the man he wanted most to beat had a firm, steady handshake and the keen, alert gray eyes of an eagle scouting for prey. And only last evening he had discovered Curtis's competence at darts, in several impromptu matches in which Daniel was bested. His skill at billiards was no less remarkable, and he did not drink even socially during any form of competition.

This was not true of the majority of his opponents, who were consuming their fair share of liquor while awaiting the traditional hunting horn to summon them to their particular positions, previously determined by drawing numbers from a whirled squirrel cage. There was a strong odor of horse flesh and whisky and sweat, as some polished their steeds' coats with spirits, and the atmosphere was one of joviality and optimistic arrogance.

The King-at-Arms and Master-of-Horse, heralded by a bugler, led the cavalcade of knights to the grand pavilion, where they lowered and slowly raised their lances in ceremonial salute to the appointed judges, whose decisions were indisputable. As the contestants paraded single-file past these officials, their names were duly noted in the roster and programs. Spectators filled every available space in the stands and along the rails. The ladies acknowledged their favorites with tossed flowers, blown kisses, fluttering handkerchiefs and scarves. Some of the knights were attended by young squires, and Scotty had wanted to be his father's, but his age and inexperience relegated him to the safer company of his mother and Fawn Haverston, who, naturally, was rooting for her father.

As the starting trumpet sounded, the first contestant raced swiftly toward the Rigg, his blunted lance aiming for the center of the tiny golden ring. His incredible feat, accomplished at high speed, received boisterous applause. His successor also

made his goal, his supporters cheered, and the judges marked
their scorecards. The third gentleman, perhaps a bit too tipsy
and confident, missed the suspended circle, and was derisively
tooted and hooted off the track. Ten more opponents tested
their skill and luck, seven were triumphantly lauded, while the
taunted losers left the field to await their next turn. Six courses
must be ridden by all contestants before the final determination
of the tourney.

Devon prayed and held her breath as Keith's first time approached, and Scotty crossed his fingers. His powerful bay
lunged foward and flashed past, his steady lance impaled the
ring, and his family and crew cheered wildly, along with some
new friends who obviously admired him.

"Bravo, Knight of Manhattan!" Devon shouted, waving her
lacy kerchief and flinging a flower from the tiny straw basket
on her arm.

"Hail, Daddy!" Scotty yelled, clapping his hands and jumping up and down on the plank platform.

Daniel followed Keith, securing his target, and his daughter
and numerous guests hoorayed the Knight of Harmony Hill.
Like his Yankee predecessor, Daniel saluted the spectators
courteously before riding back to the end of the line.

After completion of the initial run of the lists, the sequential
courses followed in rapid succession; tilting was an exceedingly
swift and continuous sport, with no intermissions or brouhahas.
The two recognized champions never missed, and a sudden-
death playoff between the Knight of the James and the Knight
of Mount Vernon seemed inevitable. This did not concern Keith,
whose primary opponent was Daniel Haverston, and thus far
their scores were tied with three hits and one miss apiece—a
phenomenon, no less, astonishing Devon as much their host.
Keith only hoped that Dan's few nips of bourbon and dogged
determination to win would be his undoing—and, ultimately,
they were.

Devon's applause for her husband only made Daniel more
eager and rash, and he spurred his nervous black stallion harder
and more recklessly. Hurt by the sharp rowels, Plato whinnied
and bolted on his hind legs, then shot forward like a wild bullet,
nearly unseating his master and definitely spoiling his aim. His
lance struck the ring at an angle, knocking it to the ground,

where it was retrieved by an attendant and held high before the judges, as proof that it was not secured. This blunder gave Daniel only three out of the six rings, while Keith finished with four. Thus, the Knight of Manhattan, while not the actual winner, had succeeded in his original goal to defeat the Knight of Harmony Hill.

Victor and still renowned champion of the Tidewater Tilting Meet was the grandly costumed Knight of the James, Richard Mallory, who had pierced every golden ring without a hitch, and was now lowering his lance at the feet of his lovely fiancée, Miss Acantha Langley, along with the white ostrich plume from his helmet, traditionally crowning her the Queen of Love and Beauty. A number of knights had been disqualified either by repeated failure to impale and hoist the gilded circle before the judges, or by being unhorsed and banned from further participation in that contest.

Showering her personal hero with rose petals and kisses, Devon was scarcely aware of the losers thundering toward the long row of conveniently mounted leather and canvas heads, to vent their frustrations and defaults and failures, whatever the individual causes, on the helpless dummies.

Wielding ancestral sabers and swords, they hacked savagely at the simulated enemies, some grinning in self-mockery, others swearing and muttering obscenities. None was more violent, however, than Daniel Haverston, whose Civil War weapon slashed his targets into leather thongs and canvas strips. Cotton and straw flew from the scalped props. Gouged eyes, noses, and mouths were reminiscent of the grisly skulls once hoisted on London Bridge to deter potential felons.

Keith declined to participate in this bizarre and medieval game, which he and his family watched from a safe distance. What tempers those Southern cavaliers exhibited in defeat! No wonder it had taken the Union four years to conquer the Confederacy. But he knew Daniel didn't mind losing to his comrades, just to the Yankee Knight of Manhattan, who had long ago won the fair lady of his dreams. His pride and masculinity must be suffering the same mutilation as the inanimate victims on the poles.

"Poor Dan," Devon remarked, cherishing the cock quill from Keith's felt hat as fondly as if it were the snowy ostrich plume from the champion's gilded helmet. "He's in quite a state. I declare, I've never seen him so distraught, never even imagined such violence in him."

"Probably pretending those dummies are me," Keith surmised. "He should be angry at himself, blaming his own desperate zeal. Spurring his mount made him lose control of it and his aim at the circle. I wonder what he'll do for an encore?"

"God knows." Devon sighed sadly.

Scotty observed the gruesome spectacle in silent awe and amazement. Fawn, who had never seen her father in such a ferocious rage, was frightened and bewildered. She cried as Daniel moved from stilt to stilt, decapitating the swaying heads missed or ignored by his now resigned friends, who were dispersing toward the stables and the springhouse for refreshments, joking and jostling one another in restored humor and camaraderie.

✦ 18 ✦

EMBARRASSED BY his macabre display, and unable to face Devon or his daughter, the Knight of Harmony Hill finally sheathed his sword and cantered off to the stables. Later, he joined the other men at the springhouse, to toast the victor and congratulate all who had defeated him, including the Knight of Manhattan. If the latter felicitation lacked bona fide warmth and sincerity, however, only they understood the reasons and refrained from comment.

Not until he had consumed several strong mint juleps did Daniel finally remark, albeit reluctantly, "I must admit I never thought you could do it, Curtis. Nor would you have succeeded had I practiced half as diligently and omitted the booze. So I did give you a slight advantage, after all, didn't I?"

"Perhaps," Keith conceded, sipping Scotch over chipped ice. "And I don't doubt your skill at tilting, Haverston. Have you won many tournaments?"

"My share," he boasted. "I was champion of the Tidewater Table three years in a row. I was also younger then."

"Weren't we all!"

Daniel frowned sheepishly. "Will you try to outperform me in the ballroom this evening, sir?"

"Is that a contest, too?"

"Just a private one, between us," he muttered, walking away, as the president of the Bank of Richmond joined the Wall Street financier to discuss economics.

Devon sat in the shade of an enormous, moss-draped live oak, reminiscing with a group of former dormitory mates from Rosewood Female Academy. All were married, with families, two for the second time, having been widowed in the war. Most were aware of Devon Marshall's journalistic achievements and admired her courage and perseverance in leaving the ravaged, bankrupt South at a tender age to seek her fortune elsewhere. *They* had remained and doggedly struggled through Reconstruction, wedding veterans in similar straits. Without betraying herself, Devon spoke of other impoverished Southern girls she had met in New York, supporting themselves as best they could: lovely, shapely former belles called Natchez and Savannah and Mobile, after their native cities, who posed in gorgeous bird costumes in gilded cages.

"Where, for mercy's sake?" they inquired in unison.

"A supper club in the Bowery, where they received five dollars per evening and tips from generous male patrons. Some concealed their identity with masks, and some even went into keeping as pets of rich Yankee bird fanciers."

"My word!" one matron exclaimed in a horrified whisper, glancing furtively about to ascertain her teenage daughter's location. "Genteel Southern ladies did *such* things?"

Devon nodded, dropping her eyes. "I interviewed and wrote about some of them later—anonymously, of course. It was a matter of survival, you understand. Oh, they tried to find respectable positions, as teachers or governesses in a city overcrowded with Dixie refugees seeking decent employment, most to no avail."

"How lucky you were, Devon, to get into publishing! To have an honorable profession backed by experience with your father's newspaper and reputation. Did you keep in touch with those less fortunate souls?"

"I'm afraid not. They went their separate ways, and I was involved in my career."

"Covering all those glamorous social affairs in New York and Washington for years, and even going abroad later in the Grant entourage! And then winning the heart of the richest man in America—oh, it's like a fairy tale romance!"

Tactfully, they did not mention the unhappy interlude with a now famous Texas politician, Senator Reed Carter, but Devon suspected that they knew about that chapter in her private life, and exclaimed, "Dear me! I never realized I had such a loyal readership."

"I kept a scrapbook," Celeste Woodbury confessed, sighing at her own dull, mediocre existence, never more interesting than it was today.

A senior during Devon's junior year at Rosewood, Celeste was a bride of a few months when her young soldier groom was killed in Tennessee. Her second spouse was a middle-aged country physician, whose poor patients often paid their bills with foodstuffs and services. They had four children crowded into a small frame house sadly in need of repairs. Although near the same age, Celeste appeared far older and more matronly, with much gray in her faded brown hair knotted on her neck and many lines in her neglected skin. She couldn't help envying Devon's youthful beauty, nor coveting her fashionable, obviously expensive costume. Celeste had learned how to turn her husband's shirt collars and cuffs, and remake her own and the children's garments to last another season or two. Lacking proper formal attire, the Woodburys were not staying for the grand ball, regretfully depriving their youngsters of the eagerly anticipated hayrides.

"Won't the kids be disappointed?" Devon asked, for the joy wagons were already being readied at the barns.

"Probably, but Mrs. Pryne's sixth baby is due at any moment," Celeste explained. "They are our neighbors on the next farm. A doctor's life, you know."

"Of course," Devon said, and the other ladies nodded sympathetically, having employed similar excuses when their own wardrobes were inadequate for the occasion.

The Richmond photographer commissioned to record Harmony Hill's most impressive entertainment since the war, roved about with his tripod and black-boxed camera, asking certain people to pose, singly or in groups. At Mr. Haverston's request, Mrs. Curtis was frequently filmed, alone, with her son, with Daniel and his daughter, but only once, at Devon's insistence, with her husband and child.

Cynically amused, suppressing his innate jealousy, Keith clapped the brooding planter on the shoulder. "Photogenic, isn't she? Could be an artist's model! And she *is* a celebrity in her own right, as you well know. I don't blame you for wanting to preserve her memory permanently, man, any way you can. In your place, so would I."

Daniel remembered this chiding sarcasm later, as Devon descended the broad central staircase for the ball, radiant in ice-blue satin overlaid with a shimmering mist of silk illusion, and embellished with diamonds and fire opals. His narrowed eyes fastened reverently on his ideal, indelibly imprinting the vision on his mind, virtually mesmerized by her glory and his adoration. Rushing toward the stairs with a raised hand to stay her midway, he beckoned the photographer to set up his equipment and capture the stunning image. Hoping his obsession was not too suggestive to the onlookers, Devon graciously consented to the pose, and then promptly and proudly joined her admiring mate for the evening festivities.

The ballroom was romatically festooned with flower-and-ribbon garlands, and aglow with perfumed candlelight. The orchestra opened the grand march with "Dixie," and the couples promenaded ceremoniously around the waxed and buffed floor. Next came the memorable Stephen Foster tunes and then the traditional Viennese waltzes, during which Keith surrendered his wife only twice to other partners. Their host had to wait until the Virginia reel for his first opportunity, and there was little time to chat in this busy, vibrant dance. Promptly upon its completion, however, Daniel signaled the maestro for the prearranged medley of Strauss, and Devon was fairly trapped in his arms. Nevertheless, she managed to keep him discreetly at bay, merely smiling at his extravagant compliments while pursuing casual conversation.

Keith took his flirtatious partners in stride, accustomed to this feminine folly on formal occasions. For some inexplicable reason, the female of the species, regardless of her age and appearance, seemed to undergo some mysterious metamorphosis in the ballroom. Dignity and discretion were modified, if not totally abandoned, and a coy coquette emerged, convinced of her irresistible charms, while the male was expected to dutifully transform into a susceptible, affected gallant. It was a ludicrous drawing-room drama in which the characters were also the audience, and he was currently playing opposite Mrs. Clinton. She begged to entertain the Curtises in Richmond again before they left Virginia, and subtly hinted for an invitation to visit them in New York. Anticipating the veiled cue, Keith smilingly reciprocated, "We're building a summer home in Newport, ma'am, and shall christen it with a grand celebration. The Clintons will be high on our guest list."

"How kind of you, Mr. Curtis! I simply can't understand the attitude some Southerners still have toward the North. If all Yankees were like you—"

Keith grinned, wondering how much she knew about his commercial interests in Richmond. "I'm afraid they're not, my dear. And maybe I wouldn't be so kindly disposed, either, had I not the great good fortune to marry a charming Virginia lady."

Mrs. Clinton thought the great good fortune was mutual. Her stout bosom heaved in a wistful sigh. "She'll be a legend in the Tidewater now. So beautiful, gracious, talented, and certainly the best-dressed and -jeweled lady here and probably anywhere she appears. In case you haven't noticed, the Knight of Harmony Hill is captivated by her charms."

"I've noticed," Keith said, casting a covert glance in their direction. "But it was the same for most of the gentlemen at your reception, wasn't it?"

"Alas, yes, including my aging Harold. But you must also be cognizant of your impact on the ladies, my dear sir. My, how they'll buzz at the teas and quilting bees!" she added laconically, rolling her puffy eyes and pursing her wrinkled mouth in a foolish attempt at coquetry. "Will you folks go hayriding later?"

"If Mrs. Curtis wishes."

"Oh, she will! That's one of the pleasures of a night-long plantation ball, especially in this state, where hayriding and bundling were supposedly both invented. And there's a full spring moon tonight to make it even more pleasurable." She winked at him. "But you'd better get on the same wagon with your wife. . . ."

"I intend to, ma'am."

"Few men here believe it, of course, but was today's joust really your first?"

"Really."

"And yet you captured more golden rings than Mr. Haverston, who's a veteran of the sport! Amazing, no less, and I suppose your fair lady inspired you?"

"She did, indeed."

"Well, you did her proud, gallant knight from the North!"

Bess Clinton tossed her pompadoured head, fluttering her feathered aigrette, reminding Keith of a plump partridge in a mating dance. At fifty, comfort and security were essential, and somehow she sensed that Mr. Curtis represented both to her husband and herself. It was nothing short of miraculous the way the Bank of Richmond received its charter over a decade ago and continued to expand and prosper under some mysterious aegis. Only Northern bankers had money to lend in those wretched Reconstruction days, and this financier was a giant on Wall Street even then. Historians listed him among President Lincoln's consultants during the Union's monetary crises, and Mrs. Clinton wanted desperately to court the favor of this powerful Manhattan mogul. She was crushed when the music ended on a flourish, signaling the end of the set, and so befuddled she thanked *him* for dancing with her.

"My pleasure, ma'am," he said, bowing chivalrously and escorting her back to the sidelines of elderly matrons, widows, and wallflowers.

By midnight a dozen or so wagons, their beds softened with hay or cotton, assembled for the next frivolity. The large vehicles could accommodate a number of people, while the smaller ones were intended for a couple only. Daniel's plans to maneuver Devon into one of the latter were foiled by Keith, who promptly lifted her onto a cotton-filled cart and whistled at the driver to move into position.

The creaking caravan rolled across the moonlit meadows

and fields, to rustic lanes marked by kerosene lanterns and pine-knot torches, accompanied by Negro attendants and entertainers strumming banjos and singing antebellum plantation songs. Soon other voices, male and female, joined the harmonizing. Devon's soft, sweet soprano and Keith's smooth, deep baritone blended beautifully in the wistful Stephen Foster ballads, and they smiled and held hands. She did very well until the first chorus of "Carry Me Back to Old Virginia," and then her native roots choked her emotionally. The tune, the lyrics, the memories were too poignant, nostalgic, reminiscent.

The moon was a great silver sphere recalling the barrage balloons that had floated over Richmond during the war, and a shooting star reminded her of the fiery rockets she had seen on dark, awesome nights. And how could she ever forget the clinking-squeaking of chains and harness, the ominous rumbling of caissons hauling cannon and coffins over this very land?

"You're not singing," Keith observed solicitously. "Isn't that the state anthem?"

"Yes."

"Well, come on, then! I've just memorized the words. Join me?" But she couldn't, and now he saw tears glistening in her eyes. "What's wrong, darling?"

They were close enough to the forest to smell the pine and hear the plaintive cry of the whippoorwills. "Just nostalgia," she murmured, lying back on the fluffy raw cotton mattress. "Virginians grow up singing that song. It's always the theme of the hayrides, just as 'Dixie' still opens the balls. I don't expect you to understand, Keith."

"I understand you're unhappy, Devon, and it worries me. No wonder Haverston tried to hop into this cart with you! He knew how all this sentiment would affect you, and hoped to comfort you in his arms."

"No, only you can do that, Keith. And I need comforting now, to shake this mood."

His face bent over hers, and her arms rose to embrace him. Their lips fused, then parted in avid ardor, as his physique pressed urgently against her thigh. "Shall we shock our driver?" he whispered, nibbling at her ears, throat, and the soft, scented flesh above her décolletage.

"Make love?"

"Uh-huh. I'm on fire."

"We can't, darling. The wagon behind us is too near."

"And transporting our disgruntled host!" His mouth sought hers again, lingering hungrily, as much for Daniel's benefit as his own. "You promised me a special trophy, Mrs. Curtis. Remember? You said our personal loving cup would runneth over."

"It will, dearest, in private."

"We can sink easily into this cotton, Devon. It'll provide adequate camouflage."

"But we'll ruin our clothes, Keith! Do you realize this gown cost you over a thousand dollars?"

"And worth every penny, judging from the Knight of Harmony Hill's expression when you appeared on his stairway, like an angel floating down from heaven. He was entranced, virtually hypnotized. God knows what he plans to do with that particular photograph! Enshrine you somehow, perhaps. He worships you, Devon."

"Well, it's not mutual, Keith, nor my concern now. In addition to this expensive Worth creation, I'm also wearing a corselet."

"But not a chastity belt." Having succeeded in banishing her nostalgic melancholy, he proceeded to overcome her prudent modesty. "I think the Knight of Manhattan is clever and agile enough to manage this escapade. And it'll be a new experience for us, milady, if we're bold enough to try it."

"Oh, you're positively wicked," Devon admonished him, giggling as they eased into the fleecy nest, so soft and resilient. "And we'll create a scandal, if anyone suspects."

"I hope so."

"That we create a scandal?"

"That someone suspects."

Devon clucked her tongue. "The scandalous Curtises who couldn't wait to make love," she murmured, gasping as he skillfully maneuvered around the troublesome barriers, and just as skillfully entered her.

And indeed it was a novel sensation, buoyantly thrilling, with the plodding mule and swaying cart stimulating his desire and aiding his technique, much as his convenient coach had served him on that unforgettable night when he had taken her virginity on the rails between Richmond and Washington.

"Well?" he prompted, pausing for second wind after her multiple delights. "Different?"

"Fantastic! Reminds me of another time—"

"Your first?"

"Mmm. Only it wasn't as much fun then."

"You weren't as cooperative, either," he teased. "Not only a rebel but a virgin."

"Would you have forced me if I hadn't been so passive and acquiescent?"

"I don't think so, although I'd never wanted a woman so much in my life." He began to move inside her again, with slow deliberation, massaging every tender and sensitive spot, repriming them both. "Incredibly, I still feel that same intense passion and urgency every time I take you."

"We share it now, beloved."

Rapt in reverie, Devon was only vaguely aware that the caravan was retracing the trail back to the manor, where others were anxious to board. Keith had lapsed into lethargic gratification, his arms loosely embracing her, his head on her breast. She spoke softly to him, touching his shoulder gently, and they emerged from their cozy cocoon together, covered with lint and smiling intimately.

"Passengers are waiting to ride, dear."

"May they enjoy it as much as we did, my love," said Keith, surveying the master of Harmony Hill. And Daniel's scowl, as he debarked from his rather crowded hay-bedded conveyance, which had trailed them at some thirty feet, distant enough to imagine and assume what he could not actually witness, somehow increased and intensified Keith's already considerable satisfaction.

⌁ 19 ⌁

THE *SPRITE* took on more provisions from the local ship's chandlery, and Captain Bowers was busily charting her course to Savannah. The crew, satiated on shore leave in Virginia, were ready to sample the taverns and wenches of that well-known Georgia port.

The incident with the children occurred the day before the scheduled departure. Daniel was in Richmond, presumably at the tobacco factory, which he had been neglecting, and was not expected back at Harmony Hill until evening. Miss Vale, who had gone in to purchase more school supplies and do some additional sightseeing, would return with him.

Scotty and Fawn pursued their mutual interests, riding horseback after breakfast, trotting the flower-bordered lanes and bridle paths, and exploring in the woods. After luncheon, they went driving in Fawn's pretty wicker pony trap with the boy at the reins, enjoying their adventures and each other's company tremendously.

Devon and Keith relaxed in the gardens, alternating between the restful hammocks supported by the trees and the comfortable lounge chairs. Devon sipped iced cherry punch, while Keith tried to cultivate a taste for mint juleps. "How in hell can such a sweet drink appeal to men?" he wondered aloud, disliking the sugar and crushed peppermint. "It only disguises and spoils good bourbon."

Devon smiled. "For Yankee men, maybe. Southerners think Scotch whisky tastes like medicine, and rum is only for sailors. They appreciate fine brandy, though, and would enjoy your French cognacs."

"Mrs. Clinton literally solicited an invitation to visit us,"

Keith apprised. "Do you suppose the Haverstons might ever do so?"

"Perhaps, if the daughter can persuade the father. Can you believe those two kids have promised to correspond?"

"Why not? They know how to write."

"You wouldn't object?"

"To childish letters? Certainly not."

"I haven't seen or heard them for a couple of hours," Devon said. "Wonder where they are and what they're doing."

"Playing, what else? Scott surprises me, though. I didn't think he had much use for girls, considering his reaction to his sisters."

"They're too little. Fawn is different, interested in things he likes. Not a tomboy, exactly, but a good companion. They're compatible and will miss each other."

"Will you miss this place?"

"A little, maybe. It has been a pleasant holiday, for the most part, hasn't it?"

"Overall," he agreed. "But our host's efforts have been primarily for your benefit, darling, not mine."

"Well, it doesn't really matter, Keith. Hardly an hour passes that I don't think of our little darlings at Halcyon. I bet Nanny, Anna, and Enid have had their hands full."

"No doubt of that. But they must be coping, for we've had no urgent telegrams. Maybe the twins are walking and talking already."

"At barely eleven months? That would be a feat even for the prodigies we produce, Daddy."

"Well, I'm anxious to get home, anyway, Mommy. For many reasons. We'll put into Savannah for a couple of days only, three at the most."

"That's fine with me, dear. I have no relatives or friends there, so if you want to skip it . . . ?"

"My connections with the Bank of Savannah are the same as those in Richmond," he informed, lighting a cheroot to modify the sweetness of the julep.

"Fifty-one percent of the stock?"

He nodded. "I just hope my Georgia investments are as well managed as those in Virginia."

Devon set her cup on a convenient wrought-iron table and

reclined in the canvas swing, enjoying the cool breezes sweeping up from the James River. She had forgotten how early summer sometimes arrived in the Tidewater, and how humid it could be so near the Dismal Swamp—a vast, miasmic wilderness stretching into North Carolina, and a former refuge for runaway slaves of both states. She was aware of the debilitating and frequently fatal fevers that periodically plagued the Virginia coast in hot weather, for her mother had succumbed to one such malady in her thirties. Caribbean hurricanes were an intermittent threat in season, heavy coastal fogs impeding water traffic could occur at any time, and Devon hoped the *Sprite* would not encounter any unexpected delays. Plans for a lavish bon voyage had been canceled at their request, for Keith felt they had been feted more than enough and a late, congenial supper would be sufficient.

"They must be, if they're returning profits, darling." She pondered the vivid azure sky above the trees, wondering if spring had come to Halcyon yet. The gardens of Harmony Hill were in prodigal bloom, a veritable Eden of color and fragrance, and virtually isolated. Her only concern was the apparent disappearance of the children. The plantation encompassed thousands of acres of land and woods, a small self-sufficient community in itself, and they could be anywhere. "I'm beginning to worry about those little rascals, Keith. I hope they're not into mischief."

He grinned at her, blowing a smoke ring. "Boy-girl mischief, in the hayloft or corncrib?"

"Don't be absurd!" she scoffed. "They're too young and innocent for *that* kind of mischief."

"Are they?"

"Of course! Maybe they wandered too far into the forest and got lost. Or toward the river and into the marsh."

"They were cautioned about those dangers before they left, Devon, and every day since we've been here. Besides, Scotty is used to the country."

"But where could they be?"

"Probably exploring that supposedly haunted basement, or some other childish fascination."

The possibility was barely uttered, before its impact struck Devon for a more realistic reason. "Oh, my God!" she gasped, abandoning the hammock. "The secret tunnel!"

"Oh, now, don't panic, Mother! They're forbidden to tamper with the seals. I suspect they're just roaming somewhere, out of sight and hearing. But it might be wise to check on them, anyway."

The manor kitchen provided easy access to the cellar, part of which also served as a larder for staples. The cook was busily frosting a Lady Baltimore cake as dessert for the guests' farewell supper when they interrupted her work.

"Rachel, have you seen Miss Fawn and Master Scotty this afternoon?" Devon asked.

"They was here 'bout a hour ago, Miz Curtis, beggin' cookies. Ain't seen 'em since, though. Me and my helper was at the separate cookhouse for a spell, and Cissy she's still there."

"Thank you, Rachel. If you should see or hear them again, please let us know."

"Sure, ma'am. But I don't think they gone into the cellar, 'cause Lil Missy ain't 'llowed down yonder."

"We'd better look, anyway," Keith told her.

"Yassuh. Jest shet the door, don't let the cats out, and watch for mousetraps. We don't want none of them dirty varmints sneakin' up here."

Cringing at the warning, Devon followed Keith down the stairs. Rats terrified her, and she was even squeamish about Scotty's white mice pets, which were kept in a cage with a treadmill.

The adventurers had been in the pantry section, all right, and their means of entry was no mystery. They had simply crawled through the narrow, top-hinged window, which was cracked for ventilation on clear days and locked against scavengers at night. A sputtering candle in a brass holder on the stone floor, and a tatter of Fawn's sash snagged on a nail, betrayed them. Devon was skeptical of Keith's suggestion that they may have just slipped in and out, using the ladder to climb back up and outside.

"Not likely, Keith. This is only a small part of the underground space here, and Scotty was too interested in the pirate-ghost stories. They certainly weren't hungry, with this hoard of vittles!"

"No famine here," Keith agreed, surveying the shelves of neatly labeled glass jars and tin cans, earthenware crocks, bins of root vegetables, barrels of flour and cornmeal, a ready supply of ham, bacon, sausage from the smokehouse, rounds of cheese, and racks of wine and liquor—all guarded by an army of diligent cats whose brethren patrolled in the barns and silos. Numerous pairs of feline eyes observed the intruders from dim corners and behind kegs and crates.

Devon was nervously quiet, stepping cautiously to avoid snapping a baited trap. "So we can rule out scrounging for food. But they could have started a fire with that candle! Oh, I could shake them!"

"We're wasting valuable time," Keith told her, picking up the flickering light. "Do you happen to know the location of that hidden passageway?"

"Essentially, but not exactly. I haven't been down here in many years." Not, in fact, since Harmony Hill's last Halloween party and midnight ghost watch, before the war. But she did not tell him that. "I think it's under the main hall and library, where the family entrance is concealed by a revolving book-case."

"Romantic, but hardly ingenious or original." Keith smirked. "Would the daughter of the house be aware of it?"

"Not at her age, lest she reveal the secret."

Calling the youngsters produced only hollow echoes of their own voices, as they proceeded to the next chamber. This was the candlery and contained molds of beeswax collected from the apiary and finished tapers suspended on long wicks attached to the sturdy beams. Devon caught the delightful aromas of bayberry and jasmine, lavender and lilac, rosemary and mignonette, cinnamon and other herbs and spices used to scent the festive candles. She inhaled appreciatively, knowing there would be no more such pleasant odors in this damp, musty environment. Here Fawn had lost a bow from her slippers, supplying another clue, for they had also taken some fresh candles for their expedition.

Truly frightened now, Devon screamed, "Scotty! Fawn! Can you hear me? Answer, and you won't be punished!"

"Don't promise that," Keith said, lighting tapers for themselves before snuffing the stub, and pushing open another heavy, creaking door. "If Scott has disobeyed me, he's in for a hard paddling."

Their lights cast elfin shadows into the large, windowless

chamber, which was divided into small barred cells, with bare wood bunks and iron shackles chained to the mildewed stone walls. "Good Lord!" Keith exclaimed. "A dungeon, Devon! No wonder Scott was so intrigued by the tales of Harmony Hill. Apparently, most are true."

"Doesn't Heathstone Manor have a dungeon?"

"All ancient castles do, because they were forts as well as family seats."

"So were Southern plantations when first established," Devon reminded him. "Besieged by Indians and pirates, later by the British twice, and finally the Yankees! They had to protect their lives and property."

"And restrain their recalcitrant slaves?"

"Slavery was not primarily a Southern institution, Keith. It was brought to the New World by the English and Dutch and French from their rubber and coffee and spice plantations! What about the Dutch patroons and their serfs in New York State? Their palatial 'wycks' are still highly visible on the Hudson River and in the Catskill Mountains. Indeed, we're living in one of their old mansions! Didn't Halcyon belong to a wealthy Dutchman? But why are we arguing this worn issue, instead of hunting the kids?"

"I'm just so damned scared and worried again, Devon. I thought we'd lost Scotty in the abduction—and now this could be another tragedy."

"I know, Keith, and I'm frightened, too. But they may be safe somewhere, with no inkling of our concern." She walked on, raising her candle higher. "I believe we're beneath the library now. The tunnel entrance should be in the east wall. Over there!" she cried, spying a stack of empty tobacco hogs-heads intricately arranged. "That's it!"

Reaching the disguised barricade, they discovered that a couple of barrels had been rolled aside, to facilitate work on the seal. A crowbar and clawhammer were used to prise off the nailed planks, providing a crawl space, and Keith marveled at the juvenile strength and ingenuity.

"They're in there, Devon. How long is the tunnel?"

Devon was frantic, trying to remember. "I'm not sure, Keith. A few hundred feet, perhaps, since it goes to the riverbank, near the landing."

"Straight, I assume?" Keith said, enlarging the access for himself. "The shortest distance between the points, and daylight should be visible at the other end, if they made it out."

"There're so many obstacles and hazards, Keith! It's a haven for poisonous snakes."

"Which means you stay here, Devon. I'll shout back to you at intervals. But I'll need more than candlelight to maneuver in that limbo. I noticed some gunnysacks and a drum of kerosene—I'll make a torch."

Fighting hysteria, Devon watched as he wrapped a tight sacking ball around a broken stave, dipped the tip in the oil, and flamed it. She knew that all reptiles, including the alligators that frequently escaped from the swamps and river inlets, feared and fled fire. "I hope the children kept their candles burning."

"They would be blind without them, Devon. And this thing will probably smoke like the devil's cigar, so pray there's enough oxygen to prevent suffocation."

"Good luck," Devon said, kissing him. "Hurry back!" She smiled and waved as he entered the long black corridor.

Keith was grateful for the ample dimensions, which permitted erect posture for his stature, and he did not need to stoop or crawl as he had imagined. Actually, the tunnel was well designed and constructed for centuries of use, and had undoubtedly been handy during the many wars in the region. Moisture glistened on the brick and hewn stone walls, which were discolored with moss and mildew. Except for some soil and water seepage through the cracks, however, the structure was remarkably sound and actually something of an engineering feat. Gargantuan spiderwebs hung like weird draperies from the cedar-beamed roofing, which had been waterproofed with pitch and creosote, and Keith had to tear and brush them aside. Spaced vents admitted some fresh air and specks of light; otherwise it was a long dark eerie hollow.

A venturesome boy's attraction to the tunnel was understandable, but not even the bravest little girl's, and Keith thought his intrepid son was the chief instigator of this trouble. Every so many feet, he yahooed to Devon, who answered instantly. But his summons to Scott and Fawn only echoed vainly, increasing his fear and dread.

Waiting impatiently in the basement, Devon could gauge

Keith's progress by the changing tones of his voice drifting
back to her, and hoped that he could still hear her tremulous
responses. Meanwhile, she had horrible visions of the children
trapped under a cave-in, or stumbling into a vipers' nest and
fanged to death. Any minute now, she expected Keith to make
some such terrible discovery.

She continued to listen and reply, until Keith's voice grew
distant and distorted, and her own weak and hoarse. Then she
paced the floor in frenzied circles, heedless of the sympathetic
female cat keeping her company. How much longer could she
endure this dreadful anxiety and suspense? Amid the other junk,
she noticed a box of pine cones and a discarded lightning rod,
and suddenly decided to devise a torch for herself. Impaling a
large cone on the spearlike finial of the thin iron shaft, she
doused it with kerosene and ignited it with the candle flame.
Then, steeling her nerves, she entered the awesome darkness.

⚓ 20 ⚓

GLIMPSING HER light through the smoky shadows, Keith yelled,
"Go back, Devon! There's nothing you can do!"

She ignored the order, and, though furious at the delay,
Keith paused to wait for her. She approached diffidently, beseeching divine guidance and protection. When they were about
thirty feet apart, an animal scurried out of a hole and directly
into her path. Thinking it a reptile, Devon screamed and dropped
her flambeau, paralyzed in her tracks. Rushing toward her,
Keith angrily admonished, "You little ninny! I told you to stay
put!"

"Don't scold me, Keith. I just couldn't wait there any longer,
doing nothing. Was that a water moccasin?"

"No, a big rat. I haven't seen any snakes yet, thank God."

As his boots stamped out her flare, Devon realized why she couldn't understand him clearly. His kerchief was tied over his nose and mouth to prevent smoke inhalation, and he advised her to improvise a mask, too. She used the fichu of her blouse, holding it in place with both hands.

"Follow me closely, Devon. And please be careful; we don't need any more accidents. Filter your breathing as much as possible. Some ventilation ducts are partially clogged with debris, and these oily fumes can be suffocating. The tunnel hasn't been cleaned recently, I'm afraid. Probably not since the Civil War."

"Any sign of the kids?"

"Not yet." He walked a few feet ahead of her, casting sufficient light over his shoulder to guide her. "But they had to have illumination to navigate in here, and I've found no candle stubs or other evidence. They must have made it through and forgot to close the river entrance. I think that faint shaft of sunshine farther on indicates we're near the end of this awful odyssey."

"I've been praying so hard, Keith."

"Me, too. I trust God was listening."

"Apparently so."

The ray of light was indeed coming from the riverside portal. The interior door to the sentry box was unbolted, and several used and spare candles were simply left. Overwhelmed with relief and gratitude, the parents looked at each other and smiled, joyful tears filling Devon's eyes. Never again would she doubt the power of prayer, the mercy of Providence.

"We haven't found them yet," Keith cautioned as they emerged from their dark, perilous journey into the bright daylight. Extinguishing his torch in the damp earth, he took Devon's hand to assist her through the thicket and around the boulders cleverly concealing the entry.

"Maybe they took the road back to the house?" Devon suggested hopefully. "Or they're playing on the landing, and the crew has seen them?"

Keith surveyed the plantation wharf, storage sheds, moored boats—and the *Sprite* anchored in the wide deep swiftly flowing James River. "Maybe," he said, leading her in that direction, swearing when he discovered that one of the yacht's dingies was missing from the dock. "Damn it! They must have tried to row to the *Sprite*."

Her fears rekindled, Devon cried, "Oh, no! The James flows into the Atlantic, Keith, and the current in the main channel is terribly swift and treacherous!"

"I know that, darling. But Scotty's handy with oars; I taught him well. At any rate, the ship's watch should have seen them. I'll try to get his attention, if I can find some signal flags. Ah, there're a couple in Haverston's riverboat."

Cupping his hands to amplify his voice, he shouted, "Ahoy! Ahoy!" until Captain Bowers himself appeared on the bridge, binoculars in hand. Deciphering Keith's message, he replied by semaphore. Devon was frantic until advised that the children were safely aboard and a sailor had already been dispatched to the manor with the information. Keith then signaled for their return to the landing, and a lifeboat was promptly manned and launched on the mission.

Pacing the wood dock, Keith flexed his fists and ground his teeth in bewildered fury. "What am I going to do with that boy, Devon? First he risks their lives in that tunnel, and then he could have drowned them in the river."

"Don't blame him entirely, Keith. Fawn is at fault, too. This is *her* territory, after all!"

"Oh, hell, Devon! Scott has been showing off for her since we arrived, how brave and clever he is, and the daring deeds he can perform. Racing his horse recklessly and climbing the highest trees on the property. I intend to blister his behind, no matter what you say."

"In private, please."

"Of course. But he must be punished for this. Don't you think Daniel will spank his daughter, too, when he finds out what happened?"

"Probably."

"They ought to get it together."

When the sheepish pair was delivered and placed ashore, Fawn was clutching a tiny bundle of clothing stuffed into a pillowcase. "Here's the potential stowaway, sir!" the coxswain advised with an amused salute.

As Keith thanked and dismissed them, Devon dropped to

her knees on the landing and embraced both youngsters, one in each arm. But Keith remained erect, legs spread in an authoritative stance and hands on hips, glowering at his errant son. "Look at me, Scott, and don't fib! Whose idea was this wild, reckless adventure?"

"Mine, sir."

"No, Mr. Keith," Fawn interposed. "It was mostly mine."

"We decided together," they said simultaneously, defending each other.

"But why the clothes, Fawn?" Devon inquired. "Surely you weren't planning to run away?"

Her reply was simple, honest, direct. "I wanted to go with Scotty."

"Without telling your father?"

"He wouldn't let me go, Miss Devon."

Keith chucked a firm hand under Scotty's lowered chin, forcing his attention. "Did you let Fawn think we would take her away from Harmony Hill secretly?"

"Sort of, I guess."

"Sort of! I'm surprised at you, son, and very disappointed. And you'll receive more than a scolding for this misdemeanor, believe me!"

Fawn tugged at Devon's skirts. "Punish me, too! We did wrong, but we just wanted to be together. Scotty can't stay here, because you're leaving tomorrow, so I—I begged him to take me with him on your big boat."

"Oh, honey! Your daddy would be terribly hurt to know you even thought of leaving him and your lovely home. Don't you like living on the plantation?"

"Oh, yes! I do, and so does Scotty. But we just didn't know how else to be together, and he said ship captains can marry people at sea. . . ."

Astonished at that statement, Devon glanced at Keith for assistance. He had to clear his throat twice to speak. "We'll settle this at the house, children. Come along now!"

He gripped Scotty's hand firmly. Devon led Fawn gently, sighing at her pleas not to tell her father how naughty she had been. "I won't, dear, if you'll promise to tell him yourself."

"Yes, ma'am. Tomorrow."

Overhearing, Keith said sternly, "This evening, Fawn, when

he comes home from Richmond."

"But it would spoil your farewell supper," she supplicated, already aware of feminine wiles. "I don't want to do that, Mr. Keith. Please don't make me!" Then she had another idea. "Tell you what, sir. You can spank me, just to make sure I get chastised. And then Daddy can do it again, after you all sail. Two spankings should be enough, don't you think, sir?"

Her sharp little mind was a keen match for his son's, and Keith suppressed a smile, maintaining a stern countenance, lest either child think him outwitted. "I'll leave your discipline up to your father, young lady."

Fawn winced, familiar with the feel of the willow switch on her bottom and legs. "Yes, sir. It'll hurt, too."

Hoping to delay the inevitable as long as possible, Scott inquired if they might ride in the pony trap once more before dark. "You may not," Keith replied emphatically. "Indeed, you may not leave our sight for more than a few minutes for the rest of the day. And don't dare try any tricks!"

"Furthermore," Devon added, "I want to speak with you privately, Fawn, while Scotty's daddy deals with him."

"Yes, ma'am."

Humbled in humiliation, the two went docilely to whatever fate awaited them. And judging from their covert glances at each other, they did not regret their exciting adventure, only the consequences of it.

Ushering his son into the library and sliding the doors together, Keith demanded an explanation as he removed his belt. "Do you realize the worry and anguish you caused your mother and me by your disobedience? It's a miracle that you and Fawn are still alive! Weren't you warned about the dangers in that tunnel and forbidden to enter it?"

"But nothing happened, Daddy."

"That's not the point, son. Next, you jeopardized Fawn and yourself by rowing out to the *Sprite*. You weren't paddling a canoe on a placid pond, Scott! You could have gotten into bad trouble on that river."

"The Hudson is bigger, and I've sculled on it."

"Not without me! Take your pants down, boy, and breech across that lounge chair."

"Can't we discuss this more?"

"Do as I say, Scott!"

"Yes, sir. But I won't cry, no matter how long and hard you hit. You can't make me cry!"

"That's your prerogative."

Scotty bore the stinging leather valiantly, without a whimper, gritting his teeth and trying to concentrate on other things. Although it hurt, he knew his father was not employing nearly the force of which he was capable. And, as on other rare occasions of corporal punishment, the administrator was suffering as much as the recipient, if not more. The lashes were fewer than anticipated, or possibly deserved, no more than five or six, during which Scotty clenched his hands and uttered no audible complaint. "Is it over?" he asked then, voice and chin quivering.

Keith nodded, replacing his belt. He had been careful not to let the gold buckle strike or bruise any flesh. The faint red stripes would not linger past the soreness of his buttocks, he knew, having received enough such discipline from his own father at that age. Most injured, as in his own case, was his boyish pride; lessons learned in embarrassment were always impressive, however temporary. Keith turned away, scanning the bookshelves, while Scotty pulled up and fastened his breeches.

"Do you understand why that whipping was necessary, son?" he asked, turning back to him.

"Because I was bad?"

"Worse than that, Scott. We're guests in this house, and you involved Mr. Haverston's daughter in your misdeeds. I don't care whose idea it was, originally, or whether or not you hatched it together; you're older than Fawn and should have known better. We could have lost you both!"

"I'm sorry, Daddy."

"You should be, son, and I trust you won't deliberately provoke such paternal discipline again soon. I don't relish it, you know."

"May I go now, sir?"

"Not outside, or anywhere else with Fawn, unless your mother or I am present. Is that clear?"

"Yes, sir." He hesitated, measuring his father's seriousness. "I really like this plantation, Daddy, and Fawn invited me to stay as long as I like. When I told her I couldn't, she decided to visit me in New York. We thought it would be fun to escape through the hidden passage, pretend we were running away."

"Pretend?" Keith knit his brows. "You were playing a game, acting out a fantasy? And did you expect to board the yacht unnoticed?"

"We hoped the crew wouldn't tell on us, until after we sailed. Then it would be too late. I was going to hide Fawn in my cabin."

"In your bunk?"

"My sea chest."

"Good grief! She might have suffocated in there."

"No, sir. I'd have propped the lid up for air. I read how to do it in a story about a stowaway. And I'd have stolen food for her from the galley, too, if Rufus wouldn't give me any."

"That's fantastic, Scott! Quite a scheme for kids your age. But you underestimated your elders; adults are never quite as stupid and gullible as you might think or hope. Mr. Haverston would have had a posse searching for you, probably with bloodhounds."

"Like the planters used to hunt runaway slaves?"

"Well, not for the same reason. We would have assumed you were just lost somewhere on the property. This is an enormous place, with plenty of roaming space."

"And freedom," Scott ventured. "Not with armed guards always watching, like at Halcyon. That's why I like it here so much, Daddy. And Mr. Daniel invited us to come back in the fall, to hunt foxes. I'd like to ride in the meets with Fawn, and I think Mommy would enjoy it, too. May we?"

"We'll see," Keith muttered. "The lower shelves on the wall behind you contain children's books. Select one and read until supper. Miss Vale is going to be mighty upset with your behavior in her absence, and she has my permission to chastise you however she sees fit."

"That'll be a thousand lines on the slate," he estimated, groaning. "Maybe a million!"

"Whatever, you'll obey without complaint."

"Yes, sir," he agreed, perusing the designated library for an appealing title.

* * *

Upstairs, in the parlor, Devon took a different course with Daniel's daughter. Despite her innocence, her attempted runaway with a young boy was food for thought. And her childish babble about a ship's captain "marrying people at sea" was even more so.

"That was a very foolish thing you and Scotty did today, Fawn. Tell me the truth, now: the real reason you wanted to go away with Scotty."

"It's a secret," she murmured, staring at her small white kid slippers, soiled from the trek through the dirty tunnel, and minus a bow. The sash and ruffles of her dainty sprigged-dimity frock were also stained and bedraggled, her coppery hair tangled and a smudge on her cheek, so that she resembled a street urchin.

"I won't tell, Fawn. I promise."

"Cross your heart and hope to die?"

Devon made the symbolic gesture. And Fawn, apparently convinced that she could trust this kind, lovely lady of whom her father seemed so fond, hesitated only slightly before confiding, "I—I love him."

"Darling, you mean you *like* Scotty, don't you? Love is a very strong, grown-up feeling that big people have for each other. It's for boys and girls much older than you and Scotty."

"And for married folks?"

"Usually. But never at your age, dear."

"A Nigra girl, one of our sharecropper's daughters, got married at eleven last year, Miss Devon. Pretty soon her tummy swoll up, big as a watermelon, and the servants said she was going to get a baby. One day later on, I heard her screaming and crying in the cabin with her ma and aunt, and she died. They buried her and the baby in the old slave cemetery, near the pasture. Then her pa went crazy and beat her husband with a chain, and drove him off the plantation, clear out of the county. Daddy had to stop him from killing the poor fellow."

"That's awful, Fawn, and I'm sorry it happened. Is that all you know about that sad story?"

"Her older sister, Miranda, said it was because Tom and Louisa were bad together in the field. Then her ma shushed her with a cornstalk and sent me home."

Devon regretted broaching the subject. Fawn was much too

young for such a heavy exposure to the facts of life, from which Southern girls were sheltered well into their teens. Planters' daughters were kept away from the breeding pens until after marriage. Cats bred at night, and hunting hounds were locked in the kennels with selected females in heat. It was highly unlikely that Fawn had ever witnessed, as Scotty had at Halcyon, anything whatever to do with reproduction, and it was certainly not Devon's place to enlighten her.

"You really should have a governess, dear. I'm surprised your father hasn't hired one for you yet."

"He tried, Miss Devon, but couldn't find just the right lady. Anyway, I'm going to boarding school in September. My teacher at the parish school says I'm smart enough to enter Rosewood Female Academy. But I wish Scotty and I could go to school together."

"I'm afraid that's not possible, child. Scotty will be enrolled in a boys' school in the North, soon. You'll be with girls only, at Charlottsville, and many miles apart."

"But we can write, can't we?" She twisted her little fingers, and Devon noticed a gold birthstone ring. "We *promised* each other."

"Of course, Fawn." But the intensity of her plea generated another disturbing thought in Devon's mind. "Remember, all this is still our secret, so I want you to be truthful. Besides being disobedient, did you and Scotty do anything else naughty today? Like touching each other?"

"You mean, holding hands?"

"More than that?"

Fawn blushed, contemplating her shoes again. "We kissed once, on the cheek."

"That's all?" Devon patted the brocade settee, encouraging the confused girl to sit beside her. As Fawn obeyed, she smiled and brushed a curl from her forehead, prompting, "Honor bright?"

"Well, in the tunnel—"

"Yes?" Devon virtually held her breath.

"We got real scared, once, so scared we both had to go to the toilet. Scotty held my candle while I did, but he looked away, so he didn't see my drawers even, which I sort of wet. But I peeked at him, and I know that was wrong, a sin, and God will punish me."

"Then why did you do it, Fawn?"

"I was curious, Miss Devon. He can stand to tinkle, and I have to squat. His body is different from mine."

"That difference is called male and female, Fawn. Boy and girl, and you should have allowed Scotty his privacy, too. Peeking at him wasn't nice, not nice at all."

"You won't tell Daddy?" she asked anxiously.

"No, darling. We made a pact, a promise, and I won't break it. But, baby, there's so much you need to know!" She needed a mother, desperately, and Devon wished Daniel had at least one prospect in mind. But he seemed totally uninterested in any other woman, although a number were obviously interested in him.

"Baby?" repeated Fawn. "Oh, golly gee, Miss Devon! I won't swell up and die, like Louisa, will I?"

"No, honey, no!" Devon hastily assured her. "I was calling *you* a baby, because you're so young and innocent. Is there anything else you would like to tell me, Fawn? Anything at all?"

"I don't think so, Miss Devon. I just hope Mr. Keith didn't punish Scotty too hard. I reckon not, because I haven't heard him cry. He's so brave, you know. And so smart, the smartest boy I know, and the best looking, too! I really do like him a lot, and he likes me. When we're old enough, may we get married and be together always?"

"Oh, sweetheart, that's still a long way off!" Devon hugged her to her bosom, thinking of her own daughters. One day, Sharon and Shannon would be this age and probably as naive and confused and bewildered about life. But they would have a mother to consult and confide in, to help solve their feminine problems—and this poor little girl had none. Devon embraced her again, maternally, as if Fawn were her own. Ironically, she might have been. . . .

☙ 21 ❧

THEIR BON voyage was as courteous and spectacular as their welcome: liveried servants in attendance; the polished landau drawn by handsomely caparisoned horses; the baggage following in a special vehicle. Daniel and his daughter stood on the landing, waving as the *Sprite* steamed down the James River and out to sea. Devon would not soon forget Dan's sorrowful expression, nor Fawn's poignancy as she fluttered her lacy handkerchief and blew kisses to Scotty, who was also visibly affected by the parting.

En route to Savannah, they put into Charleston, and Devon remained aboard while Keith attended to business. Viewing the Battery with its beautiful old pillared and galleried mansions, and the skyline limned with church spires, she wondered what might have been her destiny had not the Confederacy fired those fateful shots on Fort Sumter that April day in 1861. Would she have wed the scion of Harmony Hilll, become the mistress of that vast plantation and its numerous slaves? Probably so, to please her father more than herself. For while he had prized her intelligence and assistance in his profession, Hodge Marshall had believed, like all Southerners, that a woman was happiest in marriage and motherhood. Devon doubted he would ever have understood her desperate, unconventional flight to New York with Keith Curtis.

Miss Vale used the time in Charleston to give her pupil on-the-scene lessons in American history. Along with other pertinent information, Scott learned about the Carolina Lords Proprietors of the Low Country, their once elaborate rice and indigo plantations along the Ashley and Cooper rivers, with gardens rivaling those of Buckingham Palace and Versailles, and about the slave system and its demise.

186

In Savannah, she taught him about General Sherman's devastating March to the Sea, which had ended with the burning of this port and prefaced the South's defeat. The boy absorbed it all with scholarly interest, jotting notes in his tablet for future tests. Intermittently, however, his mind strayed back to Virginia and Fawn Haverston, and these thoughts baffled him as much as the strange sensations that periodically seized his body, particularly when alone at night. He contemplated confiding them to his father, but their filial relationship was somewhat strained since his whipping at Harmony Hill. His only consolation was that Fawn had not heard him cry, which restraint had been exceedingly difficult, and he would long remember it.

When at last the Curtises were homeward bound again, Scotty was not happy, and remained in his cabin much of the time.

Some nostalgia still lingered for Devon as the *Sprite* approached Staten Island, steaming into Lower New York Bay, through the Narrows, and finally up the Hudson River to its berth at Halcyon Landing. Suddenly, inexplicably, "Carry me Back to Old Virginia" hummed in her heart and mind and soul, and she had to suppress her emotions. Never forced to leave his birthplace, how could Keith understand her innate attachment to hers? The roots she had believed dead were apparently only dormant; revived by the long visit, they flourished again in memory, and she would have to guard against visible nurturing. New York was her home now: the present. Virginia was the past and must remain so, forever. But would it?

Her homecoming was both happy and tearful, for the babies had almost forgotten their parents. They had taken their first steps during their absence, and Devon would always regret missing this important stage in their development. Now they were toddling about the nursery, with Nanny or Enid in constant attendance. Their physical and emotional differences, so noticeable even at birth, were more so now and increasing daily.

Their first birthday, falling conveniently on a Sunday, was marked with a small family party. Compared with the many fabulous and exciting entertainments at Harmony Hill, however, Scotty found this celebration dull and ordinary. Already he missed Fawn's interesting, mischievous company and had fervently hoped a letter from her would be waiting upon his arrival home. Perhaps there was one at Gramercy Park, for he had given her both addresses and written to her at sea, posting his missives in the Charleston and Savannah harbors.

Anna baked two angel food cakes, each decorated with spun-sugar flowers and a lighted pink candle, which the twins succeeded in blowing out. Before the refreshments could be served, however, Sharon raised up in her highchair and pressed both hands into her cake. Laughing gleefully at the destruction, she reached over to similarly demolish her sister's cake. Shannon slapped at her and spoke her first positive words, "No, no!"

Keith grinned, winking at Devon. "Weren't those the same first words you spoke to me, and in the same tone? I hope she remembers them when she grows into a raving beauty like her mommy."

Devon blushed, admonishing him. "What Sharon did wasn't cute, Daddy, and she should be chastised."

"On her birthday?" Keith addressed Dr. Blake. "How does their godfather feel about it?"

Ramsey shrugged, also amused by their different characters, and as proud of them as if they were his own. "I'm neutral, my friend. But Shannon seems capable of defending herself, and she *is* going to be her lovely mother's image," he predicted, glancing fondly at Devon. "Which is not to say that her sister will be an ugly duckling. Far from it, and Prince Charming will have much ado choosing between them."

As her twin was taken off to be cleaned up, Shannon smiled, exposing her new upper teeth, and Keith couldn't resist picking her up and cuddling her. "Daddy's little darling, from head to toe, and Daddy loves her more than she'll ever know. And Sharon, too, no matter how naughty she is!"

"I bet Daddy'll never use a belt on them," Scott muttered, eating his cake and ice cream.

Surrendering Shannon to Enid, Keith immediately sat at the table beside his sullen son. "Still sulking about that, Scotty? And do you think a year-old infant deserves a licking for squashing a cake? You created a holy mess on your first birthday, too, and made me wear a silly Yankee Doodle hat and blow a tin horn for hours. Ask your mother, if you don't believe me."

"How could a baby make an adult do anything?"

"By crying when I stopped playing the game, that's how! So I kept on—and spoiled you, didn't I? You expected to get off scot-free, so to speak, for your misbehavior at Harmony Hill, and still resent your well-deserved discipline. That's your problem now, isn't it?"

"Not really."

"What, then?"

"I—I think you coddle the twins too much, sir. You're always fussing over them!"

"Always? We've been away over a month, Scotty. Babies forget easily, so we must give them some extra attention. But that doesn't mean we love you any less, and you're too bright to think and feel that way. We're a family, son, and we want to share everything, most of all our love and affection for one another. Shall we help the girls open their gifts when Sharon gets back?"

"I guess so," he agreed morosely as Nanny returned her other charge, with face and hands washed and a more practical muslin pinafore replacing the dainty organdy one.

His lack of enthusiasm turned into boredom as the feminine toys were revealed. And the gurgling, infantile antics, which so engaged the adults, exasperated him. His mother was pretending to talk through the dolls, which were named Sharon and Shannon, his father making strange noises for the stuffed animals, and everyone, including the dignified doctor, had donned crazy caps and made fools of themselves playing with balloons, whistles, and tinny bugles.

Since Karl and Lars Hummel was among the merrymakers, Scott excused himself and went out to the stables to saddle his own mount. Remembering his jaunts with Fawn Haverston, he knew his lonely rides would never be as enjoyable anymore. Kids were just more fun, and he had never met anyone quite like her before. He would write to her again this evening, saying how much he missed her and the plantation, what a marvelous holiday it was, and inviting the Haverstons to visit them at Halcyon. And would sign it, "Yours truly, Scotty." Or maybe, "Forever yours, Scotty."

That evening, lying together in the same bed in which all of their children were born, Devon sensed Keith's worry over their son. "I'm afraid Scotty wasn't very polite at the party," she apologized for him. "He totally forgot his manners."

Keith sighed. "That's an understatement, Devon. He was embarrassingly rude! And when I went to his room to say good night, he pretended to be asleep. How was he with you?"

"A little reserved," she said. "Maybe he feels he has outgrown that parental tucking-in routine. I ignored his reticence. How did you handle his pretense?"

"Oh, I couldn't let him realize I knew he was faking, and just left quietly. But I've decided it's time to send him away to school, Devon. He needs that kind of environment. We've kept him too close to us."

"He's begging me to take him back to Virginia for the hunt season, Keith."

"Let him beg! Neither of you is going South this fall, although I may have to again on business."

"I see," she murmured, moving slightly away, creating a space between them on the mattress. "Am I being indirectly chastised for Scotty's folly at Harmony Hill? Maybe you feel I also misbehaved somehow?"

"No, I just think we've all had enough Southern exposure for one year—and have more important things to do this autumn than chase foxes."

"You're so right, darling. I have articles to write for the *Record*, and tracts for the Women's Movement."

"I didn't mean *that*."

"What did you mean? If it's boarding school for the boy and business for you—what's my important mission? To help launch the Manhattan social season? Plan our costumes for the masquerades? Entertain the frumps and gossips at tea?"

"Go to sleep," he muttered. "I have to leave early tomorrow, you know."

"Alone?"

"Unless you want to accompany me on the commuter train, Mrs. Curtis. I've neglected the bank long enough."

"And I my maternal duties here," Devon said, buffing his cheek. "Good night, Keith."

"Some kiss! I got better from my daughters."

"You just reminded me of your early departure—I assumed you wanted to rest. Didn't you tell me to go to sleep?"

"Since when do you do everything I say?"

"Do you want to make love?"

"Do you?"

"Aren't you tired?"

"Are you?"

"Why are we answering questions with questions?"

"Why are we bickering?"

"There, you've done it again!"

"I'm sorry, Devon. I guess I'm just worried, afraid I've annihilated Scott. My only son!"

"Oh, Keith, that's not true! Scotty loves you and will forget that discipline at Harmony Hill. His sibling rivalry with his sisters will pass, too. Ramsey says his reaction is completely normal for a brother his age."

"Is that what you were discussing in your little tête-à-tête on the loveseat?"

"That's a hard oak settle, not a cozy settee! And it was a medical conversation."

"And is it the learned physician's opinion that our son is already in puberty?"

"The first stage, yes. Verging on adolescence."

"Don't you think, my dear, it would be more appropriate for Ramsey to discuss that subject with me?"

"I do, indeed. And he will, if you mention it to him, as I did. Talk to him on his next visit."

"I will, if I'm here, and he can stop admiring you long enough to spare me some time."

"My, you are in a foul mood! An irascible grouch, to put it mildly."

"Growling like a bear with his tail caught in a trap?"

"Precisely."

"Well, you know how to soothe the savage breast," he proposed, drawing her into his arms. "Oh, Devon, I want so desperately to feel secure about our life together! About our love and marriage and children. When any part of that security and unity is threatened, as it was in Virginia, and with Scotty this afternoon, I get afraid, then suspicious, and then ridiculous. Forgive me, darling, for being so jealous and possessive, and hurting you with cruel and stupid remarks. Why do you put up with me?"

"Shall I give you a hint?"

"Please."

No other man could so effectively melt her heart; humble her while humbling herself; simultaneously arouse her passion and compassion. Clasping him to her breast, she nurtured him in every vital way, until all was right and rapturous between them again, and as beautiful and permanent as anything could be on this earth.

"That's more like it," he said when finally they kissed good-night. "I just may want an encore before dawn."

"And I just may want one sooner, my love. . . ."

Aware of the date of his return to New York, Keith's sec-retary had flowers in the executive office and a ribbon greeting on the door. As he walked in, hat and portfolio in hand, sar-torially perfect in his custom-tailored clothes, Marnie Ryan flung her arms around his neck and planted a kiss on his smooth-shaven face, impulse overwhelming decorum. Holy Saints! What had she done? She stepped back, embarrassed and apol-ogetic. "Your pardon, sir! I was so happy to see you again, I—I forgot myself. Welcome back!"

Keith smiled, trying to put her at ease. "Thank you, Miss Ryan. It's nice to know I was missed so much."

"Did you enjoy your vacation? You look so fine, so tan and healthy."

"The sun and sea will do that," he said, flashing another arresting smile. "I know things ran smoothly here, because Mr. Hammermill kept in touch by wire, thanks to your memos." He indicated the sentimental banner on his private portal, sug-gesting its removal, although he allowed the bouquet to remain on the credenza, beside the photograph of his wife and children.

"All of this?" he asked, surveying the neat stacks of mail on his desk, many with foreign postmarks.

"That's only the personal letters, sir. Mr. Hammermill and I took care of the general business correspondence, per your instructions."

"Well, I'll have to read the rest later," he decided. "It's time for the Monday board meeting. Afterward, we'll go over your notes on those I missed."

"They're typed and in your files, sir." She gazed at him

intently, her spring suit as sky-blue as her Irish eyes, the tiny freckles barely visible across her pixieish nose. "May I say again how good it is to have you back, Mr. Curtis?"

"Yes, Miss Ryan." His voice was almost brusque with embarrassment. "Now get your shorthand book and come to the Board Room, please."

"Right away, sir."

Later, studying some transcripts of previous sessions while Marnie interpreted from her original notes, Keith caught a faint whiff of lavender never before scented on her person. When had she begun using cologne in the office? Or was it just the soap fragrance of her freshly washed hair, in which a sharpened pencil was professionally tucked?

"Repeat that last paragraph, please. I seem to have lost track in my report."

"Is something amiss, Mr. Curtis?"

"Nothing, except that our chairs are too close. We're bumping elbows, and it's distracting."

"I'll move mine to the front of your desk."

"The side will do."

Marnie obliged before clarifying the requested information from her record. She had feared that she had made some typographical errors.

"Thank you, Miss Ryan. You may go to lunch now."

"I bring it with me, sir. My budget won't allow for restaurants, not even the working girls' favorite Gosling's."

"How is your father?"

"Cantankerous," she replied matter-of-factly. "His injuries give him considerable pain. But opiates are so expensive, and addictive, too."

"He shouldn't have to suffer, though."

"Oh, he's tough enough to take it! And Father O'Toole, our parish priest, says pain strengthens the character and prepares the soul for the hereafter, should Heaven not be its destination. I gain plenary indulgences by enduring Pa's grumbling and complaints." She spoke earnestly, believing every concept and precept of her religion. "With enough such indulgences, Pa may only have to go to Purgatory."

"You're a fine daughter," Keith complimented. "Still living in that same Bowery tenement?"

Marnie nodded. "But it's not so bad, sir. I've fixed it up rather nicely, with paint and curtains. At least it's clean, and as free of pests as possible in those infested warrens."

"When do you find time for such work?"

"On Sunday after Mass, and at night."

"No beaus?"

"One, in the same block. We attend church together. But we're just friends."

"Friendship can develop into more, Miss Ryan. Does he have a job?"

"Horsecar conductor." She smiled, confiding, "He lets me ride free on his line sometimes."

"Ah, ha! Your motives are mercenary?" he teased, suppressing laughter.

Marnie was crushed. Cheating on her fare was an immoral conspiracy with the omnibus driver, pilfering from his company, and wrong for both of them. "You're right, sir. I'll confess my sin, and pay hereafter. Maybe I should make restitution, too."

"My dear, I was joking! And no merciful God would hold those few pennies against you. But to ease your conscience, there'll be another raise in your next paycheck."

"So soon? Isn't that against company policy?"

"I'm the company, Miss Ryan." He shuffled some papers on his desk. "Surely you're familiar with that old adage about not looking a gift horse in the mouth?"

"Indeed, sir. It's a favorite quote of Irishmen who frequent the race tracks."

"Then don't question my judgment, Miss Ryan. I gamble on many things: horses, cards, billiards, steamboat races, the stock market, and, occasionally, even on people."

"People, sir?"

"I gambled in hiring you, young lady, and won the best confidential secretary on Wall Street," Keith said, waving his hand in dismissal, and Marnie never lingered after such a definite signal.

PART THREE

My hopes of the future rest on girls. I believe America's future pivots on the great woman revolution.

Dr. Dio Lewis
OUR GIRLS, published 1871

If I am anything, I am a woman of tomorrow.

Kate Field (1838–1896)
Noted 19th Century journalist

It exasperates me to be unable to do anything without being accused of eccentricity.

Sarah Bernhardt (1844–1923)

A woman is a foreign land,
      which, though there he settle young,
A man will ne'er quite understand
The customs, politics, and tongue.

Coventry K. D. Patmore (1823–1896)
WOMAN

The ballot is stronger than the bullet.

Abraham Lincoln (1809–1865)

Mr. President, how long must women wait for liberty?

Susan B. Anthony (1820–1906)

Men to new joys and conquests fly,
And yet no hazard run.
Poor we are left if we deny,
And if we yield undone.

Then equal laws let custom find,
And neither sex oppress.
More freedom give to womankind,
Or give to mankind less.

from THE LADY'S COMPLAINT, published in
the VIRGINIA GAZETTE of October 15–22, 1736

If thou must love me, let it be for naught
Except for love's sake only.

Elizabeth Barrett Browning (1806–1861)
SONNETS FROM THE PORTUGUESE

✣ 22 ✤

SUMMER, AS USUAL, was unbearable in the city, and Keith spent longer weekends in the country, frequently leaving the bank as early as Thursday noon for his haven on the Hudson.

Devon did most of her writing in the upstairs sitting room, which had been transformed into a comfortable study-retreat by the installation of a desk, a filing cabinet, and bookshelves. The trip to Virginia had inspired her, as perhaps nothing else could have, to seriously begin the long-contemplated antebellum novel. She did not neglect her commitments to the Women's Bureau, however, and especially not the Child Labor Committee, which she chaired. She wrote comprehensive pamplets for the mailing campaign to congressional leaders, and excellent articles for the New York *Record,* many of which were reprinted in other publications. Research on all her projects was extensive and often exhausting, and Devon knew she could not have accomplished nearly as much without the servants, nurse, and governess. Indeed, Heather Vale's encyclopaedic knowledge of history made her a valuable consultant. The children were well cared for, and both households ran smoothly, even though Devon was absent more from Gramercy Park, where she still was not entirely comfortable unless Keith was with her. She continued to experience odd chills and premonitions in the third-floor chambers of the former mistress, though none of the domestic staff was similarly affected, not even the highly superstitious Irish maid, Briget Hollihan, who had attended Esther during the final years of her life and had no qualms about cleaning the "haunted" rooms.

Although lonely in town without his wife, Keith knew the country atmosphere was much healthier for her and the children. Manhattan became a steaming Turkish bath during July and August, so debilitating that horses and mules often collapsed in their harness, elderly citizens suffered strokes, heat-related childhood ailments were rampant, and rabid dogs created a fearful menace. The thick masonry walls of the Curtis Bank and his brownstone residence provided some insulation and relief, along with properly ventilated windows, and cool morning baths prepared him to cope with the business days. But he wondered how his secretary managed to appear so fresh and eager while performing her myriad duties. Miss Ryan must rise well before dawn to accommodate her incapacitated father's needs and still arrive punctually at the office. A single flower and sprig of fern invariably brightened her desk, and Keith thought in addition to her horsecar conductor friend, she must also have an admiring florist or vendor.

Day after day, as she ate her lonely lunch, he considered inviting her to share a good meal at a pleasant restaurant. But he dared not risk the wild speculation even an occasional such kindness might create in the Street, nor the possible misunderstanding at home. Devon's jealousy of him was no less than his of her, and he bowed to discretion in marital matters.

The Curtises spent an enjoyable hiatus at Saratoga Springs, and another at the fabulous Mountain House in the Catskills, reminiscing about previous marvelous holidays at both famous resorts. Early in September, the *Sprite* sailed to Newport with the entire family aboard, to assess the progress of their future summer residence. And though Devon had some conception of its dimensions and exterior from the architectural plans, she was astonished when they visited the actual construction site. A special wharf and warehouse had been built to accommodate the tons of imported materials, including a mountain of white Cararra marble, and European ships arrived with their entire cargoes consigned to Mr. Keith Heathstone Curtis. Hundreds of wagons and workmen, including expert Roman and Greek stonecutters hired abroad, swarmed over the property, busy from dawn to dusk, six days a week. Devon could not have been more awed if she were observing the building of the Taj Mahal, a pharaonic pyramid, or a royal castle.

"Isn't it a little pretentious?" she asked in breathless wonder, "and flamboyant?"

"That's how Newporters build their cottages," Keith apprised. "I was advised upon purchase of this land that anything costing less than a million would be scorned and even ridiculed in the community. Our contribution will qualify in excess of five times that figure."

"They don't just live and entertain in these summer palaces, Keith—they rule and hold court! But I never imagined us in such ostentatious splendor."

"Nor I, Devon. But New Yorkers are invading Newport now, and there won't be a parcel of waterfront property left in a few years. Availability was a prime factor, and I can't ignore building codes and restrictions, so I'll exceed them. It's a wise investment, financially and socially, for our children. The twins can make their debut here."

"Royalty could proclaim here," Devon murmured, still astounded.

"Well, my daughters are princesses to me."

"And your son a crown prince? Oh, the fortunate progeny of the King of Wall Street! But your first 'queen' would have been more appropriately enthroned in this grandeur, and certainly it's more befitting to her Brahmin peerage. Is this my fertility award for producing?"

Keith frowned, disliking the press-bestowed titles even more than his spouse, and chagrined by her last remark. "I was speaking paternally, my dear. Emotionally, not literally."

"I know, Keith. I'm just overwhelmed, and unable to cope with my emotions at all."

"Worried about your reception by the local grandes dames?" he perceived, uncannily. "You had no difficulty in New York, and you'll have none in Newport."

"By royal decree, Midas?"

"If necessary, milady," he bowed, self-mockery etching his cynical smile. "Only, in this case, the emperor is not naked. He *has* the proper clothes!"

His strong arm circled her waist, imparting trust and reassurance, and Devon relaxed against him. He did indeed possess the golden raiment, adorned by power and influence, that counted most in America and the mercenary world. *Lèse-majesté* would be accorded them in whichever realm they lived or traveled.

"Of course, sire," she agreed, chiding herself for doubting him. "Have you noticed the heir apparent's fascination with that huge derrick and crane?"

"He's analyzing the mechanics so he can construct a model with his erector set."

"Maybe he'll decide to study architecture and engineering at Harvard."

"Fine. I admire a broad education, as long as Scott realizes where his real responsibilities lie, which I'm confident he will." But his face donned a saturnine mask as he paused in retrospect. "He exhibited some interest in a certain Southern plantation, but I can't conceive of his ever wanting to be a planter."

"Or marrying a planter's daughter?"

That struck him like an arrow in the heart, and he automatically removed his physical support. "Are you attaching future significance to his childhood friendship with Fawn Haverston? They'll forget each other when school work keeps them too busy to correspond. Lord, but you're a romantic little soul! Your antebellum novel should have wide appeal to the ladies, especially in the South."

"It'll contain some exciting fox-hunting scenes," Devon ventured, hoping he would reconsider the invitation to ride to hounds at Harmony Hill.

"Good! Your knowledge of that noble sport should win accolades from Newport's horse enthusiasts." He consulted his ornate Swiss watch, whose dangling gold seals delighted his little daughters. "The architects and contractors are waiting to discuss some details with me. Do you want to participate?"

"I think I'd rather wait until the decorating stage," Devon shied off.

"That's at least two years away, Mrs. Curtis, and we'll need a christening upon completion, usually an elaborate house-warming party here, so be thinking of a suitable name for our cottage."

White Elephant came immediately to mind, but Devon did not voice it. She knew from her journalistic travels with the Grants that Americans were as fanciful as Europeans in naming their villas and châteaux on the Atlantic Coast. "We'll decide together, dear, when the time comes. Rufus will be serving

dinner at the usual hour," she reminded him, beckoning Scotty
to return to the yacht with her.

"I'd enjoy a New England clambake, right on our own
beautiful beach. Perhaps we could have one tomorrow?"

"I'm sure your marvelous genie can arrange anything you
wish," Devon assured him. "But I'm still curious about your
long delay in acquiring real estate on the Rhode Island Riviera."
What better setting, she mulled, for the imperious Empress
Esther!

"I thought I'd satisfied your curiosity on that point long
ago," he replied with an oblique glance. "Esther preferred Na-
hant, Massachusetts, and Bar Harbor, Maine. I had agents
scouting both locations when our marital walls came tumbling
down like Jericho, wreaking havoc and chaos. My spirit was
crushed, my life in shambles, and I had little interest in anything. I considered sailing off to some remote island, growing
a Crusoe beard, and living in a grass hut with a native girl.
But only in fancy! A lot of people were dependent on me for
their livelihood. I had inherited the 'Curtis Empire,' you see,
and I owed a great responsibility to my ancestors. Heritage and
tradition can be burdens as well as treasures, with grave duties
and obligations binding on the male heir of the dynasty."

"And you were Number-One Son?"

"And only," he said ruefully. "There was no one to succeed
me then—and if there had been, we wouldn't be standing here
now, discussing any of this, including what to call our great
white marble elephant." He smiled wryly as her eyes widened.
"No, my dear, I'm not clairvoyant, although I did pick up on
your earlier thoughts. Isn't it rather obvious, viewing our neighbors' abodes? We're surrounded by white elephants!" Several
men holding manifests and roles of blueprints were gesturing
to him, and Keith signaled back. "Now do you understand?"

Nodding, Devon hissed him quickly and waited for the boy
sauntering toward her. Resting her hand on his shoulder, she
asked, "Do you think you'll like spending your summers here,
Scotty?"

"I'll like sailing in these waters," he said. "But I'd enjoy
sailing anywhere, including on Chesapeake Bay."

"Oh? What made you think of that?"

"My last letter from Fawn. Her grandparents have a summer home on the Chesapeake, and she was there on vacation."

"Her father, too?"

"No, just her Grandpa and Grandma Caldwell and her aunt Merilee. Mr. Daniel was too busy with his plantation and tobacco factory to join them. Fawn will be going off to boarding school next week, just as I will. We've already given each other our addresses away from home. I can't wait to write to her about Newport." Reaching the private pier and mounting the gangway, he suddenly suggested, "Let's pretend we're walking the plank, Mother."

"Why, son?"

"Because that's how Fawn and I felt when we were taken off the *Sprite* at Harmony Hill. And Daddy was Captain Kidd, when he punished me. His belt was a whip, and I was tied to the mast, not leaning over a chair. Then I was confined in the brig, instead of the library."

"Oh, Scotty, you must forget that incident! Your father has suffered much remorse over his action and your attitude. You're a prince in his eyes, but even a real little prince must be disciplined when naughty, lest he become a tyrant. Wasn't Fawn chastised for her mischief?"

He shrugged, stepping along the board bridge. "I don't know. She never said, and I never asked. It was so mortifying, Mother!"

Devon sighed, following him aboard. Parenthood, never easy, was becoming increasingly difficult and complicated. Should she mention this conversation to Keith? No, it would devastate him. . . .

✣ 23 ✣

THE EMPTINESS created by the young master's absence was keenly felt by everyone at Halcyon, but most especially by his parents. The atmosphere was funereal at times, as if he had departed permanently from their lives. Devon plunged deeper into her writing and work at the Women's Bureau, and Keith into business. Already employed as future governess to the twins, Heather Vale kept busy assisting Mrs. Curtis as personal secretary, and Nanny in the nursery.

It was mid-October now, and though Scotty would be home for the Thanksgiving holidays, the parental temptation to visit him before then had to be resisted in his best interests. But Devon, conditioned by previous long separations from her child, was enduring this scholastic one better than his father. Indeed, Keith appeared so depressed for a while that she traveled to and from Manhattan with him, despite her aversion to the urban dwelling.

"It's for his own good," he insisted whenever doubts about his decision assailed him. "But maybe we should have hired a male tutor and kept him with us a few more years."

"We were both in boarding school at his age, Keith."

"But what if he's homesick?"

"Most children are their first time away from home," Devon told him. "I certainly was during my freshman year at Rosewood, frequently and intensely so, and you must have been when you entered Groton, too. But those feelings are natural and usually temporary, aren't they?"

"I suppose so."

They were in the Gramercy Park library, which was far more extensive than that of Halcyon, and where Devon and Miss Vale had been engaged in research most of the day. Now it was evening and Heather was in her room, transcribing their notes in the journal marked *Untitled Novel*.

The disturbing chilliness Devon had experienced earlier disappeared with Keith's presence, and she removed her capelet. But his floor pacing distracted her, and she marked her place in the biography of General Robert E. Lee she was perusing. "Darling, Scotty will be home in November, and again in December. You act as if he were on another continent, miles across the sea. He's just across Long Island Sound, not the Atlantic Ocean."

"I can't help how I feel, Devon. And I'm considering crossing the Sound to Connecticut this weekend."

"Now, Keith, you know the school officials discourage impromptu visits! Scotty isn't complaining about being lonesome in his letters, is he?"

"They're too brief and formal for complaints," he said, frowning. "Only slightly improvised from the examples provided by the administration to keep in touch with the family when I was there. I recognize them from my own 'Dear Father and Mother' days."

Devon suppressed a smile. "Did you expect 'Dear Daddy and Mommy'? He's maturing, Keith, a bit faster than either of us might like, perhaps, but that's life. And apparently you were no different. You just admitted addressing your parents the same way at his age, and having to be reminded of your filial duties, too."

"Don't give me that old 'like father, like son' routine again, Devon! I bet his letters to Fawn Haverston are longer, and more personal."

"Really? At Newport, you told me how quickly they would forget each other."

"Do you record everything I say, for future reference? Will I be quoted in your novel?"

"Not verbatim," she promised, winking to lighten his mood. "And no romantic boudoir talk or technique will be revealed, lest the book be banned and the love-starved females throw themselves at your feet."

But he wasn't amused. "That's evasive."

"I'm humoring you, dear, and that's a role reversal, too. It's usually the other way around, isn't it? Relax, Keith, and stop brooding. Did I tell you that Carrie Hempstead asked me to interview Sarah Bernhardt when she arrives for her American debut? Tickets for her first appearance at Booth's Theater are already sold out. She'll perform *La Dame aux Camellias* and three other plays, and I'm anxious to see them all. Thank heaven, we have a box!"

"Wealth does have its advantages, eh?"

Devon ignored the remark, for like most of his cynicism and mockery, it was directed primarily at himself. "Then we will attend the premiere?"

"Of course. Mademoiselle Bernhardt is among the few great stage actresses, in a league with Adelaide Ristori and the late Rachel, and as competent a tragedienne as either of them, although Ristori is more renowned."

"I envy you, Keith. You've seen all the international stars perform, in Europe and England, on your Grand Tour and subsequent trips."

"Oh, well. Didn't you meet the Great Ristori and her handsome Italian count, at one of the Vincent Bottas' celebrity receptions on her New York debut? Now you'll have an opportunity to compare them."

"Only their personalities," Devon said. "Carrie wants an intimate, in-depth profile of the Divine Sarah, not a criticism of her talent, and we hope she will graciously cooperate on personal details."

"Why not? To my knowledge, the Continental press has never accused her of being either reticent or discreet, and rumors about her rampant Bohemianism fill their scandal sheets. I trust you'll be more objective in your assessment? At any rate, you shouldn't have any difficulty extracting pertinent information, considering your charm and professional expertise."

"I hope that's a compliment."

He grinned at her. "It works on me, doesn't it?"

"You're a master of the double entendre."

"I'd rather be master of the double bed."

"You're that, too, and you know it."

"Thank you, Mrs. Curtis. But I'm afraid I've been somewhat remiss in our conjugal relations lately."

"I feared I was at fault, Mr. Curtis, that I'd been neglecting you somehow, though I can't recall pleading any convenient headaches or other feminine excuses."

"No, I'm the guilty party, and I apologize. The tension over Scotty has fouled up my sexual psychology. You know how damned tricky it is for the male of the species."

"For the female, too, on occasion, darling. But I'm adjusting to the situation with our son. I only wish you would, before you wear out the carpet."

"Aubussons don't wear out, my dear. They become family heirlooms, passed on for generations."

"Nevertheless, I think your nervous energy could be put to better use for both of us."

"Oh? Sounds enticing, but you may have to work some of your special magic on the old boy, to get him in the proper mood." He gazed at her significantly. "Any preference in erotic potions?"

"Champagne," she proposed. "And in lieu of gypsy violins, I'll read to you from Ovid."

"In the original?"

"No, my Latin is rather limited. But the other day, I discovered a stimulating translation of some of his most amorous poems and longed to share them with you."

Practiced voluptuary that he was, Keith had long ago committed much of Ovid's erotica to memory and could recite it to her. "I think I know the passages you have in mind, love, and they're already running through mine. We may not even need the stimulant, except as a fillip. But I'll order a bottle anyway, and a bowl of fresh strawberries sent to the master suite," he said, pulling the bellcord.

Accustomed to such exotic, nocturnal requests, the servants promptly executed them and returned to their quarters. Almost immediately, then, Devon was captured in his arms and transported up the stairs with the vigorous, masterful passion she loved and craved. Something, perhaps too-long abstinence, had suddenly inflamed him, for a spontaneous fire raged in his blood, and Devon was eager to stoke it.

Soon they were in private, on the conjugal bed, and he was quoting Ovid as he disrobed her, his sensuous voice as seductive as his foreplay. He kissed every part of her, reveling in the touch and taste and scent of her delectable flesh, all the sensations and sensibilities he knew so well, just as he knew the limit and peak of her endurance; the exact moment when urgency transcended desire and could no longer be sustained. And each time they imagined they had reached the supreme sexual summit, experienced the ultimate coital bliss, and it could not be surpassed, some instinctive gesture or bold innovation proved otherwise.

Physical parting, always slow and reluctant, evolved in languid euphoria. They smiled appreciatively at each other and smirked at the untouched French "aphrodisiac" in the frosted silver bucket. "We didn't even pop the cork," Devon murmured.

Keith laughed, touseling her hair. "Oh, yes, we did, curly top! Several times for you."

"Sexual wonders never cease for us, Keith. I realize that anew each time."

"Rejoice, Devon. Sex is a divine gift to couples blessed with love."

"And a soupçon of lust?"

"Well, we seem to have achieved the perfect balance between those two emotions, darling. Shall we toast our good fortune with some Château Rothschild, celebrate the end of my self-imposed celibacy? Was it actually as long as it seemed?"

"Almost three weeks." Devon sighed as he did the refreshment honors, placing a plump ripe strawberry in her goblet before filling it. "I was getting worried, as well as anxious. In a bad moment, my jealousy ran rampant, and I wondered if there was another woman."

"Perish the thought."

They touched glasses and sipped the excellent champagne, Devon enjoying the berry tartness in hers. Then her eyes traveled down his naked torso, observing the receding tumescence which had just given them both so much pleasure, and Keith explained, "Unfortunately, man's most significant organ can also be his most fickle one, betraying him in crucial situations. I'll try to avoid such future crises—at least until a more natural age for them to occur, physically." His free hand cupped her firm full breast, fondling the still-erect nipple. "Isn't it about time for a gynecological checkup, dear heart?"

"I'm not pregnant, Keith. My menses are regular, and the pessary's still in place."

"It's a good idea anyway, medically. I'll go with you, while we're in town. Ramsey will be moving soon, you know, to his own clinic. He has a large and lucrative practice, including many society ladies. I don't know how he manages to stay single."

"More puzzling, *why?*"

Keith thought he knew the reason for the attractive young physician's bachelorhood and wondered when Devon would realize it herself. "Would tomorrow be convenient for you?" he inquired, setting aside his empty glass. "I don't have any unbreakable appointments, and you don't need one with Ramsey. He'll take Mrs. Curtis if he has to keep Mrs. Astor waiting."

"How flattering, if true!" Devon nibbled her berry to the stem and dunked another to devour. "And though I don't enjoy those kinds of stirrups, I don't dread them as much anymore, either."

"Gentle, is he?"

"Very. And considerate, too. Warms his instruments before using them." Devon would never forget her first vaginal examination, by an elderly Greenwich Village doctor, to check her suspected illegitimate pregnancy. The painful insertion of the hard, cold steel speculum still sent horrifying shudders through her body. How frightened she had been, and how embarrassed, and then bewildered by her predicament!

"Real kind gentleman, our friend. No wonder the females flock to him."

"Some at their husband's request," she reminded. "And we can easily postpone this visit."

"No, we'll go, Devon."

"Before or after noon?"

"Before, please, and then we'll share a chateaubriand at Delmonico's."

Since he hadn't eaten heartily at dinner, Devon teased, "Did the exercise increase your appetite?"

"In more ways than one," he acknowledged, as conscious as she of his phallic response. Leaning over, he kissed her, savoring the ambrosial sweetness of her lips, which he transferred by tongue to her taut pink nipples. "In fact, I'm hungry again, now. Maybe insatiable tonight, darling. Will you nourish me?"

"We'll nourish each other," she promised. "I wonder how strawberry-flavored champagne would taste on you?"

"Nectar of the gods," he said thickly, quivering in anticipation.

❧ 24 ❧

ADVANCE PUBLICITY for Sarah Bernhardt was colossal, and her welcome included every honor except a twenty-one-gun salute. Hundreds of journalists and sightseers met the *Amerique*, on which she and her retinue had sailed from Le Havre, when it landed in New York. A band played the Marseillaise as the French consul and delegation kissed her on both cheeks and filled her arms with flowers. Her only escape from the interminable speeches and hurrahs was a skillfully feigned faint, allowing her to be promptly whisked off to her hotel. But her publicists would not permit her to renege on press interviews, and she was scheduled to receive the representatives of the most important news organs in private sessions.

Her reputation for the bizarre, the vulgar, the fantastic in her private life preceded her, and she made no effort to conceal anything. Indeed, her revelations were so candid and shocking as to question reality, and Devon wondered if she were not deliberately amplifying her fantasies, foibles, and fables to confuse and confound the obscenely greedy and relentlessly officious public.

She was thirty-six, not a spectacular beauty, but the most flamboyant, liberated woman Devon had ever met. Her figure was slender enough to play male roles, yet shapely enough to portray the most voluptuous and seductive females in history. She called her interviewer *chérie* or *belle amie* and mixed her languages, loosely translating her motto, *"Quand-Même"* as "daring to do as she pleased, regardless of possible consequences." By which she confirmed the Continental rumors of her wild exploits and outrageous behavior, both moral and professional. She was the *enfant terrible* of the theater, as well as the Divine Sarah, and she no longer cared about her peers' or critics' opinions of her.

Her personal habits, whims, and impulses were freely indulged and discussed. She admitted to enjoying a good cigar with her cognac and lit up one in her sybaritic hotel suite to prove it; to wearing men's clothes on occasion and fencing and boxing to keep trim and agile; to owning an exotic menagerie consisting of a cheetah, a puma, six chameleons, numerous monkeys, cats, and dogs. She traveled with a gorgeous white wolfhound, which often slept on her bed, and volunteered other information Devon neither requested nor intended to put in her report. This concerned some scurrilous pamphlets circulated by her enemies prior to her arrival and accusing her of torturing her animals in temperamental rages, of seducing the Czar of Russia, Napoleon III, and Pope Pius IX, and of rehearsing with the skeleton of a lovesick man who had committed suicide over her—all of which she vehemently denied as vicious and preposterous calumnies. But, *oui,* it *was* true that Emile Zola was an intimate friend and staunch defender, to whom she would be eternally grateful.

The end of the hour allotted to the New York *Record* was approaching when Mlle. Bernhardt, observing that Miss Marshall was not recording her every word for posterity, nor yet posed the perennial question, suggested, "You are saving it for the finale, *n'est-ce pas?*"

"*Pardon, s'il vous plaît?*"

"My son, Maurice. He will be sixteen before I return to France, but you do not ask about his *père,* as all the other journalists."

Feeling an empathy for her in this respect, Devon had deliberately ignored the matter, for it was a *fait accompli* on which there had been years of monotonous speculations and assumptions. The child was illegitimate, and Sarah herself was uncertain of his paternity, as she had been actively engaged in *affaires d'amour* with two noblemen during the period of conception but most promiscuously with Prince Henri de Ligne of Belgium, whom she presumed and preferred to regard as the boy's father. And though Devon had no doubt about her own son's progenitor, she could sympathize with any woman caught in the universal dilemma of her sex: the horror of choosing between dangerous abortion or defiant disgrace.

"Well, mademoiselle . . ." She hesitated as the actress's faithful friend and companion, Mme. Guerard, poured a cup of tea for her. "I had imagined you were long since bored with that inquiry, and considered it satisfactorily settled in favor of Belgian royalty."

Bernhardt affected a theatrical gesture. "The law of averages favors him, *chérie*. But what lady, single and *enceinte*, would not choose a prince over a pauper for her child's heritage? The Compte de Keratry was in disfavor at the French court because of debt, the Second Empire was beginning to crumble—" She paused, shrugging significantly, leaving Devon to draw her own conclusions, and suddenly changed the subject. "That handsome gentleman who shares your theater box, he is your *mari, oui?*"

"My husband, yes."

"How he must love you, *chérie!* In Europe he would be mistaken for your paramour. Continental men do not adore their wives in public. Their mistresses, perhaps, but not their legal spouses." Apparently delighted by Devon's modest blush, Bernhardt clasped her marvelously expressive hands before her, and exclaimed, "Ah, you are blushing, *ma petite!* Rarely do I behold such an enchanting feminine sight. You are so lovely, *ma chère*. Your mere presence on stage would captivate every male in the audience. Have you ever considered acting?"

"Never. My talent, if any, is with the pen. Writing is the only career to which I've ever aspired. Would you like to read this article before it is printed, mademoiselle?"

Her plucked brows arched in genuine surprise. No journalist had ever made such an offer to her before, and she had learned to accept, or ignore, whatever was written about her. She smiled, graciously declining: *"Merci,* Mademoiselle Marshall. *Merci beaucoup,* but no. I trust you not to slander and libel me too much."

"Not at all," Devon promised, rising with her notebook. "You've been most kind, Mademoiselle Bernhardt. I'm at a loss to express my appreciation."

"You already have, *ma belle amie*."

"How?" asked Devon, puzzled.

"By not referring once to Rachel, Ristori, or that ambitious little Italian ingenue, Eleanora Duse, who aspires to eclipse us all."

Only vaguely familiar with the latter name, with which some of her colleagues tried to provoke a jealous rivalry, Devon said, "I don't know much about her."

"Not many people do, yet. She's only twenty, hardly more than a *bébé*. But she made her debut as Juliet, at fourteen. Give the dark-eyed child time, and she'll be the next Roman idol." She lifted her hands, as if imparting a benediction. *"Au revoir, ma petite!"*

"Au revoir," Devon replied and left, wondering if the Divine Sarah had just made a theatrical prophecy about the new toast of Italy.

Manhattan society, and its assorted artistes and dilettantes, celebrated Sarah Bernhardt with an enthusiastic frenzy surpassing even London's during her British debut. The elite feted her in their homes, either ignorant or heedless of the fact that she was not received by French and English aristocracy. There was standing room only at her performances, and even matinee tickets could be auctioned for forty and fifty dollars. The applause was deafening, the curtain calls and bouquets too numerous to count, and the police cordons at the stagedoor and her hotel entrance were stormed by hysterical fans seeking a closer glimpse and touch of the Divine Sarah. They snatched feathers from her hats, decorations from her gowns and cloaks, chased after her carriages. Guards had to protect her stage costumes, jewels, furs, her person and her sanity, lest the souvenir hunters steal her blind, tear her apart, or drive her mad.

Between the premieres of her critically acclaimed repertoire, the Curtises loaned their regally furnished loge in Booth's Theater to less fortunate friends and business clients until the programs changed. Publication of Devon's story coincided with the opening night of *Adrienne Lecouveneur,* and they were surprised when an usher delivered an envelope addressed to Monsieur et Madame Curtis. Written in Bernhardt's own distinctive hand, on monogrammed and scented vellum, it contained a gracious invitation to come backstage after the performance.

"She probably wants to thank you," Keith surmised, reading the note.

"And meet you," Devon added, adjusting the boutonniere in his black satin lapel. His black opera cape, tophat, and white gloves lay on a vacant seat, but he refused to affect the gold-hilted ebony cane of the other wealthy gentlemen in attendance.

"Why?" he asked skeptically.

"Because you're far handsomer than her leading man," Devon murmured behind her program. "And she may also be aware of your many other attractive assets, too."

Keith scowled, then laughed aloud. "My beaucoup francs?"

"Shh!" Devon cautioned, finger crossing her lips. "Adrienne's death scene is next, and I understand Bernhardt is magnificent in it."

Indeed, she was superb, and Keith congratulated her in superlatives during their special audience. Impressed by his savoir faire and fine baritone voice speaking her native tongue, Bernhardt remarked that Monsieur Curtis must have noble blood, and that she had met no other *American* like him. Appraising his suave good looks and stalwart physique, she winked at Devon and opined, "Every woman should have such a leading man in her life! And every heroine such a hero! What a divine Armand Duval he would make for Marguerite Gautier!"

Unaffected by her flattery and merely amused by her theatrical coquetry, Keith bowed and kissed her hand in parting. *"Enchanté, mademoiselle, et adieu."*

Glancing at the male star of her company, who appeared bored by the feminine chatter and fawning over him, Devon caught Angelo staring intently at her, as if his dark brooding Latin eyes could penetrate the layers of her clothing, exposing her bare body on his mental stage. Was her chartreuse velvet gown too décolleté, revealing too much of her bosom? Drawing her chinchilla wrap closer about her shoulders, she slipped an arm through her husband's on their way out, acknowledging Angelo's *ciao* with a sedate nod.

In the clarence, she exclaimed, "What a performance!"

"Which one?" asked Keith. "On stage, or off?"

"Both, darling. She was certainly taken with you!"

"Just flirting, an art in which the French excel. She's not nearly as beautiful or charming as you, however. Surely you noticed Angelo's admiration, despite the bevy of Manhattan belles around him? He was actually leering, but Sarah didn't seem to mind her hot-blooded Italian lover coveting another woman. Maybe their reputed *amore* is over, and he is no longer her *amante*."

"Or never was," Devon said. "Mere publicity."

"Well, she paid you a nice compliment, displaying your clipping on her dressing table and vowing to paste it in her scrapbook. You should be proud of yourself."

"More important, are you proud of me?"

"Of course, Devon. If I'm stingy in praising your work, maybe it's because I'm jealous of the time and attention you devote to it. How is the novel coming?"

"Slowly, but rather well, I think. And so does Miss Vale. She's a great help to me, Keith."

"Do you have a title?"

"Not yet." She smiled vaguely. "I'm waiting for a divine inspiration, such as Alexandre Dumas is said to have experienced during the creation of his masterpiece."

"Perhaps a famous play will be adapted from your romance, darling."

"Oh, Keith! Even Dumas never produced another *Lady of the Camellias*. Few immortal classics are written in a century, and even fewer literary geniuses born to write them." Lightning flashed in the eastern sky, and thunder rumbled and echoed over the harbor. Soon rain was pelting the roof of the carriage and splashing against the windows. Devon gazed wistfully at the blurred street lamps, which seemed to glow in misty yellow auras, hoping a winter storm would not develop. "Anyway, it's not on my mind now."

"I know," Keith comforted, pressing her gloved hand. Their son was due home tomorrow, and they were both eager and anxious about the reunion.

For Devon time seemed to move too swiftly and erratically, days and events telescoping on another in kaleidoscopic brilliance and disarray. Scott came and went back to school, and she wept maternally on both occasions, first with joy, then sadness. He appeared exceptionally well, lean and athletic, and at least an inch taller. He was a straight-A student, and his parents' pride in him was enormous. But they had to exercise restraint in their physical emotions, for he shied away from demonstrative affections. A motherly kiss on his arrival and departure was allowed, but he plainly preferred shaking hands to his father's bear hugs. And though they realized it was typical boyish behavior at his age, they couldn't help feeling slighted, and compensated each other and themselves with more love-making and cuddling of the twins.

This season the Astors outdid the Vanderbilts with an elaborate *bal masque,* and Devon had never seen more flamboyant costumes even on the stage. Keith, who disliked such adult playacting, went as a formally attired, black-masked Beau Brummell, with an antebellum Southern belle on his arm. Devon's costume was a replica of the gown she had worn to the inaugural ball of Confederate President Jefferson Davis. The modiste had designed it, complete with hoopskirt and crinolines, from a sketch provided by her client. Rows of white chiffon ruffles, scattered with pink silk rosettes, covered the white satin skirt, which belled gracefully from a tight, pointed white satin bodice with dropped shoulders also ruffled in frothy chiffon. A stylist had coiffed her honey-bright hair in three thick gleaming curls held on the left side of her throat with a diamond barette. Her perfume was attar of roses, complementing the fragrance of her nosegay of pink sweetheart roses, and the effect was not lost on Keith. He visualized her at sweet sixteen, minus the white satin mask, dancing with Daniel Haverston at Harmony Hill.

"Doing some memory-jogging, darling?"

"Research," she said, for she had written the costume into a scene only yesterday. "How did you guess?"

"The gown, of course."

"Didn't Northern women dress similarly at formal affairs, when it was fashionable?"

"Oh, yes—but they never looked quite the same. At least none I knew then."

"Not even Esther?"

He shook his head. "Boston ladies have an image of their own, and she personified it."

Devon sighed, recalling the gorgeous, violet-eyed, raven-haired creature who had been his first love, his first wife. "I'm sure she did, especially when she captured the most eligible bachelor in all New England."

"And later lost him to an even lovelier lady from the South. I think your victory upset her more than any Southern general's ever did, and she could easier have forgiven Grant, had he surrendered *his* sword to Lee, then she could forgive me for surrendering my heart to you."

"It was mine that was forfeit," Devon wistfully reflected, "along with my body and—"

"Virginity?" he prompted at her hesitation.

"I was going to say soul."

"Oh, come now, darling! I've never wanted to possess you spiritually, and that wasn't a Faustian bargain we made in my railroad coach that night in Virginia. Unless of course, all Yankees personified Satan to you when we met. Did they?"

"I'm afraid so, more or less."

His smoky-gray eyes narrowed behind the slits in his black mask. "No wonder you stared at me so hard in the ruins of Richmond! It was certainly a hellish landscape of fire-blackened rubble, twisted iron, and tortured trees. Were you seeking some external signs, the mark of the beast? Well, it was your pure little body I coveted then, not your equally pure little soul. Later, I wanted it for keeps, along with your love and devotion, your mortal being, but never your immortal soul. And it's the same now, angel, my devilish attributes notwithstanding. Too bad you're not a Roman Catholic."

"Why?" she asked, wishing for the midnight unmasking to reveal his full expression.

"Because papists don't burden themselves with such excess baggage, my dear. They consign it to their priests in confession, obtain absolution, and repeat the process regularly with other cargoes of sin. Whereas you, my precious, have been obsessed with *The Scarlet Letter* concept of theology since our first consummation."

"Is it so obvious, Keith?"

"To me, yes. What miracle will it take to erase that invisible red ink *A* from your puritanical conscience?"

"My, how melodramatic we are! Is this what masquerades do to people?"

"Only if they assume the characters, as well as the costumes, of those they represent. And I see some Madame DuBarrys and de Pompadours here this evening, but no visible saints. No vestal virgins, either, tending the perpetual lamp at Vesta's shrine. Frankly, I doubt there's one past sixteen present, even among the debutantes on parades, at this bacchanal celebration. The late Commodore Vanderbilt could have portrayed the guest of honor—the perfect Bacchus."

"That's cynical, Beau Brummell! Exactly the kind of remark *he* might have made at the profligate courts he frequented, especially George the Fourth's."

"I'm a born cynic, madam. And maybe we should have dressed more originally and characteristically? Wings and halo for you, horns and tail and cloven hoofs for me."

"Oh, no, darling." She smiled, finally succumbing to his wicked humor. "Not the cloven hoofs, anyway! You couldn't dance nearly so divinely."

"Wait till I get you home," he warned, affecting a satanic aspect.

"*That* long? We could leave early."

"The devil has a willing subject, eh?"

"Always. An eager one, too, who rarely requires much tempting."

He laughed, waltzing gracefully to the strains of the Younger Strauss. "*Bals masques* traditionally end at midnight, you know, and we'll have to politely endure our torment a while longer."

Devon frowned as if in pain. "Torment is the right word, all right, and it's only eleven o'clock! How can you be so patient?"

"Force of habit," he replied. But even as he counseled patience and sufference, his masked eyes were covertly searching Mrs. Astor's fantastic ballroom for a convenient exit.

❧ 25 ❧

THE REFURBISHED private railroad coach, newly painted in royal blue and gold, pulled into the Washington station two days before the inauguration of President James A. Garfield, and a reserved carriage promptly transported its occupants to the Clairmont Hotel. Devon had agreed to cover the social aspects of the occasion for the New York *Record*, her first such assignment in the national capital for several years, and she was not especially keen about it. Mrs. Garfield was another Lucy Hayes in conservatism and temperance, and with as little interest in the advancement of womankind as her predecessor in the White House.

As expected, the Inaugural Ball, held in the new museum on the Smithsonian grounds, was a rather staid affair. No alcoholic beverages were served, and the dancing was confined to the sedate waltz. Quite a contrast to the glittering galas of both of General Grant's inaugurations, the fountains of sparkling champagne, the lively quadrilles and lancers, the elaborate gowns and jewels of the ladies. While Mrs. Garfield was a gracious First Lady in mauve satin trimmed with exquisite point lace, she wore no jewelry except her plain gold wedding band, no ornamentation in her severely coiffed dark hair, and her female coterie were also conservatively dressed and virtually jewelless.

Keith remarked that it was the dullest such affair he had ever attended, and Devon agreed. "Fruit punch!" He scowled, hating the sweet concoction. "And I'm surprised we're not dancing the minuet."

"I'm sure you'd dance it as marvelously as the waltz, darling," Devon complimented, for they were surely the most

220

graceful and handsome couple on the floor.

But composing an enthusiastic report taxed even Devon's vivid imagination and experience, and she resolved to decline future White House assignments during the Garfields' tenure. And she was relieved that her husband, invariably considered to be the most qualified Republican for Secretary of the Treasury, had let it be known immediately after Garfield's election that he was not interested in this or any other cabinetcy.

Their first occupation of the Clairmont penthouse as man and wife was naturally cause for celebration, for which Keith ordered a gourmet supper served in their elegant dining salon and the finest wines from his private cellar.

The city, viewed through the expansive sheet-glass windows installed in the last remodeling, was an arresting sight at night, with lights gleaming and twinkling everywhere, even on the Long Bridge across the Potomac to Alexandria. The steadily increasing population of the District of Columbia was expanding into Virginia and Maryland. There were many new government buildings, parks, and memorials, although the Washington Monument, begun in 1850, was still under construction. Observing the stark stone obelisk in the shadows of the glowing Capitol dome, Devon remarked, "I wonder if they'll *ever* finish that thing."

"Give them time, darling. It's only been a hundred years since Congress first decided to commemorate the Father of our Country, and it was supposed to be an equestrian statue then. But this town is rife with granite and bronze generals on rearing steeds and, thank the designer, this won't be another one. It's time to appropriate funds for a suitable memorial to Lincoln, too. Also Thomas Jefferson," he hastily added, aware of every Virginian's reverence of this native son. "Being a qualified architect, Mr. Jefferson could have designed his own monument."

"Historically, he did—in Monticello and the University of Virginia," Devon said, contemplating the effervescence in her hollow-stemmed goblet, the bubbles rising and popping in the air. "How long will we be here, Keith?"

His banking interests were more extensive in Washington than anywhere else, except New York. "A week or so, Devon.

My days will be fairly well occupied with business and conferences, but we'll have the nights for pleasure. You're not bored already?"

"Oh, no, dear! The Women's Movement is very active here, and the leaders keep beseeching Congress to help us."

"More like besieging, isn't it? But many of the congressmen and senators are lame ducks, who won't be returning to the next session. Besides, politicians don't pay much serious attention to nonconstituents. Women have no vote, consequently no voice in the Capitol. Save yours for the platforms of Cooper Union and Chickering Hall."

"You know I don't lecture, Keith."

"But you wholeheartedly support the ladies who do, Devon; appear on stage with them and help to produce some of the fiery material with which they bombard the state and federal capitals. And you want the franchise as much as any of them, don't you?"

"Of course," she admitted. "I think I'm as qualified to cast a ballot as any male citizen of this country."

"Well, just don't march in any bloomer parades on this trip, Mrs. Curtis. That was a ridiculous display on Pennsylvania Avenue during the inaugural ceremonies, strutting and waving flags and posters, and chanting their trite slogans. Mrs. Garfield was obviously embarrassed."

"What a shame!" Devon clucked her tongue in mock sympathy. "One thing is certain: there won't be any aid from her, except for the prohibitionists. She's already a member of the temperance organization. Imagine posting servants to guard against spiking the punch bowls!"

Keith smiled. "Sherman and Sheridan, who enjoy their booze as much as Grant, were obviously just as disappointed. But Garfield was a Union general, too, albeit a more sober one than some of his peers."

"Too bad there's no ambitious hostess to create the social rivalry with the White House that Kate Chase Sprague did with the Lincolns and the Grants. Julia appears well, plump and energetic, but poor Mary Lincoln is quite pathetic since her long seclusion in Europe."

"Still haunted by her husband's assassination, no doubt, and holding seances to contact his and their dead son's spirits. And apparently poor. It's a crime for the widow of a martyred president to live in such straits. Congress should vote Mrs. Lincoln a pension. There's a worthy issue for the feminists to address!"

Devon nodded, although she considered child labor a more important one. And what about the thousands of widows and orphans of the Civil War soldiers?

Keith reached across the table to press her hand. The candlelight, as always, enhanced her beauty and aroused his desire. "Will you do me the honor of sharing my bed, Mrs. Curtis?"

"With pleasure, Mr. Curtis," she replied, tingling with excitement, as if it would be their first intimacy there. And indeed he was treating it so, with previously ordered bouquets of her favorite flowers in all the rooms, and an exquisite gift purchased in New York but kept secret until that moment, when he presented the forty-carat star sapphire on a uniquely designed platinum chain.

"Oh!" Devon exclaimed in breathless awe. "It's magnificent, Keith! Queen Victoria should have such a jewel in her crown. However did you acquire it?"

"Tiffany's acquired it in India, outbidding the Maharaja of Jaipur's agent, who hesitated too long in the auction. They knew I was seeking such a gem, and I immediately commissioned this pendant."

"Would it be too gauche to wear it to bed?"

"Maybe a little uncomfortable," he suggested, "under certain conditions."

"And awkward," Devon murmured, remembering the time they had tried to make love while she was wearing a fabulous diamond and topaz parure from the collection of Louis XV's Queen Maria, which he had acquired for her in France. "But I shall have to find a special way to thank you...."

"It's a gift of love, Devon. No selfish motives attached. And you're all the reward I want, now or ever." And bringing her to her feet, he swept her up in his arms and along to the master bedroom.

A few days later, on a nice afternoon when she was alone, Devon decided to go riding in Rock Creek Park. A hackney conveyed her to the livery stables in the still largely undeveloped area, which was popular with equestrians, picnickers, and lovers. Bridle and buggy paths crisscrossed the semiwilderness of rustic woods, rocky hills, and a pleasant valley through which the clear, shallow stream of its namesake flowed toward the Potomac River.

Devon selected a pretty light-coated mare named Godiva, and the groom realized the lovely lady he assisted onto the sidesaddle was no novice. Not a glimpse of petticoat was revealed beneath her bottle-green velvet habit as she hooked her knee securely around the pommel and tucked her small boot into the shortened stirrup, and he inquired only if she were familiar with the bridle paths. "Slightly," Devon replied, though she had not ridden them in several years.

"Would you like a map and compass?"

"I think I can manage without either, thank you."

She started off in a slow walk, then a gentle trot, leisurely enjoying her favorite hobby. An early spring was evident in the leafing trees and plants, the impetuous birds building nests. Soon the bare redbud branches would be tinted rosy-purple, dogwood blossoms bursting like popcorn, forsythias showering their golden stars. Columbine and arbutus and wild violets were already in bloom.

Absorbed in reverie, Devon was only vaguely conscious of company. Another rider was exploring the same trail. As she increased her pace, the hoofbeats behind her also accelerated. At first annoyed by the intrusion, then curious, she glanced back . . . and caught her breath in surprise and dismay. Escape was hopeless, for the horseman was Reed Carter, and Texans had no peers in western saddles. Aware of her recognition, Reed gave a jubilant rebel yell, spurred his buff-colored stallion, and approached waving his tall tan Stetson.

"Hold up there, ma'am!"

Devon flinched as she pulled on the reins, wondering how she could explain this coincidence to Keith. "Good afternoon, Senator Carter," she greeted sedately. "Fancy meeting you here!"

"I come here often," he said. "My breed can't stay out of a saddle long, you know, and this is the only riding territory around here. I board my pony at these stables. Remember my buckskin, Rebel? Meet his son, Jason."

"After your father?"

"Yep, and nothing would please Pa more. Next to Ma and me, he loved horses better than anything else on earth. Faithful old Rebel is retired now, enjoying his leisure on my Fort Worth spread. You wouldn't recognize it now, though. More land, a good ranch house, new outbuildings and corrals. The vaqueros consider it a hacienda."

"I didn't think the Senate paid so well."

He frowned at the implication. "You know damned well it doesn't, Devon, except for the pork barrel dippers and lobby lovers."

Together less than five minutes, and already the air was crackling between them, the sparks flying. "I wasn't implying sticky fingers on your part, Senator."

"No? I know your facility with words, remember, and at innuendo. But if you weren't impugning my honesty, or questioning my political ethics, what then? Don't chaw your cud so long, honey. Spit it out!"

"Oh, Reed, you and your Texas idiom! You still enjoy confounding your colleagues with that alien lingo, don't you, and amusing all Easterners with your cow-country clothes."

"I'm a native Texan, Devon. Should I deny my heritage, assume some false Eastern image, and try to emulate those pompous Yankee jackasses braying on Capitol Hill?"

"No, just be yourself."

"You think I'm masquerading? These duds may be considered costume in Congress, as were Sam Houston's buckskins and Davy Crockett's coonskin cap, but they're dress-up out West, and I still prefer the more rugged canvas breeches and rawhide jackets. Evidently, you didn't learn much about me when we were together."

"Evidently not." They descended a slight slope, to a meadow abloom with crocus, and crossed it to water the animals in Rock Creek. "I realize you haven't mellowed much, though. You're still bitter and prejudiced over the Confederacy's defeat, aren't you? Is that why you didn't attend Garfield's inauguration?"

"Precisely. I voted for his Democratic opponent, even though Winfield Hancock was also a former Union general; at least his politics are compatible with mine. And the Democrats will recapture the White House before this decade is out. They're already even in the Senate and closing the small gap in the House. The Republicans can't ride roughshod over us so easily anymore."

The sight and sound of a scenic waterfall attracted Devon's attention. The cascade tumbled over granite boulders, creating a short span of foaming rapids before calming into crystal ripples, where they paused to refresh the horses. Dismounting, Reed held both their reins for a while, then tossed Devon's back to her, inquiring, "Where's Midas? In one of his capital counting houses?"

"Banking is not his only business," Devon retorted crisply, adjusting the ninon veil of her plumed postilion.

"How well I know! Curtis Enterprises are expanding in every direction."

"I won't listen to any criticism of him, Reed." Her jaw set warningly, and her eyes sparked angrily.

"Careful, honey, you'll set your fancy hat on fire. I see Curtis hasn't gentled you down much; you still have a hot temper and mucho defiance under all that traditional gentility. You're also still the prettiest little gal I ever knew, in or out of a saddle."

Discommoded by his candor, Devon fiddled nervously with her riding crop. "Really? I thought Melissa Hampton was your ideal and would be the new Mrs. Carter by now."

"She is," he said quietly, his mien sobering.

"Oh? I never read anything in the gossip columns."

"The ceremony was private, and only Texans were invited. It took place at the Hampton home in Austin. No doubt you remember the Judge's estate there?"

Devon glanced toward Rock Creek falls, a mere miniature of those on Gore Hampton's Colorado River property, where she had suffered the most wretched and terrifying experience of her life. Before scores of people attending one of Judge Hampton's famous political barbecues, his wild, reckless daughter, in a swift new canoe, had challenged the Carters, in a clumsy old boat, to race. During the daredevil contest, which the skillful Melissa won handily, their unwieldly craft had drifted into the treacherous Colorado current, plunged through a long stretch of dangerous white-water rapids and overturned in a vicious whirlpool. Devon had nearly drowned, and Reed had much ado rescuing her. How could either of them ever forget that horror, or its consequences?

"So where is your wife now?" Devon inquired. "I know she enjoys riding, too."

"Like an Indian sometimes, bareback. And no sidesaddle, ever. Melissa's with her father. The Judge had a heart seizure last month, and she's nursing him at his home. Their filial bonds are so strong, God knows how his death would affect her."

"No children yet?"

He shook his head ruefully, remounting. "Perhaps never. The physicians we've consulted seem to think Melissa is sterile. I know you have a son, Devon, fathered by Keith Curtis. I figured that out when the boy was abducted and you moved to his Hudson River spread. Any more heirs to his empire?"

"Twin daughters," Devon apprised. "Sharon and Shannon will be two years old in June."

He gazed at her morosely. "You could give him three kids, but not one to me. No, you miscarried my seed!"

"That wasn't my fault, Reed."

"Wasn't it? You and Carla Winston jouncing in a buggy over rough terrain, to that goddamn prairie fire, against my wishes and orders."

Another Texas tragedy vividly recalled! "We thought we could help, Reed. Other women were going...and I didn't know I was pregnant then."

"Nor even suspected it?" He looked skeptical. "You'd missed three periods, and Carla told me you bled slightly the night before, when the coyotes attacked our cabin."

"While you and your father were celebrating your election to the State House at the local cantina!" Devon accused, furious that he had brought up their marriage and apparently blamed her for its failure. "I was frightened half to death! But I still wasn't positive, and wanted to consult a doctor before telling you."

"Hell, Devon! You should have recognized the symptoms. You had a child, of which I was ignorant when I married you, although I knew you weren't a virgin."

Devon stared at him, appalled. "Nor did I pretend to virginity! You have a convenient memory, Reed. Have you forgotten that I tried to tell you about Mr. Curtis and our child, in that abandoned house on that former battlefield in the Virginia woods, when you proposed to me? But you wouldn't listen, you said nothing in my past mattered, only the future was important! Were you lying that day, camouflaging your true thoughts and feelings? If not, and you didn't care then, why now? And if you didn't love me enough to be faithful in marriage, why drag up these unpleasant details on this chance meeting, for heaven's sake?"

"First of all, it's not a chance meeting, Devon. I've been here every day, waiting for you. You rode here often when we lived in Georgetown, and I hoped you would again, while your monopolistic mogul was otherwise occupied. And secondly, I did—and still do—love you. I fell into temptation with Melissa, but marrying her was a mistake."

"Because she's apparently barren?"

"The inquiring reporter, blunt and direct. But no, that's not the reason." He was cognizant of the possible cause of Melissa's diagnosed sterility, for she had long ago confessed her adolescent pregnancy and crude abortion by a Mexican midwife to him. What he had difficulty abiding were his dark, ugly suspicions of incest with her father, both before and after their marriage. Judge Gore Hampton was an evil, concupiscent, irreligious man, and Reed hoped he would not survive long. But his daughter adored him, and would never admit or even suggest any abnormal attachment. "Our marriage was a serious mistake, that's all."

"I'm sorry, Reed," she apologized, seeing the nervous tension of his facial muscles. "I didn't mean to pry into your private life. Whatever is wrong between you and Melissa is none of my concern. But I hope you straighten it out, because I think she really does love you."

His eyes, the intense azure of the Texas summer skies, brooded under the broad brim of his high-crowned nutria hat, which along with his western suits and boots had become his political trademarks. Small wonder the female journalists were impressed. Tall, slim, tanned Senator Reed Carter of Texas was the most striking, distinctive figure on Capitol Hill, creating quite a sensation when he strolled the congressional halls, or anywhere else in Washington.

"You're so damned beautiful, Devon, and desirable. There ought to be a law against such a kissable mouth. I'd like to yank you off that cayuse and make ardent love to you, here and now, on the ground. Have you ever?"

"Have I ever what?"

"Been taken on Eve's bed?"

"That's crude, and this is hardly paradise," she rebuked him. "Stop leering at me like that, Reed."

"Like what?"

"As if you're contemplating rape."

"Maybe I am," he said with a sly grin. "It can be fun, honey, Texas-style. Wearing boots and sombrero, if you need a translation."

"Like tumbleweeds rolling on the prarie? Is that how you first betrayed me with Melissa?"

"Very perceptive, except for the prairie. It was in a valley in the hills above Austin, beside a pretty little creek much like this one . . . and I was only human, Devon."

"Animal," she muttered, consulting her lapel watch. "I must get back to the stable. My rental time is up."

"And you can't afford the extra fee?" He laughed, making a pistol of his hand and aiming it at her. "Shall I shoot you off that nag?"

Devon wheeled Godiva and cropped her flanks. Reed spurred his frisky buckskin stallion, unquestionably Rebel's son, and warned, "You can't outrun me, Devon. Surely you know that?"

"Oh, yes. I also know you won't take unfair advantage of me, Senator. You never have before."

"Perhaps I've changed," he suggested, pacing her. "Come to my senses, and realize what I've lost."

"If so, you must also realize it's much too late for post-mortems. I never lied about my feeling for you, Reed. There was always another man in my life, whom I could never forget. And it's the same still."

"For him, too?"

"For both of us. We're completely happy."

"Is that so? Then why aren't you content just to be his mate and breed his brats? You still pursue your career under your maiden name. I've seen your byline in newspapers and magazines, and read some of your pamphlets on child labor. I'm a senator, Devon. Don't the suffragists realize where and how all federal laws are enacted? Hasn't it occurred to you to enlist my aid in your ambitious goals?"

"Court your favor? No, indeed! Besides, you're supposed to be immune to favoritism and bribery."

"Especially to the lobbyists of the octopus cartels," he wryly informed. "I have an obsession in that respect."

"Indeed, you do, Senator!"

"Forget the formality, Devon. We were married, we've been naked in bed together—and you may even have enjoyed it on occasion. Our divorce wasn't amicable, but I'm not angry with you anymore. I'd like very much to see you again, be your friend, help you if I can. Could we ride again tomorrow, or meet for luncheon, and discuss it?"

"I'm afraid not, Reed."

"Why?"

"Because I'm true to my husband."

"I'm not asking you to sleep with me, Devon."

"What were you suggesting a few minutes ago, Texas-style, on Eve's bed?"

"Joking, my dear. I would never force any woman. You said you knew better."

"You're filibustering, Senator. I can't and won't meet you anywhere by design. But I would be grateful if you would give some attention to the child labor situation."

"How grateful?"

"I thought we had cloture on that, Senator."

"All right, I'll yield for the moment. May I ask if you'll be traveling to Texas in the near future?"

"Why?" she asked, with a puzzled glance.

"I'm on the Rivers and Harbors Committee, and happen to know that your spouse's agents are buying land along the proposed route of the Houston Ship Channel. He hasn't told you about his wheeling and dealing in Texas?"

Although astonished by this information, Devon tried to pretend otherwise. "He may have, I don't recall specifics. His commercial affairs are so extensive and involved."

"And becoming increasingly more so," Reed interrupted, chagrined by her quick defense of his nemesis. "I can't say I welcome his breed in my territory as much as some of my fellow Texans, however. Everybody wants progress and prosperity, it seems, and Yankee dollars are rolling south and west with great velocity. The dredging and widening of Buffalo Bayou from Galveston to Houston will give us a deep-water port inland, capable of accommodating international trade. Appropriation bills will be necessary to complete the project, and I'll have to support them."

"I see," Devon murmured, urging Godiva into a gallop.

Hoping she was playing with him, initiating a race, Reed chased her back to the livery, letting her win. Attendants took the horses, and he escorted Devon to her waiting hackney. Their goodbyes were gestures: a salute of his hand, a wave of hers. But Devon knew Reed had wanted very much to kiss her, and she was angry enough with Keith just then to wish he had tried.

⸎ 26 ⸎

KEITH HAD just finished reading the note Devon had left for him when she entered the penthouse, flicking her riding crop idly against her knee. "There you are, darling! I was getting worried—you're later than I expected."

"And you're earlier than I expected." Her tardiness was due to a long cab ride about the city, while she mulled the events of the afternoon, debating the advisability of confiding them to him. Not that she had anything to conceal, but she was miffed because he had not confided his transactions in Texas to her. For some incomprehensible reason, the knowledge imparted by Reed was more upsetting to Devon than the discovery of Keith's dealings in Virginia.

"Did you enjoy your ride?" he asked, bestowing a greeting kiss on her veiled cheek.

"It was interesting."

"Interesting?" He quirked a dark, quizzical brow.

"Informative."

"In what way?" he persisted, opening the cellaret and removing a decanter and glass.

"I met a senator on the trail."

Silence ensued. Then, drink in hand, he turned and peered at her curiously. "Is this a mystery? Should I guess his identity?"

"Do you need a clue?"

Keith frowned, tasting his Scotch. "You already gave me one, my dear. You said trail, not lane or bridle path. Shall we continue this charade?"

Her temper flared, exploded. "Damn it, Keith! Why do you keep me in the dark about your business affairs? It was surprise enough to hear about your holdings in Richmond *after* we arrived there!" Tears clouded her eyes, shimmering through the ninon mist. She rapped the leather crop on the brocade sofa in frustration, and then threw it down on the cushion. "Can you imagine my astonishment, learning about the Houston Ship Channel from a Texas senator on the Rivers and Harbors Committee!"

"Can you imagine *mine*, learning that you spent the afternoon in the Rock Creek wilds with your former spouse, who had been politically gunning for me from the day he entered the United States Senate?" he countered, swirling the amber liquid in agitation. "Any explanation as to how your 'trails' happened to cross?"

"By sheer coincidence on my part!"

"But not on the cowboy's?"

"Reed boards his horse at the stables there," she replied, removing her becoming bottle-green velvet hat. "He admitted knowing we were in town and hoping that I might ride in the park, while you were otherwise engaged."

"The presumptuous bastard! What's his game now, Devon? What's he after?"

She shrugged, unpinning her chignon and shaking her long golden tresses down on her shoulders. "I'm not sure, Keith."

"He must have given you some reason for ambushing you in the thicket, Devon."

"It wasn't ambush," she said, although she had been tempted to make the same accusation to Reed. "But he's still an avowed enemy of the monopolists, if that's news to you."

"Hardly. And since he already failed in that vengeance against me, he must be seeking other revenge. Perhaps to keep Curtis Enterprises out of his state? That wouldn't be politically expedient for him, considering its numerous advertisements begging and enticing investors in every Northern publication."

"He's aware of that, Keith."

"You must have had quite a lengthy discussion."

"Not on politics or economics, until he asked if we would be visiting Texas anytime soon!" she snapped, still disconcerted by his secrecy in the matter. "Will we?"

Keith hesitated, surveying the city from his vantage. Gaslamps were being lighted on Pennsylvania Avenue and Capitol Hill, for Congress had not yet voted the funds to convert to electric illumination. "I have no definite plans in that direction yet. In any event, I didn't think you would be interested. It's a damned long distance, Devon, through some rough country."

"I've been there before," she reminded.

"Not on the route I would travel, via the Missouri, Kansas and Texas Railroad. The MK&T serves the Middle Plains, which are still menaced by Indians and infested with outlaws. Roving tribes attack the frontier settlements, and bandits rob the banks, stagecoaches, and trains. Would you want to be in the private car of a New York banker if the James Brothers or some other desperadoes came aboard?"

"Aren't the rails protected by federal marshals, detectives, and the cavalry?"

"To some extent, primarily to guard the mail and money, but even Wells Fargo cargoes are regularly hit. And they're not the American Robin Hoods portrayed in the press, any more than Quantrill's Raiders were the benefactors of the Confederacy. They're thieves, killers, and rapists."

"Hire a bodyguard," she said, thinking he was merely trying to frighten her out of accompanying him whenever he went, "as you did for me, without my knowledge, when I first traveled to Texas."

"I would, of course. But Pinkerton's Agency only sells protection, they don't guarantee it. Even the army can't protect

the entire West, nor the Texas Rangers their specific territory."
He paused, pouring another shot of whisky. "I'm still wondering why Carter maneuvered to get you alone in the brush.
Is he single?"

"No, he married his mistress, as you did yours."

"Are you comparing our relationships?"

"I'm saying Judge Hampton's daughter is now Senator Carter's wife. Melissa's in Austin, helping to nurse her gravely ill
father."

"So the prairie wolf is on the prowl? Is that just his natural
hunting instinct, or has the bloom faded from his cactus rose
already, leaving a bed of marital thorns?"

"Some, apparently."

"Well, that's his hard luck!" He sighed, running his free
hand through his hair. "Good God! Here we go again! A Texas
coyote and a Virginia hound both pursuing the same pretty little
rabbit."

"Rabbit!" she protested furiously.

"You know what I mean! And it's ridiculous, Devon. But
even more ridiculous is my condoning the chase. Did Carter
proposition you?"

"No," she lied, seeing blood in his eyes.

"Is that truth, or prudence?"

"What do you think?"

"I think the goddamn rustler regrets losing you, and would
like to recapture his prize, legally or any other way," he fumed.
"But if he tries to jump my claim, he'll die with his boots on!"

"Oh, Keith, you're raving!"

"I mean it, Devon. And the same goes for the Virginian,
although I don't believe he's quite as dangerous or apt to
stampede as that maverick Texan."

"Claim? Stampede? I'm not your property, Keith! Nor your
chattel or pet, and I resent such blatantly chauvinistic implications! Yet you invariably resort to them in these situations."

"A matter of semantics, my dear, when I'm provoked."

"But I'm not the cause of your provocation now, Keith! I
haven't done anything to warrant it. Reed was the last person
I expected to encounter this afternoon. I couldn't outride him,
and it would have been foolish to ignore him. Besides, he
offered political aid to the Women's Movement."

"And your child labor crusade in particular? A ruse, Devon,

to court your naive trust and confidence. Senator Carter is as chauvinistic as any man in Congress and has done nothing whatever to aid the plight of women and children so far. I forbid you to consult him on anything."

"Forbid?"

"Yes, damn it, forbid! There are plenty of other elected officials for the feminists to call on, including those of New York, both in Albany and Washington. You stay the hell out of Carter's bailiwick! Hear me?"

"Yes, master. How many lashes if I disobey?"

"You know that kind of attitude irks me, Devon."

"No more than your edicts do me, Keith."

"Just don't defy me in this, madam. I won't tolerate such defiance, and that's final," he warned before she could speak again. "Where would you like to dine this evening?"

"I'd better defer that decision to you, sir. My suggestion might be out of order, and overruled." She spun on her boot heel and sauntered toward the bedroom, calling over her shoulder, "Do you wish to approve the selection of my gown, Mr. Curtis?"

"May I?" he asked, proceeding to her wardrobe.

"My only desire is to please you, sire."

Rummaging through the garments, he selected a seductive boudoir ensemble of black chiffon and lace and proffered it, grinning wickedly. "How about this?"

"I can't go out in *that!*"

"Precisely. The chef can oblige us here."

"I—I sort of fancied Dijon's tonight," she relented, taking the lingerie and tossing it on the bed.

"Did I misunderstand, dear? Didn't you just say your only desire was to please me?"

When would she learn not to threaten, challenge, or bait him! Outwitted once again, she pursed her lips sulkily. "I'd like a bath first."

"So would I, and our Roman tub is large enough for two. We've bathed together before, haven't we? You can scrub my back, like a good little helpmeet. I'll reciprocate by washing you all over. Any objections?"

"No," she murmured, unfastening the high-necked basque of her riding habit.

"You're not smiling."

"You're not undressing."

"Ah, Devon, don't pout!" He laughed, clasping her in his arms and kissing her petulant mouth. "Am I acting the tyrant and brute? I've already made dinner reservations at Dijon's, and we'll dance in the Metropolitan's new crystal ballroom afterward. You mustn't take me so literally, darling, when I'm in a foul mood."

She finally smiled at him, ruing her childish tantrum. "I'm afraid I sometimes behave more like your daughters than your wife. Poor man! What a time you're going to have with three such females on your hands."

"I can spank Sharon and Shannon," he said, "but I never quite know how to handle you."

"No?" She winked coyly, beginning to strip. "First one in the water gets an extra massage!"

Evanescent, irretrievable time, fleeing on swift wings, flashing by with the speed of light. April, May, June, and another birthday for the twins celebrated at Halcyon. Scotty home again on vacation, with a packet of pale pink envelopes addressed in a delicate girlish hand, which he kept locked up like treasure in his trunk. Did Fawn hide his letters, too? Devon wondered. What could be so precious and secretive about their childish correspondence? Did they really have something to conceal from their parents? Scotty was most impatient to visit Harmony Hill again and began to pester his mother about it.

"Ask your father," Devon advised, and he did so that very evening at the dinner table, vexing Keith.

"You just got home, Scott!"

"But I don't have anyone to play with," he complained.

"You had your classmates for nine months."

"The boys can't do much playing at school, Daddy. It's mostly work—studying and exercising."

"What about the sports?"

"They're competitive even in practice, teams against teams, including the riding. Nobody wants a loser on his side, so everybody tries extra hard to win, and that takes some of the fun out of the games. It's a chore, sometimes."

"But you enjoy participating, don't you?"

"Oh, sure. It's just that everyone wants to be a winner, better than the next fellow, and embarrassed if he's just average. Is winning so important, the highest goal in life? Some of the boys' fathers must think so, because they push their sons beyond their limits, and some break under the pressure. Four students got sick this semester and had to leave school."

Keith noted his slack appetite. "That happens occasionally, Scott. Do you feel pushed?"

"No, sir."

"Truthfully, now?"

"Well, maybe a little," he admitted. "Not that I mind the field or classroom competition, because I'm strong enough to handle both loads and—"

"Of course you are, Scott. You're an athletic scholar, and always have been. Your grades prove that. But I interrupted you, didn't I? What were you saying?"

"Nothing," he shrugged, reconsidering.

"No, I want to hear it, son. Tell me."

"Well, most of the students are rich, and their parents expect them to follow in their father's footsteps when they're old enough. They say I'm the richest one of all and will inherit the biggest bank in America. Does that mean I have to be a banker?"

"Not if you feel that way about it," Keith answered, obviously chagrined.

"But you'll be displeased if I don't, won't you?"

"Disappointed, Scott. But it's your choice, and I don't believe you're mature enough to make it yet. I didn't chart my future until my junior year in college, when I was capable of realizing both the advantages and responsibilities of my heritage. These are your restless years, son, and you'll vacillate about many things before they're over."

"I suppose so, sir." He glanced at his mother. "No trip to Virginia, huh?"

"I guess not, Scotty."

"Wouldn't you like to see the portrait Mr. Daniel is having painted of you?"

"Portrait?" Devon repeated, and Keith's head jerked up from the leg of lamb he was carving.

"Fawn wrote me about it," he innocently revealed. "An artist came from New Orleans, and he'll live at Harmony Hill until the picture's finished."

"You must be mistaken, Scotty! I suspect it's Mr. Haverston's daughter who's being painted, not me."

"Jacques Chantelle—that's the artist's name and he studied in France—already did Fawn, and her daddy was so pleased with his work...well, now Mr. Chantelle is doing you, Mommy."

"That's impossible, child, since I'm not posing for him! You've just misunderstood Fawn."

"Maybe," he agreed. "I'll read the letter again."

"Please do, dear. And for heaven's sake, be careful how you interpret whatever she writes! We would never pry into your mail, Scotty, so do please try not to confuse any information you choose to share with us."

"Yes, ma'am." As his parents' eyes met over the table, Scott sensed anxiety in his mother's and smoldering anger in his father's. "May I please be excused?"

"When you finish your food," Keith told him.

"I'm not hungry, sir."

Devon coaxed. "Don't you want dessert? It's chocolate mousse."

"The infirmary nurse says sweets are bad for the health. They cause cavities and pimples."

"Oh, dear! Don't talk about such things during meals, Scotty. You may be excused."

"Thank you." Shoving back his chair, he ran out of the dining room, upstairs to his private sanctuary, where no one intruded without permission, and he was free to think and dream and indulge his boyish fantasies.

Later, over coffee, Keith remarked, "Scott has a bad case of puppy love, and his obsession with Fawn Haverston and the plantation is beginning to annoy me. I trust you didn't prompt him about another journey to the Old South?"

"Certainly not! It's his own idea, and he has been besieging me with it. To get some peace, I finally told him to discuss it with you."

"Which makes me the scapegoat, if not the villain, in this domestic drama!"

"I think it's more of a dilemma, Keith. Scotty's, as well as ours, and will probably worsen with adolescence. He's already concerned about his personal appearance, though his skin and teeth are perfect. And he keeps brushing his hair as if he could straighten it."

"That'll change the first time a pretty young lady admires his wavy locks and runs her hands through them. It did for me, and I couldn't wait to shave and grow muscles and hair on my chest. The visible marks of manhood, for which every boy is eager and impatient."

"No more so, I imagine, than young girls for those of womanhood. Bosoms and menses. I got both at twelve."

"And your complexion is flawless, so you were spared the acne curse."

"You too, apparently. I hope Scotty will be as fortunate. He resembles you so much, Keith. His genetic inheritance is very strong—and I'm certain he'll want to be a financier, too."

He smiled at the placation. "You're no more certain of that than I am, Devon. Only time will tell, and right now I wouldn't give any odds on it. But his genes match mine in his attraction to a Virginia girl, only at a much earlier age. Probably because I didn't meet you as early in life."

"And he still doesn't know how any of that came about," Devon mused ponderously. "I worry about it, Keith."

"Why, Devon? Because Haverston knows the truth, and our kids are fond of each other? Daniel's not likely to discuss it with his daughter, even when she's older. It would mean betraying a woman he still loves—and he'd have some tall explaining of his own to do, wouldn't he?" He shook his head in wry wonder. "Maybe the planter really has commissioned a portrait of his former sweetheart."

"From memory?"

"From a photograph, darling. Many were taken of you the day of the barbecue and ball, and our host insisted on supervising most of them. He might have hired Mathew Brady, if he hadn't been Lincoln's favorite photographer."

"Oh, Keith!"

"Oh, Devon!" he mimicked. "Isn't my assumption logical? And aren't you curious? I'll admit I am."

"Are you proposing that we satisfy our curiosity?"

"It would delight the boy," he said, studying her facial reaction. "How about you?"

"Not especially. Besides, I still think Scotty is wrong about the portrait, and it's more likely of Dan's late wife, Caroline. Fawn should have a portrait of her mother, and there was none in the family gallery when we were there. A father's gift to his daughter! Doesn't that make more sense to you? It does to me."

"Any bets?"

"I don't like to gamble, dear."

"Hah! You're afraid you'd lose, *dear*, because your intuition about this coincides with mine."

❧ 27 ☙

ON THE second of July 1881, shocking news was telegraphed across the nation. President Garfield, only six months in office, was shot in the Baltimore & Ohio Railway Station in Washington by a disgruntled office seeker. He died of his wounds two months later, and Vice-President Chester A. Arthur succeeded to the presidency. As he was regarded as the handsomest, most metropolitan gentleman ever to occupy the White House, as well as its most eligible bachelor since James Buchanan, the social atmosphere of the capital soon changed from staid simplicity to elegant gaiety.

Female journalists were suddenly eager again for Washington assignments, and the gossip columnists were in their element trying to outguess the matchmakers. Devon was content to observe the national scene vicariously, from Tish Lambeth's viewpoint in the *Record,* while devoting more time to her own special interests and projects. Nothing much was accomplished in these areas, however. The road to suffrage had become a feminist Calvary, and as difficult to travel under the physical burdens and mental floggings. Every day was a *Dies Irae* testing the feminine spirit. Every public assembly had to endure some wrath and ridicule. Some members suggested that the Women's Sufferance Movement might be a more appropriate title, and Devon was inclined to agree. So much time, energy, effort, and money were expended, and the last was in crucially short supply. But courage was not lacking, and surrender was absent from the vocabulary of the gallant, indefatigable leaders. The torch bearers were heartened by the success of Clara Barton's long struggle to organize the American Red Cross, and inspired by the gains in Dorothea Dix's even longer and more relentless battle on behalf of the mentally ill.

Hearing these valiant ladies speak in Cooper Union and Chickering Hall, Devon thought they should be immortalized in the history of humanity. She winced at Miss Dix's horrifying descriptions of the insane asylums and treatment of the inmates whose only crime was lunacy, and the dreadful conditions in the orphanages and public hospitals and pesthouses and prisons. Miss Barton's accounts of the horrors she had witnessed on the battlefields in the care of wounded soldiers brought tears to Devon's eyes, and that lady's selfless desire to aid the victims of all natural calamities now was surely to be encouraged and aided by every possible means. But every crusade needed dedicated volunteers and, above all, generous philanthropists.

Devon wrote more fervent tracts for the Women's Bureau, had them printed at her own expense, and agreed to help distribute them in the financial district on a bright autumn day. Voguishly attired in a new suit of heliotrope cashmere intricately scrolled in pessementerie, and a jauntily plumed velvet cloche, she strolled bravely on Wall Street, passing out flyers announcing forthcoming meetings and accepting donations.

"Good Lord!" Keith exclaimed aloud, glancing out of his office windows, and then yanked open the door to his secretary's cubicle. "Miss Ryan, come in here!"

Marnie obeyed immediately. "Something wrong?"

"Damned right! Look down there, on the sidewalk before this bank. Do you recognize the lady in the lavender finery offering leaflets?"

Marnie had never seen more poise and elegance, except in the pages of *Godey's Magazine*. "I think so, sir. It's Mrs. Curtis, isn't it?"

"Correct! Go tell her I want to see her, at once."

"But, Mr. Curtis—"

"That's an order, Miss Ryan. On the double!"

"What if she refuses?"

"She'd better not. But give me a signal; I'll stand at this window. Move, woman!"

"Yes, sir." Marnie hurried all the way.

Keith observed the meeting. Marnie was smiling and even accepting a flyer, apparently in deference. Devon did not look up at the top floor, but stood rooted like a statue for a few minutes, talking animatedly, and then finally ascended the marble steps to the imposing bronze portal, and soon entered the executive office on her own steam, of which she had a full head.

"You summoned me, sire?" she asked, fuming.

His anger flared with hers. "What in hell are you doing now, and why the devil in this realm?"

"We need coin, and this is where the gold is, Midas! And how dare you send your secretary to fetch me like a naughty child for punishment?" she demanded, glaring at him, embarrassed for herself and Miss Ryan. "She's not a truant officer, nor I an errant pupil to be remanded to the principal!"

Keith glowered back. "I've given you thousands of dollars for your eternal, mostly infernal causes, Devon! You don't need to walk the streets for more. Why are you flaunting yourself here?"

"Flaunting? You make it sound like naked streetwalking, Keith! I'm not trying to sell myself."

"The men don't know that, Devon. Those flyers could be advertising a new brothel, for all they know."

"In that case, they'd be fighting for them."

Thrusting his hands into his trouser pockets and balling them into impotent fists, he treaded the Oriental carpet, muttering furiously, "Just the same, I won't have my wife soliciting that way! It's indecorous and conspicuous, and you might as well carry a sandwich board front and back." Pausing at his desk, he scrawled out a liberal check and handed it to her with a dark scowl. "Throw that damned bundle down the garbage chute, and take this to the Women's Bureau. It's enough to buy a thousand tickets to that lecture, or whatever you're touting. . . ."

"Oh, Keith, it's not just funds we need! Can't you understand? It's stuffing envelopes, knocking on doors, handing out circulars and literature, lecturing, demonstrating, going to jail if necessary. . . ."

"Don't remind me of that last fanaticism, Devon! We weren't married when I had to bail you out of the Tombs after that crazy march and riot in the Bowery with Miss Susan 'B. for Batty' Anthony. Do you want to end up in a cell again, with a diseased prostitute and lousy thief and sadistic matron anxious to shear your curly locks and mar your beauty with her cudgel, as could have happened then?"

"No, of course not. But if restaurants can solicit customers by advertising menus—"

"They have permits!" he interrupted. "You don't and never will! It's illegal to beg alms without a license, whatever the cause, and you could be arrested. We have a position to maintain, madam. I won't be a laughingstock on the Street just to indulge your whims."

"They're not mere whims, Keith."

"No matter. A man who can't manage his spouse is considered a milquetoast everywhere in the world, but more so in finance. For how can he be expected to influence international monetary affiars if he can't effectively control his own domestic affairs and pursestrings?"

"Puppeteers pull strings, Keith. Men who want that kind of feminine control should marry marionettes!"

"Very witty! But you know money is not the issue here. I don't care how much you spend, or give away. But I do care how and where you practice your charity. And I'm beginning to worry about our daughters, Devon. You'll probably indoctrinate them with your fervent feminist creed in a few more years and enlist them in your zealous crusades."

"And shepherd them to the polls, when they're old enough," she quipped, her eyes sparking green fire. "Maybe by then we'll be able to vote together."

Keith smiled faintly, admiring her indomitable will and spirit despite the frustrations they caused him. "I'm afraid you'll be old and gray by then, Mrs. Curtis, and our girls will be grandmothers."

"Moreover," she added, ignoring his dire predictions, "I think Marnie Ryan would be standing in line to cast her ballot, too."

"Possibly," he conceded. "But she'll never distribute propaganda before this building, or anywhere else in the district, and remain in my employ."

"You'd dismiss her?"

"Promptly, if she became a gadfly on feminism. Maybe I can't always manage my spouse properly, but I damned sure can my secretary."

"Indeed? Miss Ryan apologized for coming after me, at your command."

"Ah, but she obeyed, didn't she?" He grinned with suave complacency. "Marnie knows on which side her bread is buttered."

"So 'tis Marnie now, is it, Mr. Curtis?" she mimicked the Irishwoman's accent.

"Not in her presence."

"Butter is slippery, Keith. Be careful you don't use too much on her . . . and lose your control."

"Go peddle your papers," he muttered, scowling.

"You're not going to incinerate them?"

"That would be tantamount to burning money, considering that I paid the printing bill. Oh, you used your allowance, my dear, but where did it come from? Just don't spread your folderol in this vicinity, my lovely charmer. Tell me, did you volunteer to work on Wall Street?"

Devon nodded, retrieving the package from the leather chair on which she had deposited it, explaining, "No one else wanted it."

"Or dared to antagonize her menfolk in this exclusive and territorial male domain? Beard the lions in their dens, so to speak!" He raised his eyes heavenward. "Lord, give me patience with this woman!"

"And me with this man," Devon echoed, blowing him a kiss on her way out. "Amen."

Minutes later, knowing that he would be watching from his vantage, she waved a flyer at him and passed out a number before boarding a hansom cab. Keith laughed to himself, shaking his head, convinced that she would always be his defiant little rebel. And half-convinced that something vital and exciting and *important* would be lacking in their relationship if she wasn't.

Devon half expected a surly bear for dinner in Gramercy Park that evening. But most of the thunderclouds had disappeared from his brow, and she did not risk restoring them by confessing that en route to the Women's Bureau to deliver her husband's generous contribution, she had bade the driver to stop at Madame Demorest's Emporium and other notably feminine specialty stores and shops, where she left small stacks of circulars and pamphlets for their interested customers. It was so unfair that gentlemen had numerous places to meet for social and leisure purposes, including opulent private clubs, where they could dine on gourmet cuisine, drink and gamble, enjoy male camaraderie and ribaldry if inclined, and even take up temporary lodging. Their less privileged brothers could gather in saloons and air their grievances at political and labor rallies.

The average woman was confined to her home, to cook and clean, wash and iron, and raise children. As she must submit by law to her husband's sexual demands at his convenience, there were few small families, and many wives were pregnant annually throughout their childbearing years. Contraceptives were illegal, although available, like almost everything else, to people who could afford them. Some pathetic, barely literate and legible letters to the Women's Bureau were revelations of misery, despair, desperation. Illiterates made stealthy trips to the only refuge open to them, to complain of their spouses' penury, oppression, and brutality, of beatings and child abuse and molestation of daughters. They admitted praying for early menopause, employing drastic measures to hopefully prevent pregnancy, and dangerous attempts at self-abortion. Sympathetic counselors listened and recorded their pitiful stories, but there was little legal aid to be offered, and even practical advice had to be cautiously administered, lest it boomerang on the Movement and result in arrest and imprisonment for the advisors.

Devon never returned from a meeting without thanking Providence for her good fortune. Keith might rant, scold, forbid her public involvement, as he had this morning, and then relent in a large donation. She rewarded him with extra benefits, especially in the boudoir, and thought she was very subtle about it all. Sometimes he let her believe it, then again he advised her in no uncertain terms that he was aware of her manipulation, and she had better not overdo it.

"No rings in my nose," he warned her.

"Never, darling. Not even a solid gold one studded with

diamonds. No jeweled collars or leashes, either."

"I'm serious, Devon. And if you think I don't know you deliberately disobeyed me by strewing your propaganda along a circuitous route to that cackling henhouse on Twenty-third Street to deposit another golden egg in their badly deficited nest, if not bankrupt treasury, you're mistaken."

Shocked and surprised, Devon inquired petulantly, "Am I under surveillance again?"

Keith smiled, patting her bare buttocks as they lay in bed. "No, I just suspected it, knowing you, and now you've confessed."

"Damn," she swore softly. "You always manage to make me incriminate myself."

"Your extra bonus in bed was another clue," he apprised, grinning at her in the candlelight, which he had always preferred to darkness in intimacy.

"Oh, you're so clever! But I didn't commit any crimes, Keith, and I don't feel guilty of any. So put that in your pipe and smoke it!"

He scoffed at her impudence. "Do you realize, madam, that I could blister your bare bottom now, or whenever I pleased, with impunity?"

"Or lash me with a whip, and batter me black and blue." She nodded, aware that he was more amused than angry with her defiance. "Like the poor soul who came to the shelter this afternoon, with her eyes and face horribly bruised and a broken arm, which a volunteer nurse tried to set for her, because she couldn't afford to go to a doctor. Similar cases appear there regularly. Last week, a beaten mother came in carrying her six-year-old daughter, who had been raped. A darling little girl, hardly more than a baby, and savaged by her own father! That's what goes on in this terrible man's world! And the victims have no recourse in law—they're desperately poor, and the police don't care, the politicians don't care, only a few 'misguided, radical firebrands,' as the social reformists are labeled, seem to care. So we help these unfortunates as best we can, and we're way over budget for the year, and if you want to spank me for disobeying you today, go ahead. And later, when you're asleep, I'll bite your hand—and maybe something more tender."

"My little tigress," he murmured, pulling her back into his

arms. "Go for my heart—it's the most vulnerable part of me where you're concerned. And I guess the feminists do some good, after all. The District Attorney should know about that violated child, however. Get her name and address, Devon."

"Her mother didn't give that information; too ashamed and frightened of her husband, who threatened to kill her if she did. Fear and terror are effective muzzles. And the records are confidential, anyway, to protect those souls courageous enough to reveal their true identities."

"But there *is* a law against incest, Devon, and that animal should be behind bars."

"He should be dead and in hell," Devon cried passionately. "But Mrs. Stanton told me that the few men ever arrested on such charges are rarely even indicted, much less tried and convicted, for their attorneys staunchly defend them. 'They must support their families, Your Honor, and it was a singular incident due to drunkenness and would never happen again, Your Honor!' The judge knows the county has more vile criminals than cages to confine them, so the cruel beasts are released to prey upon their helpless quarries again and again. Tragic, sad, reprehensible, but true." She gazed at him with misted eyes. "How lucky I and my children are! I count my blessings every time I go to the Bureau, Keith, and I came to you in love tonight. Not feminine wiles or guile, only love, profound and eternal."

"Dearest," he whispered, holding her tenderly close, his lips brushing the fragrant, touseled head on his shoulder. "I'm the lucky one, and I thank God every day for you and all you've given me. The children, the happiness, the joy, the love and passion and pleasure and fidelity; I could recite a litany, but it would be endless and perhaps maudlin. And it's late, and I have an early appointment with J. P. Morgan tomorrow. Sweet dreams, precious," he said, humbly kissing her good night.

Devon smiled as the light was doused, thinking how skillfully he had averted a confrontation over his vexing summons earlier that day, humiliating both her and his secretary. But that was all right with her, and forgivable, because she wasn't anxious to debate it further, either, especially not since she felt she had already won enough points and concessions. "You, too, beloved."

* * *

All the major elevated railroads in Manhattan were completed by the end of the next year, and the iron arteries quickened the life of the island. Villages were no longer as remote and isolated as before, and more women joined the once predominately male passengers commuting to the city, ignoring the tobacco smoke and lifting their skirts over the cuspidors in the narrow aisles, which were as littered and often filthy as those of the horsecars and omnibuses, although the seats were far more comfortable and the transportation much more rapid. The countryside along the tracks was gradually disappearing, except for the large estates, as the city expanded northward, and progress burst its seams in commercial ugliness. The beauty of the Hudson and East rivers was threatened by the construction of more docks, piers, warehouses. Factories beclouded the sky with smoke and soot, slaughterhouses and tanneries befouled the air, and more neighborhoods degenerated into wretched slums controlled by Tammany Hall, whose current politicians were only slightly less greedy and corrupt than those of the notorious Tweed Ring. Boss William Marcy Tweed, most infamous Grand Sachem of the Wigwam, had died in jail some years back, and his ward chiefs had scattered to the four winds, but others had assumed their places and powers. The Democrats had elected their candidate, Grover Cleveland, to the governorship of New York, which could be a stepping stone to the presidency, and Devon thought Reed's prediction the day they had met in Rock Creek Park might possibly come true. Politics would always interest her journalistically, even though the Wyoming Territory was the only place women could vote, and she wondered what would happen to their franchise there if the territory became a state.

She pondered an article on the subject, but decided not to poke any hornets' nests. Things were running smoothly in her career, Keith compromised on matters he couldn't change, and Devon was happy in her various projects.

A major new newspaper, the *New York Morning Journal*, was established, and Publishers Row wondered how it would affect the industry. Already characterized by sensationalism, dignified editors worried that Joseph Pulitzer might try to compete with James Gordon Bennett's *Herald* in yellow journalism.

Competition was fierce in the publishing field, circulation wars were common, and Carrie Hempstead was concerned about maintaining the *Record*'s substantial feminine readership, for the public appetite craved the bizarre, the exotic, the erotic, the unconventional. They devoured the stories about Grover Cleveland's acknowledged mistress and illegitimate child; salivated over novels that touched upon obscenity and immorality, illicit love and adultery; packed the theaters when these situations were dramatized, and idolized the actresses whose private lives were as wicked as some of the heroines they portrayed. If the scandal was connected with royalty, aristocracy, high society, like Britain's most famous stage star Lily Langtry's affair with the Prince of Wales, so much the better, as Devon discovered when she interviewed the gorgeous Jersey Lily on her recent American debut. Miss Langtry was not only willing but eager to discuss her intimate relationship with His Royal Highness, whose blatant immorality had become a painful thorn in the side of his highly moral mother, Queen Victoria. Indeed, Devon and her editor toned down the lurid details, which were so profitably exploited in the opposition presses, along with the fickle lady's immediate conquest of a wealthy American socialite, Frederick Gebhard. The gentleman hosted a gala in his new paramour's honor, which the Curtises attended, and Devon was not surprised that the celebrated guest had heard of the King of Wall Street; the fickle lady was also mercenary. But Keith paid no more attention to Lily Langtry than he had to Sarah Bernhardt, nor to what was written about her in the papers, although he did read his wife's interview and everything else published under her byline.

At present, however, Devon was maternally immersed in *The Training of Children,* a manual of child care written by Helen Hunt Jackson, who was currently working on a romantic Indian novel to be titled *Ramona.* The twins grew more rambunctious with each birthday, and also more adorable. Their father continued to spoil them on weekends, doubling Nanny's and Miss Vale's work in his absence, and Devon felt sorry for them. She read to Keith from the manual, which condemned pampering, while he was down on the floor, his daughters astride his back and squealing with joy as he moved about on all fours.

"Stop that and listen to me, Keith!"

"No, Mommy," Shannon objected. "Daddy's playing horsey with us."

At Keith's pause, Sharon wailed, "Giddyap, horsey!" and his mild pitching created shrieking delight.

Devon almost yelled, "Do you hear me, Keith?"

"Hee-haw," he answered.

"That's the bray of a jackass," she said, laughing at the spectacle, "which is precisely how you look and sound now! Poor Nanny, her week's work for naught. Mondays must be dreadful for her."

"Give her another raise."

"We've already doubled her salary twice this year. It's not more money she wants, Keith, but more cooperation in rearing those little imps. Unload them in the nursery, close the door and—"

"They'll cry, honey."

"Let them! It's time for their naps, anyway."

He delivered his passengers to their nurse, who promptly tucked them in their cribs, and shooed their father out before he could weaken under their sobbing.

"They have rocking horses, dear. No need to tote them around on your hands and knees. And bucking that way— you'll injure your back."

"Is *that* worrying you?" he teased.

"Well, a wrenched spine can be painful, you know."

"And inconvenient in bed," he agreed. "I was playing that way because I've ordered a pair of Shetland ponies for them. They should be here in a couple of months. They'll be fitted with saddles, and I'll hire an expert instructor to teach our little angels."

"They're so young, Keith."

"That's the time to start, as any Virginian should know. Haverston's daughter must have started early, to become so accomplished at nine. I expect Sharon and Shannon to ride as well as their mother someday."

"Which reminds me," Devon seized the opportunity, "of another invitation to Harmony Hill for the Hunt Season. Scotty is included—but, of course, we couldn't take him out of school."

"Hardly. And it's not our son Haverston wants to see, anyway," he said laconically.

"Our polite excuses are wearing thin, Keith."

"Invent some new ones, little writer. Use your creative imagination. Unless *you* want to oblige this time?"

"Well, I haven't been on a hunt in ages."

"Tally-ho, then!"

"Accept?"

"Not for me." He shook his head grimly.

"But you know I wouldn't go without you, Keith."

"That's too bad, my dear. Because I have no desire to foxhunt in Ole Virginny—especially not with the most tenacious hound in the field chasing you."

"That's insulting!" she reproached him.

"Sorry, but we both know it's true."

"I'll send our regrets," Devon decided, eschewing further argument. He would never relent, never mellow, never reconcile himself to any other man in her life, no matter how far in the past, or distant in the future.

✣ 28 ✣

DEVON, WHO had never even in her wildest fantasies aspired to be the mistress of three mansions, was awed as the most fantastic of them all neared completion. She could not even conceive of a name for this splendid white marble palace, for an appropriate one simply defied the imagination. Moreover, it seemed a perverse mockery of modest to call such castles "cottages" and occupy them primarily during the Newport Season, as the few summer months in this most famous American resort were known throughout the cosmopolitan world.

When at last it was finished and ready for occupancy, the

grandeur seemed excessive and almost obscene. And as the Curtis ménage and retinue arrived to spend their first summer there, Devon wondered how she would ever adjust to it. The hauteur, the pretension, the flamboyance of the residences was exceeded only by the efforts of the grandes dames to best one another in their entertainments, and one could only guess at the time, energy, and fortunes expended in these social contests. Deciding that she would participate only to the extent necessary in such a community, Devon unwittingly established herself as the most reserved and inaccessible lady in the elite colony, therefore the one whose favor was the most eagerly sought. And since it was common knowledge that Mr. Curtis was not only the wealthiest of the wealthy but descended of English nobility in his distaff lineage, embracing the Curtises became the goal and ambition of Newport society.

Amused by it all, Keith remained his suave, courteous self, attending to business and pleasure with equal expertise and finesse. As always, sailing was his favorite sport and relaxation, and the graceful *Sprite* became a familiar sight on the Rhode Island waters. He patronized the Casino when interested, and escorted his family to Newport's most exclusive recreational club, Bailey's Beach, while the landscaping of his own property was in progress. The sea was his only mistress and Devon's only rival for his attentions, as he began to consult with shipbuilders on the design and construction of a formidable yacht to compete in the America's Cup Race. So when Devon complained that her tactics regarding privacy were not working and showed him a raft of invitations, he spread them out like a deck of cards on the table and advised her to select one and ignore the rest.

"What if it's someone we dislike, or don't even know?"

"Choose another, or toss them all in the garbage."

"Everything is so simple to you, isn't it?"

"Not everything," he said somberly.

"Oh? Is there a new problem?"

"No, the same one."

"Our son?"

A grave nod. "Scotty's not really happy here, Devon. I'm afraid he'd rather be elsewhere."

"It's just new and strange to him," Devon temporized. "And he lacks friends his own age."

"Only because he won't make any."

"Like his mother?"

"Hell, Devon! I don't want either of you to cultivate people in whom you have no interest. But Scott already has some acquaintances here, in the sons and daughters of our New York clique. And there are some boys from his school, too. I told him he could invite anybody he pleased as house guests, or aboard the yacht."

"Anybody? Does that include Miss Haverston?"

"We haven't discussed her," he muttered.

"Perhaps you should, Keith. Because Fawn's the one guest he really wants—and keeps hoping we'll extend the proper invitation to her family, or let him accept theirs."

"Alone? Never!"

"Then it's hopeless, for now."

"What do you mean by that?"

"Don't be obtuse, darling. You know exactly what I mean. Just wait a few years."

Keith frowned, donning his yachting cap and pulling the bill low over his brooding eyes, lest she read his mind.

Earlier that year the two families had met at Hot Springs, the oldest resort in the country, and the most popular with Tidewater Virginians since the Colonials had appropriated it from the Indians. Coincidentally, they had engaged commodious suites in the enormous Homestead Hotel, which sat on seventeen thousand scenic acres of verdant hills, pristine lakes and streams, and provided numerous forms of amusement. Spying each other in one of the excellent dining rooms, the youngsters had immediately rushed together, and there was no separating them afterward, except for the nightly retirement.

Fawn had grown even prettier in puberty, her long coppery hair cascading on her shoulders like a sun-bright curtain, and her sherry-colored eyes sparkling whenever she looked at Scott, who had also grown even handsomer than the girl remembered him, and much taller. They rode together daily, along miles of picturesque trails supervised by guides, picnicked by placid lakes and ponds and gurgling brooks with baskets prepared in the hotel's kitchens; gathered wildflowers and chased each other in the meadows and woods. Unlike their parents, however, they avoided the warm mineral-water baths for which the spa was justly famous. Keith resented the sexually segregated facilities even for married couples, and nude bathing was prohibited for everyone, except very small children with asthma, disease-twisted limbs, or other health problems.

"Damned prudes," Keith grumbled as they returned to their rooms wrapped in towels and robes. "A woman can share her husband's bed naked, but not his bath stall even partially clothed. What sense does that make?"

"It might be too distracting," Devon surmised, trying to decide what to wear to luncheon.

"For us, anyway," he agreed, winking significantly. "The baths are quite invigorating! I feel wonderfully rejuvenated and motivated. How about you?"

"Ravenously hungry," she murmured, showing a pale rose Swiss voile gown fashionably bustled and bowed and a flattering sheer straw cartwheel hat dyed and decorated to match. "Do you like this outfit?"

"Don't bother getting dressed, darling."

"It's almost noon!"

"High noon," he grinned, pressing his erection against her buttocks and blowing gently on her neck, where the curls that had escaped her protective cap were still damp. "And as good a time as any for my particular appetite."

"So was midnight, and dawn before breakfast."

Keith laughed, swooping her up impulsively. "Must be the water, Mrs. Curtis, and your irresistible charms. Any complaints about my irrepressible ardor?"

"Have you heard any, Mr. Curtis?"

"Not yet, so I just might keep you in bed all day."

"And ravish me for hours?"

"Well, as often as possible."

"Oh, Keith, I love you so much! And I adore it when we play this way. It excites me so, I feel positively wicked and wanton. But sometimes I worry about my libido, fear that I may shock you. . . ."

"And sometimes you talk too much, woman," he admonished huskily, with a silencing kiss.

Despite their vigor and pleasure in each other, however, the Haverstons' presence at the Homestead chafed and discommoded Keith in many ways. For though Daniel did not lack for company among the unattached females also vacationing there, he contrived to meet the Curtises on the grounds, in the dining rooms and pavilions, and in the ballroom every evening. But since neither man would relinquish the hard-to-acquire reservations prematurely, there was no alternative except gracious endurance. And when the children pleaded for an additional hiatus at Harmony Hill, Keith succumbed with a heavy sigh, informing Devon en route to Richmond, "One week, no more! Understand?"

"It wasn't my idea, Keith. But we are in Virginia, after all, and Scotty might not understand our rejecting their invitation again."

"All right, all right! Forget it. I'll just be glad when our place at Newport is ready. . . ." He pondered some papers in his portmanteau, while Devon wrote in her notebook. "Your manuscript is growing like Topsy, my dear. The novel will have to be published in volumes."

"If it's published," she said realistically.

"What on earth can you find to say in all those hundreds of pages and thousands of words?"

"A lot of history, a lot of happiness and heartbreak, a lot of story. It'll have to be edited, of course, but I didn't want to omit anything important to the plot or characters. The War Between the States will never be forgotten by the people who witnessed it, and will be preserved in the memory of those who didn't through books. As you know, General Grant is writing his memoirs now. Unfortunately, Lee died before he could leave his legacy to posterity."

"And so might Grant, if that malignancy in his throat spreads. But at least his royalties will help his family. I've already ordered inscribed editions for all of our libraries." He smiled ruefully, thinking of where they were headed. "I may even present a set to Mr. Haverston for *his* library."

Devon was gazing at the countryside through which the train was passing, its clicking wheels sounding like clocks ticking backward. She would have to include the fierce military action in this now tranquil green valley limned with hazy blue ridges, this hallowed earth more bloodily contested than perhaps any other in the South, for Virginia was the heart and soul of the Confederacy. How well Dan knew that, and how much he could tell her of the horror, terror, tragedy, death, destruction! The unmarked graves, the blue phantoms and gray ghosts, the terrible truth . . .

She wept inwardly, scribbling in shorthand, which Miss Vale had learned to decipher and would eventually transcribe, and when finally they arrived at their destination, Devon feared she might actually faint. For there, in the great central hall, she met herself on canvas, life-size in shimmering ice-blue satin and tulle, diamonds and fire opals, exactly as she had looked descending the stairway for the grand ball finale of the tilting tourney and barbecue. Sweet Jesus! Scotty had not misinterpreted Fawn's letter, after all; Daniel had indeed commissioned a full portrait from her photograph. And Keith was staring at it in outraged disbelief, for it occupied a place of honor in the family gallery: the niche which should rightfully have belonged to the mistress of the house, and at its base was a large bouquet of perfect red roses in an engraved silver urn, the Knight of Harmony Hill's most cherished trophy. Daniel was obviously presenting it to her now, as he would have laid his victorious lance at her feet the day he had won it, traditionally proclaiming his Queen of Love and Beauty.

Ignorant of the significance or ramifications of the painting, Scott was merely pleased that its existence verified his information, and triumphantly exclaimed, "See? I was right! And it's beautiful, Mother! Fawn thinks you're the prettiest lady she ever knew, and her daddy must think so, too!" He glanced curiously at his father, who seemed mesmerized by the lifelike image that eclipsed every other female face in the baroque frames, and was doubly enhanced by a huge, gilded mirror on the opposite wall. No other woman, living or dead, could have taken such total possession of that chamber. It was simply uncanny, overpowering.

"Oh, Daniel!" Devon cried, dismayed. "You shouldn't have done this!"

"I wanted to," he said softly, his heart on his sleeve. "The artist who painted Fawn was so fine, I knew he could capture your likeness to my satisfaction. And he succeeded! Don't you agree, Curtis?"

"Absolutely," Keith nodded, "although he was merely doing justice to his subject. My wife is an exceptionally beautiful woman! I don't suppose there's any way I could persuade you to part with that treasure?"

"None."

"Then may I ask that you forgo any entertainment for us this time? Business in Washington forces me to leave sooner than I expected."

"In that case, why deprive your wife and son? You can return later, or arrangements can be made for them to join you there?"

Keith declined, ignoring his son's obvious disappointment, which was no less so than Haverston's. "I'm sorry. My family will depart with me, the day after tomorrow."

"We're sorry, too," Daniel said, patting his daughter's shoulder, for she seemed about to cry.

Keith suppressed his true feelings until alone with his wife. "The slimy snake! Did he really expect me to fall for that ruse? And he's doing exactly what I figured he would, Devon. Enshrining you! No wonder he promotes our kids' friendship—it's his means of seeing you periodically, or so he hopes." Struck by a sudden brainstorm, he announced, "I think, rather than Harvard, Scott should go to Oxford or Cambridge University."

"No, Keith! Not unless he wants to go to either one. He's my son, too, and I won't have him sent off to England against his will."

"Then he'd damned well better overcome his obsession with Fawn Haverston."

"What about yours with her father?"

"Touché! And you're right, as usual. I'm acting like a fool again. For the hundredth time, forgive me?"

"For the thousandth time, yes." She smiled, tenderly touching his face, smoothing away the tenseness, and his mouth turned to kiss her palm.

"That truly is a magnificent painting, Devon. I'm tempted to try to steal it." He frowned, still chagrined by his jealousy. "But no doubt he'd set the hounds on me, not to mention the vigilantes. We'd be dueling at dawn."

"There are many other excellent artists, Keith."

"Yes, and I want my own portrait of you. That'll be a priority when we return to New York."

But he couldn't help wondering what comfort Haverston derived from the worship of another man's spouse, and what pleasure he obtained possessing a woman on canvas whom he could not possess in person. Like Pygmalion in love with a statue, Daniel was in love with a painting. With one important exception: Devon was not a myth, and the man also loved the flesh-and-blood woman. And, ironically enough, he probably also felt some prior claim on her, if only by virtue of having known and loved her first.

The Richmond depot was busy when they arrived to board their car, which Rufus had ready for travel, including a well-stocked pantry. And while their luggage was conveyed, Scott maneuvered Fawn behind a pillar to say goodbye. When they emerged, looking sheepish, Devon knew they had embraced and perhaps kissed on the lips. Fawn was blushing but not giggling, and Scott appeared tense and wary, as if he had just discovered a baffling fact of life. Fortunately, Keith was preoccupied at that moment, and Devon had no intention of betraying their precious little secret. For what they had discovered, she suspected, was each other. Boy and girl, and the adolescent awakening of sex.

Her heart bled for them.

Every room in the Newport cottage offered an expansive, inspiring view, and Devon could spend hours working in her study, or merely observing the sparkling blue waters and billowing white sails. If the mood prevailed, she might stroll on their private beach, or romp in the surf. The Curtises had retreated to Newport for another summer, leaving small domestic staffs to maintain their other residences. Since less than a dozen servants was considered impecuniary in the colony, and most residents had at least twenty or more, they had to hire additional help locally. Devon was constantly amazed by the air of the nouveaux riches, and soon learned the truth of Keith's earlier assurances that her genealogy was superior to the majority of their neighbors'.

"Didn't I tell you so, milady?" He laughed, glad that she had finally realized it for herself. "One former washwoman now employs thirty maids, and another snobbish dame was little more than the madam of a whorehouse. A notorious gambler now masquerades as a fine gentleman, and a new yachtsman shoveled manure from the stables of the wealthy old widow he married a few years ago, and still sleeps with her pretty young personal French maid. These, Mrs. Curtis, are America's ruling class!"

"Incredible," Devon murmured. "Appalling!"

"No, merely democratic."

Shannon and Sharon loved the beach, where they played under supervision, forbidden to go near the water alone. Even Scotty was not allowed to venture past the markers and buoys, although a very strong swimmer, and a life preserver was always handy when he went sculling. Often the entire family took to the surf, the twins riding jubilantly on Keith's shoulders as he jumped the waves, taking turns because each screamed for attention when the other was aloft. Remembering similar play with his father, Scott wondered if he had been as spoiled and demanding of his parents' time and affections. Presumably so, but he had long since outgrown such childishness and preferred to occupy himself in other ways, mostly alone, beachcombing for driftwood and rare shells, observing the seagulls and sandpipers, or building sand castles. Some of his structures were architectural and engineering feats, including models of Heathstone Manor, Halcyon-on-Hudson, Gramercy Park, his school, famous castles and cathedrals. But his favorite was a replica of Harmony Hill, distant enough from the shore to prevent destruction by the relentless tides, and so accurate in detail as to be easily recognizable by his parents. Keith searched in vain, however, for a miniature of the Curtis Bank and adjacent office building, or of anything on Wall Street.

Devon looked fetching in her bathing costumes, which conformed with the mandatory modesty of bonnets, stockings, and canvas shoes, and the sight of Keith's muscular torso in his striped jersey suits, which flaunted his manhood when wet, never failed to arouse her sexually. Dawns were glorious creations of pink and rose and salmon and silver. Sunsets were as spectacular as any Devon had seen in Texas: brilliant, gorgeous hues of crimson, saffron, magenta, burnt orange. Twilight descended slowly, like sheer draperies of mauve, lavender, violet, deep purple. They gathered around bonfires eating steamed clams, crabs, and Saratoga chips. They might cruise the Sound in the moonlight, or send the children to the house and make love on beach blankets. Devon always worried about being seen, but not enough to resist the temptation.

She liked to ride along the shore, on the hard wet sand, with Keith and Scotty, or alone if they were unavailable. Her son always cautioned her about riding too near Harmony Hill, and once she asked, "Why is it so important, dear? You don't mind your other structures being trampled, or washed away by the sea. Nothing built of sand is ever permanent, you know."

After some hesitation, he confided that Fawn might wander up that way sometime, and see how well he'd captured the plantation from memory. "We still correspond, Mother, even oftener now than before."

"You must both have trunks full of letters," Devon said. "Is Fawn as sentimental about yours?"

"I guess so, if she ties them with blue ribbon, as she claims. Fawn is graduating from Rosewood Female Academy next spring. May we go to the commencement, Mother?"

"We'll see, son."

"You always say that! Daddy, too. 'We'll see, we'll see.' But this time I'm going, if I must do it alone, and even hobo my way! I'm old enough."

"So you are, Scotty. Entering Harvard this fall! I can scarcely believe it. Boys your age do many things on their own, including travel. Some even take the Grand Tour, but I hope you'll be content to wait until after college for yours. Will you?"

He shrugged. "I'm not sure. I may not even want to go abroad alone."

"Well, an experienced guide would be with you, naturally. And a companion-valet."

"I'm not referring to an escort or man Friday."

Devon glanced at the moored yacht. "We could sail on the *Sprite,* if you prefer."

"You don't understand, Mother."

"Perhaps not, son. Do you want to explain?"

After due consideration, he replied, "Not now."

Being a coastal island, Newport was often foggy, but it was not fog blurring Devon's vision now. The sky was a sunny azure, with puffs of white clouds drifting southward like cotton blown on the wind, and she saw some things quite clearly. Rather than diminishing with time, his interest in Fawn Haverston was seriously deepening. He longed to spend his holidays with her, and his father must often seem like an ogre keeping them apart. For Keith was far more adamant than Daniel in this respect, and his attitude did not even mellow, much less alter.

"You like Fawn very much, don't you?"

"More than like," he said.

"Do you think you love her, Scotty?"

"Does it matter?"

"Of course it matters! You're teenagers."

"So were Romeo and Juliet."

Devon sighed. "I knew that was coming, and that was a play, Scott. This is life."

"Yes, Mother. My life, and Fawn's, and maybe we know ourselves better than our elders. Isn't that possible?"

"I suppose so, son. We just don't want you to make a mistake, that's all."

"People make mistakes, Mother. You and Father probably made a few, didn't you?"

"We're human, Scotty. Nobody's perfect."

"But you expect me to be?"

"No, no! But you're so young, darling. We love you, and want you to be happy. Is that so wrong of us?"

"Just parental, I guess." His crooked smile, so like Keith's in cynicism, wrung her heart. "Do you mind if we don't continue this conversation, Mother?"

"Why, no, dear," Devon said, nonplused as he spurred his mount, creating a minor dust storm that soon obscured him from her sight. So often of late, these adolescent tensions or terrors or torments suddenly seized him, and he tried one way or another to escape them. Wheeling her horse, Devon trotted back to the stables, convinced that nothing useful would be served by relating this episode to his father. Keith wouldn't understand; or perhaps he would, only too well.

❧ 29 ❧

AWARE THAT it would be futile, Keith made no concerted effort to persuade his son to continue his education in England. The boy was as obstinate and determined as his mother in wanting to make his own decisions, assert his freedom and independence, and Keith did not want a contest of wills to develop between them.

Scott entered Harvard on schedule, acquitted himself well in his studies and athletics, but shunned the more daring extracurricular activities that could have led to expulsion. Few of his fraternity brothers admitted to having a sweetheart back home or anywhere else to whom they were devoted, and Scott never confided his private life to even his closest associates. Thus, he was often lonely on weekends and holidays, when the older boys sneaked off to carouse in some of Boston's liberal fleshpots. They boasted of heavy drinking and sexual experiences at incredibly early ages, and teased the apparent virgins among them: "Saving yourself for marriage, brother? Virginity is just for the bride."

"And promiscuity will get you the clap," a divinity student warned, enlisting the aid of his New York friend who was studiously trying to ignore the ribald conversation. "Isn't that so, Curtis?"

"According to the medical journals," Scott agreed.

"Why do you read them?" inquired the self-proclaimed lecher of the dormitory. "You're not in medical school. Thomas Heming reads the Bible so much because he's a pious minister's spawn and headed for the pulpit. But why are you practically memorizing *Gray's Anatomy*? Your destination is supposed to be Wall Street, Mr. Curtis. My old man claims your old man is the biggest of the big bankers."

"I don't call my father 'the old man'," said Scott.

"You also don't answer questions," his tormentor drawled. "Christ, we're only trying to help you and the future reverend have a little fun, that's all! But keep your virginity, if it's so important to you, and beat your meat for relief. Who the hell cares!" He offered his hand, grinning. "We can still be friends, can't we?"

"Sure," Scott nodded, shaking with him. "How much do you want to borrow this time, *friend?*"

"Huh?"

"Money, Wharton. Greenbacks are the primary basis of your friendship, and loans without collateral. Your allowance never lasts long enough, at the rate you spend it."

"That's a fact! Can you spare me ten bucks? I'll pay it back next month."

Scott obliged, advising, "You already owe me fifty, Wharton. I'm going to start charging you interest."

Wharton laughed, slapping his creditor's shoulder. "Oh, you're destined for banking, Curtis! No doubt of that. And I pity the poor widows and orphans in your clutches."

"They should be so lucky," the future clergyman said. "We'd all be strapped for cash if it weren't for Curtis's generosity—and you'd be in debtors' prison, Wharton!"

True to his promise to Fawn, Scott went to Charlottsville for her graduation from Rosewood Female Academy, and his mother accompanied him against his father's wishes. Daniel couldn't have been more delighted that business kept her husband in New York. The exercises were held outdoors, as was customary for Rosewood, and Dan sat beside Devon on one of the long wood benches provided for parents and guests. The graduates were dressed in frilly white frocks, with bows or flowers in their hair, and appeared very sedate and grown-up accepting their diplomas from the headmistress. Remembering her own graduation day, Devon waxed nostalgic, and Dan longed to hold her hand. But her son was present, and she would probably have rebuffed him in any case.

"Memories?" he whispered, leaning closer.

Devon nodded. "Was I ever that young, Dan?"

"Yes, my dear, and prettier than any of them, including my

own daughter. Indeed, you don't seem much older to me even now, and certainly no less lovely."

"Oh, Dan!" she admonished. "You must need spectacles!"

"Don't you believe your mirror, Devon? Those sweet little things on that platform are mere children, none over sixteen."

"They're young ladies, Daniel, and some are already thinking of young men."

"Of course, if they're normal."

"Are you aware . . . ?"

"Mother, please!" Scott interrupted. "The ceremonies are about to be concluded."

The final ribbon-tied certificate was bestowed, to a Marlene Anne Zepple, and the school officials bade the familiar farewells to the senior class. In minutes, the honorees were off the spring-decorated stage, flitting among family and friends, chattering like magpies, and Devon decided they were not so mature, after all. Fawn looked angelic in ruffled white organdy and fluttering blue taffeta sash, a crown of white camellias on her burnished-gold hair, and her face wreathed in smiles, as she flew to her father and special guests, and was embraced by all. Then, taking Scott's hand, she led him along the campus paths to a wrought-iron bench under a chestnut tree in the garden, and the abandoned parents could only watch and smile resignedly.

"What were you saying, my dear, when Scott shushed you?"

"Nothing you don't already know, Dan."

"You seem worried, Devon."

"Aren't you?"

"A little," he admitted. "Any suggestions?"

"Only parental interference, to which I'm loath, and don't believe would be effective, anyway." She toyed with her ivory-spoked silk fan, her face shaded by a brimmed and veiled hat the same apple-green shade of her gown.

"Not if they're half as stubborn and defiant as their parents— and I mean the three of us, Devon. We're all rules in that respect."

"I'm afraid so, Daniel."

"I'm sure Fawn suspects my feelings for you, Devon."

"You haven't told her anything!" she cried, shocked.

"Not in words," he assured. "But the portrait speaks plainly enough, don't you think?"

"Yes, and I'm surprised she doesn't resent it. Her *mother* should be on that wall, Daniel!"

"I explained my marriage to you some years ago, Devon. Although Caroline and I tried, neither of us could forget our first loves, nor held it against the other."

"But she gave you such a beautiful child, Dan! Doesn't she deserve some homage for that?"

"Caroline has my undying respect and gratitude for that precious gift," he declared. "And her family has a nice portrait of her, which Fawn will inherit."

Plying her fan nervously, Devon suddenly decided, "I think it's time for my son and I to go to the hotel."

"Hotel? You're staying in Charlottesville?"

"Just for the night. We'll leave tomorrow."

"That's absurd, Devon! We're expecting you at Harmony Hill."

"I'm sorry, Dan. We only came for the commencement. I know how much Scotty wants to visit the plantation again, but we can't this trip."

"The King of Wall Street forbids?" he asked cynically, still bitter toward Keith Curtis.

"It wouldn't be discreet, Dan, under the circumstances. You know that."

"There are many rooms and servants, Devon. But if you're concerned about the proprieties, I'll invite some house guests. The Clintons would enjoy seeing you again, and Mrs. Clinton could be your chaperone. Bess is a very circumspect old matron now. Doesn't your spouse trust you? He didn't worry much about your reputation before the marriage."

"That's unfair, Daniel, and untrue. Keith has always worried about me in every respect, and it's you he doesn't trust, especially after seeing that portrait."

"Too bad I can't give him more reason than a painting," he muttered. "But I guarantee his son is not going to appreciate being separated so swiftly from my daughter."

Devon was fully cognizant of that, but she had no choice, even if he invited a dozen old ladies to vouch for her decorum in his abode. She had promised Keith not to go to the plantation without him, and she could not breach any vow whatever to him.

"I expect both kids to protest," she said.

"Am I to understand that you came to the graduation only to please Scotty?"

"Well, I'm also sentimental about my alma mater," Devon dissembled, glancing wistfully toward the cluster of pink brick buildings, some hung with English ivy, which had served as a hospital during the latter phases of the war.

"No doubt Fawn will share that sentiment now, my dear, being an alumna too. So we'll also spend the night in Charlottesville, at the same hostelry. I presume it's Magnolia Inn, since it's the best in town. We can have dinner together this evening, including the children, of course. Surely no one could criticize such a nice congenial little family celebration? If you have any reservations or objections, you'll have to explain them to your son."

He was very cavalier about it, grinning at her accusations of connivery, until Devon sighed and acquiesced in a smile of her own.

"Sleeping on the job, Miss Ryan?"

Marnie jerked upright in her chair. Her head had been lying on her folded arms on her desk, and she had indeed dozed off. "Taking an early luncheon period, Mr. Curtis."

"It's only ten o'clock!"

"So it is," she said, consulting the ornate timepiece on the paneled wall. "I didn't get much sleep last night, sir. None a'tall, in fact. Pa was in dreadful pain, and we had no laudanum. He kept me awake moaning and groaning. I don't know what to do about him, Mr. Curtis."

"I do, Miss Ryan. Your father must be put somewhere, and promptly. You simply cannot do proper work without your proper rest."

"I know, sir, and I'll stay late to make up for it. But I can't afford to put Pa anywhere."

"Not to worry," Keith told her. "I can get him into an old-age home."

"A charity ward, on Blackwell's Island, in the East River? Oh, no, Mr. Curtis! I hear they treat poor old folks badly in those places, especially if they're sick and cantankerous, like Pa."

"I was thinking of Sunset House, Miss Ryan. It's a privately endowed institution, and your father will be treated humanely. I'm on the board of trustees, so all we have to do is take him there. And the sooner, the better."

"But he can hardly walk!"

"Well, now, me foine lass," Keith mimicked, "do ye think he'd be after walking to Sunset House? 'Tis in a carriage he'll be riding, and 'tis some instructions *this* trustee'll be giving the administrators."

Marnie burst into tears and began to fumble in the desk drawer for her reticule. Keith whipped out his handkerchief and handed it to her, unable to bear her distress. "Good Lord, is my accent that awful? Don't cry, Miss Ryan. I'm trying to solve your problems, not increase them."

"You're so good and kind and generous, I never knew anyone so wonderful, and I was afraid of being fired—and would have deserved it, too, being derelict on duty."

Afraid that she was about to canonize him, Keith quickly interceded, "I'm no saint, Miss Ryan, but hardly villain enough to dismiss anyone under these circumstances. And about that early luncheon period—where's your food?"

"I was in too big a hurry to prepare a sandwich this morning," she explained, drying her eyes, intending to wash and press the fine monogrammed linen square before returning it to him.

"So you were going to skip eating today?"

"Well—"

"No sleep, no food. You'll get sick! My employees have to be alert, and especially my secretary. Get yourself together, Miss Ryan, and take the rest of the day off. I'll make the arrangements for your father, and we'll take him to Sunset House this Sunday."

"But you always go to the country on weekends, sir."

"So I'll miss this one," he said decisively.

"Your wife won't mind?"

"Mrs. Curtis is in Virginia for a few days, but why should she mind my helping you in an emergency?"

"All right, then. I'll go to eight o'clock Mass, sir, and afterward—"

"Don't you think God will understand if you miss church this once for your father's sake?"

"God might, but I'm not sure about Father O'Toole. It's a

mortal sin to miss Mass on Sundays and Holy Days of Obligation, and must be confessed. I'll get a stiff penance, at least a whole rosary, maybe several."

Keith smiled, shaking his head at such religious innocence. "Heaven forbid that I should heap such a burden on your soul, Miss Ryan. We'll go after services."

"Thank you, sir. I'm fine now and quite able to finish out the day...."

"Damn it, woman! I don't have the patience of Job. Go home and rest. And if you utter one more word of protest, I *will* fire you sans reference!"

"Yes, sir." She gathered her hat and purse and gloves, smiled at his gruff pretense, and left.

The elegant equipage standing before the shabby tenement when Marnie rushed home from the parish church that Sunday morning, made her pause and gasp in breathless admiration. A princess royal could not expect to ride in grander style! The matched bay horses were handsomely caparisoned, the attendants in livery, and the coachman informed her that Mr. Curtis was inside with Mr. Ryan. The old fellow didn't really want to go to an institution, which he ranked somewhere between a pesthouse and a prison and regarded as the end of the road for any unfortunate inmate. But Keith assured him that Sunset House was neither a lunatic asylum nor a dungeon, and finally managed to convince him that it was the best thing for him and his daughter. "So be it," he agreed, after Marnie promised that both she and the priest would visit him regularly. The footman was summoned to assist Keith in carrying Patrick Ryan and his ancient straw valise down the flight of rickety stairs to the princely vehicle.

The new patient was welcomed at Sunset House like a dignitary, assigned a private room and personal wheelchair, and he wondered if all his prayers had finally resulted in a miracle. When he was settled in with a minimum of complaint, Marnie kissed his forehead and joined their benefactor in the administration office, where the head nurse and supervisor was virtually groveling to him.

"All set, Miss Ryan?" he asked.

"Yes, and Pa seems to like it here already."

"I thought he would. And he'll receive good care, won't he, Mrs. Barnes?"

"The very best we can offer, Mr. Curtis," she assured him with an ingratiating smile.

Keith took Marnie's arm. "I'll take you home now."

"Oh, you needn't—" she began, but his look silenced her. "Thank you, sir."

At the apartment, she invited him in for a cup of tea or coffee, and was surprised when he accepted. Though small and meagerly furnished, the place was neat as a pin. The cretone curtains were washed and ironed, the bare floor scrubbed, the two single iron beds spread with cheap candlewick counterpanes, an embroidered pillow on one. As Marnie put the kettle on the stove, Keith asked, "Would ye be having something a mite stronger in the house, Miss Ryan?"

His brogue always amused her, and she replied in kind: "Sure and I might, sir. Nothing fancy, mind ye, just a bit of poteen. Pa claimed it eased his aching bones. You know the Irish and liquor, sir. 'Tis no such creature as a teetotaling mick, and that's the gospel truth. Some even go to church half in their cups, and Father O'Toole chastised this morning's drunkards from the pulpit to no avail." She fished the cheap Irish whisky out of the cupboard and placed the bottle on the oilclothed table, along with a spotless hobnail tumbler. "Help yeself, sir."

Keith poured a drink and gingerly tasted it, trying not to wince at the poor quality.

"Not very good, is it, sir?"

"Illegally distilled spirits never are, Miss Ryan. Are you sure this isn't rubbing liniment?"

Marnie chuckled. "He used it for that sometimes, I think, dosing himself inside and out." Her eyes saddened suddenly. "Oh, Pa was a rascal, all right, and a cross to bear, but I shall miss him. He was company, at least."

"He's not dead, Miss Ryan."

"He thought so when he imagined he was going to his grave, and even held his own wake. But the nice home brought him to life again."

"And you're both better off," Keith comforted. "Now you can have more leisure for yourself, and with your friend, the horsecar conductor."

When the tea was ready, Marnie poured herself a cup and sat opposite him at the table. She had no cream or lemon, and did not use sugar. "His name is Michael Shawn, and he wants to get married."

"I don't blame Mr. Shawn, a pretty girl like you."

"I'm not a girl, sir."

"Well, pretty woman, if you prefer. He must know you'd make him a wonderful wife; any man worth his salt would know that, Marnie."

"Marnie? You never called me that before, Mr. Curtis."

"And shouldn't have then," he said, sipping the sorry whisky again. "Don't worry, it'll be Miss Ryan in the office tomorrow. I just hope you rest well tonight, so you won't need any sudden respites."

Marnie flushed, still dismayed by that lapse. "I just couldn't keep my eyes open any longer, no matter how hard I tried. It won't happen again, sir."

Keith was embarrassed. "I was only teasing, Marnie. For God's sake, don't apologize for that little fault anymore." He stood. "I'd better leave now."

"You haven't finished your poteen."

"My throat can't take much more. I trust your suitor drinks better stuff than that?"

"Just beer or ale, at ten cents a pail. That's all Mike can afford."

"May I send you some decent wine, my dear, in case you have a reason to celebrate?"

"A bottle would be nice, for a special occasion, but—"

"Consider it a birthday gift," Keith suggested, while she hesitated over decorum. "You have another milestone coming up next week."

"How did you know my birthdate?"

"It's on your employment application."

"Oh, of course! How stupid of me! But I didn't expect you to remember. I don't know your vital statistics."

"They're on my insurance policies, if you're curious."

"I just keep track of the premium payments, sir."

"Behold a noncurious woman!" Keith opened the door, and Marnie heard his deep, resonant laughter in the stairwell, and felt her heart flutter and her knees tremble.

Watching the luxurious green-and-silver carriage leave, she whispered, "Goodbye, Keith." She had to say his name aloud just once, to hear it in her ears and feel it on her lips. And while she was indulging in a sinful reverie, she remembered another mistake.

Glory be! She had forgotten to return his handkerchief. It still lay in her bureau, wrapped in tissue paper now permeated with the residual scent of his fine French shaving lotion. But the carriage was out of sight now, and she could not catch it, no matter how fast she ran.

After a few moments, Marnie opened the drawer and touched the expensive white linen square, tracing the monogram and inhaling the marvelous masculine odor so uniquely his own. She knew the Scriptures, by chapter and verse, and to lust in one's heart for a married person was tantamount to committing adultery with him. God and the Holy Saints forgive her for coveting another woman's husband now, for sinning so grievously in her mind! Father O'Toole was going to lambast her in confessional, and assign the Stations of the Cross for her penance. . . .

✢ 30 ✤

SCOTT WAS preoccupied on the return trip, immersed in a history of Virginia much of the time. Devon's efforts to draw him into conversation was largely fruitless, except during meals, which Rufus prepared and served with his usual culinary skill, whether on land or at sea. Over supper on the day of their departure, the boy asked a question which his mother could not honestly answer: "Why couldn't we spend more time with the Haverstons?"

"This wasn't a vacation, Scotty. You wanted to attend Fawn's graduation, and we did."

"I also wanted to go to Harmony Hill," he reminded her morosely, "and we *didn't*."

"It seemed the better part of discretion to decline that invitation in your father's absence."

"Why? Is Daddy so jealous of Mr. Haverston, because of that portrait he had painted of you from a photograph? I think it was a great honor."

"We both have our reasons," Devon said, discommoded by his keen perception. "I don't understand your sullen attitude, son. We stayed in Charlottsville longer than I planned, and you and Fawn had some extra time together."

"But never alone," he protested.

"Of course not! Proper young ladies must be chaperoned in the company of young men. You know that! We saw the most important tourist attractions, didn't we? I thought you enjoyed visiting Monticello, and President Madison's home, Ashlawn. And the birthplaces of the explorers most responsible for opening the West, Lewis and Clark."

"Mother, I don't need footnotes on any of these figures. I've studied about them in American history."

"It was still nice to actually *see* the sights, wasn't it, rather than merely reading about them? And I know you enjoyed the stagecoach expedition to the Blue Ridge Mountains, and the picnic with Fawn, even though it delayed our return home two full days, and I had to telegraph Daddy. I did my best, Scotty, and you've no reason to be cross with me. We'll retreat to Newport again in July, and I've invited the Haverstons to visit us there."

"Really?" His face brightened, along with his mood, so typical of adolescence. "That's wonderful, Mother! Thank you ever so much."

"Don't get your hopes too high, dear. They may not accept. Mr. Haverston merely promised to consider it."

"They'll come," he said, confident of Fawn's powers of paternal persuasion, although less sanguine of his own. "If not, it'll probably be Daddy's fault."

"Oh, Scotty, you mustn't say such things! Some of your criticism would hurt him deeply—and, in fact, has already caused him considerable pain. Lately, you don't seem to admire or appreciate your father as much as a son should, and that grieves *me*, too."

"But you know he wanted to send me to England, to Oxford or Cambridge. Then he talks about a close family relationship...just how close could we be with me across the sea? Or did he imagine he could simply drown my interest in Fawn Haverston in the Atlantic Ocean!"

The train whistled through the misty blue hills, echoing mournfully on the way to Washington, then Baltimore, and evoking poignant memories for Devon. "I won't condone any more disrespect to your father, Scotty, nor harsh judgment of him," she admonished. "Mercy, you act as if you and Fawn were mature individuals, capable of making your own decisions, and already betrothed!" She glanced suspiciously at his left hand. "Where's your signet ring?"

"Lost," he answered, eyes downcast.

"I think you're fibbing, Scotty."

"If you're accusing me of lying, Mother—"

"I'm asking for the simple truth, son. What happened to the gold signet ring you received last Christmas and were wearing yesterday?"

"I gave it away. It was getting a little small for my finger, anyway."

"It could have been enlarged, you know." Devon waited for their eyes to meet. "Does Fawn have it now?"

"Yes, she's keeping it for me."

"Did some promises go with the ring, Scotty? Is it a form of engagement?"

"Maybe," he murmured, resenting the inquisition.

"Dear heaven, at your ages! And don't parallel Romeo and Juliet again! Does Mr. Haverston know about this?"

"Probably not. I don't think he grills Fawn the way my parents do me. We intended to keep it secret for a while, if possible. You're worried about Father, aren't you? Will you tell him?"

"No, *you* will," Devon said firmly.

"Only if he notices my bare finger, and asks. Lots of rings and jewelry are lost, or misplaced. And I can be as vague as Daddy is in answering some of my questions," he added defiantly.

Startled by his rebellious vehemence and wondering at his implication, Devon felt slightly ill. Sweet Jesus! Was the long-feared haunting of her past going to commence in the very same railroad coach and on the same route of its inception? How ironic, coincidental, and perhaps even fitting!

"You're white as a ghost, Mother!" Scott observed, his eyes peering at her with the color and intensity of Keith's. "I'm sorry if I shocked you about Fawn and me. But we don't plan to do anything wrong or rash, like running away together. We have more sense than that! She liked the French bonbons and stationery we gave her for graduation, but I wanted to give her something extra. And more personal."

Devon was mulling his assurances of sensible behavior with Fawn. Could she have made the same statement about herself with his father? Had *she* been prudent, wise, patient? Hardly. Nor had Keith, either.

"Are you all right, Mother?" he asked solicitously, for she had grown even paler during the pause.

"Fine," Devon assured him. "Just a bit tired, Scotty. Finish your meal, so Rufus can tidy the the pantry. Did Daddy tell you he's having another car built, to accommodate the whole family and attendants on future trips? We'll soon be able to travel across the country, now that the railroad systems are becoming so well connected."

"And the Curtises own so much stock in them," he added wryly. "As much as Jay Gould or the Vanderbilts, no doubt, if not more."

"Our wealth is a fact of life, son, which you and I must learn to accept gracefully and gratefully," Devon temporized, for she also found it incredible and difficult, at times. "Frankly, I'd like to visit the West Coast, especially California. San Francisco is considered a very progressive and exciting city. I'd like to visit Denver, too, and cross the Great Divide of the Rocky Mountains. The western scenery is absolutely spectacular, according to John Muir. He writes as well about nature as did Henry Thoreau and—" Realizing that she was babbling nervously, she pleaded a headache and excused herself to rest. Scott resumed his reading of the history of the state which currently interested him more than any other in the country, or the world.

Fawn did not come to Newport that summer, but her letters went to all three Curtis residences, for she was never quite sure where the family would be at any particular time. Scott had told her that the longest any of the "cottagers" remained on the island was four months, and the average season was about eight weeks. He had described their palatial marble mansion and the paradisiacal gardens to her as modestly as possible, but said she would have to see them to believe it. Although it was still not formally titled, Scott had various names for the Newport place: Mont Blanc, Olympus, Castle Curtis, but his favorite was still his mother's first impression of White Elephant. No matter how mail was addressed, the envelope needed only *Curtis* and *Newport* to be delivered. One such delivery contained a message explaining why the Haverstons would not be going north to visit the Curtises that year: Fawn's father had not received a formal invitation from Scotty's, and so, except for their annual holiday at Hot Springs, Virginia, they would be at Harmony Hill. Or, perhaps, a week or two at Sea Island, Georgia.

Scott showed the letter to Devon. "Didn't I tell you, Mother? They're not coming, and it's all Daddy's fault! One little gesture, and he wouldn't make it."

"Now, Scotty—"

"Oh, don't defend him, Mother!"

He stomped out of her study, just as Keith was entering, and merely glared at him, continuing on his way out of the house. "What's his problem *today?*" he asked, frowning.

Devon sighed. "The same as it was yesterday and will be tomorrow, I'm afraid."

"We were supposed to go sailing this afternoon."

"I think he'd rather be alone, Keith."

"I got that impression at the tennis and polo matches, too. He does a lot of woolgathering, Devon."

"That's natural enough, all things considered."

"Well, he'll be back at Harvard for the fall semester soon. Where are the twins?"

"Napping."

"Aren't they old enough to skip it?"

"Yes, but their siestas provide some rest for Nanny and Miss Vale. You know how active and tiring the girls can be. As for your recreation with Scotty, there's always *mañana.*" She occasionally used some of the Spanish words she had learned in Texas, as she sometimes spoke in French, to keep her languages in practice.

Keith sat in a winged Gainsborough chair with a view of the harbor. He supposed that Scott would go sculling with one of the crew of the *Sprite*, or alone. Abruptly, he said, "I'm losing my son, Devon."

"Oh, I imagine we both will, eventually, when he marries," she assuaged. "Remember that old rhyme? 'A son is a son till he takes a wife, but a daughter is a daughter all of her life.'"

"If it's true, thank God for Shannon and Sharon!" His face was anguished. "But I don't want to lose my boy, Devon. I *can't* lose him!"

"I was speaking figuratively, darling. Scotty is, and always will be, our son. Only death can really take him from us."

"But I had such high hopes and plans for him," he brooded. "Curtis and Son, Bankers. Curtis and Son Enterprises, East and West. Curtis and Son, Everything!"

"It might still be, Keith."

"Maybe, but I think Scott wants an entirely different kind of life, my dear."

"Well, it's not too late—"

He interrupted, "To try for another son?"

"Why not?"

"You know why! Besides, even if it were a boy, I'd be an old man before he was grown. No, Devon."

She hesitated, chewing her lower lip. "You may not have any choice in the matter, husband. Accidents happen, you know. In fact, I think one has happened."

That startled him to his feet. "You're pregnant?"

"I've missed two periods."

A look of horror and incredulity crossed his features, and

Devon presumed he was counting backward, trying to fix the possible date of conception.

"Oh, my God!" she cried, leaping from her desk. *"What* are you thinking?"

"Nothing," he said.

"Don't lie to me, Keith! I saw your expression, the look in your eyes! I'll never forget it!"

He came toward her, arms extended, but she pushed him away. "Don't touch me! Whom do you suspect? Daniel Haverston? Dr. Blake? Maybe even Senator Carter, during the train's short interim in Washington?"

"No, you little ninny! Whatever you saw in my face was fear, not suspicion or accusation! Fear for you to have another child."

"I don't believe you! You were mentally calculating, and I was in Charlottsville in early June. You think I was unfaithful to you."

"That's not true, Devon."

"It is, it is!" She was sobbing now, utterly distracted, and screaming at him. "Get out of here, damn you! Leave me alone!"

"You're hysterical, darling. Calm down, please, and listen to me." He glanced about the room. "Don't you keep any spirits in here, not even wine?"

"Sherry, but I don't want any, Keith. I just want you to go away, before I throw something at you!"

"How can I convince you . . . ?"

"You can't!"

She grabbed a delicate porcelain figurine off a table and hurled it at him. Keith caught it luckily, placed it safely on the Grenache marble mantel, and reached her before she could fling its mate. He restrained her forcibly as she struggled against him, weeping and writhing as if in severe pain. Keith picked her up and sat down with her, pinioning her flailing arms and holding her head against his chest. Unable to reason with her, however, he simply waited for the storm to pass. It subsided within minutes, leaving fatigue and apathy in its wake, and she murmured, "Let me up."

"Only if you promise to behave." Frightened by it all, Keith sought to inject some humor. "That was a sixteenth-century

Mennecy piece, my dear, worth a fortune. Lucky it didn't break."

"I don't care about its cost or antiquity! I hated you when I threw it and wanted to hit you."

"Smash all the art objects, Devon, if it'll make you feel better. Nothing unimportant to you is important to me. Break up the whole goddamned place, if you hate me. I'll help you. Where shall we start?"

"Just release me, please," she implored, abandoning his embrace as he reluctantly obliged.

"Have you seen a doctor, Devon?"

"Not yet. We've been here since July."

"Well, do you have any other symptoms of pregnancy? I expected you to swoon a few minutes ago, but you seemed strong enough."

"I was too angry to faint," she muttered, sitting on the exquisite Italian settee. "And I haven't had any morning nausea yet."

"You always did before. Maybe your menses are just delayed, by cold bathing or something. But why didn't you tell me the first month?"

"Oddly enough, I thought you'd notice it yourself, since you've always paid more attention to my lunar calendar than I have."

"I was worried after the twins were born, as you know. But they're seven years old now, and we were both fairly confident of our contraceptive. Overconfident, apparently, for here we are in another crisis. We'd better go back to New York and consult Ramsey."

"There's no emergency, Keith. We can finish out the season here, if you wish."

"You should be examined, Devon, and the pessary removed, if it hasn't been autonomously expelled."

"How could that happen, without my knowledge?"

"I don't know, but we have to find out," he said, knitting his dark brows worriedly. "Shall we try now?"

She shook her head slowly.

"Still hate and want to kill me?"

Cool silence as her fingers traced a pattern in the rose satin brocade, testing his patience.

"Devon, if I made you pregnant—"

"What do you mean, *if you did?*" she demanded, verging on another rage.

"Oh, God! Not what you *think,* darling. You misunderstood from the beginning, and I can't seem to remove your misapprehension."

"What about *your* misapprehension?"

"I was frightened, Devon, not suspicious. If I believed anything else, I'd be on my way to Virginia with a gun."

"Or to Texas, if Congress has adjourned?"

"Keep on, Devon, and we'll be in separate rooms tonight," he warned. "Is that what you want?"

"Right now, I don't care, one way or the other."

"Very well. Where do you want me to sleep?"

"There are forty rooms in this house, Keith, and half of them have beds. It's your choice."

"Not mine, madam, *yours!*" He rose and left without another word, but Devon sensed his barely controlled fury and saw his clenched fists.

∗ 31 ∗

IMMEDIATELY AFTER DINNER, for which Devon did not appear at the dining table, Keith took a supply of liquor to a guest chamber and proceeded to indulge in maudlin woe and bewilderment. His son was drifting away from him as surely as if they were in separate vessels sailing toward opposite horizons, and his wife seemed to be traveling in another direction, too. How could she have read anything but concern in his expression? And what could he do about it now, except hope that she would quickly dispel the erroneous notion and forget it? A helluva problem, and the solution would not be found in a bottle, but he needed the temporary solace and solitude.

Finally, partially inebriated and half undressed, he flung himself across the massive Empire bed with its heavy crimson velvet lambrequin, and fell into a fitful slumber rampant with nightmares. He tossed on the unfamiliar mattress and buried his head in the large eiderdown pillow, but the pounding in his ears only became louder, more insistent, and finally a shrill feminine voice penetrated his subconscious. It wasn't a dream, after all. There was some emergency, and Heather Vale was banging on the door and calling, "Mr. Curtis! Mr. Curtis! Wake up!"

Keith dragged himself off the bed, in trousers and socks, retrieved his shirt from the floor where he had dropped it, and opened the door.

"What is it, Miss Vale?"

"Mrs. Curtis needs you, sir. Come quickly!"

"My God! What happened?"

"I'm not sure, sir. Just hurry, please."

They ran along corridors that seemed serpentine and endless, down flights of stairs that also seemed endless, and Keith burst into the master suite at a gallop. Devon was lying on the pink marble bathroom floor, the bottom of her nightgown saturated with blood. She had awakened with abdominal cramps and managed to pull the bellcord before rushing to the commode, but was unable to reach it before the uterine hemorrhage felled her.

"Call a doctor!" Keith told the governess, for telephones had been installed in Newport's cottages several years ago. "Ask the operator for the best man in town!"

"Yes, sir! Mrs. Sommes will be up as soon as she can get dressed."

Keith lifted Devon and carried her to the bed, snatching towels off the gold-plated racks as he proceeded, to tuck between her legs and beneath her limp body. She was barely conscious, and Keith, horrified and fearful, castigated himself for impairing his senses with alcohol. But soon capable Anna Sommes was there to help, Enid was bringing a pot of strong black coffee, and there was little else to do now except wait for the physician.

Dr. Harry Morton arrived posthaste, fully aware of the importance of the people who had summoned him. And after ministering to the patient, he examined the expelled material in the bathroom, and diagnosed, "Spontaneous abortion, very early stage."

"How early?" Keith inquired.

"Eight or nine weeks."

"Will she be all right?"

"Your wife will be fine, Mr. Curtis. The expulsion was complete, and complications are rare in these cases. A week or two of bed rest should heal her rapidly. I'll leave some medication and return tomorrow. Call if you need me before then."

"Thank you for coming so quickly, Doctor. Someone will show you out."

By now the entire household was awake and anxious, including Scott, who was curious for details. "Your mother miscarried," Keith explained in the hall.

"She was with child?"

"How else could she miscarry, son?"

"May I see her?"

"Not now, Scott. She's under sedation."

Scott pondered his father's bloodshot eyes and disheveled garments. Obviously, he had been drinking, something he never did to excess. "How did it happen?" he asked.

"I don't know."

"Weren't you there?"

"No, I was in a guest room."

"Did you and Mother have a fight?"

"That's none of your business, boy! Go back to bed. It's hours before dawn."

"I'll bring her some flowers tomorrow."

"That would be nice. Good night, son."

"Good night, sir."

When Devon awoke, shortly before noon, Keith was beside the bed. He had not left the room, resting as best he could in the lounge chair. Taking her hand tenderly, he asked, "How do you feel, darling?"

Devon knew what had occurred and was reluctant to discuss it. She had experienced this same reticent reluctance after her first miscarriage, in Texas, when she was Mrs. Reed Carter.

She regarded it as a personal inadequacy and failure, too painful to dwell upon. "Better," she answered, although she felt sore and drained, and the bitter taste of ergot lingered in her mouth.

"The doctor prescribed a period of bed rest."

"Is Ramsey here?"

"No, he couldn't come that fast from New York. We called a local physician, Harry Morton. He seems competent and will visit you again today." He hesitated, groping for words. "I don't know what to say, Devon, how to handle this—"

"There's nothing to say or handle, Keith. The pregnancy is terminated." Her voice was barely audible, and she turned her eyes toward the windows, as if to ponder the unfathomable sea. "Now you won't have all those months to worry about the delivery."

"Don't punish me, Devon. We lost a baby, and I'm penitent enough, because I think that emotional upheaval precipitated it."

"It was an act of God," she murmured dully. Later, she would mourn and grieve in her heart, privately. But now she was just numb, empty, apathetic.

"Did you fall, or hurt yourself somehow?"

She gazed at him, her face blanching, her hands twisting the sheet. "Deliberately? Say what you mean, Keith. First you suspect me of infidelity, now of aborting myself—is that it?"

"No, Devon, no! Couldn't you have slipped in the bathroom, or tripped on the carpet?"

"Or jumped up and down, or probed my womb with a hatpin or crochet needle?"

Good Lord! Where was this going to lead, and end?

"I realize you're distraught, Devon, and still angry with me for your own peculiar assumptions and delusions, which I'll try to ignore. I should have been with you last night, of course, but I felt persona non grata. Just get well, darling, and regain your perspective and rationality. You know I love and trust you, and we must weather this tragedy together. It's the only way for either of us, Devon. We're a team, and no good apart. I was miserable last night and sought comfort in the bottle. Now I'm wretched with guilt and remorse for leaving you alone. You may have miscarried anyway, but at least I'd have been here and in reasonable command of my faculties. I'll never forget it, or forgive myself. Never!"

"I guess we're both too proud, Keith. But I really didn't expect you to retreat so easily under fire. You usually stand your ground until *I* surrender."

"Well"—he shrugged sheepishly—"when the bric-a-brac started flying like bullets . . . you rarely get that furious, my dear."

"Or physical? I'm glad I didn't hurt you, or that valuable *objet d'art*. I'm ashamed of my temper, Keith."

"And I of my intemperance," he apologized humbly. "I hope I didn't scandalize the servants too much. The whole household was disturbed, except for the twins, who slept soundly through it all."

"And Scotty?"

"He was awake, and curious. I told him about your mishap, Devon. He wants to bring you flowers."

"Bless him," she smiled. "He's really a fine boy, Keith, and I think your doubts and misgivings about his future are unwarranted. I wish you'd resolve your differences."

"I'm trying, Devon. We'll take him back to college in the yacht, and then sail northward while the weather is fair. The New England coast is beautiful in autumn, especially around Maine, and the cruise will help you recuperate."

"I'm not ill, Keith."

"I know, darling, but the rest and relaxation will benefit both of us."

"The sea is your panacea, isn't it? You couldn't be happy away from it."

"I couldn't be happy anywhere without you," he replied, hoping she would echo his sentiments, his sincerity. But her wounds were too raw, her emotions still in shock. A tragic fissure had opened in their relationship, which would take time and patience to close. Preventing its broadening concerned him now, while she endeavored to divert him and the tedious conversation.

"Are you still investing in western real estate?"

"Primarily Texas. Why?"

"Just wondering. You haven't mentioned the Houston Ship Channel recently. Is it still a going project?"

"Definitely, and aided considerably by the appropriations in the Rivers and Harbors Bill. Senator Carter supports progress in his state, all right, apparently unconcerned about the growing number of monopolies there. Oh, no! Texans can't own too much land, cattle, timber, or anything else. Some of the biggest robber barons of the future will come from that territory, and he'll likely be one of them." He paused at her weary sigh. "I'm tiring you with this palaver, and you need your rest. I'd better visit our daughters, before they come tearing in here." His lips brushed hers lightly, and for once Devon did not demand more, nor contrive to detain him.

The twins, frisky in red-checked pinafores and hair ribbons, came running to meet him in the wide hall of that story. Keith knelt and embraced one in each arm, while they planted moist kisses on his cheeks, and fastidious Shannon complained about his beard.

"Your face scratches, Daddy."

"Sorry, sweetheart. Daddy hasn't shaved yet this morning, been sort of busy."

"Nanny told us to be quiet and not bother Mommy, and Miss Vale gave us extra lessons," Sharon informed unhappily. "Is Mommy sick, Daddy?"

"No, sugar, just indisposed."

"What does that word mean?"

"Not quite well," Keith explained. "Mommy is resting in bed, so don't bounce and crawl all over her, like you usually do. Understand?"

They nodded solemnly. "May we go to the beach this afternoon?"

"Yes, of course."

"With you, Daddy?" asked Shannon, and her sister hung on his reply, for both adored their father.

"Well," Keith hesitated, "if your brother doesn't have other plans—"

"Scotty's big enough to watch himself in the water," Shannon advised perkily, "and he always wants to be alone, anyway! We want you to play with us, Daddy. Please, please, please?"

"All right! Hush, both of you. And don't run and scream on this floor like little hellions."

"What's a hellion?" came the inevitable question.

"Ask your governess," Keith replied, urging them off with gentle pats on their ruffled backsides. They were a constant joy and delight, his precious progeny, and he brooded over last night's loss. They would never even know the sex of the lost child, for the embryo was not developed enough for the physician to tell.

America had much to celebrate on New Year's Eve, and New Yorkers did so with their customary enthusiasm and wild revelry. Slowly but surely the country was reuniting, although bitter memories of the War Between the States and Reconstruction lingered in the Deep South. The West had become an American mecca attracting thousands of pioneers. They trekked across rivers, plains, mountains and deserts toward the sunset horizon. Hostile Indians, blizzards, intense heat—nothing could halt the westward roll of the covered wagon caravans, the armadas of prairie schooners. More forts and trading posts were constructed, and settlements established along the ever-expanding network of iron rails. If not vanishing, the wilderness was certainly diminishing. The cavalry had finally captured Geronimo, the most fearsome and elusive Apache chief, in Arizona. Civilization was on its way!

A different kind of pilgrim flocked to the East Coast, which was virtually inundated with tidal waves of immigrants. New York's recently dedicated Statue of Liberty welcomed them with a glowing torch, government officials corraled them like cattle in the horribly crowded Castle Garden Immigration Station, and the eastern outlaws of industry promptly enslaved and exploited them. And since entire families often worked together in the same factories, mines, sweatshops, the prospects for laws against child labor appeared dimmer than ever. The streets of Manhattan and Brooklyn teemed with youngsters trodding to work instead of school, and Devon knew it was the same in other large cities. What good did the pamphlets do, the memorials to Congress, the editorials of the few crusading publishers? Nothing was going to change much for women and children for decades to come.

There were some changes, however, in Devon's own life and marriage. The misfortune in Newport last summer, from which she had totally recovered physically if not yet emotionally, had never actually estranged them, although it had affected their marital relations to some extent. Keith was methodically cautious, fearful of impregnating her again, despite Dr. Blake's assurances of better and safer protection with the ingenious new French cervical cap smuggled from Europe on his recent voyage.

"Good God!" Ramsey exclaimed, upon learning of Keith's additional precautions. "Condoms, too? That's like washing your feet with your socks on, man."

"Somewhat," Keith admitted, for the sexual sensations were diminished by the prophylactic shield. "But I trusted the pessary, remember."

"One accident in seven years? You expect too much, my friend. And though your self-control is admirable, you're unnecessarily cheating yourself—and your wife—out of some significant pleasure."

"My wife? Has Devon complained to you?"

"No, never. But I'm a gynecologist, after all, with some knowledge of a woman's body. Half of their female complaints originate in bed, and the healthiest ones are usually also the most sexually active. Devon is perfectly well, Keith. And responsive, isn't she?"

"Aggressive, at times."

"Then don't treat her like a reluctant virgin. Above all, don't ration your lovemaking, like some Catholic couples, by the papal calendar. The rhythm method not only produces plenty of babies for the church, it fosters much adultery and fornication outside of it."

They were seated in the oak-paneled library of Halcyon, smoking and sipping brandy, as was their after-dinner habit on Ramsey's Sunday visits. Keith puffed a pipe, while his guest lit his second Havana cigar. A roaring fire belied the freezing temperatures and gusty winds of the February afternoon. "I don't want any other woman," Keith stated firmly, never equivocating on the issue of fidelity.

"Why would you, with a helpmeet like yours? I'm still searching for mine."

"Hell, Ramsey, you must have found somebody by now! I can't believe you're celibate."

"Of course not! I have a mistress, and may eventually marry her. If she doesn't give up on me and find someone else, as often happens in procrastination." He contemplated the blazing logs, stroking one side of his blond mustache. "Guard your treasure, man, lest some pirate steal it."

Keith chewed the stem of his briar a few moments, then laughed brusquely. "Some have already tried, and I expect others will, too. They won't succeed."

"Not if you're diligent, and as wise as I think."

"Devon *is* a prize, isn't she? A jewel more beautiful and precious than any I could possibly buy, and I'm as violently jealous of her as ever. I'd kill to keep her."

"So would I, in your place." The doctor studied the glowing ember of his cigar, before grinding it out somewhat precipitously in the black onyx ashtray and draining his crystal snifter swiftly.

"More cognac?" Keith offered, chiding. "You're quaffing it like a sailor his rum."

"Just bracing myself to hit the road." Ramsey stood, glancing about for his hat and greatcoat, reluctant to depart the warm, pleasant surroundings.

"Leaving so early, Ram?"

He grinned at the seldom used abbreviation of his first name. "There's a storm brewing, Keith. Haven't you noticed the darkening sky? Thunderclouds packing ice, and we haven't had our winter's blizzard yet. It'll be a good night for loving," he added laconically as Keith walked him to the door. "Say goodbye to Devon for me."

Karl and Lars Hummel, who could predict the weather more accurately than the naval meteorologists at the Long Island station, were packing in more wood for all the bins in the house. Devon, who had left the men to enjoy their masculine companionship, was coming downstairs as Keith started up.

"Wait there, darling."

"Has our guest gone already?"

"Yes. The weather is changing for the worse."

"Oh, darn! I wanted to ride this afternoon, and play some whist later."

He gazed at her. "I had another idea."

"Little pitchers have big ears," she reminded.

"And doors have locks."

"Ours is broken."

"Since when?"

"I'm not sure. Probably since the last time you had that same idea during the day."

"That was weeks ago!"

"So it was, darling."

"It should have been fixed by now," Keith muttered. "That's why we have handymen on this place."

As his feet seemed suddenly anchored at the bottom, Devon proceeded downward. "Since the lock is on the master suite, shouldn't the master have advised them to repair it?" she suggested, smiling at his frustrated scowl.

"All right, it's my fault. But that's not the whole point, is it?"

"Well—" She shivered, wrapping her arms about herself. "Do you feel a draft?"

"More of a cold shoulder," he complained, returning to the warm library.

"Not at all," she denied, following him. "But who was the frosty one last night, Mr. Snowman? I was frozen right out of your arms, and almost out of the bed."

"Don't exaggerate. I was just tired."

"Worried," she corrected, extending her hands to the fire. "And why the sudden ardor now? Did Ramsey give you some efficacious new aphrodisiac he discovered abroad?"

"No, just some pertinent advice."

"Oh? About what?"

"My anxiety in certain situations."

"And you decided to run upstairs—and throw caution to the wind?"

"Not all caution, darling. Just leave off my socks, for a change." At her quizzical expression, he clarified: *"Sock."*

"Oh, *that* thing. You know I hate it, Keith. But you should have struck while the iron was hot. Last night I was ready, willing, and *able*. That last condition changed this morning. You'll be relieved to know, dear, that my curse arrived on schedule, almost to the hour, not a day early or late, but exactly on the calendar mark."

"Damn," Keith swore under his breath. "Well, get the cards, while I poke up the fire. We can invite Karl and Lars in for a few games of whist. And maybe," he added with a wry grin, "get that broken lock fixed, in case we're snowbound for a week or so."

✦ 32 ✦

MARYLAND WAS as far north as Daniel would allow his daughter to live or travel without him, and then only because her mother had been a native of that state. And Virginia, for all its fine male universities, lacked comparable facilities for its females. So Fawn was matriculating at Baltimore Women's College, whose student body consisted of a small but select group of mostly Southern young ladies. Her pleas to attend Vassar or Radcliffe fell on deaf paternal ears for reasons other than location. Vassar had a reputation of fostering feminism and advocating professional careers for women, and Radcliffe was the female annex of Harvard, which Keith Curtis's son was attending.

But since Daniel did not explain his objections to these Yankee schools, Fawn could not understand his attitude any better than could Scott his father's to their relationship. They were faithful sweethearts, and their childhood notes had become adolescent love letters, sacred and secret. The long distance separating them was a difficult obstacle to hurdle, however, and Scott's impetuous attempt to do so was a fiasco. The train was late getting into Baltimore, and Fawn was confined to her bed with *la grippe*. Scott left flowers and a sealed envelope at her dormitory, then checked out of his hotel room and sat for four long, lonely hours in the drafty depot waiting for his train. It rained all the way back to Boston, there were unexpected delays en route, and he almost missed his Monday-morning classes. His parents were unaware of his impromptu journey, which he never again tried during a school term. He spent his

Thanksgiving and Christmas holidays at Halcyon, morose and miserable despite the cheery atmosphere and parental concern. Devon wondered if Fawn moped similarly about Harmony Hill and, if so, how Daniel coped with her juvenile moodiness.

It was a baffling situation, which Devon was handling better than Keith. He worried, despaired, brooded. Scott would soon receive his degree, and what then? More education? The Grand Tour? Or would he simply leave home to pursue his own life and interests, wherever they led? Manifest Destiny, defined as an irresistible impulse of humankind, was a popular concept of the day, discussed in intellectual essays and forums. Other generations called it Fate, and Keith was reluctant to surrender his son to it philosophically. What would happen to the Curtis financial empire when he retired, or passed away, if his only male heir did not succeed him? There was no logical answer, at least none he was ready to accept. His dilemma mounted and peaked in June, with Scott's announcement that he did not care to go to Newport that season.

"Just what the devil *do* you want to do this summer?" Keith demanded angrily. "Fly south?"

His answer, fired like a shot, wounded. "Yes!"

"You're a strange bird, son, and becoming a stranger in your home nest."

"I just want to visit Fawn. Is that a crime?"

"What about your mother and sisters?"

"I'm not abandoning my family, Dad! And I'm not a child, for Christ's sake!"

"Nor a man yet, either, just because you're shaving," Keith reminded, bringing a stinging rush of blood to the youth's face. "You still have a few years to go, legally and otherwise. Why are you so eager to cut your moors?"

"You mean apron strings?"

"I mean commonsense ties, and drift."

"I'm not drifting, damn it!"

"Watch your mouth, boy."

"Don't call me boy."

"What do you think you are, at seventeen?"

"How did you regard yourself at that age?" Scott fenced, still smarting over the earlier affront to his manhood. *"If* you can remember that far back."

"Why, you impertinent whelp! Do you take me for a senile old fool in dotage? I'm in my prime, and my memory is excellent. I was never disrespectful to my elders at any time, and especially not to my father. Nor did I ever try to break my mother's heart."

"My mother's a Virginian, sir. Why should my interest in a Virginia girl hurt her? For that matter, why should you object so strenuously, all things considered?"

"Point conceded," Keith muttered, flinching. "I see why you're on the debating team. You have a natural aptitude for argument."

"So do you, sire, with all due respect."

"What did you call me?"

"Sire. Aren't you the Monetary Monarch of Manhattan, Ruler of Wall Street, King of the Moneychangers?" Bowing with mocking *lèse-majesté*, he backed out of the chamber, just as Devon was entering it. He made a courteous obeisance to her, murmured, "Pardon, please," and retreated to his private realm.

One glance at Keith's furious countenance told Devon they had been at odds again, quarreling bitterly and perhaps near fisticuffs. "Another verbal duel?" she asked, dismayed.

"Yes, and his tongue is indeed mightier than his sword. He deserved to be soundly thrashed. It's a hell of a mess, Devon, and I'm perplexed."

"Why don't you relent, Keith? Obviously your word battles are not accomplishing anything, only driving him farther away from us."

"Only from me, Devon. He's not estranged from you. I ought to sever his allowance, since he wants his independence so damned much. Let him hobo his way to Virginia." He frowned, bewildered and frustrated to the core. "But you'd give him the money, wouldn't you? He's convinced that you approve of his relationship with Harverston's daughter."

Devon sighed, for it was a familiar harangue. "You're gnawing an old bone, Keith. Yes, I'd pay his fare, rather than risk having him arrested on vagrancy charges and thrown in jail. And so would you, no matter whither bound, and despite all your blustering."

"That girl is sixteen, old enough to—"

"Get into trouble?" she interrupted, her face flushing crimson. "Our son might seduce her, take her virtue?"

"It's possible, isn't it?"

"Considering his parentage, yes."

He scowled in embarrassment. "Why do you always gig me that way, and yourself? There's no comparison between us and those precocious kids."

"I hope not, dear, lest the consequences be the same."

"Dammit, Devon! How can you be so nonchalant, even flippant, about this?"

"Realistic," she corrected. "The signs are obvious, Keith, and the handwriting is on the wall. Scotty intends to marry Fawn, one way or another. Parental interference can only delay, not prevent their union. Like it or not, you and Daniel are destined to be in-laws. And your grandchildren, if any, will also be his."

"With your blessings, eh?"

"What is the alternative, for heaven's sake? Disown and disinherit him? Could you do that?"

"Of course not! But you seem to forget the real fly in this ointment, my dear. I just can't conceive of that Southerner willingly giving his daughter's hand in marriage to this Yankee's son. And if Scott should besmirch her honor—well, you know how Haverston feels about *that!* Our foolish boy could end up dead, Devon. As could his foolish father, who would have to avenge him."

"I trust such horrors won't happen," Devon quavered, visibly shaken. "Must we go to Newport this year, Keith? I'm not keen about it without Scotty."

"Nor I," he admitted. "But what else is there?"

"The same thing as before we had the cottage."

"Actually, I should go to Texas. Stumbling blocks are being put in my way there, via lost deeds and muddled titles to property in escrow, especially in Houston."

"Can't your attorneys handle it?"

He smiled at her naiveté. "Not at this distance. The obstacles are human, my love, and political. A certain senator has rallied the support of his powerful friends against Curtis Enterprises West, and they could tie us up in court for years. Texans are clever operators in junta politics."

"But what could you do that your lawyers can't?" asked Devon, knowing that Reed Carter, now the senior senator from his state, was responsible for this new strategy in his old campaign against the monopolists.

"Nothing, really. I just want to see for myself if it's worth a long legal battle."

"Oh, but Texas is so hot in summer, Keith, and Houston is also terribly humid! Wait until autumn. The climate is quite pleasant then."

"All right," Keith agreed, some of his interest in accumulating more wealth having diminished in Scott's blistering comments during their heated quarrel. His ancestors had begun pyramiding the family fortune long ago, and he had added substantially to it for his heir. But like the Pharaohs, he may only have been building his own tomb.

Scott was marking time, waiting for Fawn's response to his last letter. When it came, the news devastated him. "Much against my wishes," she wrote, "Daddy has suddenly decided to go abroad, and we are taking Grandma Caldwell and Aunt Merilee, my mother's maiden sister, with us. We are departing soon from Norfolk, but I promise, Dear Heart, to write and send postcards throughout our itinerary...."

"I—I guess I'll go to Newport, after all," Scotty told his mother, dejectedly explaining his abrupt change of plans. "Do some sailing."

"Of course, dear," Devon said, reversing her own earlier decision against the resort to accommodate him. "Your father will be so pleased."

"Is he still mad at me?"

"No, Scotty. He can't stay angry with either of us for long. But I'm afraid we both unwittingly provoke him at times and—well, he has a lot of business matters to contend with, you know, and gets short-tempered."

"I'll try not to aggravate him," he promised, his young shoulders slumped in defeat.

"A godsend," Keith pronounced Fawn's letter. "Haverston is smarter than I thought, taking the girl to Europe. We'll have our boy...for a while, anyway. Did you change your mind about Newport?"

"Yes," Devon fibbed. "The weather's nice there, and Scotty wants to sail."

"With me?"

"Who else?"

"Great! Maybe things will work out, after all, if I'm patient enough. And I won't badger him, no matter what." He looked so happy, so hopeful. "God's in His heaven, and all's right with the world."

Temporarily, at least, Devon thought, but only smiled and kissed him, increasing his joy.

True to her promise, Fawn sent a steady flow of mail across the Atlantic to her Yankee beau. She had written every evening on the ship's crossing and posted a bonanza of letters sealed in a large brown envelope when they arrived in Liverpool, England. She still could not understand her father's abrupt decision to go abroad that year, except that he had not done so since his Grand Tour after graduation from William and Mary. And while she was enjoying the travel and learning much that would be useful when she returned to college in the fall, Fawn declared that she would much rather have spent the summer at Harmony Hill, or anywhere else they could have been together.

Scott had a favorite place in Newport to read and relish her letters, passages of which he committed to memory like poetry. He took them to a certain spot on the scenic Cliff Walk, a long, rugged stone escarpment towering high above the beach, where the surf splashed and frothed over the fallen boulders below. He gazed wistfully at the restless sea, as restless as his own vital young blood; at the palatial residences, including his own family's, dominating the shoreline; and at the enchanting beauty of the landscape reflected in the mirrored depths of Easton's Pond. Here, in forlorn solitude, he could savor the precious words and promises of her pen, and try to imagine where she was on her itinerary at that particular hour.

Sometimes he ventured to distant Coggeshall's Ledge, at Land's End—a promontory offering even more spectacular vistas and privacy in which to meditate, dream, romanticize, brood. He ignored his parents' observations that he was behaving like a hermit, and shunned all efforts of the colony's matchmaking mothers to interest him in their young daughters. In a few years the Curtis scion would be one of the most eligible bachelors in the country—indeed, the world—and though not unaware of his position, Scott was neither impressed nor influenced by it.

Perplexed and distressed by his son's continued lack of interest in matters relevant to his future and family responsibilities in New York, Keith rode his own emotions with a curb bit, lest he lose patience despite his determination not to hassle the boy. And Devon feared that the situation would eventually become unendurable and erupt in some disastrous conflict, or explosion. She prayed that tempers could be contained and peace would prevail until Scott returned to Harvard.

Hurry, September!

Somehow Fawn managed to dispatch a cablegram, advising Scott of a shift in ships and schedules, which would land them in New York rather than a Southern port on their return voyage. Thrilled by this news, he insisted on welcoming the Haverstons to his home state, and Devon felt that common courtesy dictated that she and Keith accompany him to the East River pier.

"I can't," he told her. "Morgan, Belmont, and I are consulting with the Secretary of the Treasury, who arrived yesterday at President Cleveland's request. The first time in office in twenty-four years, and the Democrats are already in financial difficulty. They just don't know how to manage money, or budget the government."

"The Republicans were in the White House when the Panic of 1873 struck and lingered nearly a decade," Devon reminded, with staunch loyalty to the party of Thomas Jefferson and other great Virginians.

"That crisis was precipitated by Black Friday; the cornering of the gold market by those scoundrels Jay Gould and Jim Fisk, and President Grant was a dupe. The current trouble has to do with both gold and silver, because some idiots, led by William Jennings Bryan, think we can operated on both standards simultaneously." But he knew that she did not fully comprehend the complicated monetary system, nor any of its domestic and foreign ramifications, and there was no quick course in finance to enlighten her or any other layman. "Anyway, I'll be tied up for days in the discussions, and several bankers may have to go to Washington to consult with the President. I can't take off to entertain your Southern friends, but I suppose you should try."

"Without a host?"

"Only during the day, darling. Invite them to dinner and the theater, or whatever, in the evening, and I'll try not to be late. I'm sorry, Devon, but that's the best I can do under the circumstances. Financiers don't create the federal fiscal problems, but they must work together to try to prevent and solve them. I'm sure Haverston will understand my position and commitments, though I doubt he'll be very disappointed if I'm not around much."

So their son, handsome in a dark blue serge suit, paisley silk cravat, and polished boots, stood anxiously on the crowded dock as the Cunard luxury liner steamed into the busy harbor to its berth, on a glorious midautumn afternoon. Sighting Fawn on the first class deck, Scott waved and called enthusiastically to attract her attention, while Devon held the bouquet of flowers he intended to present to her. And what a charming picture she made in a turquoise travel suit trimmed with coral braid, an adorable French chapeau of turquoise and coral malines adorning her head, and her bright sherry-colored eyes beaming down at her special young man.

"Welcome to New York!" Scotty greeted breathlessly as Fawn came off the gangplank. "I wish I could roll out a red carpet and give you the Keys to the City." He placed the fragrant red roses in her arms. "Please accept this humble tribute, my dear Miss Haverston."

"Oh, Scotty, thank you! They're lovely! Aren't they, Daddy?"

Daniel was smiling at Devon, wishing he had acquired flowers for her from the ship's florist, and would have, had he known she'd been there. Spying a vendor's cart, he promptly purchased a nosegay of her favorite camellias and presented it with a gallant flourish. "A token of my esteem and admiration, madam!"

"How nice," Devon murmured. "Keith couldn't be here, unfortunately, but we want all of you to be our guests in New York, Daniel."

"Thank you kindly," he said. "But there are too many of us to impose, my dear, and we've decided to register at the Astor House. I hope we may get together in other ways, however."

"Yes, indeed!" Devon promised, smiling. "We'll be in touch after you're settled. I trust you had an enjoyable tour?"

"Very," he affirmed, "although I was amazed how little things had changed. Governments topple, thrones are lost, yet the Old World retains its charm and beauty, as if perpetuated in immutable antiquity. Not like America, which is constantly changing and not always for the better, I'm afraid. There's much comfort and edification in traveling abroad, and I'll not wait so long to go back."

Grandma Caldwell and Aunt Merilee looked on with curious interest about the fair and lovely lady in her elegant costume, which might have come directly from the Worth salon they had visited in Paris. Exactly who was this splendid person, and how long had Daniel known her? They would have been even more curious had they seen the beautiful portrait of her that graced and dominated the gallery of Harmony Hill.

Whether deliberate or not, Mrs. Caldwell suffered a sudden bilious attack on the evening of the Curtises' dinner in Gramercy Park, and her spinster daughter was obliged to remain at the hotel with her. The Haverstons arrived alone at the brownstone mansion, Keith was cordial, and Scott was ecstatic. Devon had not seen him so happy in months, and Daniel could hardly have missed the radiant glow on his daughter's face whenever she glanced across the impeccably set banquet table at the boy of her dreams. If ever youthful love was a visible emotion, it registered on Fawn's countenance. And Scott's expression was an equally unsubtle revelation, of which his father was acutely aware. Whatever Dan's observations, he guarded them in conversation directed mostly at Devon, keenly interested in the magnificent tapestry depicting an English fox hunt, until informed that it had been commissioned by her husband's maternal ancestors, Lord and Lady Heathstone, for their centuries-old family estate in Sussex, England.

"Oh, how interesting!" exclaimed Fawn, who had been captivated by such historic manors on their tour of the British countryside. She had wondered why the middle name of both

Mr. Curtis and his son was Heathstone; now she knew. "Just think, Daddy, Scotty has royal blood!"

"Noble," Dan corrected. "And so have you, kitten, far back in the Haverston ancestry. Nearly every colonist who came to Virginia on the King James Charter, except the bondservants, descended of English nobility. The House of Burgesses in Williamsburg, where your forefathers sat, was almost a house of lords, daughter. Noble blood was no great novelty in America then."

"And still isn't," Keith said, abruptly digressing. "I assume you plan to do some sightseeing in New York, sir?"

"For Fawn's sake, yes. And the other ladies, if they're up to it. I've been here before, of course, although not since *The War.*" He always capitalized and emphasized the word, as if there had been no other war in history; and, indeed, for Daniel Haverston there was none of such importance.

"Well, our transporation is at your service."

Servants hovered with desserts and demitasse, after which the men retired to the library for the ritual of tobacco and brandy, and Devon accompanied the young couple to the fourth-floor solarium for a panoramic view of Manhattan at night. Fawn was entranced, her memories of London and Paris and Rome and Vienna paling somewhat, for she had not experienced them with her sweetheart, whose arm stole shyly around her tiny waist despite his mother's presence. New York was far ahead of even the great European capitals in modern inventions, especially in lighting and communications. Electricity as well as gas was used in illumination, and she had noticed that the Curtises had one of the marvelous new telephones on the foyer wall, plus a private telegraph line, neither of which Harmony Hill yet possessed.

Anxious for a few minutes alone with Fawn, Scott blamed his father for Devon's constant vigilance. No doubt she had orders to shadow them everywhere, and after their guests' departure, he vented his frustration. "Why not just hire a Pinkerton sleuth to keep us under surveillance!"

"I was chaperoning Miss Haverston, not you," Devon temporized, but Keith was less tolerant of his insolence.

"You have no business even being here, son! You should be in Cambridge, Massachusetts."

"I registered by mail, and the fraternity initiations are just for new members, as you know, sir. Classes don't start until next week."

"And you'll be there in time, won't you?"

"Certainly," Scott replied. There was no incentive to remain in New York, for Fawn had to be in Baltimore Women's College next week, too.

The next morning he rushed Devon relentlessly, lest they be late for the engagement with the Haverstons, and was abashed when she accused him of being a slavedriver. "Sorry, Mother. I just don't want to keep them waiting. What shall we show them first?"

"Brooklyn Bridge, probably. That's the major tourist attraction, after the Statue of Liberty, which they saw coming into the harbor."

"Only glimpsed," he said. "We'll take them to Bedloe Island, for a better view. And, of course, to Central Park for the carriage parade..."

"Now, Scotty, I'm sure they've ridden in more beautiful and exciting places."

"Not with us, Mother dear." Was she being deliberately obtuse, or merely subservient to their strict "master"? Didn't she realize how desperately he wanted to be with his darling, how happy they were together and how miserable apart? Didn't any of their parents realize how few were the years they could be legally separated?

To Fawn's relief and Scotty's delight, Grandma Caldwell's dyspepsia still confined her and Aunt Merilee in their parlor suite, and the Curtis barouche went off with only four passengers. The young couple sat vis-à-vis their elders, a seating arrangement which pleased both males immensely. Scotty wore a sporty houndstooth jacket with his gray flannel trousers, and Daniel was dapper in newly acquired British tweeds. The ladies were charming in small-bustled, ankle-length street costumes, designed for walking and climbing in and out of vehicles, and Daniel was delighted with their company. How perfect that the King of Wall Street was not along, even though his young Prince Charming was! Cognizant of the attraction, the magnetism, between their respective heirs, Daniel wondered how much more serious and intense it might become. What if it was not mere infatuation but genuine love, as deep and death-less as his own love for Devon?

The children were chattering gaily, Fawn observing every-thing Scotty pointed out as if it were some wonder more sig-nificant than any she had seen abroad. Brooklyn Bridge interested her more than London Bridge, and Coney Island seemed more exciting than the French Riviera. What was Westminster Abbey, or Nôtre Dame, or even the Sistine Chapel, compared with St. Patrick's Cathedral with her sweetheart beside her? Central Park was magically transformed into a paradise eclipsing Hyde Park and the Bois de Boulogne. The Thames, the Seine, the Tiber, the Danube—no river anywhere was more scenic to her than the beautiful Hudson. And she admired the brilliantly striated Jersey Palisades more than she had the lofty snowclad peaks of the Swiss Alps.

Devon suspected that Fawn was responding more to her guide than her surroundings, and thought that Daniel shared her suspicions. "It's amazing," he remarked, shaking his head ponderously. "All the money we spent abroad...and I think she would have been happier just going north. I guess I'll have to take her to Philadelphia and Boston and Saratoga Springs and Niagra Falls next year. Or perhaps back to Europe, again and again, until she learns to appreciate the history and art and culture, and distinguish the difference between our civiliza-tions." He smiled yearningly at Devon, longing to clasp her small gloved hands in his. "Your world tour with the Grants must have been quite an experience."

"Oh, yes, even though I was unable to complete it." She did not explain the reason, certain he was aware that the at-tempted assassination of her first husband, Senator Reed Carter, had brought her back to America prematurely. "You must see President Grant's tomb, Dan. His funeral was the largest in the history of the country."

His features turned grim in retrospect. "I read about it, Devon. And I was infuriated by the marching order of the military units in the procession. The Virginia battalion defeated by Grant preceding his own victorious battalion, as if still in pursuit of Lee's army. What an insult to the South!"

"I don't think it was meant as such, Dan. It was supposed

to be an honor, a tribute, suggested by General Winfield Scott Hancock."

"Honor?" he scoffed bitterly. "No, Devon—a deliberate humiliation! Hancock's Second Corps was foremost in repulsing the Confederacy at Gettysburg, and especially in ordering Pickett's charge. I'm sure that son-of-a-gun never forgot his conspicuous action in routing General Lee. And when I think of the simple little funeral accorded our great hero, my blood boils and my old minié-ball wound aches. Well, you saw *his* tomb at the University of Virginia, when you and your son were in Charlottsville. Nothing so grand and glorious as the pictures and descriptions of the North's victor!

Like so many other loyal Confederate veterans, he would never forget, Devon thought. Not as long as there was breath in his body, and memory in his mind! And hell would freeze over before he would pay homage at any Union general's monument, much less the one he despised most of all. Thus, Devon decided to bypass the massive domed memorial on Riverside Drive, begun before Grant's death on a site of his own choice and still not structurally complete. Devon herself had seen it only once, on the day of the funeral, because Keith had been an honorary pallbearer.

They lunched at a quaint country inn specializing in beef Wellington and Yorkshire pudding, and Daniel ordered a bottle of vintage burgundy for the adults. Fawn begged a sip from her father's glass, and Scott longed for a tankard of ale such as the older boys at Harvard imbibed at liberal taverns to assert their manhood, but neither of their wishes was gratified. They were gone all day, returning their guests to their lodgings rather late, and making an early appointment for the morrow. Lights were twinkling everywhere in the city, and the granite lions supporting the ornate bronze gas lamps flanking the Curtis portal in Gramercy Park looked ready to roar when they entered the mansion. And indeed the master was visibly displeased by their tardiness.

Sensing his displeasure and fearing an argument centered on himself, Scott murmured, "Good evening, Father," and proceeded quickly and quietly to his room.

"It was dark over an hour ago," Keith told Devon. "Where

have you been all damned day? I was worried."

"I'm sorry, darling. There was so much to see and so much traveling around, time just slipped away."

"Really? You all had watches, didn't you?"

"We didn't synchronize them for a race."

"Just ignored them, eh? Was it so much fun being together, you forgot the dinner hour here? I dined alone, Mrs. Curtis, and didn't much enjoy it. The old lady's indigestion must have been cured overnight."

"Not exactly. Mrs. Caldwell and her daughter were unable to accompany us."

"I see." He scowled darkly. "How convenient for the four of you!"

"That's presumptuous, Keith, and totally wrong. Nothing improper happened. Ask Scotty."

"Oh, sure! That young stag was itching to get his little Fawn off alone somewhere. Did you oblige them with an opportunity?"

"So Dan and I could have a rendezvous? We never separated, they were constantly chaperoned and vice versa, even when we strolled in Central Park."

"By pairs, hand in hand?"

Now her ire surfaced. "There was no hanky-panky, I tell you! And I resent your insinuations and third degree. Do you want me to swear on the Bible?"

He glanced away, rueful in remorse. "Now you're baiting me, Devon."

"Because I think you're still skeptical, unconvinced that it was a perfectly innocent outing."

"False thinking," he denied, brooding. "I believe you, Devon. I'm just disturbed because in your apparent absorption in your company, you forgot you had a husband."

"Come now, Keith! That's absurd and untrue. I never forget about you, no matter where or with whom I am, and I've already explained our lateness in returning. Time—"

"Just slipped away," he interrupted curtly. "Well, it didn't go so fast or pleasantly for me today, unfortunately. The United States Treasury is in a hell of a mess, gold is being shipped to foreign countries at an alarming rate, and our discussions were too involved even to break for luncheon. We allowed ourselves a couple of hours for dinner, before resuming the conference at ten o'clock this evening in the Sub-Treasury Building. I rushed home to be with my family and—" He paused, shrugging.

"Darling, forgive me? If I had known—"

He gazed at her. "Are you serious? I told you about the financial emergency, Devon. Don't you remember? Weren't you listening? Or were you so excited about the Haverstons' landing in New York, nothing else registered on your mind? Now you blithely say 'if I had known—' And I shouldn't be angry or upset? Jesus Christ!"

As she stood downcast, staring at the carpet, feeling negligent and chastised, Keith picked up his hat and portfolio. "I have to leave, Devon."

"When will you be back?"

"I don't know. We may confer all night."

"If so, telephone me."

"Why wake the household? No doubt you and Scott have plans for tomorrow, and need your rest. Your beauty sleep, for the benefit of your Virginia cavalier's covetous eyes!" He donned his fine black homburg, now the sartorial symbol of masculine success, and Devon thought him the handsomest, most distinguished and influential banker in the world. "Good night, my dear. Perhaps we'll meet again tomorrow evening. . . ."

For the first time in their marriage, he left without kissing her goodbye, and Devon was forlorn and dejected. She wanted to follow him outside to the waiting carriage, mollifying and supplicating, but she vacillated too long—and he was gone. Then the butler was inquiring, "Would you like some dinner, madam? Cook kept the food warm."

"I'm not hungry, Hadley. But you might take a tray to Master Scott; he hasn't eaten since noon, except for an ice-cream cone in the Park."

"Yes, mum."

Devon sipped a claret and warm milk caudle to relax, but finally resorted to a sedative to induce sleep. She woke alone in bed, clutching his unused pillow to her aching breast. Although it was only seven o'clock, Scott was already banging on the door, poking his head inside when she didn't immediately answer.

"Are you awake, Mother?"

"I imagine the whole neighborhood is, with that racket."

"May I come in?"

"You may," Devon allowed, reaching for her negligee before rising.

Entering, Scott glanced about the chamber, assuming his father was in the dressing room. "I thought you'd be up by now, sleepyhead. We're due at the Astor House at nine o'clock sharp!"

"I'm a bit under the weather today, dear, not quite up to strenuous gallivanting again."

He almost panicked. "We promised, Mother! But if you're not feeling well, I'll escort them myself."

"I'm afraid not, Scotty. Your father—"

He interrupted, "Dad again! Where is he?"

"In an urgent meeting with the Treasury Secretary and some other prominent bankers."

"All night?"

"Evidently. He had to leave soon after we got home last evening. We shouldn't have been gone so long, son, and it can't happen again today."

"I hate banking and finance," he declared vehemently. "There's always some economic crisis, and Wall Street is either in chaos or on the verge of it. How does Father stand it—and why, when he's the richest man in the country? He's going to kill himself, Mother. Have a stroke or something. Wait and see!"

The ominous prediction stunned Devon, who ceased grooming her hair and laid the jeweled brush on her vanity table. The mirror reflected a blanched face, horrified eyes, and a haunting guilt that she was not as solicitous of her husband's health as a loving wife should be. Only yesterday she had unwittingly provoked him again, caused him unnecessary stress and worry! "Your father would like to retire in a few years, Scotty, and pass the mantle and scepter to you."

"But I don't want to succeed him, Mother. I don't want to inherit his kingdom and power and glory, and feel guilty and irresponsible and incompetent if I lack his financial genius. Worse even, fear that I might inadvertently betray the trust and confidence placed in me."

"How could that happen, with his support and guidance and expertise? He would never criticize or condemn you for mistakes, Scotty, and certainly never abandon you to the mercies of your competitors. So if that's your objection—"

"You're naive, Mother, or pretending to be."

"No, just hopeful, for his sake. We both always assumed that—" She broke off, reluctant to belabor the issue.

"Do get dressed," he urged. "I thought we might take the train to the village station today and show them our country place. We could spend the night. I'm sure they would like to meet the twins."

Her heart jumped, nearly stopped, then pounded furiously. For several terrible moments, she feared she might faint with anxiety and bewilderment. Dear God! If he only knew the wretched circumstances under which Daniel Haverston had first come to Halcyon-on-Hudson, and the cartel that had brought him back when he found Devon unwed and pregnant with Keith Curtis's child: the son born on the very same day of their bloody fight on the frozen ground. The past was gaining on them! How much longer could they ignore it?

"No, Scotty," she said firmly. "We can't entertain the Haverstons at Halcyon, or stay there even one night, without a host. We'll ride the ferries to Staten and Bedloe islands, as we planned yesterday. Perhaps, if Keith is free this weekend, we could sail to Newport—"

"They're leaving Saturday, Mother! Fawn is going directly to Baltimore, and I'll be on my way to Boston. Shit," he muttered under his breath.

"What?"

"Nothing. Just mumbling to myself."

Devon pondered the vast array of choices in her wardrobe. "I can't decide what to wear."

"God's balls," the boy groaned, impatient with her feminine whimsy and procrastination.

"I heard *that*, Scott! Where did you learn such gutter language, from your fraternity brothers?"

"I guess so."

"Harvard gentlemen, indeed!"

"They're men, Mother, and they swear even in the sacred house of Phi Beta Kappa."

"Well, mind your manners in the presence of ladies, Mr. Scott Heathstone Curtis!" she admonished.

"Yes, ma'am. Please hurry, Mother? I'll wait for you downstairs."

PART FOUR

The joys of marriage are the heaven on earth,
Life's paradise, great princess, the soul's quiet,
Sinews of concord, earthly immortality,
Eternity of pleasures; no restoratives
Like to a constant woman.
                    John Ford (1586–1639)
                    THE BROKEN HEART

Love is a proud and gentle thing, a better thing to own
Than all of the wide impossible stars over the heavens blown.
                    Orrick Johns (1887–   )
                    THE DOOR

Thro' all the drama—whether damned or not—
Love gilds the scene, and women guide the plot.
                    Richard B. Sheridan (1751–1816)
                    THE RIVALS

Love is the part, and love is the whole,
Love is the robe, and love is the pall;
Ruler of heart and brain and soul,
Love is the lord and the slave of all!
                    George MacDonald (1824–1905)
                    A LOVER'S THOUGHT OF LOVE

↜ 33 ↝

NEW YORKERS were insouciant about the climate, paying little attention to almanacs and forecasts, which were notoriously unreliable. They preferred to trust seasonal signs, and for over a week the island had basked in a beguilingly false spring. Crocuses and dandelions sprouted in the parks and lawns, budding trees and plants defied sudden frosts. Easter shoppers wore bright clothes, straw hats, and lightweight suits, and the flower vendors hawked the season's first roses, lilies, and violets.

Marnie Ryan came to work in a beige tissue-wool dress and pancake hat trimmed with artificial pansies, a revival of the Watteau fashion, which she hoped was not too frivolous for the office. It was her Easter outfit, the prettiest she had ever had, and she wanted to show it off, albeit a bit prematurely.

"Good morning, sir!" she greeted Keith with a sparkling smile, as he walked in carrying a topcoat over his arm. "'Tis a glorious day, isn't it?"

"Aye, but 'twill change by nightfall," he predicted, amused by the frilly bonnet and chiffon scarf perched on her clothes rack.

Marnie laughed, for he had become quite adept at mimicry. "You don't trust Mother Nature?"

"My dear Miss Ryan, *she* is the most fickle, unpredictable female of all! Sure now you brought along a sturdy wrap, for you'll be needing it wherever you intend to sport your spring finery this day."

"At church this evening, sir, for the Stations of the Cross. And to St. Patrick's Cathedral for Sunday Mass and the Easter Parade on Fifth Avenue."

"You'll be a lovely addition," he complimented.

"Will your family be strolling there, too?"

309

"No, we plan to attend sunrise services in the village and enjoy a quiet weekend in the country. Our son may spend this Easter in Virginia, and our daughters will dye and hide their own eggs, having outgrown the Easter Bunny myth. What are you typing?"

"Yesterday afternoon's dictation, sir. The letters will be ready for your signature by noon. There's some confidential mail from the White House and the Treasury on your desk, Mr. Curtis. Would you like some coffee?" She had made a fresh pot on the gas jet in the conveniently equipped pantry, timing its completion for his expected arrival.

"Later, perhaps," he resisted, despite the delicious aroma, and entered his office.

He broke the presidential seal and read the letter, not surprised at its contents, for the financial ship of state was foundering again, and Grover Cleveland, for whom the political Red Sea had miraculously parted to walk him into office, was now up the well-known creek without a paddle. And the Treasury Secretary's missive only confirmed the administration's straits. In a quandary over the unstable gold situation, President Cleveland, in the fashion of his predecessors, was again appealing to the monetary mentors of Wall Street: Curtis, Belmont, and Morgan. Their responses must not be trusted to the telegraph wires, however; federal messengers would be provided. And since there was only one patriotic reply to a presidential summons, Keith told Marnie to telephone the Sub-Treasury for a courier, while he composed a formal acceptance in his own hand.

But personal matters bore heavily on his mind that morning, too. Scott's brief message concerning his intention to visit the Haverstons during his Easter vacation from college was a deep disappointment to his parents. He planned to ride the train with Fawn from Baltimore to Richmond, where her father would meet them for the short journey to Harmony Hill. Though crushed by the news, Devon had defended the boy's right to his decision, and a hot argument had ensued when Keith called him inconsiderate and ungrateful, with little or no concern for his family.

"He's just in love, Keith, and you refuse to recognize that fact," she cried, concealing her own distress. "In his place, wouldn't you prefer your sweetheart to your parents and sisters?"

"I wasn't serious about any petticoat at his age! I had more common sense, and enough intelligence not to involve myself in an irrevocable courtship."

"Irrevocable?"

"A relationship that's more than platonic, Devon. The kind that usually ends in betrothal and marriage and fatherhood, though not always in that order. Scott's a paradox, simultaneously brilliant and stupid. Phi Beta Kappa, yet the key can't unlock his lovesick brain, nor turn off his one-track mind with regard to that girl. And there's no effective remedy for his ailment, because he won't try any, not even the Grand Tour. How could any intelligent young man want to miss that experience? I certainly didn't."

"He's not you, Keith, and you can't judge him by yourself. No doubt you had quite a romp through Europe, sampling the fleshpots as well as the fountains of knowledge and culture. And when finally you settled down, did you get such a marvelous marital prize? My God, we both know better! You could hardly have gotten a worse mate if you had selected her blindfolded by lottery! Esther Stanfield had a lover in Boston when she married you, and brought him to New York afterward. And whose child did she miscarry when she fell down the stairs of his attic studio the day he caught them in bed together? All those bitter, miserable years you stayed together, bound by hatred and guilt, because you believed she was severely injured trying to keep you from killing her gigolo artist!"

Dark blood suffused his features, and his black brows drew together angrily. "Goddamn it, Devon! I don't need your tirade to remind me of my wretched life with Esther. I've been trying to forget it for years."

"Then don't be so bullheadedly opposed to our son's interest in that charming Southern belle, who could not possibly cause him the grief and unhappiness that beguiling Brahmin bitch did you! Fawn Haverston is a sweet, pure little virgin, and I trust Scotty won't seduce her without benefit of clergy."

"And if you think I didn't feel that snide stab, twist the blade some more, my dear. Make the wound bleed, and then try to cauterize it with your fiery tongue. Someday you'll burn a hole in my heart that won't heal." The storm gathered momentum, climaxing in recriminations and slammed doors and separate beds, a hangover for him and a wet pillow for her.

Now, remembering the consequences, Keith was tempted to dash off a telegram informing Scott that his allowance would be severed until he recouped his senses, and if he could forget his family at Easter, he might as well forget them completely. But he feared the proud young stallion might take the edict literally . . . and Devon would never forgive him. Indeed, it might actually estrange them. Their marital walls were already shaky, and he had some serious mending to do, which he would begin with a trip to her favorite jeweler.

Within an hour the sun disappeared from the sky, obliterated by dismal clouds, and a freezing mist slanted across the island. The federal courier arrived with snowflakes on his oilskin slicker. Locking the wax-sealed letters to Washington in a leather pouch chained to his wrist, he mentioned that a bulletin from the Long Island Weather Station contained a severe blizzard warning for New England.

In March? thought Marnie skeptically. Either the meteorologists were daft or her boss was clairvoyant. But no matter, it was warm in the bank, and the janitor could always stoke up the banked furnace.

By noon frigid gales were gusting down the rivers and off the Sound, ripping at the flag on the United States Sub-Treasury across the street, hurling sleet and snow in all directions. This was no mere late, unseasonal nor'easter, but the inception of a full-fledged arctic storm that could easily and rapidly develop into a catastrophe. Snow was gathering on streets and structures, sweeping against windowsills and steps, so that the bulky stone buildings resembled mountains hemming the narrow canyon of Wall Street, and the spire of Trinity Church was virtually obscured. Pedestrians staggered against the stiff, cold, wet winds, shivering in inadequate clothing. Vehicles skidded on the slippery pavement, horses and mules lost their footing. Traffic was formidable, and there was a frantic rush to get out of town before it became hopelessly snarled. Already the mounted police, fortunately still in their winter uniforms and helmets, were seriously hampered in their efforts to keep things moving. Hoarfrost soon covered the Curtis Bank's windowpanes, impairing Marnie's visibility, and she wished she had brought along a wool jacket or shawl to work.

Keith made it to Delmonico's for luncheon, but not to Tiffany's on Union Square, and returned without the conciliatory gift for his wife. Dusting the ice crystals from his felt hat and alpaca overcoat, he said, "Business has been suspended for the day, Miss Ryan. The Stock Exchange, banks, and brokerage houses are all closing early. Our employees have also been dismissed."

"I'm not worried, sir," she said, which was not quite true. "I'm sure 'twill blow over quickly."

"I'm afraid not, Miss Ryan. I've seen these freakish spring blizzards before; they can last for days and do terrible damage. Lives are invariably lost and property destroyed. Torn-off signs, awnings, flagstaffs, garbage receptacles, and other debris are flying and crashing dangerously in the streets. Trees are breaking branches and even being uprooted in the parks and squares. I doubt you could get home safely now. You should have left hours ago."

"No matter, sir. I can finish my day's work, and it'll be much warmer here than in my flat, anyway. There's never enough heat in any tenement in winter, and those in Paradise Alley are ice vaults."

"Are you still living there? I *know* I'm paying you well enough to move, Miss Ryan. So well, in fact, my accountants probably wonder about my generosity."

"Oh, yes, Mr. Curtis! You're too generous with my salary. But I'm saving for a rainy day. And my old age."

"Old age?" he scoffed. "You're barely past thirty!"

"A bit more than that, sir, and still single. An old maid must plan for the future, alone."

"And whose fault is that, pretty lady? How many honest proposals have you rejected since the last time you lamented your spinsterhood?"

"Only two, and both fellows married others."

"Did you expect them to wait forever? Most men want a wife young enough to bear children. You have plenty of time for motherhood, but it's nice and convenient to have a husband first."

"It's nicer and more convenient to be in love with him,"

said Marnie, perusing her shorthand notes.

"I can't argue that," Keith conceded with a shrug of his shoulders, whose magnificent breadth was the bane of his tailors. "And this little debate has probably stranded us both, Miss Ryan. Cabs are impossible to hire, and the horsecars and omnibuses and els will soon cease operation. In lieu of a sleigh or skis we'd have to sprout wings to get out of here—and even the birds are dropping out of the sky."

"Like I said, sir, it's more comfortable on Wall Street than in Paradise Alley."

"Well, take your time with the correspondence. The credo of the postal service will not prevail today and probably not tomorrow, either."

Communication by wire was impaired, as ice-laden telegraph and telephone lines collapsed, barring contact with the island villages and estates. Thank God, Devon was not alone at Halcyon, there was plenty of food and fuel, and the servants would take good care of her and the children. But why couldn't this damnable weather have waited a few more days, until he was back in the country? They needed to be together again, healing their hurts in each other's arms, and there was no greater friend to love than a powerful storm. His body ached for her now, so painfully he almost groaned aloud, and he had to quickly divert his mind.

He pondered the government's fiscal problems. If a practical solution wasn't found, world economy would be affected. He and his colleagues, sometimes referred to in the press as the American Banking Triumvirate, alias the Unholy Trinity, would have to consult via the Atlantic cable with their foreign branches. Depressions recurred like universal plagues, and international bankers were expected to cure them with monetary magic and witchcraft. The Curtis Bank had assisted in performing such feats in the past...and here was yet another hot potato to juggle. Well, the hell with it! Let the muddled mints stew in their gold-smelting pots. There would be no wizardry on Wall Street today. By five o'clock the District would be one vast frozen asset, and the money monarchs would be marooned in their temples of gold and silver.

Preoccupied, his secretary had to rap several times on his door to get his attention and permission to enter. "Some people are stranded in the lobby," Marnie informed, presenting a sheaf of neatly typed papers for his signature. "Late customers, apparently, and employees afraid to leave."

"I hope the coal supply is adequate and the water mains don't freeze. It must be zero outside and not very warm in here, either. You should have a sweater."

"I'm not cold, sir."

"You're shivering, Miss Ryan."

Not from the cold, she wanted to say, but the prospect of spending the night in his presence. "No, I'm fine, Mr. Curtis. Really."

"Heat up the coffee, if there's any left. If not, make some . . . and share it with me."

"Thank you, sir. I could use a cup myself."

Subsequently, she carried in a tray with a steaming pot of coffee, served his black and started to cream hers, when he suggested, "Lace it with brandy instead, Miss Ryan. It'll help to warm you."

"Well"—she hesitated—"if you'll tell me how much."

"I'll fix it," he said, removing a squat bottle with a Napoleonic image on the label from the cellaret. "Nothing but Providence can halt this blizzard, and He seems disinclined to do so yet. Try to relax, Miss Ryan. This building is quite safe, built like a fort, to endure for centuries."

"And many generations of Curtis bankers?"

Keith nodded, his face sobering as he thought of Scott. The elements would keep him in Boston, if he had not left impetuously early for his destination. If he had jumped the gun, he might be stranded somewhere en route—another worry for his parents!

"Troubles?" asked Marnie, noting his tenseness.

"Just wondering about my son."

"That tall, handsome lad I met last summer, a certified copy of his father? Isn't he due to graduate from Harvard University this year?"

"*Summa cum laude,*" Keith said proudly. "In June, if he can wait that long."

"Why shouldn't he?"

"Sure now"—he smiled wryly—"you've heard what a young man's fancy turns to in spring, Miss Ryan?"

"He has a sweetheart?"

"Yes, in Dixieland. On his way to visit her now, perhaps, and snowbound on the rails."

"Trains prepare for such emergencies," Marnie assured him from experience. "They keep plenty of coarse wool blankets and stale sandwiches aboard. Mr. Scott won't freeze or starve, not such a vigorous youth as he, and vitalized by first love yet!"

"Oh, he's healthy enough, and his vital young juices will sustain him, if nothing else."

He set his cup and saucer abruptly aside, stood, and crossed the floor to a long window, with snow banked on the ledge and sleet pelting the pane. Rubbing a clear, round space like a porthole on the frosted glass, Keith thoughtfully appraised the elemental monster, the savage March lion ravaging the helpless island as the worst in his memory. Karl and Lars had better keep the fires burning on Halcyon's hearths, and lock the livestock in the barns with plenty of hay and oats. Was Devon frightened? Were the twins, who had never witnessed such a ferocious white beast on a rampage before? Was Scott safe, wherever he was?

Marnie was cognizant of his paternal anxiety, and sympathetic, but Keith was unaware of her compassion for him, or the personal emotions creating her own dilemma.

❧ 34 ❧

EVENING WAS approaching in a white fury, descending on a deceptively beautiful fairyland. Gas street lamps, lighted earlier in the day, glowed and twinkled through the spinning ice crystals like magic lanterns. Icicles decorated the roofs and parapets and balconies, the trees and utility poles, and the sagging, swaying, popping wires. Suddenly, almost mystically, at twilight, the bells of Trinity Church began to ring the Angelus, amazingly clear and vibrant, and Marnie marveled at the hardy souls tolling them.

"The angels must have flown down from Heaven to the belfries," she declared as other chimes sounded the evening vespers, as if echoing over distant hills and dales. "And is that the wind wailing so mournfully? My mother would swear 'tis a chorus of banshees."

His reverie broken, Keith returned to the long brown leather sofa. "You believe that old Irish superstition?"

"'Tis heresy not to in rural Ireland, and my folks were farmers, you know, until the great potato famine brought them to America. They claimed to hear the banshee spirits crying before every death in the family."

"Well, it'll hold true for some New Yorkers tonight," Keith predicted. "It's colder in here, don't you think? The janitor must be doling the coal." His hand gestured toward the black marble fireplace, with its big andirons topped with leonine brass heads. "Some wood should have been sent up by now, if there's any in the basement. Put on my topcoat, Miss Ryan."

"I'm comfortable," she insisted, her lips quivering in the lie. His garment on her body, when his scent was already an erotic incense to her senses? "Is there some dictation you can give me, sir—some work to do?"

"You're a glutton for punishment, lady."

"I—I just like to keep busy."

"Too busy," he said. "That's why there's nothing more to do now. Unfortunately, the bank library isn't very entertaining, mostly business and law books. No poetry, romantic novels, or fashion magazines."

"I'll read the papers," Marnie decided.

"They're yesterday's news, and stale. But I'm sure you'll find the *Wall Street Journal* fascinating."

A quick glance caught his humorous grin, for he still liked to tease her about her unordinary career. "Oh," she quipped, "I've already read *that!*"

"Liar." Keith laughed, drawing the latest *Atlantic Monthly* from the periodical shelf.

Marnie selected the New York *Record*, in which his wife's byline appeared rather frequently, usually in the Sunday editions, and Marnie always read her comprehensive articles and feature stories. Their social life was chronicled in all the society columns, but they seemed to attend only the most important events, with a special fondness for those connected with charity and the arts. Marnie scanned the advertisements and chuckled over the cartoons, her musical laughter tinkling like a little girl's, reminding Keith of his young daughters.

"What's so funny, colleen?"

"This caricature of President Cleveland. He's Humpty-Dumpty about to fall off the White House wall."

"And so he will, in the next election. But that's better than being ridiculed as the leader of the Rum, Romanism, and Rebellion Party, alias the Democrats, isn't it? Or mercilessly taunted in that stupid ditty, because he fathered a child out of wedlock."

Every American adult knew the snide limerick to which he referred, and even youngsters ignorant of its true meaning recited it blithely in the streets: "Ma, Ma, where's my Pa? Gone to the White House, ha, ha, ha!"

"People can be so cruel," she said.

"Especially politicians, for who else but his political enemies coined those malicious slogans?" He closed his magazine. "Is there anything in the pantry?"

"Whatever you ordered from that outrageously expensive delicatessen on Broad Street. Crackers, caviar, olives, truffles, some imported cheeses, the last time I checked. Are you hungry?"

"Not really. I was hoping to offer the refugees in the lobby some substantial nourishment, like bread and ham and sausage. I doubt they'd eat those delicacies."

"And fight over them, if they did, for there's not nearly enough to go around, Mr. Curtis. The guards might have to quell a riot."

"Can't risk that." Keith frowned. "Who knows how long they'll be confined here?"

"Not too long, please God," Marnie prayed, crossing herself.

"Ask Him for some quilts and blankets and additional fuel, too," Keith suggested, just as the janitor's assistant arrived with firewood and kindling. "Well, that was prompt, anyway . . . intercede some more, Miss Ryan. How's the coal supply?" he asked the man kneeling to build the fire.

"Not too good, sir. Lawson stopped ordering in March, figuring there was plenty to last until fall. I guess we was all too confident after than warm spell."

"Better be more cautious in the future," Keith advised. "And try to keep the plumbing from freezing."

"We'll do our best, sir. But I got to tell you, there ain't much wood left, neither."

"Shut off as many department vents as possible. Burn some of that old furniture in storage, if necessary. Help the folks in the lobby any way you can."

"Yes, sir," Briggs said on his way out.

Marnie rushed immediately to the fireplace, belying her previous assurances of physical comfort. "Oh, that feels good!" she cried, stretching her hands to the warmth and then turning her back, wishing she could raise her skirts to warm her legs in their practical lisle stockings, for she could not afford the luxury of silk hosiery.

Her childish delight amused him. "I thought you weren't cold, Miss Ryan."

"A lie, but only a little white one, and a venial sin easily forgiven in the confessional."

"The only kind you commit, I imagine. Surely no big black mortal sins, with all your piety."

Her eyes dropped hastily, guiltily, lest he see the cardinal offense of carnality in them, which was also against the Commandments where he was concerned.

"Ah, you're blushing! Are you a secret sinner, Miss Ryan?"

"Mr. Curtis, *please!* It's blasphemous to discuss religion this way."

"Sorry, my dear. Forgive my heathen ways. I was just joking, trying to make light of a heavy situation. Comic relief, as it were. Shall we discuss philosophy, psychology, history, science—what?"

"I don't know much about those subjects, sir."

"There must be a deck of cards somewhere," he said, searching through his desk. "What games do you play?"

"Old Maid," she said laconically.

"That's for kids." He shoved back the drawers, empty-handed. "Damn it, woman! We can't just sit here and stare at each other! I'll go cell-crazy."

"You mean get cabin fever, like the settlers during long winters on the frontier?"

"Close enough," he nodded, glancing at the office time-piece. Nine o'clock, and the storm showed no signs of abating; indeed it was increasing in intensity, and they were definitely marooned. "What's your usual bedtime?"

"Ten or eleven, depending on when I get my home chores done. Quite late, sometimes."

"You can use the sofa, and cover with my coat. I'll sleep on the floor, before the fire. We'll have light, barring trouble at the gasworks. Keep some candles handy, just in case." He paced the floor like a caged animal, pausing intermittently before the dark, ice-glazed windows. Eating would give them something to do, for a while. "Fix some snacks, Miss Ryan."

"Yes, sir."

She obliged with her usual alacrity and efficiency, preparing some exotic canapés by candlelight, for the gas supply to that area was suddenly disrupted, probably by an explosion in an overloaded plant. Marnie, who had never tasted caviar before, found it a wee bit salty for her liking, and she declined to eat the French truffles when she learned how they were harvested. But she enjoyed the delicious cheeses and pâté de foie gras, and the excellent Madeira from the bar.

Remembering the first time he had offered such delicacies to Devon, on the train from Richmond to Washington, Keith suddenly lost his appetite. His attention shifted to her gold-framed photograph on the credenza, and he sipped his wine in reflection. After a long, brooding silence, he said, "I guess it's time to retire, Miss Ryan."

"I guess so, Mr. Curtis. And I think I should sleep in my office."

"There's no couch or fire there," he reminded. "You'll rest better here."

Marnie doubted that, but agreed. Using his lavatory, she scrubbed her teeth as best she could on a huckaback towel and removed the pins from her lovely titian hair. Then, asking his permission to douse the candles, she lay down on the long, comfortable sofa, fully clothed except for the new spring slippers, and was quiet while he covered her with his greatcoat.

"Good night, Miss Ryan."

"Good night, sir."

Keith placed another log on the fire and poked up the flames. Then, removing only his cravat and shoes, he stretched out on the Persian rug, grateful for its luxuriant resilience and thick underpadding. A chair cushion served as pillow.

Marnie tried not to move, lest the sloughing leather disturb him, and prayed fervently for sleep. With a sidelong glance, she could admire his extremely handsome profile silhouetted in the fireglow. The warmth of her body enhanced the scent of his garment, and she wrapped the sleeves around herself and secretly kissed the collar and lapels. She knew if he would but beckon, she would crawl on her knees to him, and risk eternity in hell for one night in his arms. She agonized in desire, and moaned in torment.

If he was asleep, she had awakened him, for he asked, "Something wrong?"

"No," she murmured. "I'm sorry if I disturbed you."

It occurred to him that she may be menstruating, or just starting a period, and was unprepared and embarrassed, perhaps cramping. "If you're in pain, brandy might help."

"No," she reiterated in a tense whisper. How could she tell him that something was indeed wrong, and she was in agony, and there was no simple, easy relief? The last time she had confessed this grave problem, the priest had warned her that she must either resolve it morally, or remove herself permanently from the source. And she could do neither, no matter how hard she tried, how many votive lights she burned to patron saints, how many rosaries and litanies she mouthed like a crazed parrot.

"Well, good night again," he bade, and even his voice aroused her, its smooth, deep, sensual timbre vibrating in her flesh like a physical caress, so stimulating she could not reply without betraying her traitorous emotions.

Marnie hoped to lull herself into oblivious slumber through his regular, rhythmic breathing, but never quite succeeded. It was long past midnight, and the fire was dying away. She knew he would get cold and wanted to share the coat in the only way possible. Creeping from the sofa, she spread it furtively over him, and crawled quietly under it beside him. Miraculously, he was undisturbed; she credited her finesse to the Blessed Virgin, and entranced herself through the drumbeat of his heart. She possessed him in an erotic dream, and it must have been near dawn when the incredibly realistic experience caused her to cry out and clutch him to her throbbing breast.

Dazed with sleep, thinking Devon was having a nightmare, Keith cradled her in his arms and tenderly soothed, "It's all right, darling. You're just dreaming. . . ." He started to kiss her, still groggy and confused, and then jerked abruptly away, realizing his mistake. "My God . . . *Marnie!* You're supposed to be on the sofa! What're you doing on the floor, with me? Did you walk in your sleep?"

Befuddled herself, Marnie uttered the only logical explanation she could muster. "I suppose so."

"Do you do that often?"

"Not often. But the storm and all . . . I must've had a nightmare."

Keith sat up, shaken to the core. "Maybe I did, too. Nothing happened, I hope?"

"I—I'm not sure." She was unable to distinguish between fact and fantasy in her present mental confusion, for something sexual had definitely occurred in her body.

"Well, find out! Check your chemise."

"I—I wear drawers."

"A mere technicality, Marnie! Are your pants on or off?" He averted his eyes while she checked.

"On," she said, omitting that they were also slightly moist and wondering if she had wet herself. "I'm still Maiden Marnie."

Keith sighed in acute relief. "Are you saying . . . ?" How could he put it delicately? "You've never been with a man?"

She blushed all over. "Not intimately. It's the one thing I have in common with the Virgin Mary."

"Then you're still status quo, thank heaven! But you should fall in love and change it, Marnie. Sex is a wondrous thing, and you should have experienced it by now. I can hardly believe you haven't, even once, at your age."

"Nor ever shall, probably."

Her loose hair rippled on her shoulders, red as the glowing coals reflected in her blue eyes. "I doubt that, Marnie. You're a very desirable woman, with an appealing figure. A man would have to be impotent not to want you."

"Do you?" she asked, shocked at her boldness.

"Well, I'm human, Marnie, and not gelt. But love and lust are not the same emotions, you know, and I'm in love with my wife. I've never been unfaithful to her, and don't believe I ever could be, technically, even if I tried. That's how it is, and this is a strange conversation for a boss and secretary to be having at this hour of the night. Blame crafty Mother Nature, for it sure as hell couldn't have happened otherwise! Could it?"

She shook her head in agreement. But the cruel witch was still screaming and raging outside, and they were still immured together, and Marnie knew she had to make a decision, now or never. "Is two weeks sufficient, Mr. Curtis?"

"For what?"

"Notice."

"You're not serious?"

"I am, sir."

"Why?" he demanded.

"I'd rather not say."

"I insist, Marnie. Tell me."

She remained silent, and he persisted. "If it's a question of more money—"

"Oh, no!"

"Have you had a more attractive offer, from one of my piratical competitors? I'll match and surpass it; give you an officership, if that's your ambition."

"You don't understand, sir."

"No, I don't, Marnie. Please explain?"

"I—I just can't stay, Mr. Curtis."

"That's no answer!"

"It is, for me."

"But what will you do, where will you go?"

"To St. Louis, probably, and into the convent with my elder sister," she said in a barely audible voice, refusing to meet his incredulous gaze. "Become the bride of Christ. That's what nuns do, you know; give themselves to God and the Church. They receive the symbolic gold wedding band when they take their final veils and vows."

"Nonsense, Marnie!"

"No, 'tis the gospel truth."

"I mean, it's nonsense for you to consider such a life for yourself. And so suddenly! You certainly weren't thinking of religious immurement a few hours ago. Have I unwittingly offended you somehow? If so, I humbly and sincerely apologize, and beg you to reconsider."

"You've done nothing," she assured him, her ragged nerves on the edge of hysteria. "It's me, it's me!" She burst into tears, wrenching, racking, abysmal tears.

Reacting with his usual chivalry to feminine distress, Keith sought to console her physically, with strong-arms and gentle voice. At his touch, her precarious control melted like wax in fire, and she began kissing his hands and face and lips with wild abandon, unaware that he was too stunned to respond in any way whatever. Bewildered moments passed before comprehension grappled with reality.

"Marnie, for God's sake! You're delirious! *Marnie!*" He shook her gently, then rather firmly, until she retrieved her senses and retreated into horrified shame and mortification, rolling onto her stomach and burying her face in his coat. "What got into you?" he questioned, still astounded by the entire incident.

"The devil," she answered. convinced that Satan had actually possessed her for a time, tempted her beyond all endurance, and she would now have to seriously consider the rites of exorcism with Father O'Toole.

"We can forget this, Marnie. Forget this whole goddamn crazy night, and never refer to it again."

She sobbed in anguish, mumbling incoherently into the woolen folds, inhaling his scent.

"I can't understand you, Marnie. Uncover your face and sit up. We'll discuss this like mature adults, and then seal it forever in the dead file."

Dead file? She wanted to die, she wished she were dead and in Hell, where she belonged. She had behaved like a bitch in heat, a slut of the streets; a vile, reprehensible creature who might have, however unwittingly, lured a married man into adultery! She *must* have been possessed by demons, or temporarily insane. And what abbey would want such a wanton, loony sinner?

"Sit up, Marnie."

She obeyed, reluctantly, afraid she would seem ugly and repulsive to him now. "It's no use, sir. Talking won't help. I did a terrible thing."

"Delirium, Marnie."

"Bedeviled," she insisted.

"Whatever." He shrugged, unable to mollify her. "But nothing really wrong happened, Marnie."

"It could have."

"The point is, it didn't."

"Because of you, not me."

"All right, flog yourself. Don your hairshirt and suffer your martyrdom. You're still the best confidential secretary on Wall Street, and I don't want to lose you. Wear sackcloth and ashes in the office, repent if you must, but stay with me. I won't accept your resignation, Marnie, nor give you a reference to go elsewhere."

"Nunneries don't require references, just baptismal certificates."

"You still want to marry Jesus?"

"If He'll have me."

"And what will you be then?" he asked, exasperated. "Mrs. Christ?"

"Sister Marnie."

"And chaste forevermore."

"Yes."

"Let me tell you something, Marnie. You have a vital, passionate nature, and chastity is not going to be easy for you. What will you do, when you want more than spiritual embraces? Resort to your self-torture kit?"

"Dedicated nuns practice sublimation."

"Oh, Marnie, that's unnatural! Sufficient for some women, I suppose, but difficult for you. When the right man comes along, and you fall in love—"

"Stop it!" she cried. "You're not fooling me. You know the truth now, even if you didn't before. And if you imagine I could ever forget my deplorable conduct tonight— Oh, Holy

Mother of God, pray for our sinners, now and at the hour of our death, amen."

"Is that the rosary?"

"Partly."

"And you have one in your purse, no doubt?"

"Always. It's a Catholic's *vade mecum*."

"Why didn't you recite it earlier, my dear, while lying on the sofa?"

"I should have. Oh, I should have! But *your* guardian angel protected you from temptation, for you were as wooden as my beads."

"You think so?"

"Isn't it true?"

"Not quite," he admitted. "My marital fidelity has never been harder tested."

"Well, you passed the test with flying colors. Your wife should pin a heroic medal on your chest. *Semper fidelis.*"

"You're fluent in Latin, aren't you?"

"It's the language of the Church. I studied it in parochial school and used to sing High Mass in Latin. A choirgirl, you see. My mother must be turning over in her grave, and my father—" She paused, fraught with yet another cause for remorse. "Oh, poor Pa! What will happen to him if I leave your employ? Will they put him out of Sunset House, on the street?"

"Certainly not! You surely don't think I'd use your ill father to hold you in your job, if you're determined to quit? He'll be cared for the rest of his life. I promise you that, no matter what."

"Thank you, sir."

Keith glanced at the windows, bleak silver rectangles in the frozen dawning. "Good morning, Miss Ryan! We're in exceptionally early today, aren't we? Shall we brew some coffee and get to work?"

"Immediately, Mr. Curtis. Oh, yes, immediately!"

✣ 35 ✣

MANHATTAN ISLAND was paralyzed in ice and snow for two days. Rationed coal and crackers sustained the refugees in the Curtis Bank lobby. When the last stick of firewood was consumed on the hearth in the executive offices, chopped-up furniture, newspapers, magazines, and reams of stationery were burned. They kept perfunctorily busy during the day, and their second night together was without incident. Marnie kept a discreet distance on the sofa, sleeping in his greatcoat. Keith was covered with the heavy velvet draperies, angry with himself for not resorting to them earlier. But Marnie was obviously under an emotional strain, suffering intermittent conscience seizures over her contretemps, and Keith suspected that she had not totally rescinded her mental resignation from his employ.

Then, as suddenly as it had arrived, winter departed, and spring returned again. A warm, bright sun gleamed incongruously on the white desolation, the howling winds calmed to soft whispers, and the city roused from its frozen lethargy. Rescue squads, working with picks and shovels, exhumed some two hundred bodies, which were transported to temporary morgues to await identification and burial. Four victims perished on Wall Street, including the elderly flower lady who had sought shelter under her cart. Many perished in doorways and empty shipping crates and vacant sheds.

Luckier survivors, including those in the two Curtis buildings, departed as the streets became passable, although the gutters and sewers overflowed with melting snow and slush, and the sanitation department was far behind in its removal of debris and dead animals. Telephone and telegraph lines would be inoperative for days and perhaps weeks, and Keith trusted that Devon would remain at Halcyon until he could get there when the Hudson River Railroad resumed operations. Sailing was infeasible, for the *Sprite* was frozen solidly in her berth, possibly even damaged, and the captain and crew were unreachable. The fate of his material possessions did not concern Keith, however, only that of his family. He imagined Devon must be frantic by now, unless she had heard from their son before the disaster struck.

Keith could not recall a more joyous reunion with his wife. Their marital quarrel was instantly forgotten at sight of each other, and forgiven in a loving embrace. The twins hugged and kissed him too, babbling simultaneously about the excitement during his absence. Some shutters were ripped off the windows, thick tree branches had snapped like matchsticks in the fierce gales, and the handymen had beaten a path back and forth to the woodshed. The collie bitch had whelped her latest litter sired by her mate, Bounder, and all were sheltered in the house, along with Calico and her new kittens; and a stray colt and bully calf had to be fetched back to their mothers and bedded on hay in the barns.

"Let me tell it!" cried Sharon, pushing at her sister.

"No, I want to!" said Shannon, jumping up and down for her father's attention. "Listen to *me*, Daddy!"

"Oh, she's so prissy," from Sharon.

"And *she's* a tomboy," Shannon complained. "Tore her stockings again today—that's the third pair this week. And she slides down the banister, Daddy, whenever Nanny or Miss Vale can't see her."

"Hush, both of you!" Devon ordered. "Don't be tattletales, and go to your rooms and finish your lessons. Daddy and I want to be alone."

They obeyed, albeit reluctantly, bickering all the way upstairs, and Devon sighed in dismay. "They've been incorrigible since the storm—I was tempted to put them in solitary confinement. You must take them to task, Keith. *Why* can't they get along better?"

"They will, when they're older," he assured her, sensing that their daughters' misbehavior was not her real problem. "No word from Scott yet?"

She shook her head, fighting tears. "None. You?"

"There's no outside communication to or from New York yet. We just have to believe he's all right, Devon."

"He's never been thoughtless, Keith, and surely he realizes how worried we are?"

"Of course, darling. It's just that he can't contact us, any more than we can him."

"Is everything all right at Gramercy Park?"

"Fine." He nodded, omitting that he had not been stranded there. "I missed you, sweet. For God's sake, let's not fight over Scott anymore! It's his life, and we'll have to let him live it."

"I hope you mean that, Keith?"

"I do, Devon. If he wants to marry Fawn Haverston and plant tobacco at Harmony Hill, or work in her father's factory in Richmond, so be it! I just want him alive and happy. If he loves that girl, then he should have her. Every man should have the woman he loves, and who loves him, if possible. How could I have bucked Scott on that issue, considering my own experience and actions?"

Her eyes misted, for she knew better than anyone else on earth what that concession cost him. "I guess we can expect a wedding then, in the not-too-distant future."

"Very likely," Keith agreed, slipping an arm tenderly about her waist. "This has been our winter of discontent, hasn't it?"

"So it seems, dear. But spring has come again and this time, please God, to stay."

By the time Scott's letter arrived from Richmond, he was back at Harvard and preparing for his final examinations. The blizzard had been less severe in Virginia, and the train from Baltimore to Richmond was almost on schedule. He had, in fact, been quite worried about his family in New York and had tried to wire them, but the lines were down.

"See, darling?" Devon said, reading the letter aloud. "He didn't forget us, after all."

"Thank the Lord he's safe! What else does he say?"

"Nothing much."

"Read between the lines."

"They're blank. I don't think he has proposed to Miss

Haverston yet, however. If so, it's their secret. But he knows he's not of age, Keith, and couldn't marry without our permission. And Fawn would need her father's, too, for another year, at least."

"Not in every state, Devon. According to my attorneys, a boy of eighteen and a girl of fourteen can wed in North Carolina without parental consent."

"Oh, but surely they wouldn't elope?"

"Even so, it could be annulled, because they're not residents of that state."

"Would you take legal action?"

"No, but Daniel might."

"I doubt it, Keith. Once they're married—"

"And have slept together," he finished for her. "It would take a mighty foolish father to seek to annul a possibly pregnant daughter's union, wouldn't it?"

"I don't even want to consider that prospect." Devon shrugged. "Dinner will be ready soon. Would you like a drink first?"

"Several, my dear. And maybe you should have some fortification, too. Parenthood can be difficult, beyond rompers and pinafores."

"I'm afraid so," Devon agreed. "How shall we cope when Sharon and Shannon are in their teens?"

"One adolescent at a time," Keith advised. "Fortunately, we don't have a baker's dozen. Being female, the twins are going to double our troubles as it is."

"Keith! What does their sex have to do with it?"

"Oh, don't ruffle your feathers! You know girls mature sooner than boys, and our audacious darlings won't be laggard in that respect. They're already too precocious for their pantalettes."

"They wear bloomers."

"Merely a figure of speech," he explained, unwittingly reminded of the feminine distinction Marnie Ryan had made in her lingerie the night of her contretemps. And suddenly he needed a drink even more than he had thought. . . .

Despite the girls' clamoring to ride the train to New York with their parents, they were left in the competent care of their nurse and governess. Devon needed a respite from motherhood, and an opportunity to be one hundred percent wife for a while. She also wanted to do some spring shopping and deliver some revised material on child labor to the Women's Bureau and the Sorosis Club.

The next day, as she was preparing to leave the house in Gramercy Park, the telephone bell sounded in the foyer. The butler answered it, and said: "It's for you, madam. A gentleman."

"Did he give his name?"

"No, mum. Just asked for Mrs. Curtis."

"Thank you, Hadley." Devon picked up the instrument. "Mrs. Curtis speaking. May I help you?"

The voice was unfamiliar, its tone rather querulous and apparently muffled in attempted disguise. "I'm sure your husband told you this, ma'am, but in case he forgot, you might like to know where he spent the two nights of the blizzard, and with whom. In his cozy office, that's where, and with his secretary, that's who, while other folks trapped in the bank were cold and hungry." Silence hummed loudly on the recently repaired wires, while Devon assimilated the information, which he seemed to be reading from a prepared and rehearsed statement. "Did you hear, ma'am?"

Devon knew she should cut him off, but was afraid he would only call again, perhaps repeatedly, to make sure she got the message. "Yes," she replied, replacing the receiver on the hook and bowing her head against the wooden box attached to the wall.

"Something amiss, madam?" asked Hadley.

"Just a crank call," Devon said. "Henceforth, I shall refuse to speak with anyone who refuses to state a name and purpose, Hadley."

"Yes, mum."

Devon surmised that the informer was a disgruntled employee, with a grudge against the Curtis Bank or Marnie Ryan's position in it. But what was Keith's reason for not telling her about this?

She took the literature to the Bureau and to the Club, so the appropriate committees in each could study it before relaying it to the printer, and returned home promptly, declining several luncheon and shopping invitations. Too restless to read or work on her novel manuscript, and disinclined to wander aimlessly in the house, she used the golden key to admit herself to the sacrosanct Gramercy Park. A couple of nannies were pushing perambulators on the still-dormant grass. Devon greeted them, admired the babies they were airing, and inquired after the parents, who were also neighbors. She strolled the garden paths for a while, then sat on an ornamental iron bench in the sun. Trees and shrubs, nipped in impetuous bud by the recent freeze, were bare of leaf or bloom. She watched a pair of robins gathering twigs and straw to build a nest and wondered how they had survived the storm in which so many of their species were lost. As the golden disk moved lower in the western sky, toward a crimson horizon, she locked the gate behind herself and crossed the street to the Curtis residence. The master would be home soon!

He arrived somewhat later than usual, with the inevitable portfolio. Devon kissed him and made conversation during dinner and afterward, as they relaxed before the fire in the library, his feet on the ottoman while he smoked a pipe. "Were you this comfortable the evenings of the blizzard?" she asked, affecting nonchalance.

"Hardly," he replied with a curious glance. "Why?"

"Just wondering."

"I know that tone in your voice, Devon. What are you wondering about?"

Despite her resolve to be casual and sophisticated, her impetuous tongue betrayed her. "An anonymous male telephone call I had today."

"Obscene?"

"Well, it had obscene implications."

"That's against the law, and the operator should have severed the connection. Did you report it?"

Finesse failed her again, and she blurted out, "The message concerned you, Keith! Your whereabouts during the storm. Why did you let me believe you were *here?*"

"I don't recall discussing it at all, Devon. But I was marooned at the bank along with some other people."

"Including Miss Ryan?"

"Yes. Is that what the call was about?"

She nodded, twisting her hands nervously. "I heard it was cold in the lobby, but cozy in your office."

"Cozy? We damned near froze, Devon. The fuel supply was inadequate, and we burned broken furniture and papers before the crisis was over."

"If it was such an ordeal, how could you forget to mention it? I just assumed you were at home. Why did I have to learn otherwise from some malicious stranger?"

"Vengeful underling, no doubt! Some disloyal, cowardly bastard who probably expected to get Marnie Ryan's position, and hopes that you will insist on her dismissal now. The stupid fool doesn't know me very well, if that's his aim. Too bad he didn't send you a note, so his handwriting could be analyzed by an amanuensis—but, of course, he knew how easily that could be traced. Nevertheless, he'll be found out, through a detective, and fired with no chance of ever working in another bank or business in New York, or anywhere else, if I can help it."

Devon toyed with her wedding band. "Did you sleep with Marnie Ryan, Keith?"

"Is that what you think?"

"What did *you* think, when I stayed over in Charlottsville," she countered, "even though Scotty was along and I informed you of my delay by telegram?"

"You're accusing me of infidelity, Devon!"

"And you're being evasive!"

"I did not make love to Miss Ryan," he denied, doggedly. "Oh, God, to be accused and not guilty! How ironic!"

"Rather like being suspected and innocent, isn't it?"

"We went through *that* in Newport, Devon. You misunderstood me then, and now."

"How eloquently you plead your case, while evading a direct answer to my question regarding your secrecy about this matter!"

"You make it sound like a sordid intrigue, Devon: a deliberate and planned liaison, rather than a freakish accident of the weather. I didn't do anything wrong, but I know how your vivid imagination can run wild. You're fantasizing now, confusing fact and fiction. Do you imagine we indulged in a two-day orgy?"

"Would you convince me that the lady's virtue is impregnable to your formidable masculine charms? Or is that a bad choice of words?"

"Damned bad!" he muttered between his teeth. "And I resent it, on her behalf and mine."

"Oh, Keith, how noble you are, and how blind! Marnie Ryan is in love with you, and I can't believe you are totally unaware of that fact. I realized it the day I met her."

"Did you, indeed? Well, your astuteness and feminine intuition notwithstanding, the fact remains that nothing of that nature happened between us, and I'd like to murder the vicious malcontent who disturbed you this way. His motives are clear to me, as they should be to you. But you're still skeptical, aren't you?"

Devon gazed at him miserably, unable to reconcile his failure to personally inform her with her reluctance to credit his belated explanation. Her emotions were in conflict and turmoil, spinning on a tempestuous carousal that threatened to hurl her off into alien space. Confused, bewildered, despairing, she abruptly announced, "The National Suffrage Association is meeting in Washington next week, and I've decided to attend."

"Oh? A rather sudden decision, isn't it?"

"The Child Labor Delegation needs more support."

"I see. Will they be consulting the issue with Senator Reed Carter?"

"Presumably, since he's one of the few members of Congress not beholden to the industries that exploit helpless children, therefore willing to receive us."

"And if I object?"

"I composed the memorial, Keith. I think I should help to present it, if the opportunity arises."

"Very well. I have urgent business in Washington, with the Secretary of the Treasury. We can travel together, in privacy and comfort, and stay at the Clairmont."

"I'm afraid I'd feel hypocritical, riding in a private railroad coach and occupying a penthouse in my husband's hotel," Devon demurred. "The other ladies are traveling by common carrier and sharing rooms and expenses at the Willard, this year's convention headquarters."

"In that case, I'll spare you any such embarrassment," he said ruefully, "and leave early. Perhaps I can finish with my capital commitments before you even arrive. Is that satisfactory, Madame Crusader?"

"It's sarcastic, cynical, and typical of your attitude toward any of my outside interests," she reproached him. "But please don't discommode yourself for my benefit."

"Nor you for mine, Mrs. Curtis. Afterward, I may go in another direction. West! The corporate problems are multiplying in Texas, via injunctions and other legal rigmarole, and must be expedited. A special car can be chartered for counselors and assistants."

"Including your highly capable secretary?"

"Would it matter?"

Devon rose, smoothing her silken skirts. "Not if you prefer to keep *that* secret, too," she retorted, smarting. "Are you coming up?"

"No, I'm going to the club."

"May I ask which one?" He belonged to three: Harvard, the prestigious Union Club, and the equally exclusive New York Yacht Club.

"One or the other"—he shrugged—"and I'll spend the night. You have your henhouse, don't you?"

"We don't roost at the Sorosis Club!"

"Only because you lack the facilities, my dear. No men have seen fit to endow an accommodating boudoir coop for the cackling members to lay their rebellious eggs in as yet, and I sure as hell won't be the first to sponsor a building fund."

"Nor I to solicit your financial aid," she quipped, glaring furiously as he prepared to leave.

"Good evening, madam." He bowed perfunctorily, donning his homburg, as if taking leave of a stranger.

Devon wanted to scream in protest, stamp her foot in outrage, throw something to release her terrible tension. Somehow, she controlled her violent impulses, lifted her chin with dignity, and bade him a sedate, "Good night, sir."

As he took only his briefcase, no overnight portmanteau, Devon thought he was bluffing and expected him back shortly. Then it occurred to her that he didn't need a robe or nightshirt, for he slept nude, and probably kept some male necessities, such as clean shirts, underwear, socks, shaving and grooming paraphernalia, in his club lockers. Nevertheless, she assured herself, he would be home tomorrow, humble and apologetic, as usual; she would graciously and magnanimously forgive him, as usual; and then they would make up in bed, as usual.

But she was mistaken, and her confidence badly shaken. Hadley received an early-morning call, and soon Rufus Brady arrived to assist in the preparations for an apparently lengthy journey, which Devon observed in disbelief and dismay. Was he going to Texas directly from Washington? Surely he would not do that without inviting her along! And why not, since she had refused to accompany him in the first place? Some answers came via the instrument that had precipitated the trouble between them, when he chose to bid her farewell on the telephone, thus avoiding another possible scene, and after her initial shock and anger, Devon was devastated.

"Take good care of him, Rufus," she adjured as he carried out the fine monogrammed leather luggage to the waiting hackney. "It's going to be a long trip."

"Yes, ma'am." Assuming that Mrs. Curtis was aware of the pertinent details, Rufus did not supply any, and Devon dared not ask curious questions, for, like the butler, Keith's man Friday was fiercely loyal to him. Finally, at the door, Rufus presented a thick manila envelope to her. "From Mr. Curtis, ma'am."

"Thank you," Devon murmured, waiting until he was gone to break the wax seal.

There was a terse office memo scrawled in his hand, and a sheaf of crisp greenbacks direct from the vault. "Pin money for your trip. Have a nice time. Keith."

Dear God, what had she done this time? Annihilated him with her accusations? Wounded his pride and ego, emasculated his manhood? Pain pierced her heart like an arrow, and remorse overwhelmed her. Her eyes blurred, the note and money fell to the floor. She had never felt so forlorn and miserable in her life.

ϫ 36 ϩ

WOMEN OF all ages and backgrounds crowded the lobby of Willard's Hotel. Bright, stylish spring costumes mingled with dark, sober, matronly garments and plain hats. The delegates came prepared for eight days of meetings, speeches, and receptions. Every prominent feminist was in attendance: Miss Susan B. Anthony, Mrs. Elizabeth Cady Stanton, Lucy Stone, Clara Barton, Julia Ward Howe, Kate Field, Jenny June, Madame Ellen Demorest, Harriet Tubman representing her race; the pioneers in education, journalism, medicine, law, civil rights; and the aspiring politicians. They assembled in Albaugh's Opera House to pass numerous resolutions to advance womankind in all fields of endeavor, to elevate her status in and outside the home, and to achieve justice and equality under the Constitution. A major goal was the nomination of a woman for the presidency at the forthcoming convention of the Equal Rights Party, in Des Moines, Iowa, and Belva Lockwood, a brilliant Washington attorney, was the unanimous choice for this particular honor. But it was an unrealistic ambition, as unattainable as Victoria Woodhull's aspiration back in 1872, and destined for the same ridicule and failure. The only political road open to them was through the men in state and federal government, and it was strewn with prejudicial obstacles and barricades impossible to hurdle without the ballot.

Devon was somewhat surprised to find the abolition of child labor rather far down the list of priorities on the convention's agenda. Not many important speakers addressed this issue, and only a handful of dedicated social workers appeared seriously interested and involved in it. And yet, except for the franchise, it was the only other goal requiring legislation to implement. The realization sent her to Senator Reed Carter's office in the

337

Capitol, only to be further dismayed and disappointed.

"Well, well!" he greeted her with a broad smile. "This must be the millennium—the mountain coming to Mohamet. You're not an illusion, are you?"

"Oh, Reed, don't run on so! You knew I was coming. After all, I called your aide earlier for an appointment. He *did* tell you?" she questioned, placing some neatly printed papers on his desk.

"Yes, but not the purpose of your visit. Have a seat, and tell me yourself."

Devon sat down, and he remained standing a few moments, impressively tall and slim in a fawn-colored western suit with saddle-stitched lapels and pockets. Before he took his swivel chair, Devon caught the familiar odors of leather, bay rum, and tobacco, which seemed to emanate from every Texan she had ever met, regardless of his location or position.

"What's this?" Reed inquired, tapping the material she had brought.

"A petition for legislation against child labor," she replied. "We call it *The Children's Declaration of Dependence*. Appropriate, don't you agree? Every child has a birthright of *dependence* until a certain age."

"That's true, of course. But it's the duty of the parents to grant that birthright, Devon." He scanned a few of the sheets, noting the number. "Do you want this memorial presented to Congress?"

"Very much, Reed! And you offered to help this cause once, remember?"

"That was seven years ago, Devon! And I expected to hear from you soon afterward. Why the long delay?"

"I've been busy on other projects," she hedged. "And so have you, according to the political columnists."

"Just doing my job for the people of Texas," he drawled. "Are you alone in Washington now—or is your Yankee Cerberus still fiercely guarding his treasure?"

"He's not a three-headed dog!" Devon protested.

"A figure of speech, honey, and not without merit in my opinion." He leaned back in his leather chair, crossing his long, booted legs on the big oak desk, which had some cigar burns, penknife nicks, and a whittle or two. "I repeat, is Curtis with you?"

"Not at the moment, obviously." Her answer was deliberately vague and ambiguous. "Will you please study that resolution, Reed, and see if you consider it worthy of a hearing, at least?"

He nodded, studying her instead, and missing nothing. She was still the loveliest, most feminine and charming woman he had ever known, and never more attractive and appealing to him than now. The way her green eyes sparkled behind the misty veil of the adorable hat perched on her thick honey-colored curls; her flawless, pale-ivory skin and irresistible coral lips; the desirable body he knew existed beneath the elegant Paris ensemble of buttercup *peau de soie*. She was a symphony in gold, a ray of sunshine on a gloomy day.

"You must have found that elusive fountain, lovely lady. No visible wrinkles, not even a silver thread among the gold, and no more in need of feminine harness than when we met."

"Blondes don't show gray, Senator. New York sun is kinder to the complexion than that of Texas, and any woman willing to put forth some effort can remain slender. Also, love and happiness are highly effective cosmetics."

He smiled wryly. "And you have an abundant supply?"

"Ample, to be sure."

"Then you'll be forever young and beautiful, an eternal goddess, while the rest of us mortals slowly degenerate."

Except for a touch of gray at his temples and a few more crinkles about his vivid blue eyes, he looked much the same to Devon. "You're not exactly in a state of decay, Mr. Carter. But I didn't come here to discuss immortality. I realize your time is valuable and don't wish to waste it frivolously. Will you oblige me on this petition?"

"It'll have to be referred to the Judicial Committee," he apprised. "I trust the ladies at the convention are aware of parliamentary law and procedure?"

"The leaders and legal advisors are, yes. But surely you have congenial cohorts on that committee, after all your years in Congress?"

"I'd be a sorry politician if I didn't have a friend or two on every important committee in both houses," he told her, picking up a pencil and twirling it thoughtfully. Then, indicating the stacks of folders on stands, in wall shelves and glass-doored cabinets, "I'm fairly inundated with petitions from my constituents, Devon. I couldn't oblige them all if I remained in office the rest of my life."

"Then why did you volunteer your assistance in my cause that day in Rock Creek Park?" she demanded, returning his intent gaze.

"I'd have promised you almost anything then, Devon, and delivered to the best of my ability, if—"

"If what?" she interrupted.

"If you had shown some interest in my office to help, and some cooperation. It's the duty of the Senate to advise and consent, you know. but you cut me cold, Devon, and I never saw or heard from you again until today. You come prancing in here like the prettiest little palomino mare in any horse show, lay down a twenty-page document, which you not only want fashioned into a bill but apparently introduced and passed in a matter of weeks. Months, at the most. Holy smoke! You sat in the congressional press galleries enough to know it just doesn't work that way."

"Are you reneging on your offer?"

"No." He shook his head slowly. "But I'm not a magician, and legislation is not accomplished by sleight-of-hand. How many years have I devoted to antitrust bills? And today there are more monopolies than ever! Oil, whisky, sugar, glass, copper, rubber, coal, beef, farm machinery, iron, steel, nuts and bolts, stoves, creosote, linseed oil—and recently, even school slates! And right now companies are organizing huge rice, cotton, and tobacco trusts. Read the *Wall Street Journal,* where your husband is so prominently featured. The Curtis Enterprises, East & West, are perhaps the most gargantuan, monopolistic monster of them all!"

Her eyes dropped momentarily to the silk-gloved hands in her lap. "I don't meddle in his business affairs, Reed." Then she faced him again. "If there's a beef trust, the cattle industry must be involved in it."

"Mostly through the packing industry," he acknowledged, "in Chicago, Kansas City, and St. Louis."

"But they couldn't exist without the cooperation of the ranchers, could they?"

"It's a mutual dependence," he explained. "Meat producers must have markets for their product, and Texas steers head north every day. Not many are trailed anymore, however. They're shipped on the monopolists' railroads."

"Including some of your longhorns?"

"Most of my cattle are driven up to the local stockyards. As you know, my spread is only a few miles from Fort Worth. There are some packinghouses there now, too, and I try to do business in my own state whenever possible."

"Naturally. And did you try to hamper the railroad octopi, as you seem to consider them, in the spreading of their iron tentacles through Texas?"

"I'm not against progress, Devon, just the continuing monopolization of it by a few crafty ruthless greedy people, among whom a certain Manhattan giant stands head and shoulders, with most others in his shadow."

"You misjudge him, Reed," Devon said, defending Keith to Reed as she had to Daniel, as usual and always. "He's not like that, really."

"My dear, you view him in a different light, and from a different angle. I know his history, remember. The Curtis fortune began with banking in America, but it wasn't confined to it. Their interests expanded with ambition and avarice, and a dynasty was well established by the time of his father's death. Keith has turned it into a vast financial empire. How else could he have become the wealthiest man in this country, if not the entire world?"

Devon was pensively silent, pondering a painting of Sam Houston in fringed buckskins, whose image she had seen in the Governor's Mansion in Austin. Beside it hung a likeness of Reed's father, Jason Carter, a friend of the great Texas hero, and who had sat in Congress with him.

"You recognize the Raven?" he asked, using Houston's famous sobriquet.

"Of course. And Jason, too. I didn't know you had these portraits, Reed."

"That's because you've never been in my office before, Devon. You never visited me here, even when you were Mrs.

Senator Reed Carter. Frankly, I find your presence now somewhat incongruous and ironic."

"So do I," she murmured, standing. "I have to get back to
the convention. Clara Barton is scheduled to speak on human-
itarianism, and I'm curious to see if the pitiful plight of the
most helpless victims of all inhumanity is addressed."

Reed left his chair and walked to the door, blocking her
exit. "Have dinner with me this evening?"

"I have another engagement, Senator."

"Break it."

"I can't," she said.

"Not even in the interest of your cause?"

"I'm sorry, no."

"Where are you staying, Devon?"

"Convention headquarters."

"The Willard Hotel? Why not in your husband's Washington
hostelry? The Clairmont is far more elegant and exclusive and
expensive."

"How would you know?"

He laughed. "Oh, I've been there, Devon. Melissa wanted
to move into the Clairmont, after the house in Georgetown was
sold out from under us."

"Why didn't you?"

"I couldn't afford the rental on my senator's salary, and
refused to let Judge Hampton pay it. But I wouldn't have
resided under that particular roof under any circumstances. It
was humiliating enough to finally learn who actually owned
that fine red brick mansion Carla Winston supposedly located
for you and me, at such reasonable rent, when we first came
to Washington. I have a small place in Alexandria now, just
across the Potomac. Not much, but at least it's on Southern
soil. A Virginian should appreciate that."

"How does your wife feel about it?"

"Tolerant," he said. "Most of her time is spent at the Hampton
estate in Austin."

"Is the Judge still living?"

"No, he died two years ago. Melissa lives with his memory,
his ghost."

"She must be terribly lonely."

"It's her choice." He shrugged. "She won't adopt any kids,

though Texas orphanages are full of them. I've just about decided to leave the Senate on the expiration of my present term, and settle on my ranch. If Melissa wants to live there with me, fine. If not . . ." He sighed.

"Seeking sympathy, Reed? Don't tell me *you* are lonely? The ladies of the press idolize you, and the capital society matrons lionize you."

"Oh, yeah. I'm forever escorting somebody's sister or niece or daughter to this or that social affair, and usually bored stiff. The female population of this territory is amazingly large, but I've yet to meet one who can interest me more than a few hours."

"Keep trying, sir!" Devon suggested, her hand reaching for the knob and stopped by his.

"What do you think I'm doing now?"

"Well, you haven't succeeded, Senator."

"Devon, you're alone in Washington this time, aren't you? I doubt you'll tell me why, but I don't really care. Curtis was here last week, in conferences with the President and Treasury Secretary—everybody on Capitol Hill knew that. I assumed he was still in town, but apparently he isn't. What's the story, honey? And don't look at me so innocently! Being a journalist, you know damned well what I mean."

"I must leave, Reed. Clara Barton is an excellent orator, and I don't want to miss her speech.

"You can read it in the papers."

"I'll scream," she threatened as his arms captured her. "I'll—"

His mouth stifled further protest, stealing her breath, and she could feel his strong sexual arousal even as she struggled against him. Not until her teeth repulsed his invading tongue did he cease kissing her, although he did not relax his hold. "Why, you bloodthirsty little wildcat," he muttered, grinning into her furious eyes.

"And you damned prairie wolf on a sneak attack! Would you like to explain some scratches and toothmarks to your colleagues?"

"Oh, now, what's a little kiss, darling? We've done much more, haven't we?"

"In marriage, Reed! How dare you do such a thing now?"

"Sheathe your claws and stop spitting at me, kitten. I wanted to kiss you, but you sure as hell didn't cooperate. I won't be able to debate and certainly not filibuster for a few days, due to a sore tongue."

"Good! I hope it swells up and chokes you."

"Really? I couldn't do your petition much good then, could I?"

"I don't expect you will, anyway."

"Not with that attitude."

Defiance flared through her indignation. "Well, I'm not about to compromise myself in bed with you, Senator, even if I have done so in the past."

His arms fell away from her, and he stepped back slightly. "Is that how you regarded our lovemaking?"

"Not always, Reed. But that's what it would be now, and no cause on earth is worth marital infidelity."

"To Curtis, you mean. You were unfaithful to me with him, weren't you? Turnabout is fair play, Devon."

"Not to me, Reed. And Keith would kill you for even touching me."

"Well, he knows where to find me, just as I know where to find him. But I didn't shoot up Wall Street, and I don't think he'll shoot up the Senate, either. Surely he's more civilized than that, although I'd like a crack at him on the wild range."

"I should have brought some chaperones with me," Devon said, ruing her indiscretion. "I was a fool to come here alone—and to no purpose."

"I wouldn't say that," he drawled. "Your memorial is in a senator's hands. That's a long way from the Chamber floor, or even a committee, but closer to a hearing room than when you came in here, Madame Delegate."

"May I go now, please?"

Reed smiled, refusing to believe she was as angry and outraged as she seemed, and opened the door with a flourish. "No dinner this evening, eh? It's just as well, I reckon, considering my mutilated mouth."

"I should have bitten your tongue off!"

"You damned near did, honey. But I forgive you. No hard feelings, honestly. And I'll keep you advised on the progress, if any, on this other business."

"Address all information to the Women's Bureau, on Twenty-third Street, New York City," Devon said curtly, ignoring his proffered hand.

"Yes, ma'am." He affected grave formality, but Devon heard him chuckling as her high-heels clicked and her silk skirts swished through the maze of marbled corridors.

The Ladies Press Corps dined ceremoniously in Willard's new and famous Peacock Alley Restaurant. Devon occupied the same banquet table with many of her old journalist friends on the capital scene: Gail Hamilton, stout and aging now, but still an effective political writer; popular Mary Clemmer Ames, who had covered the White House since Abraham Lincoln's administration; Olivia Briggs, perennial queen of the gossip columnists, whose byline was her first name; and pert and pretty Nellie Hutchinson, whom Devon had always liked and admired. All had reservations for a premiere at Ford's Theater that evening, but the New York *Record*'s representative begged off and retired to her room instead.

Rain was falling, and she watched it from her windows, which were misty and blurred in the street lights. Gentle spring showers were rare in Washington; most were violent, with rampant lightning and roaring thunder, befitting the frequent tempests on Capitol Hill. Traffic was heavy on Pennsylvania Avenue, as the nightly celebrations got underway. It was said and written in truth that Washingtonians consumed more liquor per capita than any other Americans or foreigners anywhere, and that only Paris, London, and New York had more brothels. Life on the Potomac was hectic, a merry-go-round of chaos and confusion, but the politicians thrived on it. With the possible exception of Senator Reed Carter, of Texas, who claimed the social aspects merely bored him.

Mother in Heaven, why had she gone alone to his office! There was no way to rationalize such rashness to Keith, and no sense in trying. The kiss was an assault, an affront, a violation and invasion, and she wanted only to forget it. She was too surprised initially to know what, if anything beyond outrage, she had felt in his arms again; but if it wasn't revulsion, neither was it desire. This was an emotion only her beloved could arouse in her—and where was he tonight, and with whom? Traveling toward Texas, or already there, and alone, or with Marnie Ryan?

Oh, how she missed and wanted him! Gloom and loneliness accompanied her to bed, where she wept before falling asleep and sobbed even in her disturbed, unhappy dreams.

✢ 37 ✢

THE BRIEF NOTE, delivered to Scott's dormitory one week before commencement, both surprised and puzzled him.

Dear Cousin Scott,

I would like very much to meet you before your return to New York. Please come to Stanfield House, on Louisburg Square, at your convenience.

Fondly,
Your Cousin Sabrina Carlton.

Scott pondered the old vellum stationery, its original whiteness now yellowed with age. His parents had never told him of a relative in Boston, or anywhere else in the United States. The American branch of his father's family were supposedly all deceased, as were his mother's people in Virginia. Yet here was someone claiming kin, whom he could have visited during his sometimes lonely years in college, had he known of her existence. *Why* hadn't they mentioned her? But perhaps they had, and he had simply forgotten.

His childhood memories before the age of eight were somewhat vague, with only the most outstanding events lucid and in sequence. He remembered that his father had been with him more than his mother, who was frequently away, occasionally for long periods of time, on "journalistic assignments." Scott learned to adjust to her absences, and almost forgot her during one very long interlude in Texas. As he learned from his geography and national maps, Texas was indeed a long way from New York, and he could understand why his mother had to live there to do her job properly. But why, with all his father's riches, did she have to work at all? When he asked this question of his father or governess, his childish curiosity was promptly diverted into other channels: a new toy, his pony, his pets on the estate, or some amusing distraction. They played games and sports, did a lot of sailing, some traveling to big cities where his daddy had business, and even journeyed abroad for several months. In England, he met some of his Heathstone relatives, and a few of the Curtis clan in Scotland, but he was too young and interested in other things to be much impressed.

Did Sabrina Carlton have some connection with his paternal or maternal ancestry? If so, why hadn't she tried to contact him before? Perhaps she had been abroad and unaware of his presence in Cambridge. Beacon Hill residents, and particularly those of Louisburg Square, were not only wealthy but socially elite. He had not noticed that name in the Boston journals, but then he rarely read the society pages of any newspaper, not even the one with which his mother was associated, although he did read her serious material. And he was looking forward to the publication of her novel of the antebellum South, tentatively scheduled for next spring. Scott had a deep love and affection for his mother and took great pride in her beauty, charm, and intellect.

Although fairly familiar with the Bulfinch architecture of Beacon Hill, Scott had a strange sense of *déjà vu* upon arriving at the Louisburg Square address on the stationery. Gazing at the red brick walls and lavender-paned windows, he felt he had seen this particular bow-front house in a picture long ago. But where, and when?

An elderly servant in an old-fashioned mobcap and bibbed apron admitted him. She nodded when he gave his name, said he was expected, and should wait in the parlor while she fetched Miss Carlton. Was Cousin Sabrina a young single lady, he wondered, or an older spinster like Fawn's aunt Caroline?

The parlor was sorely in need of redecoration. The blue velvet upholstery of the Queen Anne furniture was badly worn and faded, as were the draperies and carpet, but family heirlooms and antiques suggested past elegance and affluence. Scott assumed the ornately framed portraits were ancestral, and the one above the Adam mantel immediately arrested his attention, for the beautiful female face was also curiously familiar. He was studying it, feeling strangely haunted, when Sabrina Carlton entered and greeted him enthusiastically. "My dear Cousin Scott! How kind of you to accept my invitation! I couldn't be more delighted."

Scott bowed over her hand with impeccable manners, inhaling her almost overpowering essence of narcissus. "It's a great pleasure to meet you, Cousin Sabrina." She was quite attractive, he thought, and very much resembled the lady in the portrait, only considerably older, and again the other image flashed to mind, with no positive recollection of its source.

"Do sit down, please." She indicated a cabriole-legged armchair and seated herself on the sofa, gracefully arranging the folds of her iridescent silk gown."

"I'd have called before," Scott explained, "but I didn't know I had kin in Boston."

"I've been in Europe, dear. I just returned last month, read your name in this year's list of Harvard graduates, and wanted to meet you." She had an unusual contralto voice, hypnotic amethyst eyes, and a fascinating smile.

"I'm pleased and flattered," he said, displaying much of his father's suave charm, and even more curious as to why she had been kept secret. Was Cousin Sabrina the family closet skeleton, and if so, on which side?

"My, how handsome you are, just as your daddy must have been at your age! I didn't meet him, you see, until he was somewhat older than you." Anticipating his visit, Sabrina had carefully removed any photographic evidence of the Curtis couple, including their engagement and wedding pictures, leaving Esther's portrait because it could easily be mistaken for herself in her youth.

But Sabrina was lying about living abroad recently. Except for a couple of voyages to Europe to prospect for a potential keeper, she had been right there in Stanfield House, sponging off the senile proprietor now totally confined to her bed and at her ruthless niece's mercy. Sabrina kept the poor soul sedated and might have suffocated or poisoned her, except for the monthly stipends from the Boston branch of the Curtis Bank, most of which she spent on herself. But Aunt Hortense could not live forever, and then the largesse would cease. And though Sabrina would inherit the Stanfield property, she could not maintain it and herself without supplementary support. Her previous scheme to extort a comfortable fortune from Keith Curtis had failed, when she could not produce Cousin Esther's alleged incriminating letters to her mother, accusing her husband of threats on her life, and he had merely laughed at her demands. After years of searching for the elusive evidence, Sabrina concluded that Aunt Hortense had destroyed it to preserve her daughter's reputation. She was fairly desperate about her future when fate directed her attention to the columns of Harvard University's current graduating class, and decided that Scott Heathstone Curtis might possibly be a bigger bonanza for her than his father, and cunningly dispatched her invitation to him. Now, having successfully lured the fly into her web, the spider contemplated her next procedure.

"Your family will attend the commencement, of course?"

"Yes, ma'am, including my twin sisters, Sharon and Shannon. They're sailing up on our yacht and are probably already at sea."

"And will they be spending the summer in Newport again this season?"

"You know about our Newport cottage?"

Sabrina smiled coyly. How raven black was her hair, apparently dyed, for some gray should be visible by now. But the eyes under the dark winged brows were as vividly purple as those in the portrait above the fireplace and the illusion that kept recurring in his mind. "I've read about it, Scotty—if I may call you that?—and it's a marble palace."

"Well, most of them are there," he said modestly, "and Mother thinks ours is much too grand."

"Is she so modest and unpretentious? What a cross to bear, considering her position!" It was a venomous fang, and Sabrina quickly applied an antidote. "I'm sure your mother's a lovely lady—brilliant and perceptive, too, considering her journalistic accomplishments."

"Yes, she is," Scott proudly affirmed. "Maybe you'd like

to visit us sometime, Cousin Sabrina?"

"Darling, how sweet! But I shall wait for an invitation from your parents. Would you care for tea?"

"No, thank you. I must get back to school. We're having a fraternity party this evening."

"And you can't miss that!" Sabrina walked him to the door. "I noted the honors beside your name, Scotty. The same as your father's when he graduated from Harvard. I'm so anxious to renew my acquaintance with Cousin Keith, on that auspicious occasion. We haven't seen each other since you were a tyke."

"You're related to the Curtises, then, and you and I are second cousins?"

Sabrina hesitated. "Well, you might call us kissing cousins, dear."

"Won't Father be surprised?"

"Won't he, though!"

Shaking his proffered hand, Sabrina suddenly decided to kiss his cheek, unable to resist the impulse with any handsome man, particularly one who was also young and wealthy. How she would enjoy seducing this probable virgin! The seduction of Keith Curtis's son would be an ironic victory from the grave for Cousin Esther, she thought, and sweet revenge for herself if his obstinate father failed her again. Oh, things might work out for her, after all!

❧ 38 ❦

THE *SPRITE* arrived ahead of schedule, providing extra time for sightseeing on the twins' first visit to Boston. For weeks their governess had been tutoring them in the history of Massachusetts, and they had a fair comprehension of its importance in the pilgrim colonization, the American Revolution, and the birth of the nation.

"How pretty they are!" Devon remarked as they left the yacht in Renoir-blue taffeta dresses with Breton jackets, frilly pokebonnets tied under the chin, and bowed white morocco slippers, swinging dainty tasseled reticules containing initialed handkerchiefs, combs, and coins.

"Adorable," Keith agreed. "But they don't look much like twins, or even sisters, except for their clothes."

"For their sake, I'm glad. They'll grow up as individuals, not duplicates of each other. Every woman should have her own identity. Her own distinct character and personality, too."

"You forgot freedom and independence."

"That's understood, dear. Isn't the Statue of Liberty female?"

He smiled at her wit, for they both knew his reference was to her activities in Washington while he was en route to Texas. Keith had read her accounts of the Women's Rights Convention in the New York *Record*, and was aware of her participation in the march to the White House, where President Cleveland deigned to receive them, and that they had also virtually stormed Capitol Hill, where they were jeered as "the Bloomer Brigade." But none of this bothered him as much as the knowledge that, despite his objection and forbiddance, Devon had personally delivered her memorial on child labor to Senator Reed Carter's office. Keith had been too incensed at her admission of this to demand details, and she had not volunteered any beyond the contents of the petition, brilliantly conceived and executed as a declaration of *dependence* for minor children. Nor had Devon inquired about his trip west, after surmising that Marnie Ryan had accompanied him.

"That lady in New York harbor is made of metal and stone," Keith muttered now. "And you exhibit some of those same qualities at times too, my dear."

"But putty and malleable as wax at others." She winked. "Didn't I melt in your arms last night? And don't I usually at your touch, except when you belittle or ridicule my sacred beliefs and keep secrets from me? I still don't know what happened with your secretary during the blizzard. . . ."

"Nothing happened," he insisted wearily.

"Nor on your westward journey, either? Wasn't she on the same train?"

He gazed at her intently. "Did you have another anonymous telephone caller?"

"No, I rang your office myself during your absence. Miss Ryan didn't answer, and they said she was away. I never called again."

"Why not?"

"I just assumed—"

"Ah, yes! You're good at assuming, aren't you, albeit not always correctly where I'm concerned. Why didn't you ask me? Miss Ryan was on the same train, Devon, but not in my car. And she did not go all the way to Texas, only to St. Louis. Some nuns, including her sister, met her at the depot there. Marnie has entered the convent."

Devon was incredulous. "That pretty, vivacious creature! What kind of nun will she make?"

"Probably a very fine one. She prayed and fasted all the way to Missouri." Reciting her *mea culpa* was her explanation, when declining to dine with him, or even sit comfortably during the day in his luxurious coach. Indeed, she would not even sleep in a Pullman berth, but remained in the chair car, sipping plain tea or water, and either reading her breviary or telling her rosary beads. "Surprised?"

"Astonished, Keith. She seemed so happy in her career, so content working for you. Why would she leave so suddenly for such a life?"

"Religious calling." He shrugged, seeking his deck lounge and removing a cheroot from his gold case.

Devon glanced at the heavens. "I feel terrible, Keith. I've agonized over this, wondering if you were—" Her voice ebbed, and she was caught in an emotional riptide, from which he rescued her.

"Having an affair with her? I know, Devon. And I know what it's like to be tortured that way."

"Then you understand and forgive me?" she beseeched. "I promise it'll never happen again, darling!"

He smiled ruefully. "Oh, yes, it will, Devon! For both of us. We'll always be jealous of each other, and probably always without cause."

"Absolutely without cause, Keith! Poor Marnie. I hope you didn't tell her of my foolish suspicions?"

"Of course not, Devon."

"I'm so ashamed, Keith."

"You're just female, my dear."

"That's no excuse for behaving like such a witch," she lamented. "No justification, either."

"Try to forget it, Devon. No real harm done. But I'm relieved to have it over and behind us."

Devon still felt guilty, however, and her conscience hurt. "Oh, Keith, I trust you didn't fire her over me?"

"The lady resigned, Devon. She was an excellent secretary, with officer qualifications, and should rise high in her order. Sister Marnie will probably be a Mother Superior someday."

"I just can't visualize her in a black habit," Devon said, unable to conjure the image. "Such a lovely face and figure! So much gorgeous titian hair. They shave their heads, you know, and bind their bosoms."

His brow creased in a grave frown, precluding further conversation about it. "Why didn't you go touring with our daughters and their chaperones?"

"I've been here before, and history doesn't change."

"Nothing in Boston changes much," he observed. "The population is largely immigrant Irish now, but Brahmin aristocracy still rules, the Puritan influence lingers, and this city still regards itself as the hub of the universe. Hell, everybody knows it's actually New York!"

The *Sprite* was moored on a scenic stretch of the Charles River, some distance from the main port and its boisterous activity, and many of the famous landmarks were visible: the gilded dome of the State House, the grasshopper weathervane of Faneuil Hall, and the steeple of the Old North Church from which Paul Revere conveyed his famous signals.

"Is it?"

"Did you think it was Richmond?"

"Why, no, dear. I thought it was London or Paris or Rome," she replied with affected naiveté. "Are we going to visit our son this afternoon?"

"He may be off campus, Devon. But Scott knows we've arrived, because I sent him a message, and I expect him to visit us."

"Maybe the Haverstons are in town."

"That shouldn't keep him from his family. Just give him time. The final week of college is pretty hectic."

Scott came before sundown, looking fit and glad to see them. "Mother, Dad," he said, embracing Devon and shaking Keith's hand. "I meant to come earlier, but there were some commencement rehearsals."

"We understand," Devon assured him. "Are you excited about tomorrow? We certainly are, and so very proud of you."

Keith echoed her sentiments, and asked, "What are your plans for this evening?"

"Some of my friends are dining at the Union Oyster House. Since it was Daniel Webster's favorite bar and eatery, maybe they think some of his genius will rub off on them."

Keith laughed. "We thought the same thing, in my day. Go with your pals, by all means."

At that moment the twins romped into the main salon, babbling about their adventure, the most exciting part of which seemed to be their ride in the celebrated swan boats of the Public Garden. Their tongues froze at sight of their brother, whom they had not seen in months. The age and sex difference between them did not foster a close sibling relationship, and sometimes he seemed like a stranger, this tall young man with his serious mien. But he caught their hands and surveyed them with a brotherly smile. "Well, if it isn't my cute little sisters, come to watch Big Brother get his diploma!"

Shannon, who had difficulty keeping a secret, gleefully announced, "We have presents for you, too! We helped Mommy shop for them at a huge store on Broadway."

"And Daddy's giving you money," informed Sharon, not to be outdone in spoiling surprises. "Oh, you should see all the gold and silver and greenbacks and jewelry in Daddy's bank, Scotty! He showed us the vault one day. Shannon was scared the heavy door would close and lock us in, the fraidy-cat! But I like the bank and wish I could go there often. If I was a boy, I'd work there when I grow up!"

"Girls can work in banks," Devon told her, glancing significantly at Keith. "Can't they, Daddy?"

"If they're smart enough," he replied as the ship's bells rang the dinner hour. "Go to your cabins, kittens. You're having supper there this evening."

"Is Scotty spending the night?"

"No, so tell him goodbye now."

They did, then headed for the portal where their nurse and governess waited.

"Good grief!" Scott exclaimed. "How long are they going to have a nanny?"

"They're a bit much for Miss Vale to handle alone," Devon explained, "so Nanny will probably be with us for a while yet. Are you thrilled about graduation, Scotty?"

"You already asked me that, Mother."

"And you never answered."

"Well, sure. The whole senior class is enthused, and have been celebrating for several weeks."

Keith grinned. "Not too enthusiastically, I hope?"

"How did your class celebrate?"

"Traditionally, more or less."

"Raising hell?"

"A little."

"And sowing wild oats?"

"Our share. How often does a man graduate from college? We roared like young lions in the Cambridge and Boston streets, and some got uproariously drunk."

"You're scandalizing your son," Devon admonished him. "He would never behave that way—would you, dear?"

"I haven't so far," he answered, "and with good reason. Miss Haverston wouldn't approve."

"Will Fawn be in the audience?"

"I'm afraid not, Mother. Coincidentally, our schools are holding commencement on the same day. But Cousin Sabrina might attend mine."

Keith jerked forward in his chair. *"Who?"*

"Sabrina Carlton. I learned just last week that I have a second cousin here. She invited me to call at her home on Louisburg Square, and I did."

Devon stifled an audible cry. Her eyes darted swiftly to Keith's, seeing astonished fury in his, as he emphatically declared, "That woman is no relation to you, Scott. No kin whatever to any of us!"

"Who is she, then?"

"No one of importance to this family. Just an old acquaintance from the past."

"Whose past?"

"Mine, unfortunately. What did she want?"

"Just to meet me, she said. There's a portrait in her parlor, painted presumably when she was quite young. And I think I've seen another youthful painting of her, when I was small, but I can't remember where. . . ."

Keith knew immediately, as the clock turned backward to the darkest time of his life: the abduction of his small son from his Hudson River estate, by his first wife's artist-lover, Giles Mallard. A seminude of Esther was in his shack in the Bronx woods, where he had taken his lured victim in a cleverly disguised van, to hold for ransom. But when Keith and the Pinkerton detective, Carla Winston, had finally located his hideout, Mallard was dying of a tubercular hemorrhage. He had apparently been bartering his meager art collection in the surrounding villages for food, wine, and medicine, while planning his crime. But not the cherished painting of his beloved paramour, Esther Stanfield Curtis, the first sight of which had shocked Keith almost as much as the discovery of her infidelity in Mallard's studio on Tompkins Square. The gorgeous bitch reclined languidly on a purple velvet drapery, her sultry violet eyes shadowed by long, dark lashes, an enigmatic Mona Lisa smile on her sensuous lips, and her raven tresses cascading on her bare shoulders; somehow the misty veil over one cherry-nippled breast and voluptuous hip only enhanced her nudity. Although destroyed on the spot, the image was still vivid and indelible in Keith's memory. And now he realized that it was subconsciously imprinted on his son's mind, too.

"Don't try, Scott. Sabrina Carlton is nothing to you, believe me, and there's absolutely no need to ever see or even think of her again."

"But why? She seems like a nice person and is anxious to meet you again. I invited her to visit us, in Newport, since she expressed an interest in our cottage there."

Devon's face blanched, and a strange, sad sigh escaped her tremulous lips. "Oh, Scotty, no! You didn't make friends with her?"

"You're pale, Mother. Are you suddenly ill?"

"A bit queasy," she murmured, fanning herself.

Was she pregnant again? Remembering her miscarriage in Newport, which had disturbed the entire household, Scott glanced questioningly at his father. "Is she—"

"Expecting? Not to our knowledge, Scott. She's just upset by your news, and so am I. Promise me you'll never call on that Carlton creature again."

"Didn't you hear me, Dad? She'll likely be at my graduation. And, frankly, I don't understand your attitude. Is something wrong—something I don't know about?"

"No, nothing," Keith denied.

Scott almost shouted, "You're lying!"

"How dare you speak to me that way!" Keith rebuked him. "I'm your father, boy!"

"And who is my mother—Sabrina Carlton?"

Rage darkened and distorted Keith's features, and his smoky-gray eyes glared intensely. Scott had never seen his father so angry, nor his mother so pallid. Then, suddenly, he was seized by his jacket lapels and shaken so vigorously his teeth rattled. "Devon Marshall Curtis is your mother, you insolent pup! And if you don't apologize to her immediately, I'll dismantle your anatomy! Do you understand me, Scott? I'll take you apart!"

Terrified, the boy dropped to his knees and bowed his head humbly in Devon's lap. "I'm sorry, Mother. I lost my head—please forgive me? I—I wanted this to be a happy reunion, all grievances forgotten, and now..."

"It's all right, darling." She patted his trembling shoulders. "Your father lost his temper, too. He didn't mean what he said, Scotty. He would never really hurt you—you know that." Her fingers fondled his thick dark curly hair, which he tried so hard to subdue in simple waves. "And it *will* be a happy occasion, dear. We won't let this little squabble spoil anything. No, of course not!" But Scott felt hot tears falling on his face and clutched at her skirts as he had in childhood, when he feared he had lost her love and affection through some unforgivably bad deed. "There, there," Devon soothed in lullaby tones.

The time she had been dreading since his birth was at hand: the moment of truth. But they could not tell him on the eve of this important milestone in his life! That would be unspeakably cruel, a terrible blow from which he might not recover. It must be postponed a while longer....

Keith observed the poignant scene, sharing Devon's dilemma and burdened by his own sense of guilt and remorse.

"Stand up, son," he urged, reaching down a hand to assist the stricken youth to his feet. "If you'd like a punch at my jaw, go ahead. I deserve it."

Scott shook his head miserably. "I shouldn't have hurt Mother that way, or mouthed off to you. I'm really a lucky fellow, with wonderful parents, and maybe I should have my carcass kicked every so often to make me realize and appreciate my good fortune. Will you settle for a handshake, Dad?"

"You bet," Keith agreed, giving him a paternal hug. But he knew, even without Devon's frantic eye signals, that the vital information must be delayed. "And I'm sure your mother will settle for a kiss."

"Yes, sir," he obliged, as Devon opened her arms to him. "Then I'd better get back to the dormitory, before those practical jokers play any more pranks on one another. The seniors act like they're conducting fraternal hazing rites on freshmen, and I guess that's typical, too." He smiled sheepishly. "Well, see you tomorrow!" he waved, running to the gangplank.

Keith supported Devon to their stateroom, where she experienced an emotional catharsis that wrenched his heart and soul. When finally it passed, he offered her a glass of sherry, which she drank like a nepenthe. "Esther is still haunting us," she despaired. "Still wreaking her revenge!"

"Sabrina Carlton is a live bitch, Devon, and I'll have to deal with her somehow."

"You should have paid her off the first time she came to us in Gramercy Park, Keith. No matter how much money you give her now, she'll still have the advantage. The club and the upper hand! She could hold Scotty hostage, literally. Isn't her scheme obvious?"

"Oh, yes, certainly! Perpetual blackmail. But we can foil her by telling Scott the truth. We had the opportunity just now, Devon, and I considered it but was afraid you'd panic. And no telling how he might have reacted in his mood, either. Oh, God, we should have told him long ago, when the twins were born, and he asked questions about his own birth and baptism."

"He was just a child, then!"

"Children often accept the facts of life easier than adults, Devon, and are definitely less vulnerable to the consequences than impressionable adolescents. *'Cousin'* Sabrina is banking on his ignorance of our affair and our reluctance to enlighten him. She's a greedy, vicious, conniving witch, and I was wrong thinking we were rid of her. No doubt she's living off the trust fund established for Hortense Stanfield, which will dry up with her demise. That parasitic whore is aware of this, and hoping to ensure her own future through our son."

"Analyzing the problem won't solve it, Keith. How can we possibly meet her tomorrow?"

"I don't think we'll have to, Devon. Meeting Scott has served her purpose. She expected him to tell us, which he did, and now she expects me to negotiate her silence, which I won't. We'll weigh anchor immediately after the ceremonies, and initiate that long-overdue conversation at sea, where Scott can't walk away from us. That cunning slut will be left holding an empty moneybag, off our backs and on her own again, where she belongs."

"Oh, I hope so, Keith!"

"Trust me, darling. And don't cry anymore, please. Put aside your fear and guilt and agonization. We didn't do anything so terrible, you know; certainly nothing to suffer and atone for the rest of our lives. We fell in love, that's all, and Scott will just have to understand."

But that wasn't all, Devon thought mournfully. And would the boy really understand?

She nodded, watching Keith pace the cabin. He was worried, too, and distressed. Perhaps desperate?

⚜ 39 ⚜

ON THE way to the Union Oyster House for a farewell celebration with his fraternity brothers, Scott wondered what it was about Sabrina Carlton that upset his parents so. Why had his mother paled at the mere mention of her name, and his father's face gone livid with rage? And if she was no blood or marital relation, why was it imperative that he shun her even as a friend? Scott puzzled about it through the excellent seafood supper and the boisterous merrymaking afterward. Renting open carriages, the graduates raced up and down Commonwealth Avenue, through Quincy Market and around Dock Square and the Boston Common, waving pennants, yelling and singing at the top of their vigorous young lungs, until a mounted policeman caught up with them. Irish and indulgent of their youthful shenanigans, he persuaded them to calm down and return to Cambridge before duty forced him to lock them up for disturbing the peace. And though Wild Wharton wanted to defy the law and continue the spree, confident that Curtis's father would bail them out of jail in time for the Harvard ceremonies, Scott's diplomacy prevailed in ushering the rowdies back to the dormitory.

But sleep eluded him for hours, during which he tossed restlessly on his single bed, and he wondered if Fawn was restless tonight, too. What rotten luck that their schools were holding simultaneous commencements! But even more important and worrisome, how were they going to manage to be together for the summer, the way they wanted to be together, without arousing parental suspicions and objections? If only they could get married! But that happy solution was still in the future, unless they floated convention, and Scott was aware of Fawn's preferences in this respect. She wanted the traditional rituals: the lavish betrothal ball and accompanying parties, the formal wedding and honeymoon. He couldn't deprive her of those romantic girlish dreams, nor did he think her father would let him or anyone else do so. And it would be grossly unfair to her, anyway, for Fawn would make a beautiful bride. Visualizing her descending the great central stairway of Harmony Hill in her bridal costume—radiant, glorious, angelic—Scott struggled with the inevitable thoughts and emotions aroused by such visions. Oh, Lord, how much longer could he, must he, endure the pain and torment and longing for her and the physical consummation that would make their love complete?

As he lay gazing at the shadowy ceiling, in a hypnotic state between sleep and wakefulness, his mind drifted gradually back to childhood and his father's Hudson River estate. He saw himself romping with his dog at the far end of the property, where it bounded the road to the village, and pausing to speak with an artist whom he had seen there before and become friendly with. The man had a strange red beard that looked false or dyed, his paint-spattered hat and clothes were dirty, and he coughed and spat a lot. He was sketching a picture of Halcyon's woods and picturesque pond with its pair of graceful white swans gliding serenely in the dappled sunshine. A gaudily painted van, rather like a medicine wagon, was partially secluded in a nearby lane, and he offered to take the child to a carnival. But it was only a trick, and they ended up in a filthy cabin somewhere in the woods. . . .

As if struck by lightning, Scott sat bolt upright, suddenly remembering where he had first seen a portrait of the same black-haired, violet-eyed lady in the parlor of the Beacon Hill house to which Sabrina Carlton had invited him. It was in that isolated, wretched shack! That miserable, stinking hovel strewn with decaying food, liquor bottles, and other garbage. Was it possible that the same artist had painted both of them? Scott wished he had noted the signature. There must be some connection, for it was simply too bizarre to be mere coincidence. And perhaps Miss Carlton was more than just an old acquaintance from the past, as his father claimed. It was an intriguing mystery, which Scott hoped to solve before leaving Boston.

Along with hundreds of other graduates, Scott Heathstone Curtis stood in the Harvard Yard in his cap and gown, diploma in hand, family and friends beaming proudly upon him. Miss Vale had come to witness the high scholastic honors bestowed on the scholar she had tutored so many years, and Nanny to keep the twins from wandering off into the crowd. The girls had squirmed through most of the event, impatient with the pomp and circumstance: the seemingly endless parade of figures in long dark robes and tasseled mortarboards across the stage, where even more strangely garbed faculty sat; the handshaking, ovations, speeches, and even the band playing the same tune over and over again. Later, after the shouting and the black caps flying up in the air on the campus, Sharon and

Shannon were more than eager to return to the *Sprite*, which was ready to sail to New York, and their father was asking their brother why his luggage was not yet aboard.

"I'm not finished packing yet, sir."

"Then I'd better send Rufus to help you."

"That won't be necessary," Scott said. "I thought I'd stay here a few more days, take the train home."

"That's absurd, son. We're all going home together. And since when do you prefer traveling by rail to water?"

"I'm just not ready to leave yet, Dad."

His mother looked distraught again. "But we've planned a party on board tomorrow, Scotty! A joint celebration, for you and your sisters. It's their birthday, you know."

"Yes, and they don't need Big Brother sharing their special day. I'm sorry, Mother. I—I have some unfinished business here."

"In that case, we'll wait for you," Keith decided abruptly, "however long it takes. Can I be of assistance?"

"I can handle it, sir."

"Very well. You know where to find us."

"We'll have the party in the afternoon," Devon informed. "Please try to be there, dear."

"I will, Mother." He kissed her cheek. "Goodbye, everyone! And thanks again for coming."

Keith said nothing until he and Devon were alone. "What do you suppose he meant by 'unfinished business'?"

"Something at school, I suppose."

"His tuition was prior-paid in full, and he certainly couldn't be in debt to his friends. He has been *their* banker for all of his semesters."

"I guess we won't know, Keith, unless he chooses to tell us," Devon said. "And he's not at all talkative, is he? Did you notice how his eyes kept scanning the audience indoors and out, as if he hoped Fawn might appear by some magic?"

Keith frowned. "No, he's more realistic than that, Devon. She couldn't be in two places at once. I think he expected someone else."

"Sabrina? Oh, surely not!"

"He invited her, didn't he? I'm afraid I reacted too strongly to his mention of her. And forbidding him to see her again—

God, that was a bad mistake! It probably just whetted his curiosity. I erred, Devon."

"Then do something, Keith!"

"Like what? Fall into her trap? I didn't before, and I won't now."

"Our son wasn't the bait before," Devon reasoned.

"And he won't be now, either. We'll straighten it all out when he comes aboard."

"What if he doesn't?"

"The *Sprite* is not sailing without him," he told her emphatically.

"Oh, Keith, you can't shanghai him!"

"Don't panic, darling. If he's not here by midnight—well, let's not jump to conclusions. He might simply want one last fling with his fraternal comrades. After all, they are going their separate ways and may never get together again, except at class reunions."

That sounded logical to Devon, and perhaps she was worrying needlessly. But the dark shadow of Sabrina lingered spectrally in her mind, as haunting as that of Esther, and she could not dispel the eerie feeling that one was working insidiously, sinisterly, through the other.

⊰ 40 ⊱

SABRINA, WHO had been waiting expectantly for several days now, was becoming increasingly anxious and angry. Keith should have come to her by now, checkbook in hand. Why was he delaying? And what if he didn't come at all? Goddamn him! she thought furiously. She'd make him squirm and smoke for ignoring her, and pay double for keeping her in suspense!

Each morning she had dressed for company, grooming her dyed black hair in a becoming pompadour and rouging her cheeks and lips with carmine, pleased with her reflection in the mirror and convinced that she did not look her age. Thanks to diet and discipline, her figure was still as fine as ever, with high-thrust conical breasts, slender waist, and curvaceous hips. Why, she was a handsome woman in her prime! Even that callow youth had found her attractive on his first visit, for he had certainly stared at her hard enough, obviously comparing her to Cousin Esther's portrait. It was strange, the fascination young men had with beautiful older women. Sabrina had discovered this long ago—in Paris, London, Rome, Vienna. Two of her keepers had been younger than she, and many of her lovers considerably so. One of the few men of any age she had been unable to seduce—and ironically the one she had most wanted to—was Keith Curtis. Her inordinate vanity attributed this failure to his bitterness about the late wife Sabrina so remarkably resembled, both in appearance and character. She was inspired by the famous concubines of history, particularly the Mesdames DuBarry and de Pompadour, both of whom had fascinated royalty into their fifties, and remained the influential mistress of Louis XV until their respective deaths.

Hortense Stanfield was having one of her maniacal fits today, shrieking and shouting obscenities at the housekeeper, who was endeavoring to bathe her. Her piercing screams and curses echoed through the house, and Mrs. Henson couldn't seem to calm her.

Finally, aggravated to the limit, Sabrina went upstairs with a rolled newspaper, which she used as if correcting a disobedient dog, and forced her aunt to swallow a liquid opiate. "You're too easy on her, Maude," she reprimanded the servant. "Cuff her when she acts that way, or let her lie in her own filth. She's crazy as a loon, you know, and you can't reason with lunatics. Why do you try?"

"She's sick, Miss Sabrina, and suffering so. I pray a merciful Providence will take her soon."

"He will, soon enough." But not, Sabrina hoped, while she still had need of the old harridan's charity from the richest man in America! "If she's unruly when she wakes, sedate her again. Put it in her tea or broth, and spoon it down her throat, if necessary."

"Sometimes she clenches her teeth, Miss Sabrina, and won't open her mouth."

"Then pour it through her nose! Just don't choke her." *Yet,* she thought. "Understand?"

The servant nodded, more afraid of her imperious mistress than the pathetic patient.

The heavy brass knocker sounded as Sabrina descended the stairs, and she composed her features into a pleasant expression before answering, hoping it was the King of Wall Street. She was surprised but not too disappointed, for the son, not the father, stood on the stoop.

"Why, Cousin Scotty! I didn't expect you on this special occasion. Come in, please."

"I wondered why you didn't attend the commencement," he said, trailing her rustling taffeta skirts to the parlor."

"My poor dear auntie had a bad time today, and I just couldn't leave her."

"Aunt?"

"You didn't know about her, either? Yes, Aunt Hortense is an invalid, and I'm helping to care for her."

"How kind of you! Is she very old?"

"Past eighty."

His eyes were drawn almost magnetically to the alluring face in the gilded frame dominating the room, as he marked similarities and made comparisons.

"I really missed not seeing Cousin Keith again," Sabrina interrupted his calculating study. "I trust you told him about our meeting, dear?"

"Yes, ma'am."

"What did he say?"

"Nothing much," Scott lied, sparing her feelings.

"Really? How odd! Actually, I thought Cousin Keith would have called on me himself by now. I know his yacht has been in port a while. How long will your family remain?"

"Only until I'm aboard," he replied. "They're waiting for me right now."

"I see," Sabrina murmured. "And I can't believe they would ignore me, knowing I'm in town. I'm hurt, Scotty, deeply hurt by this treatment. And puzzled, too."

"I'm sorry, ma'am."

"Your father can be very stubborn, Scotty. And infuriating, at times."

"I'm afraid so," Scott agreed, aware of these particular paternal traits, which often vexed and bewildered himself. "But he says you are an acquaintance, Miss Carlton, and we're not related."

"Perhaps I should call on him."

"I wouldn't, in your place, ma'am. You may not be kindly received."

"Why not, Scotty? Would they be angry with you for visiting me again?"

"Probably."

"Then why did you come?" she asked slyly.

"To say goodbye, Miss Carlton."

Sabrina shook her head sagely. "That's not quite true, is it? You're curious about my connection with your daddy, aren't you? Well, there is one, dear boy! And how foolish of him not to have told you."

"I don't understand."

"You will, later. But it'll take a while to enlighten you, Scotty. Sit down, get comfortable. We'll chat over some nice burgundy."

Sabrina took some perverse pleasure in his nervous hesitation, as if he weren't sure now that he really wanted to satisfy his curiosity. But the naive rabbit was already in her snare, and she wasn't about to release him in innocent ignorance of the facts. Evidently, Keith had no intention of dealing for her silence. Well, she'd have her sweet revenge, if not his money! There was nothing to stop her now.

The wine tasted strange even to his inexperienced palate, rather bittersweet, but Scott drank it gratefully. Sensing some dreadful revelation, he needed fortification, and Sabrina obligingly refilled his glass. She knew precisely how to handle her quarry to her advantage. After the third potion, his eyes began to glaze and his tongue to stutter. "Wha-what do you have to t-tell me?"

Sabrina only smiled and replenished his goblet, which he raised to salute the haunting portrait. "T-to the lady in the woods!"

"Who, dear?"

"Her, up there, with the Mona Lisa smile. I saw her long ago, wh-when I was just a tyke."

"Really? *Where* did you see her, Scotty?"

"I just told you. The woods. A-a shanty somewhere. An artist t-took me in a gaudy circus wagon."

Sabrina skillfully probed his memory. "When you were abducted from your father's country place?"

"Is that wh-what happened?"

"Don't you remember?"

He gazed at her blearily, gulping more of the peculiarly appealing wine. "I—I guess not. Can you help me, Cousin Sabrina?"

"Maybe. Was the lady in the woods on canvas?"

"Uh-huh. Like that one over the fireplace. Is it you?"

"My alter ego, some people think."

"Tell me more," he entreated.

"Not now, darling. You're a mite tipsy and must sober up first. Come upstairs with me."

He rose unsteadily, his legs wobbling like a sailor's too long at sea. "I—I can't walk very well. . . ."

"Sabrina will help you," she offered, coming to his aid. "Sabrina understands."

"Nice Sabrina," he mumbled, as she supported him up the stairs, one arm around his waist. "Sweet Sabrina," he added, sniffing her French perfume, a most lascivious blend of narcissus and musk.

Maneuvering him to her chambers, Sabrina eased him onto the bed. Then she moistened a towel in the washstand pitcher and bathed his flushed face. Hoping he was not too inebriated to respond to further ministrations, she began to undress him, from his shoes and socks to his underwear, and he was a novice in the hands of an expert. Artful kisses, intimate fondling of his genitals so responsive in potent adolescence, this could be a gratifying experience for her, too! How long had it been since her last virile young stud? This one might be a virgin, but he was ready and willing to change that status. And with his conscience effectively dulled, he might not even remember how it had all come about. Such a handsome face, such a marvelous, athletic physique! And it was her privilege to initiate him in the sexual rites, as every youth should be initiated, by a mature and skillful seductress. No virginal girl could teach him as she could, nor thrill him as she would!

"Does this feel good?" she asked, stroking his lean, flat belly to his erect manhood.

"Uh-huh." His eyes were closed, his breathing heavy.

"Tell me what you like, sweetie, and I'll do it. Anything." Her tongue flicked over his burning flesh like a live flame. "Sabrina will play with you, Scotty, give you so much fun! Do you want to have fun with Sabrina?"

He groaned, shuddering in intense desire and anticipation of more satisfying pleasure.

"Of course you do," her lips coaxed against his, improving his boyish kissing. "Have you ever lain this way with a girl before, Scotty?"

"No, never."

"Poor innocent lamb. Had to amuse yourself, didn't you? And that's not nearly so good, is it? Sabrina knows all about these things, Scotty, and will show you. Oh, you'll enjoy being inside a nice warm female! There's just nothing better for a male, as your daddy could surely tell you...." She ceased her manipulations long enough to strip herself and mount him, supervising the insertion and deliberately inducing his prompt climax. Like any normal youth, he would be eager for more, and she could take her time educating him for her own benefit as well as his, especially in the art of self-control. In the throes of his first coital ecstasy Scott embraced Sabrina, moaning and quivering as his passion subsided. Almost immediately afterward he passed out, and she lay beside him and pulled the sheet up over them. Scott slept for two hours and awoke in darkness, disoriented. Not until Sabrina lit the bedside candle did he realize where he was, and with whom.

"Oh, Jesus! What happened, Cousin Sabrina?"

"We had fun, Cousin Scott, because you wanted to so very much. That's all, and it's perfectly natural. Nothing to be ashamed of, or recant. We'll have more fun, all night long. Would you like some more wine?"

"No, I'm afraid I drank too much earlier. It's awfully strong, Sabrina. I've got to get out of here!"

"You can't yet, dear—not until you're completely sober.

Your parents would be shocked and might suspect your revelry. For you have been reveling, you naughty boy!" she chided, tweaking a dark curly lock on his forehead.

Scott was not thinking of himself, however, but of Fawn Haverston. His lovely, precious little sweetheart! They had sworn to be first with each other in this respect, and he had broken his vow. With a woman twice his age, yet! How could he confess his betrayal, or face her again under any circumstances? More wine might assuage his horrible guilt and remorse, he thought, accepting another glass from the same decanter brought from the parlor while he was asleep. As Sabrina poured, a practiced shrug flipped the sheet off her body, and Scott averted his eyes. But she withheld the wine until he looked at her, his eyes focusing on her magnificent, full-nippled breasts with rekindled passion.

"Is this your first sight of a nude female, Scotty?"

"Except for art," he acknowledged sheepishly.

"Paintings and statues are to admire," Sabrina smiled. "Flesh is to enjoy. And you *did* enjoy mine, darling boy. Now we can enjoy each other, as often as possible. Drink up, lover. Then we'll play some more, for I know you want to. Don't deny yourself, or me." She lowered the linen on him, so that he was also fully exposed. "Oh, don't blush! You could pose for Adonis, and I'll be your Aphrodite. You don't think I'm too old for the part, do you?"

"It's just mythology," he said tactfully. "And you do have a nice figure."

"And pretty face?"

"Yes, you're very attractive." He did not add 'for an older woman,' and Sabrina was grateful.

"Why, thank you, darling!" She drummed her fingers playfully on his stalwart chest, which boasted a fair crop of hair for his age. "When will you take your Grand Tour?"

"I haven't decided yet."

"Why not begin this summer, and I'll accompany you. I know England and the Continent quite well, Scotty. I lived abroad for many years, you know."

Her audacity astonished him, but more so her proposal. "You can't be serious, Sabrina. Father would never approve of such an arrangement!"

"Of course not, my sweet innocent. It would be our secret. We could even travel on the same ship from New York, if I went incognito, and we ignored each other until at sea. We could play a delightful little intrigue!"

"No, Sabrina. There's someone else, a girl in Virginia, and I love her very much."

"Are you betrothed?"

"Secretly."

"Then it hasn't been formally announced?"

"Not yet."

"That's good, Scotty, because you are not ready for marriage yet. Surely you realize that? A man should know a lot more about life before he settles down with a wife and children. Your father certainly didn't rush to the altar without his qualifying experiences!"

Suddenly Scott remembered why he had come to this house today, and gotten sidetracked. "What about my father, Sabrina? I thought you were going to tell me downstairs, before I drank too much."

"Oh, it'll wait, Scotty. Right now, I think another lesson in lovemaking is more important to you. You'll need far more practice to be a knowledgeable husband in bed, and especially if your lady is still virginal on the wedding night."

"Were you ever married, Sabrina?"

"Twice, laddie. My mates didn't live up to my expectations, however, so I simply divorced them."

"Any children?"

"One, a puny little girl, who died early."

"Was my father one of your spouses?"

"Would I call him Cousin Keith, if he had been?"

"Then what was your relationship?" He stared into her amethyst eyes, which she coyly veiled in the shadows of downcast lashes. "Lovers? Were you his mistress?"

"No, although I certainly would not object to accommodating him that way. It's a long story, Scotty, too long to go into now," she hedged. "Forget it and concentrate on yourself, the present. Life is just beginning for you, and you have barely sampled its wondrous banquet. Finish your aperitif and lie down, and I'll give you joy untold, rapture unbound. A feast of the supreme pleasure you could enjoy regularly, if we went abroad together. Also," she winked, "if you remain in Boston and study for your master's degree."

"You're wicked, Sabrina."

She laughed throatily, pretending to box his ears. "Wanton, darling. And my wantonness intrigues you, doesn't it? You've had a taste of honey, and you crave more. Well, your daddy would understand that, for he dipped into his share of fleshpots, believe me. So perish any qualms about your youthful yearnings. Ah, look at yourself down there! Throbbing, aching, raring to go again. And your tutor is offering another course, but this time you must pay more attention, my eager tyro, and cooperate."

"I—I really should leave," he stammered.

"But you won't, Scotty. You'll stay and play and play until exhaustion. . . ."

There was no vigor like the vigor of youth, no lust or sexuality like that of adolescence. Now Scott knew what the other boys meant when they boasted about their sexual prowess, how they couldn't seem to get enough sex no matter how often they indulged. A few brief interludes of rest, and he was chomping at the bit again. And it seemed so natural, so instinctive to gratify himself with a knowing female. Sabrina called him a fast learner and complimented his technique, encouraging him to obtain maximum, mutual pleasure.

"Oh, honeyboy," she cried, squeezing him inside her. "Oh, you're driving me wild! Ride higher, faster . . . there, there, I've done it!" She groaned and clutched him to her tumultuous bosom. "My precious pupil, my wonderful young lover! Do you know what you've done for me?"

Scott nodded and continued. They were both intent upon achieving another such erotic zenith, her hips undulating sensuously with his, when the violent pounding on the door interrupted the inherent, atavistic rhythm just as Sabrina was approaching the savage delight. "Oh, shit," she swore. "Who in hell could that be, at this hour!"

"Let me finish," Scott pleaded, and she did before sliding out from under him and donning a frayed scarlet silk wrapper. "Stay here, sugar."

But it was too late. Mrs. Henson had already admitted the

unexpected visitor, who saw Sabrina emerging from her rooms. His agility was equal to his son's as he raced up the staircase, pushed her aside, and flung open the door. And though stunned, Scott leaped up and tried to scramble into his clothes, becoming partially entangled in his breeches. His father looked like a giant in a towering rage, and he whirled on Sabrina in colossal fury. "You goddamned whoring bitch! I ought to kill you for this!"

"Like you tried to do Esther, when you caught her with Giles Mallard?"

"Shut your mouth, or I'll shut it permanently!"

Shifting his attention to the befuddled boy, he demanded, "Was *this* your unfinished business?"

"I—I drank too much," Scott said, fumbling with his fly, "I didn't know what I was doing, at first."

"At first? How long have you been here?"

"Hours, I guess."

"Wallowing with this old sow all that time?"

"I slept some, after I passed out."

"How much liquor did you drink, for God's sake?"

"Not all that much, I didn't think. And it was wine, but powerful."

Immediately suspicious, Keith tested the contents of the cut-glass carafe. The aroma of anise, the bitter sweetness of wormwood—only a naive boy would not have detected the adulteration. And stepping swiftly to the adulterator, Keith slapped her violently across the face. "That burgundy is mostly absinthe, and you're an even worse pig than *she* was, Sabrina!"

She soothed her smarting skin, glaring at him defiantly. "I doubt that, Cousin Keith. I think Esther would have cuckolded you with her own son, if possible. But why are you raving so? He needed some experience with a wise woman. Whoever heard of a male virgin at his age? You sure weren't! Esther told me you admitted to sex at fourteen, with a housemaid. And in Europe, fathers take their sons to brothels to learn from older women."

"This isn't Europe, you cunning slut. And you not only seduced a minor, you beguiled him with a witch's brew! There are laws against that, and you could be arrested."

"Only if you press charges," she challenged, "and I don't

think you will risk such a scandal."

"Try me."

She shook her head at him, smiling smugly. "Better check with your wife before you summon the police."

"Hear me, Sabrina Carlton! Not another cent of my money comes into this house, until you go out of it."

"I'm Hortense Stanfield's guardian," she apprised.

"Only until the court can appoint another one, which, I assure you, will be soon."

"But I'm also nursing her, Keith."

"How? By drugging her senseless! I'll have a physician look into that, too."

"She belongs in Bedlam."

"And you belong in Hell where, if there's a God in heaven, you'll spend eternity! At any rate, your days here are numbered."

"How will I live?"

"Ply your trade, prostitute. There are plenty of sailors on the waterfront. I don't care if you starve to death, just remove your whoring carcass from this property. And that's final, madam!"

"Is it, Mr. Curtis?"

"Absolutely. Take my advice and give up your schemes to blackmail me, unless you want to end up in prison. You may have the dubious satisfaction of seducing my innocent son, but that's all you'll have!"

"Well, it was more than you think, for both of us! And if I'm a swine, your young boar certainly gorged himself at my trough. Nor was he any more reluctant to lose his virginity than other normal young men, which shouldn't surprise his lusty and lecherous sire!" Her mouth twisted in a taunting jeer. "You don't know what you've missed, Papa. Ask sonny, he'll tell you."

Perplexed by their scurrilous satire, Scott tried to ignore it. He was sitting on the edge of the rumpled bed, tying his shoes, when Keith handed him his jacket. "Come on, son. Let's get out of this sty!" Then, noticing a goblet on the commode, Keith picked it up and tossed the polluted dregs into Sabrina's face on the way out. The gesture could not have been more contemptuous and insulting if he had spat on her.

⚜ 41 ⚜

"Is THERE anything you'd like to say?" Keith asked as the hansom he had kept waiting left Louisburg Square and rumbled along the narrow cobblestone streets of Beacon Hill. Gaslamps glowed on the mellowed brownstone and brick residences of Boston's elite, on the pretty flowering trees and quaint windowboxes and patrician doorways.

Scott's young shoulders slumped in the seat beside his father, who appeared preoccupied and even more unhappy than himself. "What can I say, sir? You saw what you saw, and I've no logical excuse or explanation, except possibly temporary insanity. I lost command of my faculties after the third glass of that wine, which I thought tasted rather odd, but then I'm not a connoisseur like you."

"It was adulterated slop," Keith said, wishing he had dealt more harshly with Sabrina. "Try to be a little more discriminating in what you drink hereafter, son. I thought I had warned you about Mickey Finns and similar traps before you went off to school."

"You did, sir, but I forgot. And I hardly expected to be doped by someone who claimed to be a relative. Besides, the mood I was in, I might have drunk hemlock."

"Contaminated absinthe can be as fatal, too. And were you suicidal when you went to that piranha, after my specific request not to do so again?"

His head ached excruciatingly from the lingering effects of the vile concoction. Intending primarily to confuse his mentality and remove his moral inhibitions, Sabrina had erred somewhat in the preparation of her virulent recipe. For while familiar with adolescent sexuality, its prurient vulnerability and intense

374

urgency in which self-gratification triumphed over all other instincts, she had failed to allow for his inexperience with any kind of vice. Thus, even in his residual misery and mortification now, Scott realized that he had been an easy mark and gullible prey. But it was hardly a personal sacrifice, he thought ruefully, considering his cooperation in his own corruption. He was a culpable accomplice, an eager culprit, and except for parental intrusion and rescue, he might still be in that house, that room, that sinful bed. . . .

"I was curious and rather depressed," he admitted dolefully. "But I didn't expect anything like that to happen. I was seeking something else—I'm not sure what, exactly. Answers to a riddle, maybe. Pieces to a puzzle." He shrugged in bewildered confusion. "You see, last night I suddenly remembered where I had seen another portrait of Miss Carlton like the one in her parlor. . . ."

Ordering the driver to take them to the Public Garden, Keith settled back with a heavy sigh. "That's not Sabrina Carlton in that painting, Scott. It's her close cousin, Esther Stanfield, my first wife."

Thinking, hoping he had misunderstood, Scott repeated, "Your *first* wife? Isn't my mother—?" His voice cracked, and his skull was virtually splitting now, as if his brain would either disintegrate or explode.

"No, I was married when I met Devon Marshall, in Richmond, after the War Between the States." Keith paused ponderously, uncertain how to continue, how to divulge years of crucial information in minutes or even hours; how to compress nearly two decades of desultory time and events into a concise, sequential compendium. It was a monumental task, and he was not sure he was equal to it just then, nor that he should even attempt it in a public conveyance on the streets of the city where it had all begun with his regrettable marriage into one of its Brahmin families.

Scott pressed his palms to his throbbing temples, but the pain was fierce, relentless. Moreover, the jouncing vehicle was making his stomach queasy. "Is this leading to some kind of confession?"

"Revelation, son, which should have been made long ago.

But there never seemed to be an appropriate time, and I'm afraid that this may not be, either. We had planned to tell you together."

"When?" he interrupted harshly, his temper aggravated by his physical discomfort. "Just *when* did you plan to tell me what appears to be fairly obvious now, Father? I was born out of wedlock, wasn't I? You and Mother had an affair, and I was the unfortunate result!"

"Not unfortunate, Scott. A great gift and treasure! Oh, God, how can I explain it to you? Make you understand the problems and ramifications of our love, present the true and complete story..."

"Why bother, at this late date? I'm not a child anymore, and I don't want a glorified fairy tale. I can figure out the pertinent details for myself."

"Not all of them, Scott. Nor everything involved. My first marriage was a misalliance, a *mariage de convenance* for the benefit of her family, whose fortunes were severely depleted in the Panic of 1857. And though unaware of this when I proposed to Horace Stanfield's daughter, it wouldn't have mattered, because I loved her and believed it was mutual. But I was wrong, and merely hoodwinked by a clever, beguiling witch. Esther was in love with someone else, an indigent artist whose handiwork you mistook for Sabrina Carlton. I was her lover's cuckold during our engagement and for two years after our wedding. I caught them together accidentally in his Manhattan studio, on which my money was paying the rent and buying his food and wine."

Tense silence ensued, during which the steel-clad hoofs clopping on stone created an anvil chorus in Scott's ears, and he had difficulty assimilating the dumbfounding news. Feeling worse by the moment, he stammered, "So ... so you divorced her?"

"No, I couldn't."

"Why not, for crissake? She was an adulteress keeping a gigolo!"

"More like a whore supporting a pimp," Keith reflected grimly, "for she was soliciting commissions for him among our friends. Certainly I had the necessary grounds for divorce, but there were complications. I fought with her paint dauber,

Esther tried to separate us, and was hurt in a fall down the attic stairway. And there's more, son. Much more."

"I—I think I've heard enough," Scott stuttered. "Stop this hack, I want to get out!"

"You haven't heard the half of it yet," Keith told him as they arrived at the Public Garden. "And we're here now, so get out. Some walking and fresh air will do you good." He jumped down and offered his assistance.

"You want I should wait, sir?" the cabbie inquired as Keith gave him a generous gratuity. "I can see the lad's a mite in his cups. Need some help?"

"I can manage, thank you, but wait at a distance. I don't know how long we'll be here."

"Righto, governor."

The park was a large, pleasant oasis in the heart of the city, and Keith guided his wobbly son toward the nearest fountain. Before reaching it, however, Scott staggered and clutched at a handy lamp post. "I—I feel sick, Dad. Oh, Jesus, I have to vomit. . . ."

"Go ahead. Stick your finger down your throat, get as much of that poison out of your system as possible. That's the best antidote and remedy for it."

Another wave of nausea brought vomitus spewing without manual aid, and Keith supported his heavy body lest he tumble face down into it. Scott threw up until there was nothing left in his belly but bile, and still he continued to retch as if to expel his viscera. "I'm dying, Dad! Puking up my guts!"

Keith commiserated. "No, son, it only seems that way. I know, I've been there. And believe me, you'll feel even worse tomorrow. Is it possible you've never been drunk before to-night, either? Your first serious encounter with liquor and sex on the same occasion?"

"Uh-huh," he groaned.

"That must be some kind of record for a Harvard graduate! Can you make it to a bench?"

"I guess so, with help."

"Of course." The thirty-odd feet seemed the distance of a football field, but he finally negotiated it with paternal assistance and slumped down on the slatted-wood bench, arms and legs sprawling at various angles. "Wait here, Scott, and try not to fall off. I want to wet my handkerchief and clean you up."

Sprinting to the fountain and back, Keith laved the cool damp linen over his face. "Feeling any better?"

"Some."

"Relax and breathe deeply. It'll alleviate the nausea almost as well as smelling salts. I learned that long before your age, from my older college friends. We took some nocturnal swims in the swan boat ponds, too, knowing we'd either sober up or drown. Would you like to try it? I won't let you drown."

"No, I'll be all right. I'm getting oriented, at least. I know where I am. Hell, I'll never forget it!"

The landscape was familiar to any Harvard student, for it was a favorite haunt on weekends and holidays. They met and entertained girls there, by accident or design, when they could find a secluded rendezvous under a tree, or on the grassy esplanade along the Charles River.

"Did you study any botany here?" his father asked, referring to the academically labeled specimens.

"That wasn't one of my subjects."

"Nor mine," Keith smiled in the camouflage of moon shadows and scattered gaslamps. "But that's what we called some of our escapades in the Public Garden. A lot of biology was also studied beneath the weeping willows."

Scott grimaced at the sour, foul taste in his mouth. "Did you do much biological experimenting?"

"My share," he said. "Is Fawn Haverston the only girl you've ever thought about, seriously or otherwise?"

He nodded ruefully. "And now I've lost her, because I broke my promise to Fawn, and can never face her again. I'm not fit to wipe her shoes."

"Why, son?"

"*Why?* Sabrina Carlton, that's why!"

"You think you're the only young man ever seduced by an older woman? It happens frequently, Scott, and you didn't stand a chance of resisting an experienced harlot like Sabrina Carlton. I'm just surprised that you were so totally innocent and gullible. You must have been the only monk in the fra⸱ nity house."

"Just about, and they teased me plenty, when they sneaked off to brothels and taverns. But I've read *Gray's Anatomy* and some medical journals . . . and you warned me about prostitutes and venereal diseases."

"And rightfully so. But most boys manage to find nice girls, who are also friendly and obliging."

"Friendly and obliging, maybe, but hardly nice! *Nice* girls don't do that before marriage."

"Whoa there, boy! Hold on just a damned minute. What class are you putting your mother in?"

Scott swallowed, tasting gall on his tongue. "I'm sorry, sir. I forgot."

"Well, you'd better never forget again, either in my presence or hers! It would kill her, to think you even remotely entertained that stupid, medieval notion about our premarital relationship. You are not aware of all the facts, so don't try to judge us. Above all, don't dare compare Devon to Esther. There's absolutely no comparison between them, and never could be. I see I must reveal more than I originally intended, to divest your naive mind of some vile misconceptions and rash conclusions. Are you sober enough to listen and comprehend?"

"I haven't lost all of my wits and savvy," he replied wryly. "I'm sensible enough to realize that I'm illegitimate. A bastard!"

"You are no such thing, Scott! A bastard is nameless. You're my son, and you have my name. You had it through adoption even before your mother and I could legally wed. So get that wild idea out of your head. You are our child, and nothing can change that."

"Do I have a birth certificate?"

"Not every birth is recorded, Scott."

"Especially not the illegitimate ones," he suggested bitterly. "No wonder I was baptized so late! Am I even a statistic in the Bureau of Census?"

"Certainly! These things happen, Scott. I handled it as best I could, on the advice of my physician and attorneys, and always in your best interest. I'm hoping you are mature and intelligent enough to credit me with this discretion, for your own sake, as well as your parents'. Your health and happiness are our primary concerns. Do you believe that, son?"

"I don't know."

"Will you at least try?"

"Do I have an alternative?"

"Yes, you do, Scott. You can renounce your birthright, disown your parents, deny your heritage. But you'll still be our son and heir, according to every law of nature, man, and God. So if you think the Creator made a mistake somewhere along the line, you'll have to consult Him about it. You were divinely given to us, and the divine gift of life cannot be returned. It can be taken back, but only at His will. Think about it, son. Think about it long and hard, before you make any serious personal decisions."

Scott glanced at the vast imponderable heavens, as perplexing as infinity and eternity. "You said there was no comparison between your wives. How were they so different?"

"All ways, but specifically in character. To say that one was good and the other evil is too simplistic, for the first was the opposite of the second in every respect. Devon was chaste, honest, true; Esther was a wanton liar and cheat. Devon was never mercenary, Esther was never anything else. Devon loves me, Esther loathed me. Devon makes me happy, Esther made me miserable. If this sounds like a litany of Devon's attributes and virtues, it is. I couldn't have a better mate, nor my children a better mother."

"I assume she was a virgin?"

"Yes, until I deflowered her."

"So how did a carnal Yankee meet this pure and perfect flower of Southern womanhood?"

"Curb your sarcasm, son. This is as difficult for me to talk about, as for you to hear. I was speculating in Richmond. Reconstruction was under way, and there were bargains in ruined real estate, including her late father's burned-out newspaper building on Main Street; the lot was too small to interest me, however. She was alone and penniless, with some press experience, and she wanted to come to New York and try for a career in journalism. She came aboard my railroad car during my absence, naively assuming that I would accommodate her as a favor, since she couldn't afford the fare. She was young, beautiful, eminently desirable even in her pitiful clothes. I wanted her, and she was desperate."

Scott stared at him, shaking his head incredulously. "And

you took advantage of her desperation? Why didn't you just give her a pass? You own stock in half the railroads of this country!"

"I was a different man then, Scott. Unhappy, disillusioned, betrayed, with a semi-invalid spouse who blamed me for her accident and was determined to wreak her revenge. I didn't care much about anything for years. Money was power, and women a convenience. I was distrustful of them, cynical about their motives, while ruthless and relentless in mine. I even wore my meaningless wedding ring to discourage any serious female interest, although Miss Marshall wasn't aware of it until I removed my gloves. The poor child seemed relieved, innocently trusting in my marital fidelity. Jesus, what a rake and scoundrel!" he reflected remorsefully. "But it all boomeranged that very night, for I fell deeply, desperately, eternally in love with her. The angel had, in effect, conquered the devil."

"And came under his magic spell?" Observing his father's profile in the moonlight, Scott did not find this conclusion at all unreasonable. Still a virile and exceptionally handsome man in middle age, he must have been incredibly charismatic in his youth: every young maiden's image of Prince Charming and Knight in Shining Armor combined. Certainly he possessed the riches of a kingdom, the courtly manner, the mystique and savoir faire!

"If you prefer that terminology, yes. But what could we do about it? Mrs. Satan was firmly ensconced in our brownstone hell in Gramercy Park. Esther was twenty-seven then, hysterically paralyzed, and ruled her domain with an iron glove and sadistic vengeance."

Intensely interested and curious now, Scott surmised, "So Mr. Satan propositioned the fallen angel to become his mistress?"

"Oh, you do have a keen wit, my boy! And your deduction is accurate. I did propose an arrangement, which she automatically rejected. I chased her all over New York, from job to job, until finally she couldn't elude me any longer, nor resist my satanic temptations. But no two mortals in this world were ever more in love, Scott. We needed each other and had to be together as much as possible, whatever the consequences. When she became pregnant with you, I offered Esther a tremendous fortune to free me. In desperation, I even tried to frighten and intimidate her into a divorce. Nothing worked. She wrote letters to her mother—the sick old lady still residing in Stanfield House on my generosity—accusing me of threats on her life. She was insanely jealous and maniacal in her suspicions. It was a hopeless situation, a long, bitter, diabolical vendetta that endured until her death of paresis, many years later."

"Jesus God! Was Mother a helpless martyr all that time, living in the shadows of your hellish life? Secluded in the country! Was Halcyon *her* Hades?"

Keith drew a heavy breath, sighing as if it were his last. "That's enough, Scott. The rest is too personal and private to discuss and might only further confuse, rather than clarify, matters. It's almost dawn, anyway. Devon must be frantic, wondering what happened to us. She knew I was going out to look for you, and that I expected to find you exactly where I did. Sabrina Carlton is aware of the salient facts and secrets, you see, and hoped I would pay her not to reveal them to you. And if that doesn't convince you of that creature's caliber, nothing could!"

That gave Scott pause. "Must Mother be told about my disgusting behavior with her?"

"That's up to you, son. But she's very perceptive and probably suspects much more than you imagine."

"Or will, when I don't go south anymore. I might as well take the Grand Tour, try to forget Miss Haverston."

"Because you feel unworthy of her?"

"I *am* unworthy of her," he declared. "My touch would defile her now."

"That's preposterous, Scott! Not one man in a thousand goes to the alter virginal. It's not something to be proud of, or boast about, but you can't lament it forever, either. Masculine nature betrays itself, and you weren't entirely responsible for your seduction."

"Nor completely guiltless, either! I didn't fight her, Dad. I surrendered fairly easy. The absinthe wine might have helped to lure me into her bed, but I wasn't anxious to leave it. Hell, no! It was fun, and I enjoyed it."

"Naturally. She knew every trick of the trade, and your prior pleasure was apparently limited to self-abuse. It's not the same satisfaction, nor instinctively designed to be. And I seriously doubt it's any criterion for a successful marriage, Scott. A husband ought to have some sexual knowledge and experience before his wedding night, lest it become a total fiasco."

"In that case, why not thank my mentor instead of condemning her? Why were you so damned furious?"

"Because of the circumstances—her age, intentions, and tactics," Keith appraised. "It was deliberate entrapment, and a professional whore bent on blackmail is hardly to be congratulated! Sabrina should be in jail now."

"Or in a hospital? You were angry enough to harm her bodily, weren't you?"

"She deserved a good beating."

"And even death?"

"You think I'm capable of murder? Every human being is, Scott, with sufficient provocation. God knows Esther drove me psychologically to the brink of it on several occasions, and Sabrina is her incarnate. But my sins and broken Commandments don't include homicide, son. Not so far, anyway." He stood and reached down a hand to encourage the reluctant boy to his feet. "We'd better rejoin the family crew. You need some bunk time, badly. I trust you're sailing home with us?"

His legs were steadier now, his head somewhat clearer. "Yes, sir."

"Fine." Their boots crunched on the pebbled path to the public station, where they boarded the hansom again and headed for the *Sprite*. "And then what?"

Scott gazed pensively at the Charles River, shimmering like quicksilver in the dawning light, and the tall masts of the ships in harbor. "Europe, I suppose."

"And afterward?"

"Wall Street, probably. Curtis and Son, Bankers. Isn't that what you want?"

"Nothing would please me more, Scott. But I thought you had other plans for your future."

"I did," he answered ponderously, "but no longer. I can't ask Miss Haverston to marry me now."

"Do you still want her?"

"More than ever, and likely always will."

"Then have the courage of your convictions, son! Go after her, do your damndest to get her."

"With my background? Her father would show me the door,

if he knew. Maybe even have me tarred and feathered and run out of Virginia on a rail."

"Oh, for God's sake! Are you recanting your orgy with that whoring hedonist, or brooding over my premarital affair with your mother?"

"Both. They're honorable people, Dad."

"So are we, boy! And for your further information, Daniel Haverston is aware of what you seem to regard as 'the awful truth' about your birth. I won't go into detail," he said at Scott's astonished silence. "Devon's a native Virginian, remember, and she lived in Richmond. Our acquaintance with the Haverstons is no mere coincidence, Scott. And why do you think he has that life-size painting of your mother at Harmony Hill? Not just because he admires her beauty! The honorable Mr. Haverston was once Miss Marshall's fiancé. He's still desperately in love with her, and wouldn't hesitate to take her from me if he could."

Would amazements never cease! "If they were betrothed, what happened?"

"Devon broke the engagement when she realized she didn't love him enough for marriage."

"Was that before or after she met you?"

"Before," Keith said. "That was between them, and I had nothing to do with it. It's another story."

"This seems to be an endless one, Dad."

"Because it's life, son, and not over yet. It'll go on to eternity. That's how your mother and I feel about each other: till death do us part. And if you believe it could be the same for you and Fawn, make your dream a reality. I don't think her father would object or interfere too much. Even so, he can't do so forever. But perhaps you should give it more time, just to be sure of yourself and her. If it was meant to be, Scott, it will be, somehow. Ultimately."

"Are you some kind of prophet?"

"Just an authority on eventuality," Keith said wryly. "I should be, don't you think, after the length of time I pursued my ideal?"

Scott could only nod, for the cabbie was drawing rein at the designated pier. And there was enough morning light to recognize his mother on the bridge, her binoculars scanning the shore. He suspected she had waited up all night, wondering and worrying about them, and wished he had any other reason, any other excuse, but the truth.

Keith smiled and waved at her. "What did I tell you? That's not Dolph Bowers up there, but the *real* captain of our ship. A few more hours away, and she'd have had the police searching for us. Salute her, son!"

"Aye-aye, sir!"

✦ 42 ✦

TO SCOTT'S RELIEF, his mother asked no pertinent questions, and he retreated immediately to his cabin, crawled into his berth, and slept for six hours straight. He woke in the midst of his sisters' birthday party, as several crew members were entertaining them by dancing the hornpipe to the accompaniment of a concertina. He dressed and went to the main salon to watch. But the music did not soothe his residual headache, and the mirth and merriment grated on his still raw and ragged nerves. He left the scene, shoulders slumped and hands thrust into the pockets of his white sport trousers. His legs felt as rubbery as those of the sailors executing the traditional jig, which amused the other celebrants to laughter and applause.

"The party isn't over yet," Sharon fretted, gazing after him. "Why is Scotty leaving? We haven't even lit the candles on our cakes!"

"Your brother doesn't care for any refreshments," their father explained. "He isn't feeling very well."

"But we haven't opened our presents yet, either!" complained Shannon, who enjoyed an audience on such occasions. "I don't think Scotty likes us much."

"Oh, darling, of course he does!" Devon promptly assured

her. "But he's grown up now, and you can't expect him to be excited over juvenile parties."

"He doesn't act excited about *anything!* And he looks a little green—is he seasick?"

"A bit, perhaps."

"He didn't even give us a gift," Sharon pouted.

"Scotty was too busy with college work to shop," Keith temporized, "and you have plenty of presents." He indicated the table heaped with brightly wrapped packages. "Why don't the rest of you go ahead with the fun? Daddy wants to check on your brother."

He found the boy on the portside promenade, pondering the far horizon of the Atlantic Ocean. "What are you contemplating so seriously?" he inquired gently.

"I'm not sure, Dad. My head isn't on straight yet. So damned much went wrong so quickly."

"It's not the end of the world, son."

"For whom?"

"I thought we had settled all that in the Public Garden. What happened with that evil serpent can't be undone, Scott, but it didn't exactly knock the earth off its axis, either. It's not Doomsday. And you can't simply crawl into a grave or cave and stop living!"

"How much of the debacle has Mother surmised?"

"Enough, son. I told you she has an uncanny perception. She figured out where you were most of last night. Neither of us was much surprised, however, except that you were so easily duped by Sabrina Carlton. While we knew you were fairly naive, we didn't quite realize the extent of your naiveté. Naturally and understandably, you fell into the trap of an unscrupulous expert at trapping male prey. She tried to lure me with the same kind of raw flesh bait ten years ago."

Astonished at this new discovery, Scott cast him a curious, oblique glance. "Another confession, Father? Unless I forgot, you didn't confide *that* last night."

"I figured you had enough to handle, in your condition, and further revelations would only addle you more. But yes, the cunning witch came to Gramercy Park one morning while I was away and virtually threatened Devon with public exposure of Esther's supposedly incriminating letters, which I *did* mention to you, unless I set her up in style abroad. I went to the hotel where she was staying, to call her bluff, and—well, she was wearing a revealing negligee, offered me some probably doctored absinthe, which I declined, and then spread herself invitingly on the bed."

"But you were too strong and clever to be tempted and hookwinked?"

"I was also not an innocent adolescent! I had encountered her brand of mercenary bitch before; my first wife, and Sabrina's first cousin, was a past mistress at that old game. My mistake then was in thinking I had trumped Miss Carlton's high cards, and especially the ace she believed she had in her hole, and spoiled her dreams of perpetual blackmail and extortion. I had almost forgotten about her, until she surfaced from her subterranean slime and viciously victimized you."

He scowled, still amazed and mortified by his gullibility, and staring into the deep green water, as if he could find his lost innocence in its unfathomable depths. "And succeeded so well!"

"Scott, you had sex with a strumpet, that's all."

"She's a nymphomaniac, and it was an orgy."

"That doesn't make you a satyr."

"That's how I feel, though."

Keith sighed, shaking his head. "And now you consider yourself dissolute—a roué unfit for a decent girl, and so must forget Fawn Haverston?"

Scott nodded gravely, and the very thought of giving her up intensified his agony—his sense of guilt, depravity, betrayal, loss of honor, and bitter remorse. "That should please you, sir."

"Well, it doesn't, Scott."

"But you never wanted me to marry her," he accused.

"That may have been true, once," Keith admitted. "When I feared I was losing my only son, that you intended to sacrifice your family and the Curtis heritage, to embrace the Haverston dynasty. Devon was more realistic in that respect, however, and finally convinced me that every person must chart his own course in life, and ultimately sail his own vessel, come storms or high seas. And as we pursued ours, so must our children be allowed the same opportunity and privilege. A birth certificate is not a bill of sale; it conveys certain responsibilities, but no rights of ownership. That, she insisted, would be tantamount to the kind of slavery over which this country fought a long, terrible war. A brilliant and persuasive lady, your mother."

"What difference does that make to me now? I'm at war with myself, Dad; in conflict with my personal creeds and codes, ethics, and integrity. I have to regain all these things again, in order to like and respect myself. It's a helluva dilemma, which won't magically disappear in a trip to Harmony Hill, a summer in Newport, or hiatus at Halcyon. Maybe in a long sojourn abroad," he shrugged. "Travel is supposed to be efficacious, isn't it?"

"The Grand Tour has many beneficial effects, Scott. But it's not a panacea for what ails you now."

"Just the same, I've decided to take it. I'm sure you know how to arrange the details for me. Perhaps, in a couple of years, when I return . . ."

"Fawn will be nineteen by then," Keith reminded. "She's a lovely, vivacious young lady. Do you imagine she's going to wait around for you all that time?"

"If she loves me, she will," he said hopefully. "If not, then it's better that we realize it soon. Tragic mistakes are made in impetuosity—or, as the romantics say, in the bloom of first love."

"You think that describes your relationship with Fawn? First love, and the bloom will fade and disappear if you're apart long enough?"

"I don't know," he said miserably.

"Do you care?"

"Of course! Desperately. I hope she'll wait for me. I even hope she'll beg me not to go, but I can't ask her to do either one, because I can't bare my reasons."

"Oh, Scott! I'm stymied. I don't know how to advise you on this, because you're attaching too much importance to a not terribly important incident. Why not talk with your mother? Perhaps she can give you some feminine insight that I can't: put herself in Fawn's place and imagine what she might think and do in the same situation."

"I can't, Dad. I just can't discuss this with Mother, knowing the truth about you and her, and how I got into this world to begin with."

Keith frowned almost angrily. "You still don't understand *that*?"

"Yes, I do, and that's the trouble. I don't condemn either of you, or hold anything against you. But that was your life, your affair, and you made your own choices and decisions. I have to make mine with Fawn. It's not really the same problem, you know. It's quite different, in fact. No comparison, actually, for you had obstacles and impediments which I don't, therefore reasons and excuses I lack. Why should I burden Mother with this—or even you anymore? Please, sir. If you don't mind, I'd just rather be left alone, to deal with it myself."

Keith waited irresolutely, endowing his attitude with burgeoning maturity. But he was also worried that another impasse might be developing between them, just when he had imagined the filial chasm was narrowing, the barriers finally eroding and even vanishing.

"Very well," he acceded, lest his persistence erect new walls, dig deeper canyons. "Just don't continue to brood and shun your family. Above all, don't do anything rash and foolish."

Scott smiled sheepishly. "Like jumping overboard?"

"Good Lord, no! That's not what I meant at all. Were you considering it?"

He shook his head slowly. "Actually, I was wondering if I'd ever feel like eating again."

Keith clapped his shoulder, immeasurably relieved. "You will, son. Take a few turns around deck, inhale some of this invigorating sea air. You've always been a good sailor; no reason you shouldn't continue to be and—"

"I know," he interrupted, surveying the restless, eternal waves sparkling in the brilliant sunlight. "It's not the end of the world, and there's a lot of it I still have to see. Many courses to charter, seas to sail, and much wilderness to conquer."

"Wilderness?"

"My own, primarily," he affirmed seriously. "The personal, private territory of Scott Heathstone Curtis: the intricate province of Me. Life is a wilderness, isn't it? And youth? And love? And marriage? And fatherhood? All unexplored, uncharted wilderness to be individually traversed and conquered?"

Keith looked at him with new understanding, perception, pride, and satisfaction. "That's right, Scott. And you're going to succeed in all those areas. You're going to do just fine."

"Thanks for the vote of confidence."

"I *am* confident, son." A thoughtful pause. "And now I'll make a suggestion, which is entirely up to you. We are planning a short season in Newport, because we intend to go abroad. Devon wants to visit Heathstone Manor in Sussex, and the twins are anxious for a long ocean voyage. If you'd like to sail with us, as far as Liverpool or Southampton, welcome. You can begin your Grand Tour in England or Europe, or wherever you please, and alone, except for the customary and optional attendants: valet, aide, guide—one, all, or none as you prefer. But believe me, you should consider at least one helpful companion. You'll have much more leisure and far less harassment, with someone to handle the necessary exigencies. But you needn't decide now, Scott. Take your time. We won't be departing until late August, and our itineraries will be quite different."

"Sounds interesting, sir. Practical, too. And I'll probably be aboard the *Sprite,* across the Atlantic, anyway. After landing . . . well, a couple of fellow graduates are taking their tours this year. I could contact them and arrange to travel the Continent together."

"Good idea," Keith agreed, approving his desire to take command of himself, assume his own responsibilities. "No young man should ever have parental chaperonage on his self-discovery odyssey. I certainly didn't, nor would want you burdened or hampered with such excess baggage. May I inform your mother that we might have another passenger along on the first lap of the voyage?"

"Yes, sir. I'll try to get better acquainted with my sisters, too. It's hard to believe they're ten years old today, and we barely know one another. I'm sorry I didn't get them any presents."

"I think they'd appreciate their brother's love more than any material things, Scott."

"I'll show them, later," he promised. "But no cake or punch now, please. If Rufus has any ginger ale in the galley, however—"

"Always. I'll tell him to bring you some, iced, out here. Come inside when you feel like it."

Keith returned to the main salon, which was festively decorated with bright balloons and crepe-paper streamers, for the ceremonial blowing out of the glowing pink candles on the identically frosted cakes and the reviewing of the feminine booty. He met Devon's anxious eyes with a reassuring nod, and saw her visibly relax and happily resume her maternal pleasures in presiding over the celebration.

"Daddy, can we do the hornpipe?" asked Sharon, simulating the posture. "The sailors will teach us how."

"It's not very ladylike, honey."

"Oh, pooh! That's what you said about the Irish jig and the Highland fling!"

"Well, it's true. Ask your mother."

"Mommy wants us to learn the Virginia reel," said Shannon, her dainty slippers tapping the floor rhythmically. "And the waltz."

"Which you shall," Devon apprised, "in dancing school, along with the schottische and polka and whatever other craze is popular in ballrooms when you enroll."

"When will *that* be?" inquired pragmatic Sharon.

"As soon as we arrive in Newport, where they have excellent teachers and classes in all the social amenities."

"What does that mean?"

"Shame on you, Sharon! You know Miss Vale has taught you those words and insists upon their practice."

Shannon grinned at her sister's chastisement. "Oh, Sharon doesn't pay much attention to the lessons in decorum and etiquette, Mommy. She's a hoyden, after all."

"I'm not, either! You're just a sissy."

"That's a term applied to shy or timid boys," Shannon corrected eruditely. "You don't study your vocabulary very well, so you make low scores on your spelling tests. And you're an absolute dunce in French!"

"But I beat the bloomers off you in arithmetic!" Sharon

gleefully gloated. "Miss Vale says I have a head for mathematics. You like to read fairy tales and make up stories for your English compositions. And you get higher marks in history, but who cares? *My* themes are about real people and things and events. I'm interested in what's happening today, not a hundred or thousand or million years ago. You want to be a writer like Mommy, when you grow up. *I* want to work in Daddy's bank, if he'll let me."

"Hey, hey!" Keith intervened with mock gruffness. "Stop your bickering, girls, or I'll paddle you both and deliver more than the ten customary strokes, too! Can't you at least behave on your birthdays, for goodness' sake?"

Their governess looked on in dismay, reluctant to discipline them before their parents on this special occasion, and thinking that their brother had been easier to govern in some respects, although never an angel even in retrospect. And, of course, there had been only one of him! "You may *not* dance the hornpipe!" she spoke up sternly. "And if you don't mind your manners immediately, you may *not* watch the display of fireworks this evening, either."

It was an amazingly effective threat, for they both loved such spectacles, which neither had yet witnessed at sea. "Yes, ma'am," they murmured obediently, not daring to poke their tongues at each other even behind Miss Vale's back, convinced that she had invisible eyes in her head.

The family gathered on deck at dusk to observe the pyrotechnics supervised by the capable crew. The twins were forbidden to participate, lest they set each other or themselves afire. They sat on canvas chairs with their parents, Shannon beside her mother and Sharon next to her father, clapping and cheering and screaming with delight as the firecrackers exploded in chain reactions, the varicolored rockets streaked across the starry, scintillating sky, and the sparklers glowed like miniature torches attached to small metal spears on the bow. When Devon remarked that other ships in the vicinity might think theirs in trouble, Keith assured her that seamen knew the difference between fireworks and distress flares and smokestack signals. And she suddenly remembered how the United States cruiser carrying the Grants on their world tour had celebrated their distinguished guests' birthdays, the Fourth of July, and New Year's Eve.

Corks were popped on several bottles of champagne, and potions poured for all adults, including off-duty crew members. Only Scott declined his glass, preferring to toast the occasion with ginger ale, and excusing himself to retire at the same time his sisters were taken, protesting, to their cabins.

Alone with her husband now, Devon readjusted her cashmere shawl about her shoulders, for the night air was breezy and quite cool even for June. "Poor Scotty," she sighed. "He's miserable, Keith."

"Still somewhat hungover, darling. That was potent poison he ingested."

"I could murder Sabrina for what she did to him!"

"And I should have," Keith muttered, lighting a cigar. "But he'll survive, Devon. He may not soon forget and will undoubtedly suffer some more emotional hemorrhaging, but he'll survive. I think he has the requisites and capacity for survival: the character, strength, determination, and purpose. Indeed, I'm convinced."

"But why must he be put to the test so young?"

"How old were you, when faced with life's first serious crisis and challenge?"

"Twelve when my mother died," Devon reflected.

"Then the crucible of war and your father's suicide and poverty and desperation in rapid succession. And then me, and all that followed! If our son inherited only a tenth of your survival instincts, we have naught to worry about, Devon. He'll come through with flying colors."

"You're surely not implying that his experience with that dreadful creature will make him a better man?"

"No, just a man. A callow, naive boy entered that house on Louisburg Square, but a different one emerged."

"What a horrible lesson in maturity!"

"Yes, and I regret not acting earlier to prevent it. But it happened, Devon. It's an immutable fact, which we can neither ignore nor dwell upon. Sabrina Carlton got him drunk and seduced him. That's the crux of the matter; an oversimplification, perhaps, of what seems like a complex problem to us all now."

"She drugged him, Keith!"

"Essentially, although absinthe is considered a liqueur, not a narcotic. What it did was remove his boyish inhibitions and

stimulate his libido beyond control, and she knew precisely
how to take advantage of the situation. A much older and wiser
man would probably have succumbed to her wily tactics just
as easily."

"You didn't, when she tried them on you—or so you told
me the night you went to her at the Hoffman House."

"The circumstances were different, my dear. I was wary
and prepared for any tricks, she aroused only disgust and con-
tempt in me, and it was like confronting Esther again. And the
whole goddamn travesty was replayed last night! Sabrina showed
no shame or remorse or mercy, and laughed when I called her
a pig, among other well-deserved epithets. She said Esther
would have cuckolded me with my own son, given the opportunity, and she was probably right. When I cursed her and
threw the wine dregs in her face, she *was* Esther and everything
evil that woman represented. It was as if Esther had risen from
the dead and stood incarnate in that room with its rumpled bed
and dirty linen, half naked and smiling that same secret, enigmatic smile that taunted me for a trusting, gullible, amenable
fool. God, I wanted to kill her! Smash my fist into her face,
strangle her with my bare hands, crush out her vile life, and
condemn her to hell for all eternity! I lusted for her blood, not
her flesh. Her blood, that's all, and nothing else. And I fear I
would have tasted it, had I not gotten out of there promptly."

He shuddered, and Devon saw him grimace in the light of
the Japanese lanterns strung gaily across the deck. Was he
remembering Esther's many provocations that had driven him
to the narrow edge of such desperation and despair, once even
in Devon's presence?

"But you couldn't, Keith, because you're not a killer. And
the vicious cousins can't hurt us anymore, either in body or
spirit. Sabrina is out on the street, and Esther is back in her
grave. I think her ghost has finally been laid to rest and will
cease haunting me in Gramercy Park. If she was working through
Sabrina, or vice versa, their spiritual contact has been broken.
We're free of the wicked witches, Keith. Finally and at long
last, free of them!" She clasped his hand and held it confidently
to her bosom. "I know this, darling, because I feel it here and
now, in my heart. Suddenly, it's like a heavy weight, a suffocating incubus, has been lifted from my person. Is it the same
for you?"

"Yes, and I think we'll have some peace and tranquillity in that respect, Devon. No more threatening shadows lurking in the past—not for us, anyway. All we need be concerned about is our children's future. But that's the lot of parenthood, I guess, and the price we pay for the privilege and pleasure of it."

"The kids will be all right," Devon told him with confidence. "Bumpy roads and pitfalls and storms ahead, maybe. But didn't you just assure me that our boy is a survivor? Well, why shouldn't our girls be, too? They're all our progeny, aren't they? Born of your seed and nursed at my breast! Life may occasionally disappoint them, but never defeat them, any more than it did their parents."

She was never more courageous or convincing than when endeavoring to comfort, encourage, sustain, or inspire him. Nor more loving and beloved. Smiling, Keith drew her out of her lounge onto his lap, kissed her reverently, and held her in a long, blissful serenity.

EPILOGUE

Pains of love be sweeter far
Than all other pleasures are.
John Dryden (1631–1700)

As unto the bow the cord is,
So unto the man is woman;
Though she bends him, she obeys him,
Though she draws him, yet she follows;
Useless each without the other!
Henry Wadsworth Longfellow (1807–1882)
HIAWATHA'S WOOING

All other things to their destruction draw,
Only our love hath no decay;
This, no tomorrow hath, nor yesterday,
Running it never runs from us away,
But truly keeps his first, last, everlasting day.

Let us love nobly, and live, and add again
Years and years unto years, till we attain
To write threescore: this is the second of our rein.
John Donne (1571–1631)
THE ANNIVERSARY

THE FINAL decade of the nineteenth century promised to be the most fabulous and flamboyant in the country's history. America's progress, posterity, and greatness seemed not only assured but destined for every region of the vast land. The East, humming with enterprise and energy, was second only to England in industrial development. The West, virtually tamed and free of hostile Indians, encouraged civilization of the formerly impregnable and dreaded frontiers, and more and more territories requested statehood in the Union. The railroad and telegraph systems reached nearly every remote area now, and sensational new inventions continued to astound the populace and the world at large. The United States won the majority of grand prizes and gold medals at the Paris Exposition of 1889, and global travelers journeyed across the Seven Seas in steam engines first designed in America, to view, study, and write about this amazing economical phenomenon capturing universal attention and curiosity, and beckoning thousands of immigrants to its golden shores. The Statue of Liberty was the most beautiful, bountiful, seductive lady on the planet Earth.

New York had more millionaires than ever before, and their numbers were steadily increasing in Chicago and San Francisco, too. Mechanical wonders abounded, increasing production in every major industry and endeavor, from architecture to mining to textiles. Singer's electric sewing revolutionized the garment factories. The Bessemer steel I-beams enabled the design and construction of tall buildings on iron skeletons; an eleven-story edifice rose at 50 Broadway on this architectural principle, and the modern "skyscraper" was born. Astronomers could now study the sun through Hale's newly invented spectroheliograph. Edison was working on an ingenious method to produce motion

pictures and another to transmit radio signals. George East-
man's wondrous box camera created a sensation and the popular
fun-fad of "taking snapshots" for family albums. Gilt and gold
and glamor and glitter claimed the theatrical limelight, and the
more flamboyant personalities became the toast of the town;
Lillian Russell and Diamond Jim Brady reigned supreme in the
brightly lit Broadway theater district and at the renowned Rec-
tor's Restaurant. Affluent and socially elite New Yorkers took
their pleasures in the sixty-thousand-dollar parterre boxes in
the "diamond horseshoe" section of the Metropolitan Opera
House, where fabulous jeweled tiaras and stickpins were
commonplace, at the yacht regattas in Newport, the horse races
in Saratoga, and internationally famous spas.

Devon felt privileged, not only to be alive and healthy in
this glorious era, but an integral part of it, and her interest in
the future never palled or waned. None of the great European
capitals and cities she had visited seemed more exciting or
fascinating to her than New York. Indeed, most others appeared
to have reached their zeniths, while Manhattan was still only
ascending hers. Fictionally, she compared them to staid, complacent old ladies in antique costumes beside this young, restless, ambitious, dazzling ingenue determined to steal history's
spotlight. It was a fairy tale and fantasyland combined and
come true!

Her antebellum novel, *Gallantry's Last Bow,* had been published to some critical acclaim and much commercial success,
especially in the Old South, where it seemed likely to endure
as a popular classic. Of the many satisfying reviews, Devon
was proudest of those in the respected Dixie newspapers and
literary magazines, and of the numerous congratulatory letters,
Daniel Haverston's was by far the most complimentary. Keith
smiled gingerly when she first read it to him, wondering how
the Virginian felt about the dedication: "To my Beloved
Husband, Keith Heathstone Curtis, with eternal love and devotion." Did Dan imagine Devon as the beautiful and spunky
heroine of *Gallantry's Last Bow,* and himself as the handsome
and gallant hero? Did he wonder, and possibly still hope, about
the uncertain ending, which seemed to promise a continuation
of the romantic story?

Already Devon and Heather Vale were accumulating information and data for an even longer and more comprehensive work encompassing broader aspects of the American historical scene. She envisioned even greater accomplishments by the end of the century, and hoped along with other serious writers to record them for posterity. Foremost, she anticipated the advancement of the Women's Movement regarding suffrage and child labor. Whether or not she eventually witnessed and realized these dreams and goals, Devon knew she would continue dreaming of them, working for them, and writing about them. And she would have done so, even without Keith's encouraging compliments about her talents upon reading *Gallantry's Last Bow*. Never mind his criticisms that she had perhaps romanticized the War Between the States too much, and was perhaps too partial to the Confederacy in her depiction of it, her history was accurate and her style highly readable, and he only wished she had penned the novel under her full name rather than just her maiden one. But this, she explained gracefully, was also a loving daughter's posthumous tribute to her father.

"I'll add 'Curtis' to the next one, darling," Devon promised, scribbling in her voluminous research journal.

"Are you composing a love scene?" Keith inquired interestedly, observing her intensity.

"No, some details of that terrible Johnston flood last year, in which over two thousand people were drowned. I should have gone there afterward, to personally interview some survivors, and maybe I shall before I actually include that chapter in the book. I wish I had witnessed the opening of the Oklahoma Territory to civilization, too. That Land Rush must have been very exciting!" Lifting her eyes from her ever-mounting notes, she questioned, "Did you have some agents out there staking claims for Curtis Enterprises West?"

"No, my curious pet. My representatives are mostly in Texas, purchasing vast tracts of land around a Gulf Coast town called Beaumont."

"Why Beaumont?"

"Oh, there's some petroleum prospecting going on down there, and my geology consultants think it's a likely prospect. Texas has just about everything else of value, why not black gold?"

"But you already have oil interests in Pennsylvania and Ohio, Keith! Why, you're John D. Rockefeller's biggest competitor in that business."

"Well, don't imagine the Rockefellers will remain static in their explorations, or that they won't find ways to circumvent the Sherman Antitrust Act."

Devon looked rueful. It was one of the ironies and injustices of politics that Reed Carter's long and assiduous efforts to legislate against cartels had finally been realized in another senator's bill. Disillusionment with the whole democratic process had prompted him to resign his seat in the Senate, retire to his ranch near Fort Worth, and concentrate on raising the new, increasingly popular white-faced Hereford cattle. The benefits Texans derived from his years in Washington would be remembered best and longest in his native state, along with those of his father, Jason Carter, a friend and contemporary of the legendary and revered Sam Houston.

"Why the sad face, Devon?"

"Not sad, Keith, just puzzled. I find it ironic that Senator John Sherman of Ohio gets all the credit for that important legislation. Reed deserved to have his name on the act, at least as co-sponsor, since he not only supported it but drafted the original concept."

"A superfluous reminder, my dear. And Carter's version might have prevailed, had he been less obstinate and determined to exclude every conceivable loophole; able to forget his bitter vendetta with Wall Street, and yours truly in particular, enough to realize that his rigid bill could never be passed in toto, without some modifications. Compromise and flexibility are inherent and essential in politics, but that filibustering cowboy could never accept or adjust to these facts and conditions, nor his stony nature yield to them. Therefore, he failed in his purpose, and muffed his opportunity. Like many of his breed, that Texan has a six-shooter mentality."

"Reed had a political credo, in which he honestly believed, Keith. Ethics and ideals. Principles and convictions."

"Upon which he must now rest, rather than political laurels and accomplishments and statesmanship! I'm just relieved that he finally muzzled his big mouth and hauled his controversial carcass back to Texas, riding on one of my iron horses, and will probably never be heard from nationally again." He paused, realizing how his sarcasm must sound to her, and sheepishly sought to modify it. "But then, he never liked publicity much anyway, did he?"

"Loathed it, actually. Ranching was always his preferred life. And his greatest love."

"Next to you, macushla?"

"I don't know," Devon shrugged, "and probably never shall."

Keith pondered her uncertainty, wondering why she should be concerned at all about this man so long out of her life, or care that his political career had not been exactly illustrious. After all, few politicians became luminaries, stellar stars in the Potomac galaxy; most dimmed quickly once they left the Capital constellation, including some presidents, and only historians bothered with the mediocre figures. Unfortunately for the Texan, his performance in the Senate was something less than spectacular.

"Ah, but you'll always know about the Virginian! We both will, won't we?" Keith sighed, still somewhat incredulous that his son and Haverston's daughter were officially engaged. The wedding date was already set and preparations underway for the elaborate event at Harmony Hill. And, in a fateful way, Devon was observing them from her vantage in the family gallery, where her life-size painting continued to occupy the place of honor. "We knew that when we attended the announcement parties, didn't we? Your portrait is a permanent fixture in that house, Devon."

Unable to divest the master of the manor of his obsession, Devon had simply resigned herself to it, and wished her spouse would do the same. "Well, if it makes Daniel happy—"

"It would make me happier, in one of our homes," Keith muttered jealously.

"Don't you like the portrait you commissioned of your wife and daughters?"

"Yes, of course. It's excellent and lovely, and I wouldn't part with it for anything. But there's something about that other one—"

"The 'something' is the fact that it belongs to someone else," Devon rationalized. "But don't envy Daniel whatever pleasure it gives him, Keith. If ever he marries again, the lady will promptly remove it."

"Come now, darling. I'll wager a million that our future in-law will remain single to the end of his days. I doubt he'll ever even take a mistress on a permanent basis, despite his long and friendly relationship with a certain comely Richmond widow."

"Where did you hear that?"

"New York and Washington have no monopoly on gossip," he grinned. "Rumors spread everywhere."

"Especially via ladies' clubs," Devon surmised, "and Mrs. Henry Clinton is president of most of them. She's big in Richmond."

Keith laughed. "In other places, too. Her bosom juts like the *Sprite*'s prow, and her behind is as broad as the fantail. Add to those afflictions a voice about as pleasant as a rusty foghorn."

"Shame on you, making such unchivalrous comments about that matriarch of Virginia society!" Devon admonished him, clucking her tongue in a suppressed giggle. "But poor Bess is somewhat hefty, isn't she?"

"She could be weighed in tonnage! Lucky corset staves are steel now, lest whalebones prove inadequate under so much pressure per pound, and rupture. But still she frolics and flirts! Guess what she asked me while we were dancing at the betrothal ball?"

"For an assignation?"

"You know ladies never ask gentlemen for that! No, she wanted your secrets for staying young, slender, and beautiful. I said you practiced table exercises called push-away, but she misunderstood. 'Don't you mean push-ups, sir?' I corrected myself and explained that your physical regimen includes dieting." Pride and admiration beamed in his appraisal of Devon's youthful beauty and trim, curvaceous body. "You're still the most charming little belle I know north or south of the Mason-Dixon Line," he drawled, mimicking the Southern cavaliers. "Ah, yes, ma'am! Still light as a feather on your feet and in my arms."

"Then why don't you carry me to bed oftener, kind sir?" she played the traditional games with him.

"Because we're usually there when the urge overtakes me, fair lady. Four-poster convenience, you know; boudoir bounty. And we're not quite as impetuous as we once were, although I might refute that any minute now."

"Oh, Keith, I hope marriage will be as wonderful for Scotty and Fawn as it is for us! They do seem deeply in love, and anxious for the nuptials. Heaven knows they've waited long enough for each other!"

Keith conceded that. Scott had remained abroad almost two years on his Grand Tour—time which must have seemed an eternity to the anxious young lovers, and during which their feelings were put to every challenge and test. At one point midway in their separation, Devon received a long letter from Daniel expressing grave concern over his daughter's health. He was worried about her lack of appetite and loss of weight, her apparent lack of interest in the young men and social affairs of the Tidewater, her apathy and insomnia and melancholy moods. He wrote that Fawn received mail fairly regularly from Scott, but that she feared all of her correspondence was not reaching him in his many moves about the Continent. Between the lines Dan indicated his willingness to give them his blessings, and ultimately cabled his consent across the Atlantic.

In his London hotel when the message arrived, Scott immediately booked passage to America, and the respective families stood together on the Battery pier as the ship docked in Manhattan, tears of joy glistening in the ladies' eyes as they welcomed him home. After brief stays in Gramercy Park and at Halcyon, the group sailed to Newport, where they spent the remainder of the summer. The reunited couple glowed with happiness and optimism about their future together, surprising no one when they confided their serious intentions. The Curtises feted the Haverstons in their white marble palace, but the formal announcement was appropriately postponed to be made at Harmony Hill. And in the sunshine of Fawn's presence, the shadow of Sabrina Carlton faded from Scott's mind and conscience, enabling him to finally relegate the adolescent episode to its proper place in the scheme of life.

"Granted, but what else could they do, with an ocean between them? I suspect that was Scott's strategy all along, not only to see if Fawn would wait for him, but to force himself to wait for her."

"Fawn's going to be a stunning bride," Devon predicted, visualizing the image, "and Shannon and Sharon will be adorable bridesmaids, in pink organza, although they're not exactly keen about the identical costumes." The twins had decided at age twelve to cease dressing alike, and their wise parents had not objected. "They've already informed me that they want different gowns for their debut. I can't believe that time is not so far away, Keith."

"A few years, Devon. My God, don't make them grow up faster than necessary."

"They're fairly grown up now, Daddy. Face it. They'll be graduating from finishing school next year, and one day sooner than you expect you'll be giving them away, as Dan will be doing his little girl in June."

Keith frowned, reluctant to think about this possibility and far from resigned to it. "Well, I hope it'll be a double wedding, so I don't have to go through it twice."

"But you likely will, dear. They don't do anything else together much, why should they marry in the same ceremony? Anyway, it's a very special occasion for a girl and should be uniquely her own. Furthermore, you know Sharon wants to work in the bank for a while, at least."

"I'm still pondering that, Devon. But I might as well concede, since my son is apparently determined to be a planter. That's what I find most incredible about all of this! *Where* does he get his agrarian blood?"

"Through infusions of love," Devon suggested. "Fawn loves the plantation, and he loves Fawn."

"As simple as that, eh?"

"I think so. If she were a banker's daughter—" She paused significantly.

"I suppose so, honey. But Scott will be in finance one way or another, or at least associated with it, when he inherits his share of the Curtis estate. Imagine his surprise when my will is read, to discover that he even owns stock in the Bank of Richmond!" He smiled slightly, as if playing a practical joke on his male heir.

"Don't talk about such things, don't even think about them! You're in your prime."

"Of course, and I feel fine. But it'll be an ironic quirk of fate for Scott, and I wish I could see his face when it happens."

Devon tensed, loath to continue the conversation. "Hush, Keith! I don't want to hear any more about it. Besides, I have a fitting this afternoon and mustn't be late. How are the tailors coming with your and Scotty's suits?"

"On schedule. His first striped trousers and cutaway, and he'll be a handsome groom."

"Like his father was," Devon said wistfully, remembering their intimate, private wedding at Halcyon.

"I wore a plain dark business suit, Devon, and you a simple blue silk gown," Keith reflected. "We had no audience or reception. Do you ever regret our simplicity and informality?"

"Never, darling," she assured him. "Anyway, we didn't have time to make lavish plans, did we? And we had waited so long for the actual legalities. . . ."

"So long," he agreed somberly, "I had almost given up hope. Almost, Devon, but never quite. You know why? Because I knew we belonged together the night you left Richmond with me. Destiny took a damnably long, circuitous route in fulfilling our future, but it was fulfilled. That's the important thing, after all. Isn't it?"

Devon went to him, and immediately his arms welcomed her. "The *most* important," she whispered, as his mouth lowered on hers. "Nothing will ever be more important in my life, Keith, if I live to be a hundred."

"Nor in mine," he vowed. "And I intend to be around when you celebrate your centennial birthday, Mrs. Curtis. I promise you that."

"You'd better be, Mr. Curtis. And just think of all the marvelous celebrations we'll enjoy meanwhile."

"I am thinking," he admitted, kissing her with rapidly rising passion. "Forget that modiste's appointment, or be late. I'll shock the servants by carrying you upstairs."

"You think that's still possible?"

"What?" he asked, lifting her easily off the floor.

"To shock the servants." Devon chuckled, thrilled as always by his verile, impetuous ardor. "I think they enjoy our impulsive behavior. I sense them watching us now, in fact, and smiling."

"Good."

"Good," Devon murmured later, in bed and in his embrace. "So good, Keith. . . ."

"Still, after all these years?"

"Always, and sometimes I think it's even better than ever.

Maybe sex, like vintage wine, improves with time?"

Keith laughed, fondling one of her thick, lustrous curls, twisting it playfully around his finger, as he was wont to do after intimacy. Her head lay on his chest, and she could hear the steady rhythm of his heart, which only minutes ago had sounded like thunder in her ears. "What it improves with, my sweet, is practice. And deepening love and appreciation of life. And knowing, just knowing what we have together."

"Oh, yes, dearest! *Just knowing . . .*"

Life was wonderful at any age, she thought. Love was wonderful at any age. For them, it was heaven on earth, or its closest approximation, and all that Divine Providence could bestow on mortal humanity. Devon believed this sincerely, as she believed that it would continue through the years, and forever after, in Eternity.